D0445924

Surrender the Wind

Surrender the Wind
Copyright © 2009 by Rita Gerlach

ISBN-13: 978-1-4267-0072-9

Published by Abingdon Press, P.O. Box 801, Nashville, TN 37202
www.abingdonpress.com

All rights reserved.
No part of this publication may be reproduced in any form,
stored in any retrieval system, posted on any website, or
transmitted in any form or by any means—digital, electronic,
scanning, photocopy, recording, or otherwise—without written
permission from the publisher, except for brief quotations in
printed reviews and articles.

The persons and events portrayed in this work of fiction are the
creations of the author, and any resemblance to persons living or
dead is purely coincidental.

Scripture taken from the
Holy Bible, New International Version®. NIV®.
Copyright© 1973, 1978, 1984 by International Bible Society.
Used by permission of Zondervan. All rights reserved.

Cover design by Anderson Design Group, Nashville, TN
Cover illustration by Taaron Parsons

Library of Congress Cataloging-in-Publication Data
Gerlach, Rita.
Surrender the wind / Rita Gerlach.
    p. cm.
ISBN 978-1-4267-0072-9 (alk. paper)
I. Title.
PS3607.E755S87 2009
813'.6--dc22

                                        2009014259

Printed in the United States of America
1 2 3 4 5 6 7 8 9 10 / 14 13 12 11 10 09

Surrender the Wind

by
Rita Gerlach

Abingdon Press fiction
a novel approach to faith

Acknowledgments

Words seem inadequate when it comes to thanking all the people who have supported me in the completion of this novel. But let me assure you, these are not mere words on a page. They come from my heart.

To my husband and best friend, Paul, who at times acted out some of the colorful characters in this book and gave me a clearer vision as to their nature. His hilarious impersonations of the old and often confused seadog, James Bonnecker, and the odious Constable Latterbuck, often sent me into gales of sidesplitting laughter. For his support and encouragement, I am forever grateful.

To my sons, Paul and Michael, for their understanding when I forgot to take something tasty out of the freezer for dinner due to a day's immersion in my writing.

To my mother, Rose, who believed in me and prayed I would find a publisher.

To my editor, Barbara Scott, for taking a chance on me and championing this novel.

To the staff at Abingdon Press for their hard work and the designers at Anderson Design Group for producing a stunning cover.

To my friends at His Writers Writing Group for their boundless support.

To author Bonnie Toews for all the encouraging emails.

To Sandi Riggs and Mary Ann Quinn for their prayers and friendship.

And last, to all those who read this novel, many thanks. May this story bring you some respite from the hectic world we live in and inspire you to surrender your trials and troubles to the One who loves you with an everlasting love.

I hated all the things I had toiled for under the sun, because I must leave them to the one who comes after me. And who knows whether he will be a wise man or a fool? Yet he will have control over all the work into which I have poured my effort and skill under the sun.

This too is meaningless.

—Ecclesiastes 2:18-19 NIV

Prologue
The Wilds of Virginia
October 1781

On a cool autumn twilight, Seth Braxton rode his horse through a grove of dark-green hemlocks in a primeval Virginia forest, distressed that he might not make it to Yorktown in time. He ran his hand down his horse's broad neck to calm him, slid from the saddle, and led his mount under the deep umbra of an enormous evergreen. Golden-brown pine needles shimmered in the feeble light and fell. In response to his master's touch, the horse lifted its head, shook a dusty mane, and snorted.

"Steady, Saber. I'll be back to get you." Seth spoke softly and stroked the velvet muzzle. "Soon, you'll have plenty of oats to eat and green meadows to run in."

He threw a cautious glance at the hillside ahead of him, drew his musket from a leather holster attached to the saddle, and pulled the strap over his left shoulder. Out of the shadows and into bars of sunlight, he stepped away to join his troop of ragtag patriots. Through the dense woodland, they climbed the hill to the summit.

Sweat broke over Seth's face and trickled down his neck and into his coarse linen hunting shirt. He wiped his slick palms along the sides of his dusty buckskin breeches and pulled his slouch hat closer to his eyes to block the glare of sun that peeked through the trees. A lock of dark hair, which had a hint of bronze within its blackness, fell over his brow, and he flicked it back with a jerk of his head. Tense, he flexed his hand, closed it tight around the barrel of his musket, and listened for the slightest noise—the soft creak of a saddle or the neigh of a horse. His keen blue eyes scanned the breaks in the trees, and his strong jaw tightened.

Shadows quivered along the ground, lengthened against tree trunks, then crept over ancient rocks. Within the forest, blue jays squawked. Splashes of blood-red uniforms interspersed amid muted green grew out of earthy hues.

A column of British infantry, led by an officer on horseback, moved around the bend. His scarlet coat, decked with ivory lapels and silver buttons, gleamed in the sunlight, his powdered wig snow white. An entourage of other lower-ranking officers accompanied him alongside the rank and file.

Without hesitation, Seth cocked the hammer of his musket to the second notch and pressed the stock into his shoulder.

"Wait." Daniel Whitmann, a young Presbyterian minister, pulled out his handkerchief, mopped the sweat off his face, and shoved the rag back into his pocket. "Wait until more are on the road. Wait for the signal to fire."

Seth acknowledged the preacher with a glance. "Pray for us, Reverend, and for them as well. Some of us are about to face our Maker."

Whitmann moved his weapon forward. "God shall not leave us, Seth. May the Almighty's will be done this day."

Seth fixed his eye on the target that moved below. He aimed his long barrel at the heart of the first redcoat in line. No fervor for battle rose within him, only a heartsick repulsion that he would take a boy's life, a lad who should be at home tending his father's business or at school with his mind in books. The boy lifted a weary hand and rubbed his eyes. The officer nudged his horse back and rode alongside the boy. "Stay alert, there!" The boy flinched, stiffened, and riveted his eyes ahead.

A muscle in Seth's face twitched. He did not like the way the officer cruelly ordered the boy. With a steady arm, he narrowed one eye and made his mark with the other. He moved his tongue over his lower lip and tried to control a heated rush of nerves. He glanced to the right, his breath held tight in his chest, and waited for the signal to fire. His captain raised his hand, hesitated, then let it fall.

Flints snapped. Ochre flashed. Hissing reports sliced the air. The British surged to the roadside in disorder. Their leader threatened and harangued his men with drawn sword. He ordered them to advance, kicked laggards, and shoved his horse against his men, while bullets pelted from the patriots' muskets.

Seth squeezed the trigger. His musket ball struck the officer's chest. Blood gushed over the white waistcoat and spurted from the corner of the Englishman's mouth. He slid down in the saddle and tumbled off his horse, dead.

"Fall back!" Redcoats scattered at the order, surged to the roadside, slammed backward by the force of the attack. The fallen, but not yet dead, squirmed in the dust and cried out.

A redcoat climbed the embankment, slipped, and hauled back up. His bayonet caught the sunlight and Seth's attention. The soldier headed straight for Whitmann.

His hands fumbled with his musket, and Whitmann managed to fire. The musket ball struck the redcoat through the chest. A dazed look flooded the preacher's face.

Seth grabbed Whitmann by the shoulder and jerked him away. "Don't think on it, Reverend."

He shoved the heartsick minister behind him. A troop of grenadiers hurried around the bend in the road, their bayonets rigid on the tips of their long rifles. They faced about, poured a volley into the hilltop, and killed several patriots.

A musket ball whizzed past Seth's head and smacked into the tree behind him. Bark splintered, and countless wooden needles launched into the air. His breath caught in his throat, and he pitched backward. Blood trickled from his temple, hot against his skin. He rolled onto his side, scrambled to a crouched position, and slipped behind a tree. Beside him, Whitmann lay dead, his bloody hand pressed against the wound, the other clutched around the shaft of his rifle, with his eyes opened toward heaven.

"Retreat! Retreat!" The command from a patriot leader reached Seth above the clamor of musket fire. With the other colonials, he ran into the woods. His heart pounded against his ribs. His breathing was hurried.

He glanced back over his shoulder and saw that he must run for his life. Redcoats stampeded after him through the misty Virginia wilds. His fellow patriots scurried up the hill ahead of him and slipped over the peak. With unaffected energy, he mounted the slope to follow them and ran as fast as his legs could carry him over the sleek covering of dead leaves. He had to catch up. Exhausted, he forced his body to move, crested the hill, and hastened over it, down into the holler of evergreens.

Without a moment to lose, Seth leapt into the saddle of his horse, dug in his heels, and urged Saber forward. The crack of a pistol echoed, and a redcoat's bullet struck. Against the pull of the reins, the terrified horse twisted and fell sideways. Flung from the saddle, Seth hit the ground hard, and his breath was knocked from his body. For a tense moment, he struggled to fill his lungs and crawl back to his fallen horse. His heart sank when he saw the mortal wound that had ripped into Saber's hide. Desperate for revenge, Seth grabbed his weapon and scrambled to his feet. But the click of a flintlock's hammer stopped him short.

"Drop your weapon, rebel." A redcoat stood a stone's throw away, his long rifle poised against his shoulder.

Seth opened his hand and let his musket fall into the leaves. Soldiers hurried forward and confiscated his knife and musket, shot and powder horn. Saber moaned, and from the corner of Seth's eye, he saw his faithful mount struggle to rise.

The redcoat that held him at gunpoint glanced at the suffering horse, and a cruel light spread across his face. Helpless, Seth watched the redcoat take the musket from a soldier and aim. The forest grew silent, and Seth's quickened heartbeat pulsed in his jugular. He clenched his teeth and shut his eyes. Then his musket ended his horse's misery.

At the blast, Seth jerked. He stepped back from the putrid smell of rum and sweat, from the pocked face that glistened with grime, and from the eyes that blazed with sordid pleasure. A firm voice gave orders to make way as an officer on horseback cantered toward him. The Englishman dismounted, took Seth's musket from the rum-smelling buffoon, and turned it within his hands.

"Iron. Smoothbore barrel. Maker's mark." The officer examined the craftsmanship of the wood and forged brass. "Walnut full stock. Board of Ordnance Crown acceptance mark on the tang. Regulation Longland, I'd say. A quality piece by American standards."

Seth bit his lower lip and clenched his fists. "I cannot kill any of your men. It's not loaded. You have my shot and powder. Return them to me."

The officer handed the musket over to an Iroquois scout. "A gift. Show it to your people. Tell them the king of England wished you to have it."

"We captured a rebel." The redcoat who shot Seth's horse threw his shoulders back.

Colonel Robert Hawkings stood nose-to-nose with the soldier. "You think yourself worthy of some reward? One prisoner is something to boast about?"

Corporal John Perkins nodded. "Better than none at all, sir."

"Out of my sight, you foul-smelling oaf."

Perkins shrank back, red-faced. Hawkings planted himself in front of Seth and met his eyes. "Your colonials killed several of my men, including our major. Not only are you a rebel, but a murderer as well. You'll hang for it."

Seth stared straight into his enemy's eyes. "It would be better to suffer the noose than be under the bootheels of tyrants."

Blue veins on Hawkings's neck swelled and he struck Seth across the face. Seth's head jerked from the force of the blow. Slowly, he turned back and spat out the blood that flooded his mouth.

Nearby a younger officer watched. His expression burned with arrogant pride. Seth noticed the tear in the man's jacket and saw a stream of blood had stained the white linen beneath it.

To the rear, another man stepped forward.

"Colonel Hawkings, trade this prisoner for one of our own." He spoke in a quiet, controlled tone.

Hawkings's brows arched, and he spun halfway on his heels. "Captain Bray, you have no satisfaction in seeing a traitor hang?"

"Hanging is for those who have been tried and sentenced. This man has not had that afforded him."

"He deserves nothing in that regard."

"Our government has given prisoners of war the rights of belligerents, sir. They're not to be executed."

"You doubt my authority in this matter?" Hawkings said.

Bray's frown deepened. "No, sir, only your better judg-ment."

"Stand back. I'll shoot this rebel myself."

Hawkings drew his pistol, pointed it at Seth's head and cocked the hammer. Stunned, Seth's breath caught in his throat. His body stiffened in a cold sweat. .

Bray lunged and cuffed Hawkings's wrist. "He's unarmed."

Hawkings shoved Bray back. "Take your hands off me. You dare defy me?"

"We are Englishmen and Christians. Let us abide by the rules of just conduct."

Hawkings grabbed Bray's coat and yanked his face close. "I am the officer in charge. I can do anything I wish."

"Shooting an unarmed man is murder," Bray said.

Hawkings paused. His expression grew grave as though he considered the word *murder* with great care. A moment later, he lowered his pistol. "Murder, you say? Well, I've had enough blood this day. I know my officers shall agree this man is guilty and that hanging is a more just and merciful punishment. Perkins, secure this rebel under that tree, the one I mean for him to swing from at dawn. Let him listen to its branches creak all night. Perhaps that will humble his rebellious heart."

Hawkings strode off. Perkins grabbed hold of Seth and tied his wrists together. Seth lowered his eyes, stared at the ground, and refused to give Bray any sign he was grateful he had stood up for him.

"If I were you, I'd mind my place, Bray."

Seth lifted his eyes to see Bray turn to the man who taunted him.

"Have you no honor, Captain Darden?" Bray said. "A man must speak up for justice."

Darden pulled away from the tree he leaned against. "If you do not take care to show respect to Colonel Hawkings, you'll regret your interference. You should know what meddling could do, after what happened at Ten Width."

Seth let out a breath and frowned. What did these men know of Ten Width, his grandfather's estate in England? Yanked forward, he caught Darden's stare. Within the depths of his pale-gray eyes burned hatred. A corner of Darden's mouth curled and twitched. To stay silent, Seth bit down hard on the tip of his tongue.

They led him to the oak, where he struggled with the understanding he'd die young at twenty-six. Under the shadow of the tree's colossal branches, he cried inwardly, *Let the sighing of the prisoner come before thee; according to the greatness of thy power preserve thou those that are appointed to die.*

Seth's burdened heart hoped heaven heard him, but his weakened flesh doubted.

❧

The sky hung inky-black, burdened with stars. The moon, umber and maize, cast its light over twisting leaves. With a heavy heart, Seth gazed at the vaulted heavens and made out the constellation Lyra. "Where is God my maker, who giveth songs in the night?" he murmured, his eyes gathering together the stars that made its shape. What lay beyond those heavenly places? Was he prepared to meet his end?

He had lived in the Virginia wilderness, fighting alongside a handful of patriots from the Potomac Militia after a gut-wrenching farewell to his father, Colonel Nathan Braxton, and his younger sister, Caroline. Caroline was but a child then, and the war-torn colonies were no place for a motherless girl. He thought of her, with brotherly longing, far away in England, glad she was at least safe, fed, and clothed, living in their grand-father's house.

A frown quivered at the corners of his mouth. She had no idea her brother was a prisoner of the British army, assigned a traitor's death.

When the soldiers settled down before the fire and stretched out on the ground to sleep, Seth laid his head against the rough bark of the oak. A thread of blood that had seeped from the wound on his temple felt cold against his skin. Though his death was promised on the morrow, something stronger rallied his courage. He refused to accept such a fate and opened his eyes to study his surroundings. The campfire was low and gave little light. Behind him, the forest brooded in darkness.

He thought of ways he might escape and, with much tenacity, he loosened the ropes that dug at his wrists. That's all there was to it—break the bindings and with care and caution vanish into the dark.

He twisted and turned his hands and strained hard against the cords. A slight change happened, but not enough to free him. He repeated the process again with added determination. Through the gloom, he saw Bray walk toward him. He relaxed his struggle, so as not to give away his plan.

"I'm sorry you are to die tomorrow." Bray crouched in front of him. "I did what I could to prevent it."

Seth pressed his mouth hard, and turned his head the other way. "What is one rebel more or less to you?"

"A human life is precious."

"Not in war."

"Are you thirsty?" Bray yanked the stopper free on his canteen.

Seth nodded. Bray put the opening to Seth's mouth. The water tasted cold and sweet, and he was grateful for it.

"I'd give you something to eat, but we have nothing. Well, nothing you would want. Our men were starving, and your horse . . . I'm sorry."

Seth pushed down his rage and swallowed hard.

Bray pinched his brows together. "Tell me your name."

Seth hesitated, then replied in a short breath. "Braxton."

"Braxton? An English name."

"It was once."

"Have you family in England?"

"My grandfather and sister live in Devonshire in some ruin of a place, where he eats his beef and subjects her to his politics."

Bray made no sign of offense at Seth's bitter remarks. "Is Caroline Braxton your sister?"

A jolt gripped Seth at his sister's name. "You know her?"

"I do. She told me she had family in Virginia."

"Is she well?"

"The last I knew, she was well."

"At least I've been afforded some comfort before I die."

"You'll not hang," Bray whispered. "I owe it to Caroline to help you."

Bray drew his knife and slipped the blade between the cords and Seth's flesh. Seth strained to pull the ropes open to give

Bray room to slice. Soon the bindings broke and he rubbed his bruised skin.

"They'll hang you instead of me," he said.

"Trust me, I'm safe." Bray glanced back at the sentry and set the knife back in its sheath. "There is more to tell, but we have no time. Perhaps we'll meet again someday."

With the cloak of darkness to cover him, Seth slipped away. Moonlight marked his path. He went heel-to-toe and stepped through the tangled maze of leaf and root. He traveled several miles before the faint rim of the land leveled off into green fields. To the east, toward the bay and river, seams of fog wove through the bottomlands. Through the trampled battlefield, Seth trudged and paused to glance at the outworks the British had abandoned—the empty trenches and redoubts.

When he reached the heart of the encampment, he moved on toward a farmhouse. He entered through the front door into a sparsely lit room, where lay row upon row of injured patriots. He made inquiries among the men and learned from a wounded solider that his father had fallen in the early hours before Cornwallis surrendered.

With bleary eyes, and his head wrapped in a bloody bandage, the lieutenant smiled up at Seth. "I know Major Braxton. I saw him fall not five yards from where I stood. He fought bravely. I cannot say, lad, whether he is living or dead."

At these words, Seth's hopes sank and he leaned down. "Do you know where I might find him?"

"Could be among us wounded."

Seth thanked him and went on to look for his father. After a desperate search, he found Nathan's body, battered and bloody from battle. He lifted the blanket that covered him. Blood stained the linen shirt, waistcoat, and navy-blue jacket. In his father's hand, he saw the glimmer of a gold locket. He knew it kept safe his mother's portrait. He took it and shoved it into his pocket.

He curled his hands into fists and dug his fingers into his palms to steel himself against the pain. Grief broke through, clawed at his heart, and pummeled him. He silently wept and lifted his father's body into his arms.

"Grandfather will never understand the man you were," he whispered against his father's cold cheek.

He laid him back. His hand trembled, along with his heart, when he touched his father's eyes and closed them.

1

Devonshire, England
Winter, 1783

Juleah Fallowes stepped out of the carriage and gazed up at the full moon above a dark, spear-like chimney that belonged to Ten Width. Her deep brown eyes, flecked with russet, drifted over to a candle set against the blackness of the ivy-covered walls that glowed from inside Benjamin Braxton's bedchamber window. A chill swept through her—from the wind and from a sense of what she might find beyond the frosted glass.

The lantern outside the door sputtered against the winter night. She gathered the sides of her hood closer to her cheeks and entered the dark foyer where a servant met her. Benjamin's physician, Doctor Yates, donned his hat and nodded to her. She pushed back her hood, and her hair fell in auburn twists about her face and shoulders. The long ride from Henry Chase had left her chilled, and she hesitated to remove her cloak. When she caught the way Yates's eyes roved over her blushed face, it gave her more reason to keep her womanly figure concealed.

"There is nothing I can do, Miss Juleah." He grazed her arm with a sinewy hand and withdrew it slowly. "He shall not last the night." Grave, he looked into her eyes one more time and strode out the door to his horse.

When the door finally closed, Juleah shed her dove-gray cloak, mounted the stairs, and entered the room. Benjamin lay in his bed. Propped up against high pillows, he made slight efforts to breathe. Caroline, his granddaughter, Juleah's closest friend since childhood, sat by his bedside and looked up at Juleah's approach. Her jade eyes were teary, and her face pale as the lace cuffs on the faded dress she wore. At first, her expression was one of grateful relief, but then changed to fatigued sorrow.

Caroline hurried away from the bedside. "Oh, Juleah. I'm glad you came."

"I am here for as long as you and Squire Braxton need me." She squeezed Caroline's hand.

With despairing eyes, Juleah saw the bluish lips and heard the faint gurgle of liquid that filled Benjamin's lungs. He coughed, and Caroline rushed back to him and held a cloth to his mouth that caught the blood-streaked mucus. She washed his lips with a moist sponge and spoke quietly in an effort to soothe him. Waves of steel-gray hair fell back from his forehead along the pillow, his eyebrows winged upward above hazel eyes.

The clock on the mantelpiece sped past the half hour. Juleah stood at the window and pressed her back against the grooves in the jamb in a poor attempt to abate the churning in her belly. She gnawed her lower lip, while watching Caroline lean over to lay her cheek against Benjamin's hand. Juleah was troubled that he lay dying in a drafty bedchamber on a grim, wintry day at twilight, to face the sort of emancipation most men fear, with only his granddaughter to comfort him. His sons were all gone, and his grandson lived in the wilderness of America. Wind rattled the panes, shook off the hoarfrost that encrusted the trees, and rushed down the fireplace flue. Frigid gusts blew over the coals of the fire and scattered wispy breaths of silvery ash onto the flagstone hearth.

"How cold and lonesome a tomb will be," Benjamin muttered.

Juleah turned to see sorrow flood her friend's eyes.

"Do not speak so grim, Grandfather," Caroline said.

Benjamin turned his head to her. "I suppose, child, you'd rather me think of heaven, that it must be warm and bright and make one forget the cares of an earthly existence."

She nodded. "Indeed, I would."

"Then for your sake, I shall make every effort to do so." He reached his hand over and she took it. "I have asked you and Juleah to sit with me, with the intention you must hear what is about to take place. You both are to witness all that I say and promise you will stand upon it when I am gone."

"I will, Grandfather." Caroline pressed his hand against her cheek, and her eyes sparkled from the tears she forced back. Juleah felt sorry for her and dreaded the idea she, too, would lose her parents someday.

Benjamin's gaze shifted to Juleah. "And you, my girl? Do I have your word?"

"You do, sir," she answered, her heart in her throat.

Carriage wheels crunched over the gravel in the drive, and she leaned closer to the window. Below, Philip Banes, Benjamin's long-time lawyer, stepped out, careful to avoid the muddy snow. She drew away and went downstairs to meet him.

From the dimness of the entrance, Juleah watched Caroline's serving girl, Claire, open the front door and, with a quick curtsey, show Banes inside. At the foot of the staircase, Juleah waited, while Banes handed over his cloak and slapped his leather gloves inside the bowl of his hat.

"This had better be important—and worthy of my time. I shall double my fee for the trouble."

She stepped up to him and looked at Banes squarely. "He is dying, Mr. Banes. Please keep that in mind and show compassion for his suffering."

While Claire trailed behind them, she led Banes up the staircase to Benjamin's bedchamber. Banes hesitated before going further inside, glanced around the room, then rested his eyes on Juleah. Firelight flickered across the dull oaken floor and reached the tips of his buckled shoes.

"The squire usually offers tea, Miss Juleah. Today I hope he offers a glass of brandy to warm my arthritic bones."

"Claire, please bring Mr. Banes a pot of tea." She stirred the coals in the hearth with a poker and prayed his time at Ten Width would be short-lived.

Banes touched the serving-girl's elbow. "I'd prefer warm brandy."

Straight as a rod, Claire shook her head. "Aside from tea, sir, all we have is cider. I'll warm that for you."

She turned to go, but he stopped her with a wave of his hand. "If you do not have something stronger, I'll have nothing at all. I had hoped I would not have to drink the expensive elixir within my flask and could keep it for the frigid journey home."

"As you wish, sir," Claire said.

A rancid scent of approaching death mingled with the breath of the fire and the intrusion of wind. Benjamin's rattled breathing arrested Banes, and Juleah saw him wince.

"Dear me, Miss Juleah. How thin and pale Benjamin has become. And Miss Caroline looks poorly."

Juleah drew him aside. "Please, Mr. Banes, do not worsen Caroline's distress any more than it is by commenting on her appearance at such a moment."

Banes gave her a curt nod and set his portfolio on the table near the hearth, beside a high-backed chair once a deep indigo, now faded to gray.

"You are right, Miss Juleah. But I've never seen Benjamin look so bad," he whispered. "Indeed, it won't be long now."

She pressed her mouth together hard. If only Banes would keep such comments to himself. A naked branch rapped against the window. Her skin went cold, as if a hundred icy fingers tapped up and down her body.

Banes put his hand over his heart and approached Benjamin's bedside. "I am here at last, sir."

Benjamin fixed his eyes forward. "The roads were poor?"

"Frozen, hard as stone. Pitted with potholes the size of stew kettles." Banes moved to the hearth. "You must excuse me, Benjamin. It is needful for me to sit by your fire. The cold has gone straight to my bones."

"My life had been a small flame, giving little warmth." Benjamin's voice quivered. "Soon the wind will blow upon my soul, and my body will turn into something like the gray, gritty ash in my hearth."

Juleah saw the pained look on Caroline's face, equal to the regret she felt that Benjamin would speak so bleakly. Grieved to see her friend suffer, she reached over, took Caroline's arm, and looped it within hers. They sat together close in silence.

"I cannot help but think of Elizabeth," Benjamin said.

"First wives are the most missed." Banes held his hands out to the fire. "How long has it been?"

"Fifteen years next month. She was the jewel in my crown."

With ascending sorrow, Juleah looked up at the ceiling. She traced the cracks with her eyes to distract herself from the conversation.

Benjamin sighed and looked over at his granddaughter. "I had to bring you back with me when the rebellion started. You understand, don't you, Caroline?"

She gave him a weak smile. "Of course, Grandfather."

"You were far too young to be exposed to the brutality of war and had no mother or older sister to care for you."

"You spared me much suffering."

His frame began to shudder. "I tried to convince your brother to leave with us, but he turned his back on me and strode away angry. It was the last time I saw him. You must tell him how sorry I am."

She nodded. "I will. I promise."

"Where is the current Mrs. Braxton?" asked Banes, laying out more papers. "Shouldn't she be present?"

Juleah cringed that Banes would ask. She knew it would exasperate Benjamin's suffering to speak of his present wife. She remained silent, turned, and met Caroline's eyes.

"She is not available, Mr. Banes," Juleah said. "There is no need to say anything more about her."

Banes drew out his spectacles and curled the stems over his ears. "Most unusual, indeed."

Benjamin gathered the blanket in his fist and squeezed. "I sent her back to Crown Cove, where she belongs."

Banes's eyebrows arched. "Sad that she is not at the side of your deathbed, Benjamin. A devoted wife can ease a man's passing. At least you have these two young ladies here."

Uneasy with the conversation and concerned for Benjamin's feelings, Juleah looked over at the old man. By his expression, she knew that the terrible feeling of not knowing what lay ahead had seized him. He returned her gaze, and her heart stretched out to comfort him.

"What shall it be, Juleah? Suffering and eternal separation from perfect love? Or blank oblivion?" Tears stole up into the corners of his eyes.

"Neither, sir. Rest easy. You are not forsaken." She knew nothing else to say.

"You are good, Juleah. You've been a sister to Caroline and a daughter to me."

Banes cleared his throat. "May we proceed to the business at hand?" He pulled a writing table up against his knees and spread the parchments out. "I made the changes you requested in your letter. I had no idea your grandson had come into your favor. When did this happen?"

"Seth has never been out of favor with me. It is I who am out of favor with him." Benjamin's eyes were misty and he turned them back to Caroline. "I repent that my allegiance to the king separated my family. The bulk of my estate is Seth's. What I've promised you and your son shall stand, Caroline. You must help Seth make the right decision. You must write to him and urge him to come."

Caroline gripped his hand. "I'll do everything in my power to convince him, Grandfather."

Banes stood from his chair, with document in hand. "Do not allow your hopes to rise high, Benjamin. Why would he quit his life in America for here?"

"His inheritance will not require he stay."

"He will face prejudice and even harbor some of his own."

Banes rubbed his eye with his finger and sighed. Once more, he dipped the nib into the ink and tapped the shaft against the rim of the bottle. The quill scratched over the parchment.

Mingled with the vines that rapped outside the window and the fire that crackled in the room, the sound dominated.

"Shall I read it back?" Banes asked.

Benjamin nodded and shut his eyes in preparation to hear his final wishes, his firm treaty before God and man.

"In the name of God, amen. I, Benjamin Braxton of Ten Width, in the Parish of Clovelly, in the County of Devonshire, squire, being weak in body but sound and disposing in mind and memory, thanks be to God, for the same do make and ordain this my last Will and Testament as following. First, I commend my soul into the hands of God Almighty, my Creator, hoping through the merits of Jesus Christ my Savior, to receive free pardon and remission of my sins, and my body I do commit to the earth. As touching my worldly estate, as God hath been pleased to bless me with, I do dispose of the same as follows. I bequeath unto my grandson, Seth Braxton, and to his heirs and assigns forever my estate at Ten Width where I now dwell. If my grandson, Seth Braxton, has no descendants, or refuses this inheritance set forth, my estate is to be bequeathed to my great-grandson, Nathaniel Kenley."

"To my granddaughter, Caroline Braxton Kenley, I discharge the sum of £250 a year during her natural life, to be paid on the first of January after the date hereof. My will is that my grandson, Seth Braxton, shall pay the said principal sum of £350 to my great-grandson, Nathaniel Kenley, so soon as he shall come of the age of one and twenty years. To my wife, I leave £100 yearly for her natural life."

Banes rose and brought the quill and parchment over to the bedside. "I need your signature, Benjamin." He helped him grip the shaft between his fingers.

Juleah sensed within herself the wretched reality of her own mortality and all those she loved. It troubled her, as she watched, with her hand firm in Caroline's. She rallied against it, took a deep breath, and whispered a prayer. "I am the resurrection and the life." Caroline heard her, and laid her head on Juleah's shoulder.

Benjamin's hand trembled, and he brought the tip of the quill down above the parchment. A moment and he hesitated. Then he scrawled his name along the bottom.

2

Virginia, July 1784

Seth walked the river path, where the peace of the countryside had returned. As he neared home, his spirit lifted. He stood still for several moments and estimated what war and time had done to his father's house. Thick green ivy covered the facade. Airy roots clung to the mortar between the stones. Grass grew tall, encroached with thistle, brown and brittle. The oak beside the house, and the rope that hung from it, the one he had swung on as a boy, looked exactly as he remembered, although one limb was black from a lightning strike.

He hurried up the steps, crossed the porch, and pushed the door in. Dirt and leaves were everywhere as if the place had become a living part of the wilderness. The July heat drove him to the river. He stripped off his clothes and sank into the shallow rapids. While he rested his head back against a rock, the current whirled around his body. His hair soaked up the water, grew darker with it, and clung to his neck.

He watched a nighthawk mount the sky against a mammoth thunderhead. A red-winged blackbird sang in the cattails, leapt up, caught a cicada in its beak, and flew off. He remembered how, three years earlier, a plague of black locusts swept the east. Ruby-eyed, with jeweled transparent wings, their incessant whirl had been deafening. Tonight crickets and tree frogs chirped and clicked in a chorus. He soaked in the peaceful timbre, while he listened to the murmur of the river as it cascaded over the rocks.

He would have stayed longer, but he grew weary of the lengthening shadows and made his way back up the path. Surprised to see a chestnut horse in front of his house, Seth halted. He gripped his hand around his musket, the new one he purchased a week after Yorktown.

Upon the step sat a young horseman in a moth-eaten, blue regimental coat, old leather breeches, and a tricorn hat. Beside him, a dented tin lantern glowed and cast a yellow fan across the crude planks of the porch.

The lad in muddy boots pulled off his hat and turned the rim between his fingers. "Captain Braxton?"

"Who are you?" Seth asked.

The lad eyed the weapon. "A messenger. Name's John Sanson. My employer, the best lawyer in Annapolis, has been looking for you for months."

Seth settled his musket at his side. "Has he?"

"Yes, sir."

"A Maryland lawyer, you say?"

"Yes, sir."

Disinterested, Seth proceeded up the steps and scraped the mud off the soles of his boots against the iron rod by the door.

"I've brought a letter." Sanson pulled it from his bag and handed it over. "I'll be going, unless you have a reply."

"I won't know until I read it." Seth glanced at the handwriting on the front. "Come inside. I'll give you what meat I have."

Sanson smiled and strode up the stairs to the door. "Thank you, sir. I haven't had a meal since yesterday, just hard biscuits."

Seth moved to the table inside the dimly lit dwelling. After he lit a candle, he blew out the match and tossed it into the fireplace. The young messenger looked hungry, so he poured him a tin of water and gave him a plate of cold venison.

Without a word, Seth broke the scarlet seal on the letter and unfolded the page. A moment later, he folded it back up and set it on the table near the candlestick.

"I have no reply," he said.

Sanson nodded, finished his meal, and went out to mount his horse. "A girl waits for me on the other side of the river. It's easier to travel by night than in the heat of day."

Seth followed him outside. "Below the hill, you'll find a shallow place. You'll know it by the dead willow lying in the water. It's easy to cross there."

The lad climbed into the saddle, tipped his hat, and galloped off. Seth sat on the step and stared up at the crescent moon above the treetops. It bathed the land in a cool blue haze. The night sky and the trees that moved in a soft breeze caused his heart to grow heavy. He would be unable to sleep again. His mind was troubled, his thoughts cluttered. The letter declared that he had inherited his grandfather's estate. If the land were in America, he would not hesitate to take it. But England? How could he? He had rightly lifted up arms against the British. How on earth could he consider leaving his home in Virginia?

But then there was Caroline.

The last time he saw his sister, she was a child of twelve. He remembered her smile, the mass of wheat-colored curls that toppled over her head, the bright green eyes. At eighteen, he entered the Continental Army. He recalled how she cried, how her arms stretched out to her papa when her grandfather took her away.

Who cared for her in England now that his grandfather was dead? What had become of her? Did she care she had a brother, a rebel at that? He must think through everything with a rational mind and assume nothing.

Weary, he brushed the sweat off his brow and marked the moon above the inky treetops. A meteor shot across the sky and awe filled him.

At midnight, he stood and went inside. The letter sat on the table, and with hands upon hips, he stared with a lengthening face at the open pages.

Frustrated, he blew out his candle and went soberly to bed.

❧

It took Seth two days to make a decision. At nine in the morning, he headed across the Potomac to the village of Point of Rocks on the Maryland shore. From there, he traveled through the rolling fields of Frederick County and turned southeast onto the Annapolis Road. Four pennies and seven silver dollars lined his pocket.

Out in a field of golden summer wheat, a farmer waved to him. Seth jumped the fence that separated the farmer's land from the road. "Do you have a horse to sell or loan?"

"I've got a gray better for riding than work. You can have her, saddle and bridle, if you're willing to pay," the farmer said. "Come on up to the barn and I'll show her to you."

Seth looked the horse over, then emptied his pocket of two silver dollars. "Will this be enough?"

The farmer's brows shot up. "For that old nag, aye. She's slow, but she'll get you where you need to go."

Seth climbed into the saddle and ran the reins through his hands. The sway of the mare's back had a wide girth—not at all like Saber, who had once been all muscle and brawn. He allowed the sad memory to be fleeting and settled back, for the journey would be long.

The road was hard and dusty, and alongside it purple thistles grew among knee-deep rows of snowy Queen Anne's lace. The day would be hot from the way the stems bent hook-like, with the heads turned downward, eager for the earth's dew.

Riding along, he dragged off his hat and mopped the sweat off his forehead. The hours slipped by, until night fell and he settled down in a field under the stars to sleep.

He reached the bustling town of Annapolis late in the afternoon the following day. Rain clouds hovered over black slate roofs and church steeples, but had not yet blessed the thirsty earth. Along the busy, cobbled streets, Seth moved his horse. He rode past St. John's College and neared the waterfront where tall ships were moored in the Severn River, their creamy sails furled. Seagulls darted and whirled between the black lines of rigging.

He reached inside his waistcoat pocket, drew out the letter, and glanced at the address. John Stowefield's house stood out from the rest by reason of its bright red door with stark black fixtures and the numerous pots of scarlet geraniums out front.

After he tethered his mount, he bounded up the stairs and approached the door, tired and sweaty from the long journey and perpetual heat. Removing his tricorn hat, he frowned at its tattered appearance, brushed it off, and tucked it beneath his arm.

When the door opened, he was shown inside Stowefield's office, a room with large mullioned windows, where the sunlight seeped through the draperies. Stowefield sat at his desk dozing, his steel spectacles low on the bridge of his nose. His hair, a mass of gray locks, matched a pair of bushy eyebrows. His housekeeper nudged him on the shoulder and he shook and sputtered awake.

"What is it, Partridge?"

Seth waited inside the doorway. He smiled at the pronouncement of the woman's name. She resembled the bird, with her tiny eyes and spherical face, stout neck and body, the way her arms hung away from her sides when she walked.

"Mr. Braxton here to see you." Partridge folded her hands over her apron. "You must rise from your nap."

"Braxton, you say? Well good." Stowefield shifted in his Windsor chair. It creaked beneath his weight. "Bring us coffee, Partridge. Make it strong."

With a quick jerk of her head, Partridge turned. "I'll make the best coffee for you, sir."

Stowefield let out a heavy sigh. "You see, Mr. Braxton? Whenever a handsome face new to Partridge comes to my house, she's flustered. I promise, the tray she brings will be more substantial than my usual coffee and buttered bread."

Hat in hand, Seth stepped forward and extended his hand. He had no riding gloves, and frowned a moment at the red chafing over his knuckles made so by the leather reins. "I hope I haven't come at a bad time, sir. It's late in the day."

Stowefield stood to shake Seth's hand. "Aye, 'tis late, but too early to doze off at one's desk. Makes one look the sluggard at his trade. I stayed up late last night playing Whist with a client. Sinful, I know, and I should repent of it."

"Whist, sir?"

Stowefield smiled and his eyes enlarged. "Yes, Whist. Do you play?"

Seth shook his head. "I'm not inclined to sitting room games."

"I imagine it's not a game younger men enjoy these days. Others are more challenging. The ladies for example?" He wrinkled his nose and let out a snort meant to be a laugh.

Seth smiled and changed the subject. "You sent me a letter concerning my grandfather's estate."

"I'm glad you've taken my advice and come."

"Only that, sir."

Stowefield dragged off his spectacles and put them on his desk. "What do you mean?"

"I'll not take his property."

Stowefield raised his brows. "But it's been willed to you. You're the legal heir. It'd be foolish not to take it. Think of the fortune you'd have."

"I have my father's land."

"And what will that bring you but a pocket of scratch? You'll be in the poorhouse by winter. This drought will wipe out many a landed gentleman."

"A landed gentleman I'm not, Mr. Stowefield."

Stowefield cocked one brow. "Well, not in English terms perhaps. But that is beside the point."

"I've other plans besides planting."

"Such as?"

"I want to breed horses and restore the house."

"Noble goals they may be, but . . ."

"It will take some time to raise the money, but it's my ambition to raise the finest racers and hunters in Virginia."

Stowefield sighed. "Well, your grandfather has left you enough to raise a hundred or more."

Seth lowered his eyes with a frown. "I don't want his money. I'll raise the funds on my own. A few good seasons and . . ."

Stowefield raised his hand. "You're too young to know what is wise to do. I mean no insult by it, but you need sound advice. You cannot let your feelings or prejudice rule you in this matter. I know you fought for independence, and I hear you paid dearly for it. But a man has a duty to his family no matter what country he may live in or what political allegiances he may have."

"And it is for that reason I'll not go to England. How can I live in a country I rebelled against?"

"Have you forgotten your sister?"

"No, sir, I have not."

"What will she do now that she's alone?"

"I would hope she'd come home and live with me until she weds."

A look of consternation rose on Stowefield's face. "Forgive me for saying so, but I think you may be uninformed on such delicate themes."

"In what way, sir?"

"You expect her, a woman, to journey across the ocean alone? America would be unfamiliar to her now. She has lived in England for a long time."

"It would be her decision, of course."

"She'll have wolves prowling at her door. Have you thought of that?"

Seth shifted on his feet. He had an obligation to his sister, and he was fighting it.

Partridge brought in the tray. Coffee, sliced apples coated with cinnamon and sugar, and baking powder biscuits with pats of bright yellow butter were upon it. She had used the best china and silver.

When she left, Stowefield sipped his coffee. He looked at the black brew and licked his lips.

"I say. This is the best coffee Partridge has ever concocted." He glanced over at Seth and grinned. "No doubt it's for you and not for an old man like me."

Seth smiled at the compliment, but said nothing in reply. He, too, enjoyed the little repast she provided.

"As I understand it, you've had no contact with your grandfather since the beginning of the war." Stowefield picked up an apple slice between his fingers and tasted it. "He left our country with Caroline in seventy-six. Is that correct?"

"Yes, that's right, she without our mother and too young to suffer a war."

Stowefield popped the rest of the apple slice into his mouth, chewed it, and washed it down with his coffee. "Benjamin remarried years ago. Did you know?"

This new twist added sober surprise in Seth. "No, sir."

"Well he did, and at his advanced age. The woman was comely for her years, but poor, so this letter states. He married her out of loneliness, no doubt. New love is rare when one is old." Stowefield set his cup on the table. "Beggars cannot be choosers."

Seth let out a short laugh.

"I know what you're thinking." Stowefield winked. "How can I, an old man, say as much? Experience, I can tell you. Whether a wife be a titled lady or a milkmaid, it is she who makes a home out of four lonely walls."

Seth shrugged. "Some men prefer four walls that are his alone, no matter how dark or lonely. Marriage for some is bondage, for others freedom. I suppose my grandfather couldn't do without it."

"She brought a son into the marriage by her first husband." Stowefield, refilled his pipe, lit a match, and put it to the bowl. "I learned he's a man about your age."

This brought a rise of pain. To him, he and his father had been replaced. Seth clutched his fists hard, stood from the chair, and stepped over to the window.

"That's not unusual. Why should it matter to me or to my inheritance?"

"It's of no importance," Stowefield replied. "Indeed, it's common. Your grandfather left his widow an annuity of one hundred pounds per year. More than generous for them to live comfortably on."

"Then why does there seem to be a problem?"

"I'm afraid if you do not lay hold on your inheritance this gentleman might try to claim it for his own. He may leave your sister in a situation where she's forced to marry where she does not wish. I have no doubt Benjamin's stepson is hell bent on having his way if he craves more money, and things could be complicated, if not compromised."

"How would you know this, sir?"

"My profession is the law, Mr. Braxton. My hobby is detection." Stowefield squinted his eyes and tapped the side of his nose with his forefinger. "It is the wording of the letters that paint the picture. The story holds the keys to determining which course of action your grandfather's stepson would most likely take. Do you see?"

"I think so." Seth shifted on his feet. "Who are these letters from?"

Stowefield settled back in his chair. "One is from Mr. Banes, your grandfather's lawyer. The other is from your sister, Caroline. It is but simple facts she discloses, and her urging for me to convince you is profound."

"Is it?" Seth moved back to the chair but remained standing.

"Indeed so. A letter is enclosed to you as well." Stowefield handed it to Seth. He stood up and moved toward the doorway. "I'll provide a few moments for you to read it. Perhaps later you'll have an answer for me."

Seth waited while Stowefield left the room. The door clicked shut. Upon Seth's neck, the heat of the evening sun poured through the window. The letter lay in his calloused hand. He stared at it a moment, at his name scrolled in a feminine hand on the front. He broke the seal and unfolded the pages.

My Dear Brother:

I pray Mr. Stowefield has been able to find you. I hope you will listen to his advice with an open mind. Before Grandfather died, he begged me to write to you and ask that all injuries be forgiven. He lived this last year in relentless anguish and rued the past.

I married a good man, but he has left me a widow, with a young son, age two years. He's a fine boy and brings me joy.

I am sure Mr. Stowefield informed you that our grandfather remarried several years ago. His widow is cold in manner and never was a mother to me. I never see her, and I believe she is a sick woman. Her son says if you are alive, the government would refuse to acknowledge you as heir and brand you a traitor and rebel. I do not believe this, dear brother. He says you are undeserving under the grounds of treason for having fought in the Revolution. Mr. Banes has assured me otherwise.

Therefore, my dear brother, I beg of you to come to Ten Width. Come at least for a time, and then, if it is your wish to return to Virginia, I shall understand.

My friend, Juleah Fallowes, Mr. Stowefield's niece, has stayed with me following the days after Grandfather's death. She has provided a shoulder for me to cry upon. Without her, I'd be alone in the house except for two servants and my little lad. I cannot bear the sorrow here.

So much has happened in my short life. Things I cannot tell you until I see you again. You must send me word of your decision, and hopefully your arrival.

Your devoted sister, Caroline

When Mr. Stowefield returned, Seth sat in the chair with the letter in his hand. Contemplative thoughts stirred his mind and he felt them expressed upon his face. The setting sun spread the copper light of twilight inside the room, and for a moment, he watched it play over the wood furnishings.

"Mr. Stowefield," he said. "I need time to think."

"I understand that principle, sir." Stowefield tucked his spectacles inside his waistcoat pocket and sighed. "But if you think too long and hard on the matter, you'll find a way to talk yourself out of it."

"Wisdom demands caution, sir," Seth replied. "A man who makes his steps too hasty and bases his decisions on feelings may fall into a pit."

Stowefield chuckled. "You're a farmer and a scholar."

"I'm not good at either profession. Nonetheless, I thank you for the compliment."

"Forgive me for asking, young man. But doesn't it feel grand to have become so wealthy?"

"No, I feel doubtful."

At once Stowefield's brows shot up. "That's most incredible, sir."

Seth stood and picked up his hat. "I must be leaving. Direct me to a cheap inn if you know one."

Stowefield threw back his shoulders. "I'll do nothing of the kind. My house is large and I'd be honored if you'd be my guest."

"I cannot impose upon you."

"Why waste your money on an inn? You'll not find a finer table than mine, nor better conversation."

Though reluctant, Seth agreed to stay. Partridge told him she was pleased to wait upon him, and showed him upstairs before dinner. The glow of the candle fanned out before them as they climbed the staircase. The room stood at the far end of the house.

"Have you a good coat with you, sir?" Partridge's voice was motherly, her gray hair spying out from beneath her white mobcap. "The wise gentleman brings a good coat with him when away from home. If you give me your traveling suit I'll brush it for you and polish your boots."

Seth pulled off his boots and handed them over, then his coat. She was short, stout about the middle, and waddled over to him to take them in hand. "These are fine, Mr. Braxton." She held them out and studied them. "Soon you'll have finer."

"I can't be sure of that, madam," Seth told her.

"No one knows what the future may hold, Mr. Braxton, save for the good Lord. We hope for the best." She headed through the door and turned back to close it. "I'll put your boots out here in a half hour, so as not to disturb you."

That night the windows in Stowefield's house stood open. The boxwood and roses from the garden scented the tepid air, and candlelight bathed the room in a haze of gold. The interior of the house was stuffy and warm, with that musty smell old houses seem to have.

As he descended the staircase, Seth heard laughter. Dressed in his best navy blue jacket and beige breeches, he entered the dining room. Stowefield introduced him to his guests and he bowed. They were Stowefield's generation, some fat, some lean, gray, and wrinkled. The ladies wore heavy powder upon their faces, and the gentlemen dressed as natural men, a trend admired in Ben Franklin when he won the hearts of the Parisians.

They supped together on a simple yet delicious meal of roasted chicken, pole beans, and potatoes. Partridge stood back near the door and wrung her hands while she watched Mr. Stowefield carve the birds she had prepared. They were burned on the outside, and she fretted they were spoiled.

"I fear they're ruined, Mr. Stowefield."

"In spite of their charred appearance," Stowefield said as he popped a piece into his mouth, "the meat is delicious and succulent, Partridge. Nothing to fear."

Still, Partridge bit her lower lip and wiped her hands over the front of her apron as Stowefield placed the chicken on his plate.

"It's a fine table you set, Mrs. Partridge," said Seth, tasting the bounty. "I've not had food this good in a long time."

"Thank you, sir." She dipped with a broad smile and left the room looking happy.

"I imagine camp food was not to a man's liking," said Stowefield.

"Not to mine, sir, the little we had."

"It was the same in the French and Indian War, I assure you. Bread as hard and tasteless as wood, and not a good ale to wash it down with."

"You served in that war, Mr. Stowefield?"

"Indeed I did, and I have a few scars to prove it. I shall not tell where."

The group laughed. The middle-aged woman to Stowefield's left, Mrs. Jenny Bayberry tapped him on the shoulder with her spoon.

"We've heard the stories a thousand times over, John Stowefield, so much so that we know them by heart. Let us talk of other things."

"Well, all right. Our young guest, ladies and gentlemen, served in the Revolution," said Stowefield. "Is that not so, Seth?"

"I was among a group of Virginia sharpshooters, sir."

"Virginia is proud of her sons." Stowefield drained his glass of wine and lifted the decanter in front of him to refill it. "As is Maryland. Our Frederick riflemen were praised as the best sharpshooters of the war."

"A hero sits among us," Mrs. Bayberry exclaimed. She was a widow, and older than Stowefield by her look, her eyes gray and misty with cataracts, her face a collage of wrinkles.

"Ah, ma'am, I would not say that." Seth smiled. "I did my duty, that's all."

"You're too modest, Seth Braxton. Our Mr. Stowefield was a rich lawyer before the Revolution. Dedicated to The Glorious Cause, he forfeited his plenty to aid the rebels in their struggle for independence. You no doubt gave up much as well."

Seth bowed his head to the lady. "We all did, ma'am."

"Indeed, Mr. Braxton. I lost two sons in the Revolution and my husband. I warned he was too old to go off fighting. A stubborn man was he. I rued the day he and my boys left. I'm sure your mother is glad you lived."

The memory of his mother caused Seth's smile to waver. "My mother died before the war, ma'am."

Mrs. Bayberry's expression was empathetic. "Well, fortunate for you, you have a sister. But no wife? What a pity. For you're young and handsome. You cannot deny ladies wait upon your attentions."

"I can deny it with confidence."

He did not enjoy such open conversations regarding love and hoped the subject would change. His experience with women was his own, private, something he felt a man should not boast about. Still, he had not known what it felt like to be in love.

Mrs. Bayberry's mouth fell open. "Perhaps you simply have your eyes closed to it. You'll have them opened in due time. We should be grateful our infant country and England are on good terms, else no one would inherit a smidgen from their relations on the other side of the ocean. Some of us would've been cast off."

Stowefield cleared his throat and looked up from his plate of food. "Shall we have a toast to our brave lads?" He raised his glass.

With a gentle acknowledgment of their revolutionary heroes, the guests drank, and then coughed from its strength. Seth remained quiet during the rest of the meal, but politely answered every question directed at him. Most came from Mrs. Bayberry, the spokesperson for the group. He was not in the mood for chitchat with strangers, and the conversation put him in a sullen mood, thinking about his parents, the war, his sister, and the decision he faced.

Afterward, tables were set up for card playing. Moodily, Seth stood by the window. Over the mantle hung a group portrait, and when his eyes met those of the woman in it, he was struck by the beauty and skill of the painting. The color of the eyes, the way the artist caused them to glisten and express feminine joy, captivated the viewer.

The subject was unlike any he had seen. She wore a slight smile upon a face naturally beautiful. No powder, rouge, or wig concealed her. Her hair, long and dark, brown as the color of oak leaves in autumn, lay soft across one shoulder. Her left hand held the flow of hair at her breast. A band of blue ribbon pulled her heavy locks together near her forehead, and from under the front of the ribbon, delicate curls framed her face.

A gown of white linen, accented with blue taffeta ribbon at the belled sleeves, graced her feminine frame. Her shoulders, round and smooth, were bare. Her right hand lay in her lap, touched by a flow of soft creamy lace. Within it, she held a spray of purple heather.

Then there were the eyes, the depths of which drew the admirer. The artist's attempt to capture the facets of color held Seth's gaze in rapt attention. Sparkling full of spirit, clear amber struck Seth with the noonday sun. He wondered how they would appear in real life. Would the light play over them and her soul be revealed?

Stowefield drew up beside him. "I see you admire the painting."

Seth's eyes remained transfixed, as he studied the contours of the woman's face. "Who is she?"

"My niece Juleah. Lovely creature, wouldn't you say?"

"Yes, she's pretty."

"Mather Brown produced the painting earlier this year in London. He painted John Adams and his daughter Nabby's portraits."

"I've heard of Mr. Brown."

Stowefield turned and lifted his brows. "Have you?"

"Even Virginian planters can be kept abreast in the arts. Who are the children beside her?"

"Ah, her sister, Jane, and brother, Thomas. Jane is a fine girl, and I daresay she shall be as pretty as Juleah. Thomas will be a strapping young man when he's older."

"Do you see them from time to time?"

"No, but we correspond throughout the year. Juleah will not forget her uncle. I commissioned the portrait a year ago and received it this week. I had no idea she had grown so lovely, and with womanly wisdom showing in her eyes."

Seth studied Juleah's face deeper and discovered how quick his heart was to beat. "Yes, except there is no true smile there, but a sadness."

Stowefield pinched his eyebrows together. He drew off his spectacles, held them out before him, and leaned in for a closer examination. "I had not noticed."

"You can see it in her eyes. She may have smiled for Mr. Brown, but the expression in her eyes shows pretense."

"You may be right. Most likely she was bored sitting. Or, she may have been thinking of some unrequited love."

Seth turned away. His manner was cool, but beneath it, his blood raced. It disturbed him that Juleah's image had such a strong effect upon him. Her beauty and natural allure were undeniable, and he thought about the possibility he might meet her in England . . . if he were to go.

"Caroline mentioned your niece in her letter," he said.

"Yes, they are great friends," Stowefield replied. "If you do go to Britain, perhaps Juleah will be of comfort to you also, as she is to your good sister."

At this, Seth stiffened and set his mouth. His genial smile vanished, and he could feel, down to his marrow, the cold and pained look that flooded his eyes. "I doubt there's a woman so lovely or modest, or graced with enough womanly wisdom to be of any comfort to me, sir. Women do not wish for friendship in a man."

Stowefield let out a laugh. "On the contrary. My late wife was my best friend and I hers, right from the start of our courtship."

"My father spoke the same of my mother. I hope I'm as blessed, but I doubt it."

He excused himself, and wished Mr. Stowefield and his guests a good night. He went upstairs to the guest room and pulled off his boots. That night, Seth lay in bed staring at the pattern the moonlight made against the ceiling. He thought to no end, torn between two worlds.

He needed to see his sister again to be sure she was well and to set his affairs in England in order. It was his duty. Then he envisioned those yearning eyes that belonged to Juleah Fallowes.

Frustrated with it all, a prisoner to obligation and conscience, he asked what care did he have for England, for his grandfather's estate, for the love of a woman?

3
Ten Width, September 17, 1784

I love thee, I love but thee with a love that shall not die
Till the sun grows cold and the stars are old
And the leaves of the judgment book unfold
—Bayard Taylor

A knot gripped Seth's stomach. After a long sea voyage, he stood on English soil in the port town of Penzance in Cornwall, in the land of his ancestors, long dead, long forgotten. The sun ruled the zenith, touched upon his face. Its caress warmed his skin, chased off the chilly wind that blew across the southern harbor, but that was all.

After he handed up his ticket to the coachman, he stepped inside the bleak interior of the coach. He was glad to see he was the sole occupant, with as much room as the cabin he slept in crossing the Atlantic. Only this smelled of people instead of seawater.

He pulled off his tricorn and set it next to him. The whalebone buttons on the bands of his breeches were cold against his knees. He hoped his cloak would keep him warm into the night.

The door shut, and Seth, seated to the right and forward, leaned toward the window. A magenta light peeked through the clouds, while veils of mist fell over frost-laden fields. From the chimneys of houses blew smoke from hearth fires.

What kind of reception would he receive at Ten Width? A strange name was this for a manor. He had been told Ten Width was founded upon rich farmland, banked by thick forests teeming with game and a blue lake to the east. The house was old, built in 1603. Originally, the acres were ten miles in width, thus the name Ten Width.

Would he find the house in ruins? Crumbling walls, no doubt, broken windows, lichen-covered stone, airless, unused rooms smelling of age. Yes, the house would be dark and bleak, and he dreaded it.

These troubling visions made him frown, and he cursed his obligation as Benjamin's heir to a house he had never seen, in a country he had not been born to. During his journey over sea and land, he had come to realize that other magnets drew him to England. Those eyes, the parted mouth, drew him to a woman he had not met in the flesh, but in paint and canvas in a candlelit room. The lips, even now in his memory, whispered. The eyes cast a suggestion; the face enticed.

Seth rebuked his foolishness to dwell on an image, an interpretation of an artist's brush. For all he knew Juleah Fallowes was not as her portrait. What did he care? Outward beauty was fleeting. What mattered lay inward.

Four miles east of Penzance, the coach rolled over the sandy highway situated atop the hills above Marazion. Below, Seth saw the spire of the Church of Saint Hilary jutting skyward. The coach wheels drowned out the sigh of wind. The tide had gone out in Mount's Bay, and from the highest point on land, Seth gazed at the granite island of St. Michael's Mount rising out of the sea. The sun spread a plane of sapphire across the water, alighted lances against the rocks and the ancient castle atop the island. What kind of person would live in such a place? It would be lonely, and to be surrounded by the sea, depressing. He preferred fields of wheat and corn, deep forests, the whisper of the Potomac. In a castle surrounded by rock and water, a man would go mad, or fat and idle. He'd have no fields to plow; life would be dull and listless, absent of singing birds, replaced by screeching gulls, no great bass to fish from the river, no deer to hunt.

Soon the island passed out of view. The coach swayed and dipped along a road lined with villages and headed inland to cross the barren heathlands of Bodmin Moor on to northern Devonshire.

At nightfall, the coach slowed, came to a halt in front of an inn outside of Baxworthy. The sign outside the black lacquered door read The Black Mare, and it swayed with the breeze upon rusty hinges.

The coachman jumped down from his perch, and a moment later a woman ordered him to go easy with her baggage. Under the glare of the coach lamps, he opened the door, pulled down the step, and handed the lady up, followed by a boy and his sister. The woman wore a large bonnet clustered with blue ribbons and a thick bow beneath her chin. She plopped into the seat across from Seth and gathered her children to each side of her.

"Good eve, sir." Her breath hurried, and she gathered her cloak closer about her. "My, it is fine weather to travel in, is it not? Chilly, but fine."

"Yes, madam," replied Seth. A snap of the reins and the horses moved off into the center of the road and headed on. The left wheel dipped into a pothole and the coach lurched to the side and soon righted.

The lady passenger, now Seth's companion for the journey, glanced at him somewhat puzzled. Fidgeting, she wished to break the silence between them.

"My children and I are not far from home. I shall be happy to sit before my own fire. We have come from my sister's house, Lowery Cottage, just outside of Milford. Are you familiar with Lowery Cottage, sir?"

Seth lifted his hand from under his chin. "I'm afraid not."

"Oh? Well, it is a fine place to be sure. My sister's husband is the vicar there, and the church sits nearby in a pretty glade. May I ask where it is you are journeying to?"

"I'm on my way to Ten Width."

The lady sighed. "Ten Width?"

"You know this place, ma'am?"

"Know it? Indeed, sir, I do."

"Is it far from here?"

"Within the hour, I'd say. Did not the coachman say as much?"

"He said we would arrive in daylight. I see now he was wrong."

"That is true. The coach was an hour late picking us up."

"I hope your family shall not worry," Seth said.

"I am sure my husband is anxious to see us home. Ten Width is known well within our county. The squire died last November, and so mysterious a man he was in his later years. There were no parties at Ten Width like in years past. Everything was kept quiet."

Seth listened in an effort to absorb the information she put forth. "I imagine he wanted his privacy."

The boy stared at Seth with boyish curiosity. "Mother, do you suppose the gentleman carries a brace of pistols with him under his coat?"

The mother squeezed her son's arm to silence him. "You must forgive me for asking. But by your speech, it is evident you are an American. Is it from there you hail?"

"It is, ma'am. I was raised in Virginia."

She put her hand against her heart and sighed. "Virginia. I hear she is pretty alongside her neighbor Maryland. I find it laudatory they are named after noble women. Don't you?"

Seth nodded and settled back against the seat. "Yes, but deceptive as well. Their wildernesses are treachery and beauty combined . . . like women."

The lady laughed, and her son continued to stare over at Seth with interest.

"Sir, do they have highwaymen in Virginia and Maryland?" the boy queried.

"I've met none, young sir," Seth told him.

"Were you a soldier in the last war?"

The mother snatched her son's hand and shook it again in reproof. "You mustn't ask the gentleman such questions, Thomas. It is not proper." Her hazel eyes softened when she looked back at Seth. "I suppose it is natural for my boy to be inquisitive."

The right corner of Seth's mouth curved. "I was a patriot. I think here in England it would be wise I not bring it up."

The boy's eyes widened. "Have you fought with Indians?"

"I had a few encounters, yes."

"Is it true the savages eat the flesh of their enemies?"

"Where did you hear that, young sir?"

"I read it in a book. My father keeps it in his library."

"Well, don't believe everything you read." Seth put his elbow up on the windowsill and relaxed. "Indians are a noble people, great warriors, and skilled hunters. To the surprise of some, they're more civilized than people imagine."

"Someday, I'll go to America and see them for myself." The boy held out his hand to shake Seth's. "My name is Thomas Fallowes. This is my mother, Lady Anna, and my sister, Jane.

Jane's twelve. I am eight. Jane is very shy of strangers, sir. That is why she has not spoken to you."

"I see. Have you any other brothers or sisters?"

"One other. Juleah is the eldest," said Mrs. Fallowes, her tone proud.

What had been the chance of this? Slim to none. Could Juleah be anything like her mother; fine figured, pale of skin, soft in gesture and manner, yet lacking beauty? Anna's hair was dove-gray, which matched the color of her cloak. Delicate lines graced the edges of her eyes. Her mouth was thin and pouty. She looked nothing like her daughter, according to Mr. Brown.

"Your name, sir?" the lady asked.

He gave her a nod. "Seth Braxton, at your service."

The lady looked stunned, bewildered, intrigued, while her large eyes stared back at him through the dim light. "I should have realized you are Benjamin's relation."

"His grandson to be exact."

"My goodness, sir. You should have said so."

"My apologies. I didn't think it mattered."

"Oh, it does. So many whispers these days as to your grand-father's dying, about your dear, unfortunate sister, Caroline. We mustn't discuss the intimate details of your family, nor the reason you have come of a sudden. But I find it by chance we should meet, for we know the same people and are somewhat neighbors."

Seth nodded. "Yes, it is coincidental."

"You must come dine one evening and meet my husband, Henry, and our daughter Juleah."

Again, Seth inclined his head. "I'd be honored."

"Caroline must come as well. We've not seen her in a long time. I suppose the grief of losing her grandfather has done it."

"Yes," Seth agreed. "I suppose that must be the reason."

"It takes a long time for a woman, Mr. Braxton. We are sensitive creatures. I shall have my husband send forth an invitation as soon as you are settled."

With a crack of the coachman's whip, the horses pulled the coach up a single steep street into Clovelly, a medieval hamlet of thatched cottages.

The lady pulled her children close. "Clovelly at last. We are proud of it, Mr. Braxton. It is the most beautiful seaside village in England."

Here the lady and her children disembarked. A carriage awaited them, sent by Sir Henry Fallowes to carry his family the rest of the route up the winding roads that led to their home six miles northeast.

Farewells being said, Seth watched Lady Anna set off with her children. He would see them again, for it was inevitable he and Juleah Fallowes should meet.

Having disembarked, Seth made his way down a narrow street that pitched sharply toward the sea five hundred feet below the village. He could hear the waves lap against the quay and pound the rocks in the windswept harbor. He looked down and saw a stone breakwater, curved like a pirate's hook into the sea. A seawall was draped in seaweed and the dark brown nets and traps of fishermen draped over the seawall.

He paused and asked a man seated in his doorway, which way to Banes's house. Up the path he must return, go past a row of quaint cottages along a cobblestone street, and walk north for a quarter of a mile to a bleak timber-and-plaster house at the side of the road. From his coat pocket, he took out the address given to him and checked it against the brass plate fixed beside the door under the glare of a lantern. Sea air had turned the plate green. He walked up the stairs, raised his fist, and knocked on the door.

The door opened. A servant stood inside, one hand firm upon the latch, the other holding a candle. The golden flame cast a light over Seth's face, and the housekeeper hesitated, obviously wary of the man who stood outside. She took a firmer hold upon the door and closed it until only her oval face showed.

Seth dragged off his hat. "I'm here to see Mr. Banes. Is he at home?"

"He's abed. Come back tomorrow."

"I'm Squire Braxton's grandson." Seth took a step forward. "Mr. Banes expects me."

Her jowls wiggled. "I don't care who you are. The hour is too late for my master to see anyone."

"Late? It is but six of the hour."

"Mr. Banes concludes business by three on Saturday afternoons. Go on with you." She lifted her nose in the air and went to shut the door.

Seth put his boot in between the door and the jamb. "Listen here. I'm not leaving until I see Mr. Banes. I've had a long sea voyage and traveled overland from Penzance. Now, will you rouse him from his chamber, or shall I?"

The woman narrowed her eyes. "If Mr. Banes gets angry, you're to blame."

She mumbled under her breath, hoisted her skirts above a pair of stout ankles, and ascended the staircase. Then she disappeared down an upstairs hallway. To the right a double door led to a sitting room. A fire simmered in the hearth and gave warmth to the paneled room. Seth went in and warmed his hands in front of the fire. The floorboards creaked under someone's weight upstairs. A moment later Banes came into the room, followed by his disgruntled housekeeper.

"Bring tea, Winkle, and bread and cheese."

Banes wore an old burgundy dressing gown over a linen shirt and breeches. Upon his head, he wore a cap with a gold tassel that dangled from the top.

"Winkle says you claim to be Seth Braxton."

"I am he, Mr. Banes. I'm sorry to disturb you, but you asked that I see you straightaway upon my arrival."

"Have you proof of your identity?"

From his breast pocket, Seth retrieved a letter and handed it over. Banes put on his spectacles and took it in hand. He moved to inspect it in the light and nodded.

"Yes, this is the letter I sent. But anyone could come by it."

"I've another addressed to you from Mr. Stowefield, since you are in doubt."

Banes glanced over the missive from his colleague. He raised his brows and folded the note. "I believe you are who you say you are."

"It took some convincing to get me here, Mr. Banes. As you probably know, my grandfather and I were not on the best of terms."

"I know something of it."

Slices of brown bread and a hunk of good English cheese were brought in. Banes poured Seth a mug of ale and handed it to him. Seth lifted the mug and drank. The ale tasted bitter and he set it aside.

"Ten Width is a few miles from here?"

"Five and one-half, I believe. Possibly more. I've never taken the time to notice." Banes dug his knife into the cheese.

Seth picked up his hat to leave. "I'll not intrude upon you any longer. You can find me at Ten Width if you should need to speak to me."

"I'll see to it you have a mount. Take this note of introduction with you." Banes scratched a line across a sheet of paper.

A light smile moved from a corner of Seth's mouth. He took the note and tucked it inside his waistcoat pocket. "I'm used to living rough, sir. I can walk."

"A horse will get you there in better time. Will you be settling here for good?"

"I have land of my own in Virginia."

"I hear it is a swampy place, full of a rabble of veterans of your revolution."

"Veterans, yes. You've been misinformed as far as rabble."

"Perhaps. The question is how you'll convince Englishmen otherwise." Banes rubbed his nose with the back of his hand and sloshed his bread through the butter. "Thousands of loyalists left America to resettle in Britain. Have you heard that Sir William Hershel discovered a new planet? He named it Georgium Sidus, meaning George's Star in honor of our king."

"The ancients also named the stars, Mr. Banes. But they did it for God's glory and not for the glory of any earthly king. I'm sure King George is pleased, though, and doesn't flaunt the honor."

Seth was not surprised at the reaction to his comment, the frown, the rapid blink of the eyes, and the hard setting of the lips.

"A comment I would expect from a revolutionary." Banes tossed his bread down on the plate. He stood and tightened the sash of his dressing gown. He tugged on the bell cord and within a moment, Winkle appeared in the doorway. "Winkle, be a good woman and go around the back to Finley. Tell him to bring my horse for this gentleman."

Winkle dipped and went her way, the gloom of the hallway swallowing her up in its dark cavernous hole. Banes shuffled out into the hallway. "Take care of footpads along the road. Have you a pistol?"

"I do, sir."

"Good. Stay to the high road and you'll have no problems." Banes stepped out into his narrow hallway and turned back to Seth. "I must warn you that a fever has spread through the county. Keep your loved ones safe at Ten Width, for I hear it is a strong contagion."

He ushered Seth to the front door and closed it as soon as Seth stepped foot outside. It had been a cool meeting, but Seth put it behind him. He mounted the horse and it sighed under him. The man, Finley, stood back and stared at Seth. He brushed his hands over his shirt and walked off. Seth kicked the horse's sides and it cantered down the road, one side lined with stately trees, the other open to the sea below. The breeze strengthened, churned up the dry leaves scattered over the ground, and rustled the bracken that grew alongside the road.

Near his destination, with less than a mile left to go, Seth slowed his mount and reined in atop a hill. The horse shook its hairy mane, snorted, and flicked its ears. It paced uneasily, and Seth tried to soothe it with a touch of his hand, roping the reins around his fist.

Through the gloom, he could see the great old house, standing on the opposite hillside. Tall poplars grew to the left and cast long spiky shadows across the lawn as the breeze twisted and turned their waxy leaves. So this was it, the ancestral home of the Braxtons. If it were not for Caroline, he would not have come. He would have let this place rot.

Seth nudged the horse on. Outside the gates, he brought it to a halt. Wind whispered forlornly through the trees. The horse paced, turned round, and with a click of his tongue, Seth moved it slowly down the drive. When he reached the door, he dismounted, looped the reins over the post, and glanced over brick and mortar, ivy and window.

He scraped the mud off his boots along the stone step and climbed it. No one greeted him as he had hoped, and he had no key.

He drew in a long breath, raised his fist, and knocked upon the door.

4

In those moments when Seth rode toward Ten Width, Juleah sat at Caroline's sickbed. She rubbed her eyes with the palm of her hand, sighed, and pushed back the tendrils of hair that had fallen over her face. Normally, it was fixed in a mass of long tresses that hung about her throat and down the nape of her neck. Tonight her hair hung loose along her back, dark as the chestnuts in the bowl near the fire.

She bit her lower lip. Would Seth Braxton ever come to Ten Width? Caroline told her what she remembered of him, that he was everything good and amiable. After Caroline had written to Seth, Juleah advised patience. Caroline needed her brother, yet Juleah had a certain aversion toward a man who had taken up arms against England and killed her countrymen on the battlefield. What kind of subversive attitudes would he bring? Would not the gentry snub Caroline for having such a relation? Were not all Americans wild and ill-mannered?

Caroline refused to believe anything other than Seth being a kinsman who would redeem their legacy. And so, Juleah refused to say anything that would dampen her friend's vision of her estranged brother. Tucked up in bed, Caroline moaned and Juleah turned back to soothe her. She lifted the cool rag off the girl's forehead and with the back of her hand touched her skin. The fever had broken.

Caroline gazed up at Juleah with misty eyes. "Will you bring my son to me?"

Juleah brushed back Caroline's hair. "Yes, soon."

The bedchamber door opened. Candlelight shot across the floor, over the fawn counterpane. Claire crept up to Juleah and motioned her aside. "Mave Proctor waits to speak to you."

"Did she say why?" Juleah moved with her to the door and out into the hall. Claire replied by the direction of her eyes. In the dim light stood an older woman.

Mave stepped forward and grazed her hands across the front of her outdated frock.

"Miss Juleah, I am sorry to be the bearer of bad news. I came as quickly as my old limbs could carry me. The child has died. Hetty said she woke this morning and he was burning up, died in her arms."

Blood rushed cold from Juleah's face and sank to her soles. Her chest tightened. Her throat constricted. "How could this be? He should have been safe there by the sea."

Mave bit her lower lip. "You would think so. Hetty is beside herself. Mind, she is not to blame."

"It's unbelievable." Juleah's eyes filled. She covered her mouth with her hand to stifle a sob. "Poor Nathaniel." She took in a ragged breath. "Poor Caroline." Rallying her wits, she reached out and took hold of Mave's sleeve. "Why did you not come and tell me he was sick? Why did you wait?"

Mave let out a squawk. "I didn't. I came to Ten Width after I got word from Hetty Shanks. Perhaps it's a blessing in disguise. Miss Caroline's young and to have lost her husband would've made bringing up a child hard."

Shocked by such icy words, Juleah let go of Mave. "To have lost both husband and child is harder."

"They've taken the young master to the church. He'll be taken care of proper and put beside his grandfather. When Miss Caroline is better, she can go there, but for now she should stay put, being so sick."

"You're not lying, are you?" Juleah desperately wanted to hear a different truth.

Mave's mouth fell open and her brows arched. "I wouldn't do such a thing."

"You swear?"

"On my late husband's grave and the Bible."

"Where is Hetty? Why didn't she come and tell us instead of you?"

Mave lifted her chin. "Does it matter?" She then held out a grimy hand, nails yellow with ridges, skin thin and blue with age.

Juleah stared down at the fingers that wiggled greedily. "You want money?"

Mave placed her hands upon her ample hips. "I had to trek all the way out here risking life and limb in the glooming to bring the news. Hetty was too afraid to risk the dark. A farmer was good enough to give me a lift in his wagon. I got to give him something for his good deed, now don't I?"

Juleah took the black satin ribbon from around her throat and handed it to Mave. "Is that enough?"

Beneath the glare of candlelight, Mave examined the ivory cameo attached to it. "It'll do." Then she slipped away down the servants' staircase.

Heartbroken, Juleah leaned against the wall and wept. The sound of a rider coming down the lane toward the house caused her to hurry to the window. Had Dr. Yates returned? She drew back the heavy drape and searched the road. Darkness cloaked the rider.

"Whoever is it now?" said Claire, as she stepped out into the hall. "I'll slap the bolt across the door. He'll soon weary of his knocking."

Juleah glanced up at the moon. Its light touched her face, softened the contour of her mouth, and widened her pupils in the glass. "You best answer. It may be Yates."

"I doubt that, Miss Juleah. He told me he would not be back."

Juleah let the edge of the drape fall. "What if it's your new master? You wouldn't want him angry with you."

Claire's eyes widened and the thin line of her mouth parted. "I hadn't thought of that." She hurried away, down to the door.

Juleah turned back inside Caroline's bedchamber. She left the door open and listened to the echo of the rider's knock. Settling down at the edge of the bed, Juleah picked up Caroline's hand and squeezed it.

"I have something to tell you," she said. "You must promise to be strong."

Caroline stared up at her with eyes full with fear.

✍

After waiting some time, Seth lifted his fist again but did not strike, for someone pulled on the handle. The heavy oak door opened and a pair of brown eyes peered out.

"What is it you want, sir?" When Claire moved closer under the glare of candlelight coming from a sconce on the wall, caution flickered in her eyes. He drew off his hat and stepped forward.

"Is Caroline Braxton at home?"

Claire knit her brows. "Yes, sir. But she ain't takin' any visitors."

Claire's beau, Will, hurried around the side of the house to take the saddled horse. At first he set down the lantern he carried. By its light, Seth saw how young Will was. He had to be no more than nineteen.

"Open the door and let the gentleman in, Claire. Can't you see who stands on the threshold?"

"No, I can't see, Will." She shook her head at him and pursed her lips. "Don't order me about, neither. I ain't your wife. And until I am, I'll . . ."

Despite her reproof, Will smiled. "He's Seth Braxton. Let him in, Claire. He's the new master and wishes to see his sister."

Claire blinked her eyes at Seth and let out a slow breath. "Beg your pardon, sir." With a curtsey, she moved back to allow him entrance.

Seeing her embarrassment by the blush upon her cheeks, Seth handed her his hat and gently smiled. "It's all right, Claire. How were you to know?"

She glanced down at the mud on Seth's boots. "You must be tired and hungry, sir, after riding long."

"Yes. Didn't the household receive word I was coming? I sent two letters."

Claire shook her head. "No letters came into my hand, sir. They always do, and I give them to my mistress."

"Is there no one else who would have come by them?"

"No, sir, but not to worry. I'll tell Miss Caroline you're here."

"You have my thanks, Claire or soon to be Mrs.—?"

She lowered her brown eyes. "Just Claire, sir."

"Well, Claire. You'll have to show me many things here, you and Will."

"Yes, sir. I'll get your room ready right away, and bring you supper."

"Please tell my sister I'm here first."

Claire stepped forward. "Yes, sir. If you go into the library, there's a good fire to warm you."

"I'll wait here," he said, disturbed by the look of worry in Claire's eyes.

Claire nodded and left him to stand in the foyer. Seth pulled off his gloves. Uneasy and alone for the first time in his grandfather's house, a strange sense came over him, as if many pairs of eyes from the past watched him.

A painting hung on the wall to the right of him. The moon escaped the cover of a cloud and its gentle rays came through the glass in the window. It brightened the room enough for him to see the painting was Ten Width.

Movement came from the hallway above. He glanced up. The rustle of a woman's skirt glided across the floor. Amber light shone across the lady's cheek from the candlelight. Seth realized by the color of her hair, she could not be his sister.

Startled by what his eyes beheld, his breath caught in his throat. She came down the staircase in a frock of brown muslin; a touch of white lace edged the bodice and touched her bare skin. Her free hand ran along the balustrade, fingers delicate and smooth. Here he beheld the girl in the portrait, the face he secretly admired.

The same eyes, yet, through candlelight, a pair of amber gems edged with dark lashes took him prisoner. Above them, her brows arched in a graceful line against milky skin. To see her living and breathing made his heart race and he could not help but stare.

Once she had drawn closer, he could tell she'd been crying.

As for Juleah, Seth Braxton was nothing like what she had imagined. Where were the cruel eyes, the lined face that had gone unguarded from the sun? He should be an ugly man, a repulsive vagrant. Instead, he was handsome, his face arresting.

Kindness marked his expression, yet his eyes were turbulent and potent, the darkest blue she had ever seen, interrupted with flecks of slate. Brooding and fathomless, Juleah felt them upon her, and she glanced away.

He bowed and kept his gaze upon her. "You must be Juleah Fallowes."

Amazed by this deduction, Juleah's lips parted. "How did you know me?"

"I saw your portrait in your uncle's house."

"It is of no likeness to me now, I'm sure."

"If I told you a living person is better to behold than what an artist may render, we might stand here for the next hour debating."

She frowned. "I doubt we would, Mr. Braxton."

"Have I upset you? Have I said something offensive?"

"No, not at all." Juleah swallowed the tight feeling in her throat.

"Where is my sister? Why hasn't she come down?"

"I'll tell her you've arrived, to prepare her, if you do not mind waiting outside her door."

A wail followed and startled them both. The sobs went on a moment and stopped. Juleah lifted her skirts and turned to rush up the stairs. Seth stopped her with a touch of his hand.

"Tell me what has happened. Is that her?"

Juleah looked at him, her heart broken, her face heated as if with a fever. "Her child has died. He was only two years old and her whole world. You must let me go to her."

Seth pulled back his hand and moved past Juleah up the stairs.

When they reached the bedroom, Seth hurried over to his sister. Juleah's heart lurched to see Seth go down on one knee at Caroline's beside. At the touch of his hand, Caroline turned her face to see him.

"Seth?" Caroline lifted her hand out of his and touched his cheek.

"After so long, you know me?"

"There, above your right brow is the scar in the shape of a half-moon. Remember when we were children, you chased me up a hill and I threw a stone at you to stop your teasing? Remember how I cried, for the wound bled badly and I thought you would die?" Her body shuddered, and her voice quivered with the force of tears.

"Yes, I remember," he said. "I deserved it."

"Is it you! Oh, Seth!" She threw her arms around his neck and embraced the brother she had longed to see again.

Juleah slipped out. While she closed the door behind her, her heart ached. For the Braxtons, one tragedy led to another. What salt to the wounds would this new turn of events add or remove?

5

*L*ate into the night, Seth and Caroline sat upstairs together. The glow of the low fire colored Caroline's face, and the joy of her brother's arrival moved her to get out of bed and gather her strength. Claire helped her dress, and now Caroline sat with her legs pulled up beside her in the chair. Her face was lined deeply with grief, and Seth wondered what he could possibly say to comfort her.

"I'm sorry, Seth," she moaned. "You've come at such a sad time, and I'm not well."

"There's nothing to forgive."

"Oh, there is more than you know."

Disturbed by what she meant, he looked at her a long while. "I wish I had come sooner. Perhaps I could have done something."

"You must not feel that way." She looked over at him with a struggle. "I'm glad you are here."

He went on to change the subject. "I cannot believe how you've changed. You are not the little girl I once knew."

"Indeed not. And you . . . you are not the lad I romped with. I remember how strong you were as a boy. You'd lift me up into the oak tree near the house so I could climb with you. Father would get angry and command us down."

"He was afraid you'd fall. The tree is still there."

"Is it? Has the house changed?"

"War aged it, but it still stands."

"I'm glad to hear that. Did you suffer in the war?"

"Hardship was unavoidable."

"I cried when Grandfather told me Father died at Yorktown." Caroline drew her hands up against her breast. "Where is he now I wonder? In heaven, you think?"

"Yes, in heaven with our mother."

Caroline closed her eyes. "I hope it is true, for I imagine heaven is a beautiful place where there is no sorrow or pain. Perhaps when we go there we are children again, like my son."

From his breast pocket, Seth pulled out the locket and gold chain. "Father carried this with him through the war. It is now yours."

Caroline took it from his hand and opened the front. "It is Mother. She was gentle and kind. Why are those we have loved taken from us too soon?"

He looked away. "I cannot say."

Caroline closed the locket and put it around her neck. "You and I must tell each other everything. And if you decide to send me away, I will go."

Seth leaned forward and picked up her hand. He could tell by the expression in her face that the gesture comforted her. "Send you away? I'd never do that."

"People will be cruel, and they'll say terrible things about me that will embarrass you."

"I'll not let a harsh word toward you pass any man's lips. I don't care how they treat me. Wagging tongues will never cease, no matter where you go. Besides, I'll be the one to embarrass you, being a Yankee."

Claire set a tray on the table. She lifted the cover off a platter of food. "I suppose it's been a while since you had good home-cooked meals, sir."

"It has, at least by womanly hands."

"Perhaps you can persuade Miss Caroline to eat something."

He looked over at his sister. "I cannot eat alone, Caroline."

Claire spoke up desperately. "Please try, Miss Caroline. It'll strengthen you."

"What about Juleah?" Caroline said.

"She had a bite to eat in the kitchen with Will and me. Don't you worry."

Claire bent and lifted the blanket that had slipped off Caroline's lap, set it over her mistress, and left the room. It satisfied Seth to know a servant cared so much for his sister.

With no more hesitation, Caroline lifted the spoon, but set it back down. "I cannot eat." Her face stiffened with sorrow and he saw her struggle to push back tears.

"Caroline."

She wiped the tears from her eyes. "Let us talk, Seth. It will help me. Was it a shock to inherit Ten Width?"

Seth nodded. "More than I can say."

"Grandfather blessed you before he died."

"Did he? I'm surprised."

"He repented of the breach between him and Father—and you."

"People seem to wait until the final hour to make amends."

"At least he made them."

"He may have reconciled his sin with God, but not with me."

She reached over and touched his hand. "It's never too late. Try to forgive him. He was stubborn and opinionated, but he took good care of me."

Seth paused to sample the coffee Claire had brewed, which tasted better than the gritty concoction he was accustomed to. "Have you been happy here?"

"The happiest when I had my son. I'll never be happy again. They took him away and he's gone. How shall I live without him?" She trembled and buried her face against his arm and cried.

He held her a long while, until she exhausted her sorrow. Then he helped her back into bed. A candle softened and the room darkened.

"Seth," she said, a plea in her eyes. "Please, I must talk more with you."

"I am here. Say anything you wish, Caroline."

She turned her eyes straight ahead and looked as though she saw the painful past.

"Four years ago, I fell in love with a man named Jeremy Kenley. His father had other matrimonial plans for him, and he threatened to disinherit Jeremy if we were to wed. I was not good enough for him, too poor in Sir Charles's eyes, too meanly born. But we continued to see each other.

"One night, we gave in to our passions, and I conceived a child. You are shocked by this and must hate me now?"

He pulled the chair closer. "Hate you? I could never do that."

"Then you will stay with me, even a little while."

"Of course I will."

She looked at him and shivered. "I am relieved. Tell me about the war and all you went through."

He glanced down at his hands, imagining the traces of gunpowder burns. "We will have plenty of time for that. You must tell me the rest."

She drew herself up higher on the pillows and turned to face him. "Jeremy came to Ten Width week after week and was sent away. I sent his letters back too."

"Why? If he loved you . . ."

"I did not want to shame him, nor did I wish to feel the sting of rejection. I had been a virtuous young woman, yet in one night I fell prey to temptation. Harsh consequences were certain for both of us. Ten Width became my prison. Depression clung to me. At night I cried myself to sleep, and when a new day dawned, I faced it with dread. I did not know what to do. Then one morning I saw Juleah walking up the drive. I realized I had to confide in my best friend. When I told her about the child, I was moved to tears by her kindness.

"She told me I had to tell Grandfather, that he loved me and would make things right. Then she urged me to tell Jeremy. I felt ashamed, and I told her I could not do it. She insisted it would be wrong not to. If I did not tell Grandfather and Jeremy, she swore she would. So, I dried my tears, took hold of my friend's hand, and we walked together into the study. I shall never forget the way Grandfather looked up at us, knowing a grave matter was at hand.

"At first, he was distraught, but said what was done could not be undone. He ordered me to pen a letter. Jeremy arrived the next day. He fell on his knees in front of me, gathered up my hands in his, and kissed them. We were married in the village church the next morning. He was willing to risk everything for our love and the sake of our child.

"Now he is gone, and so is my Nathaniel." Tears surged in her eyes and trembled on the tips of her lashes. "I wish God would take me to heaven."

Her tears and words sliced through Seth like daggers. When she fell asleep exhausted, he quietly left the room and went downstairs. Running his hand across his face, he stood by the fire to think.

"Is Miss Caroline asleep, sir?" Claire asked in a soft voice, by the door.

"Yes, and soundly, I think."

"I'll say good night, sir." She went to leave the room, but paused by the door. "We're all grateful you've come to Ten Width. You being here will help Miss Caroline. She's been through a difficult time."

"I'll need your help, won't I, Claire?"

"Yes, sir. Your room is ready. It's the first door on the right down the hall upstairs." Claire held out her arm in that direction. "It was the squire's room. Shall I show you to it?"

"No, I'll find it," he said.

Claire gave him a quick curtsey and left.

After he kicked a coal back into the fire, he walked over to the window. He gazed outside at the rain and gloom. His heart grew heavy and he was homesick. He turned. Juleah's head of dark curls lay pillowed upon her arms on the settee. For a moment, he stared at her with some consternation. Why was she sleeping here? He dared not wake her, not knowing what a man should do in such a case.

A north wind swooped down hard upon the house, against the windows now dark and covered with rain.

Curled up in the folds of a woolly blanket, Juleah looked beautiful and peaceful. He gazed at her face, at the soft eyelids, the dark lashes that brushed against her skin as she breathed through parted lips. He imagined she had been untouched by hardship, unacquainted with hunger. Life had to have been easy for such a woman. Her hands were soft, absent of scar or callous. By them, he supposed she had never done a day's work in her life, never hauled water from the river or kneaded bread dough, never washed her own clothing or scrubbed a floor.

No, not with those hands. She had been pampered and waited upon, and it was in such a woman's mind that life should not be any other way.

The room grew colder, and he placed more logs on the fire. Within moments, warmth permeated and held, and the scent of cedar filled the air. Before he left, he reached down and brought the throw closer around Juleah's shoulders without touching her.

His mind restless, he headed for the room once occupied by his grandfather. He held the candle high to study the room. He supposed it had remained as Benjamin left it, his books with worn covers, a great oak clothes cupboard, and a model sailing ship in a hand-blown bottle on the mantel. A large four-poster bed stood in the middle of the room against the wall. Faded curtains hung from its canopy and a satin bolster stretched across the head.

He opened the cupboard stuffed with clothes. They were worn and outdated and smelled of dust and age. The presence of the man remained, something Seth could feel and see while he looked at the coats and linen shirts that hung from the rod. He would have Claire clear them out in the morning and give them to the poor.

He pushed the door shut, turned, and stared at the bed where Benjamin had died. He could not think of that. The room already had a sense of loneliness, as if the walls had been etched through the years with the names of those who had come before him. They left, each one at the appointed time, leaving behind a beloved spouse, children, or lovers. Lives lived out through the years in forlorn hope and solitude. Yet, there were happy times, love shared, and children, like his father, born in this room.

He set the candle on the table and began to undress. He put his boots at the foot of the bed and decided to keep his breeches and shirt on for the night. The fire crackled in the hearth, yet the room was frigid and numbed his fingers and limbs.

Before he settled down, his eyes caught something lying across the back of a chair, something white and fine. He lifted it up. It was a woman's chemise. The heady scent of lavender rushed to his head. On the chair were two books: a small New Testament and Shakespeare's sonnets. He picked them up, opened the covers, and saw Juleah's name. She had been sleeping in this room.

With a sigh, he set the books down and opened the door. The gloom and the chilly air struck him. He started to call Claire, but hesitated. She had gone to bed, and Juleah was asleep downstairs.

He lay back down with his arms behind his head feeling wretched. She slept on the settee, while he lay comfortable in a large feathered bed. He watched the light of the fire flicker above him. Then he got up and pulled his boots back on.

❦

The blanket had slipped below Juleah's shoulder. It pulled her dress with it, and revealed her skin. For the second time that night, Seth drew the blanket up over her. Not meaning to, his fingertips brushed against her. She moved and opened her eyes.

"Forgive me, I startled you." He pulled a chair up opposite her, sat, and leaned forward. "What are you doing down here?"

She drew her legs in and sat up. "I fell asleep. The fire was warm and I dozed off." She rubbed her eyes. "What time is it, please?"

"After midnight."

"So late?"

"That settee must be hard as the floor. The bed upstairs is more comfortable. You should have it, not I. I can sleep anywhere."

Juleah shook her head. "But you are the new squire."

"I am also a gentleman."

"You should have the best room."

"An English custom?" He smiled at her.

"It would be improper for me to stay in that room." She pushed aside the throw and stood. Her hair fell over her shoulders along her bodice. "I will go to the room next to Caroline's."

"Then I wish you to sleep well." He folded his hands together and looked over at the crimson coals that glowed in the fireplace.

Juleah stepped past him, and he noticed her feet were bare. "I'll try. Goodnight."

A breath of wind swept against the windowpanes, and Juleah slipped out of the room. A moment more and a door upstairs closed.

$\mathscr{L}$♥

In the morning, Seth rose and crossed the room to the window that faced east. Brushing aside the curtains, he regarded his grandfather's estate in the light of day. Green fields and hedgerows dripped with dew that glistened in the sunlight. Sheep grazed on a hill, and a flock of swallows flitted against the pale sky.

He ran his hands through his hair, pulled it back, and tied it into a pigtail.

From the blue-and-white china basin on the wash table, he splashed cold water over his face. Claire knocked on his door and entered.

"Good morning, sir." She set a tray of coffee and buttered toast on a side table and prepared to leave.

Seth turned to her. "Claire, I discovered last night that Miss Juleah slept in this room before I arrived."

"Yes, sir. The room has a better view and the mattress is down-filled. The other rooms are colder, sir, and the furnishing aren't as suitable for a lady."

"What do you mean?" he said concerned.

"Not as pretty, sir," Claire answered. "Except for Miss Caroline's."

"I see." He handed the chemise over to her. "This belongs to Miss Juleah. Please do not tell her I found it."

Taking the garment in hand, a rush of scarlet colored Claire's cheeks. "Oh, I won't, sir."

Seth wiped the shaving cream off his face with a towel. "If I'd known she'd been using this room, I would have taken another. It would have been best to let her stay where she was."

Claire bit her lip, lowered her eyes. "I should've told you, sir. 'Tis my fault."

Seth glanced back at Claire's guilt-ridden expression and felt sympathy for the girl. "Do not be hard on yourself, Claire. Everything is settled now."

Juleah was sitting in the window seat when he came downstairs. The window was open and she was throwing out crumbs to the sparrows that hopped along the sill. Seth wished her a good morning and she turned.

"How do you like the house, Mr. Braxton, now that it is light?"

"I've no heart for it. I'm out of my element and would rather be back in Virginia plowing fields and raising horses. But, I felt obligated to my sister, and I'm glad to have come when I did."

She gathered her hair in her hand. "Your arrival has eased her grief and given her hope."

He rubbed his jaw to ease the razor burn.

She pulled at a loose thread on the seat cushion and twisted it between her fingers. "They say war hardens a man, that he loses sensitivity."

"The things I saw and did in war taught me compassion if nothing else," he said. "The Lord knows we need it."

"I did not mean to imply *you* had lost sensitivity." She yanked the thread until it broke. "I have said the wrong thing."

"You dislike Americans, don't you?"

"I lost my brother in your battle for independence."

"I'm sorry."

Juleah turned back to the window, pushed it wider and threw out a handful of breadcrumbs from the dish on the sill. "This is a subject we should not discuss."

He smiled over at her and hoped to ease the tension between them. It ebbed and flowed, like the tide. "Politics is a volatile subject of conversation."

She tossed him a glance over her shoulder. "Unless you know the person well enough."

"Even then it can be touchy."

"Indeed." She touched the edge of the ribbon on her bodice, dropped her hand when his eyes follow her gesture. "Ladies are not encouraged to talk of such things with men."

"You are free to speak your mind to me anytime you wish."

A smile grew in her eyes. "I apologize if I gave you the impression I would not."

A gentle laugh tugged at the corners of Seth's mouth. "I believe you. Tell me your mind now. Does it bother you that a rebel inherited an English estate?"

She gave him a shrug and dusted the dish out with her hand. "No more than what you'd feel if an Englishman bought land next to yours in Virginia. It doesn't matter, as long as people are good neighbors and conduct themselves honorably."

Seth inclined his head to her. "*Touché*, Miss Fallowes."

Was she always quick to speak to a man in this fashion? Where had her boldness come from? Did she have to prove herself to him, that she was not the timid English girl that kept her eyes down, that only spoke when spoken to, that did not laugh in public or interject her opinion?

"I have spoken my mind too swiftly." She trailed off, those fascinating eyes of hers meeting his again. "It is a flaw, I am told."

Seth shook his head. "I doubt you have many. What some call an imperfection may be a strength."

Juleah stood and stepped aside from him, for he was close. "I would think it would be hard to break ties and journey to a country not your own."

"I broke no ties. Both my parents are buried on a hillside that overlooks the river. For now, I've lent my fields out for planting."

"Your father would be pleased. I imagine he was a good man."

"He was the best of men. If he had lived, things would be different."

It was a delicate subject, to talk of the past war and the loss it had brought not only to his life, but hers. Before he could divert the topic, a change in Juleah's expression went from genial and warm, to pale and distant.

"My brother would have made a difference if he had lived, too." Sadness edged in her voice.

Seth's feelings for her surfaced, and he picked up her hand and held it a moment. "I suppose we're equals on that account. We've both felt the pain of losing people we love."

She withdrew from his grip. "I shall never understand."

He watched the glow of the morning sun play over her face and hair. He paused and drew in a breath. "Does anyone besides Claire and Will know about the loss of my nephew?"

"The sexton at the church, the woman who cared for him, and Mave Proctor. Unfeeling creature. She asked for payment right after she told me the news."

"How much from your own purse?"

Juleah's hand went to her throat. Her fingers moved about, as if she searched for the piece she treasured. "I gave her a brooch choker. It was all I had at the time."

"I'll get it back for you."

"It is nothing and worth little."

"Still, I'll have it returned."

She thanked him with a slight nod.

"What kind of boy was Nathaniel?"

"He was sweet, inquisitive, easy to grow attached to, easy to love."

"Did you know Caroline's husband?"

"Briefly. Jeremy's father would not agree to a marriage. They were forbidden to see each other."

"So they ran off?"

"Yes. The squire and Sir Charles tried to find them, but were unsuccessful."

"They were shunned after they returned, and Jeremy was cut off. Am I right on that account?"

"Yes, by Sir Charles." She angled her head.

Seth said nothing for a moment. He watched the light cross the floor, listened to the fire crackle in the hearth. "You'd think Sir Charles would have been glad his son made right by the woman carrying his child."

"Caroline was considered below Jeremy's station."

"And what about my grandfather's stepson? Did he try to help?"

"No," Juleah answered tersely. "He agreed with Sir Charles."

A muscle twitched in Seth's face. "From what your uncle told me, he's apt to take advantage of grieving women." The look of displeasure on her face did not escape Seth.

"In the end, Caroline returned when the squire fell ill," she went on. "At least they made amends before he passed away. Benjamin was happy about the child and eventually accepted Jeremy. One afternoon a letter arrived for him, and he insisted it was urgent he leave. He was found two days later wandering in a farmer's field. He died the next day."

Seth lowered his head. "My sister has suffered. Has a doctor been to see her?"

"Four days ago. Dr. Yates said her fever was infectious, that Nathaniel should be removed from the house. Little good it did him."

"I'd like to speak to him."

Juleah stood and stepped toward the door. "William can go."

"No, I must. Where can I find the good doctor?"

"I expect at The Sea Maiden tavern. Otherwise, you should find him at his house outside of Clovelly."

Seth called for Claire. "Tell Will to saddle a horse," he told her as she waited inside the doorway. "Tell him he's to show me the way to The Sea Maiden." He then turned back to Juleah. "You'll stay until I return?"

"Yes, for as long as Caroline needs me."

"I should tell you, I met your good mother, brother, and sister on my way here. They were returning from your aunt's home. Won't your mother wish you home soon?" He looked down into her face and felt such pleasure that he shifted back.

"Henry Chase is a little over two miles from Ten Width. My mother says I am close enough for her not to worry."

For a moment, their eyes held. Something passed between them—a rise of passion that almost overwhelmed them both.

Seth retrieved his hat, slipped on his overcoat, and beheld Juleah in the glare of the morning light. "I'll be back within a few hours."

She took a faltering step toward him. The color in her cheeks heightened. He tried to understand why the sight of her should affect him so, cause his heart to ache in his breast. He could not help but lift her hand and kiss it, realizing it did not matter.

He turned out the door and down the stone step to mount the late squire's horse, Jupiter.

6

Above mossy bluffs The Sea Maiden appeared ghostly amid the fog that drifted inland from the sea. Washed of color, it appeared like a damp black-and-white etching set on a plain of dew-drenched grass. Smoke from the chimney whirled over the thatched roof. Outside the door, a tarnished lantern sputtered—a lemon star against a curtain of bleakness.

Will's horse sighed and he brought it to a halt. "Be on your guard, sir. Rough men frequent this place."

Seth drew rein and dismounted. "Come in with me, Will. You're old enough."

"I'm nineteen, sir." Will's eyes shifted from Seth's back to the tavern. "If it's all the same with you, I'd rather not."

"I'll buy you an ale. Surely there's a roaring fire within."

"Aye, and enough horse thieves sneaking around, too."

Amused at Will's caution, and the way his eyes enlarged, Seth choked down a laugh. "If it gives you ease, keep to your pistols and guard our horses. But I cannot see why you want to stay out here in the chill."

The cold caused Seth to shiver and he turned up the collar of his coat against the wind. He strode toward the tavern door, avoided the puddles of mud and horse dung, and closed his palm over the pommel of his flintlock before he entered.

Brassy lanterns on wrought iron hooks hung from blackened rafters. Ashy logs and pinecones crackled in a stone fireplace. English sausages were heaped on the patrons' pewter plates with potatoes and eggs fried in savory grease, with enough brown bread and smoked herring to feed a troop of redcoats. The aroma filled the air and tempted Seth. His stomach growled, but he set his mind on finding Yates instead of breakfast.

The tavern-maid approached him. With a bright smile, Pen showed him to a table. The tresses of her flaxen hair fell over her throat. But Seth would have none of her. He wanted information of the doctor's whereabouts. In answer, she turned her large sapphire eyes toward Yates.

"He's been here an hour, having not yet begun his daily rounds to his titled patients." The chatter between her customers kept her from being overheard. "He owns that black gelding stabled in the lean-to."

Seth glanced over at Yates. The doctor sat alone in a booth near the fire and called for a pint of cider.

"Both his stomach and mood are wanting, sir, even though it's midmorning," Pen said.

Seth leaned back against the smooth oak bench. The doctor's clothes were immaculate and fitted snug around a gaunt frame. "The profits of his practice are apparent by his clothes."

"Hmm, too fine for a man of his station, sir." She whirled round to fetch Seth a mug of morning cider.

"Are there no other doctors in these parts besides him?" Seth asked.

"He's the only doctor for miles. He attends the poor when they've money to pay or a dressed goose to offer."

"That is typical, don't you think?"

"I suppose. But he's a hardhearted man. I guess he has to be or else he'd give in to the suffering of folks and quit. He's made a living."

"So, he prefers to serve the rich?"

"He says so; but like I said, if there's money or meat he'll do only what's required if the weather is fine and he's up to it." She leaned down and glanced over at the surly doctor. "When he's had too much ale, he mutters, 'Bleed them until they recover. Summon a clergyman or undertaker if they don't.' "

"Thanks for the information." Seth stood and stepped over to Yates's booth. "You drink alone, sir," he said standing at the edge of the table. "May I join you?"

Yates squinted up at Seth from his pint and plate. "You may, if I might know who it is I'll be conversing with. You're a stranger by your speech."

"I am, sir."

"Your name?"

"Seth Braxton of Virginia . . . and of Ten Width."

Yates raised his bushy eyebrows. "The old squire's grandson? Accept my condolences. Your grandfather was a good man."

Seth inclined his head. "I thank you, sir."

Yates was a man about his father's age, with dark hair turned gray and a narrow, drawn face heavily lined. His fingers were long and bony, covered with veins and dark spots. His deepset eyes were a bleary hazel that appeared insensitive in a grim face.

Yates made a swift gesture with his hand. "You may have a seat."

Seth sat opposite Yates. "Forgive me for interrupting your breakfast."

Yates dove his fork into his plate and skewered a hunk of sausage. "You should try it. 'Tis the best English breakfast in the whole of Devonshire."

"I haven't come to eat. I need to speak with you."

"About?"

"My sister. Her fever broke yesterday, but she is weak, as you know since you were there several days ago."

Yates twisted his mouth, as if he were a man of some importance. "I expected her illness to linger." He raised his mug, put it to his lips, and swallowed a large portion of the cider. "I assume she had the child removed from the house like I told her?"

"She had, but the child has died, taken by the same fever that plagued my sister. Caroline is beyond grief. I fear it's harmed her soul and her desire to live."

Yates settled back and leered over at the fire. "Call a preacher."

Shocked by Yates's lack of sympathy, Seth narrowed his eyes. "I intend to. But what a preacher cannot do for the body, you can." He grew irritated with the doctor's flippant attitude, but hid it well. By his cool manner, the man was unwilling to do anything that might inconvenience him.

Yates frowned. "I warned her. Mave Proctor is a witch, who finds the lowest of nursemaids for the upper crust. I suspect that nursemaid is her apprentice. I warned Caroline not to send the child to them. He should've been sent to Sir Charles Kenley, regardless of their estrangement." Yates leaned forward. "The women of the village, even some aristocrats, insist on having Mave Proctor attend them when their time comes. I do not like it."

"A woman knows best," Seth told him.

"Humph. Husbands should order their wives to have a doctor attend them. Midwives are risky and nursemaids indecent. Bad business for me, you see. I tried to explain to Caroline the danger, but she would not listen."

Seth scrutinized the captious doctor. "If these women are as careless as you say, shouldn't you have intervened?"

"Little I could do." Yates shrugged. "Their business is legal."

"But when a child has died in their care . . ."

"It is not uncommon. Even in a skilled doctor's practice, it happens. I'm not surprised the child contracted the fever and succumbed to it. Those unskilled harpies are careless in the extreme."

Seth leaned forward. "My sister would never give charge of her son to the kind of persons you describe."

Yates smirked. "What do pampered women know? I don't trust those ill-begotten nursemaids whose methods of caring for children are tainted by the devil."

With mounting irritation, Seth pushed his pint aside. "Harsh words, sir."

"Harshness often proclaims the truth."

"You are wrong, sir, for I believe it is written that love does that."

Yates huffed, shifted his mug from one hand to the other. "One must show prejudice in my practice against old crones."

Seth threw him a stiff glance. "They burn witches in England, so be sure of what you are accusing them of."

Yates lifted his mug, drank, and wiped his mouth with the back of his hand. "Certainly I will."

"I want you to come back with me to Ten Width and attend my sister."

Yates drew in his lips as if to think. "I'm weary and should go home."

"I'll pay you whatever you ask." Seth was firm, and heads turned within earshot of their conversation. "What is your fee? I'll double it."

"It is not a question of a fee, Mr. Braxton. My time is precious, and I'm afraid I'd be wasting it by seeing her today. I'm expected at a wealthy client's at noon."

Outraged, Seth shoved himself away from the table and stood. "Caroline is your patient, is she not?"

"There's naught I can do, I tell you." Yates replied low, but his tone grated.

"I think there was naught you could do from the start, sir." Seth gathered up his hat and placed it on his head. Before he turned to go out the door, he looked down at Yates with a steely stare. "I'll hold you accountable if anything happens to her."

"There's no negligence on my part." Yates looked aghast. "Do not dare accuse me of it."

Seth leaned his hands on the table. "I do dare."

"I have no desire to travel to Ten Width today in the rancorous drizzle and the miserable mud. My other client will have a warm fire, warm brandy, and a hot meal awaiting my arrival. More than I can say for Ten Width."

"Your words are insulting, sir."

Yates turned away. "Perhaps tomorrow I'll feel differently."

"Tomorrow, sir? Do not bother. You'll never again attend my sister or any member of my family if I can help it."

He tossed a coin down for the serving girl. Many pairs of eyes watched him pass through the door. An oath slipped from his lips, and he repented of the harsh word he spoke under his breath once the biting wind hit his face. Yet anger stirred his blood and he clenched his fists with its force.

Yanking the brim of his hat down closer to his face, he went to get his horse. He plunged his booted foot into the stirrup and mounted Jupiter. With Will, he traveled afar off from that dismal place. His pulse pounded and his mind raced.

7

In the weeks that followed, Seth worked on the estate, met with Banes and bankers, and settled legal papers until he was too weary to do more. Juleah stayed on and spent her time with Caroline. But in the evenings, after they dined, she sat with Seth in the sitting room talking.

Early one morning, he rode off with Will toward the small stone church outside the estate. The air nipped at Seth's face and smelled of rotting leaves. The scent of scythed hay overtook him as they galloped past harvested fields within reach of the old medieval chapel. Staggered gray headstones jutted up from the soaked earth.

Seth had no fear of such a place. He had seen death before, along with the graves of brave soldiers topped with the red Virginia earth and the green sod of her fields. Here was a lonely place, a quiet eternity, and he wondered at the stillness. It would not always be so, his heart told him.

While his mind mused over the ancient echoes, he lifted his eyes to a gray-haired man walking toward him. He turned and, with a gesture of his hand, asked Will to stay behind.

The knees of the man's breeches were smeared with dirt, the rest of his attire careworn. Light touched upon the baldness of his head. Wisps of hair floated alongside his broad ears and wrinkled face. He was a short man, thin and lanky, round in the middle. His hands, grimy with dirt, dangled at his side. In one of them he held a spade.

"Good day to you, young sir." He hailed Seth with a wave and a smile.

"And to you." Seth removed his hat. "You are the caretaker of this place?"

With hazy blue eyes, the man glanced over at the rows of somber chiseled tablets. "Aye, I am."

The gardener swept his arm outward at his churchyard. "One day all these shall be raised, some to eternity, others to . . . well, you know."

"You believe that's true?" Seth inquired respectfully.

"Don't you, young sir? If you don't, then you are a man most miserable."

"I do believe it. But I have times when I wonder; then I think of my father."

"Ah, he was a man of faith, was he?"

"He loved God, yes."

"All men are doubters some time or another. I've my moments; then I look at the Lord's handiwork and find I cannot deny what my eyes see and my heart feels. Flowers of the fields bloom in spite of the sadness in the world."

Seth nodded and smiled at the man's simple outlook on life. A pebble poked under his boot. Pausing, he bent and picked it up, turned it over in his hand, and threw it into the nearby grove of trees.

The old man leaned closer. "If you haven't figured it out, I'm a horticulturalist of sorts. I study these plants and trees the entire year. I observe their cycle, their birth and dying. I've taken notes over the years. Tending a garden is similar to tending men's souls."

Seth understood what the old fellow meant when he compared gardens to souls. His father had taught him the same: the seeds, the earth, rain, and sun. The tender care, the harvest, the dying and rising.

"But this is a graveyard. Don't you find it a depressing place?"

"At times." The elder brushed off the dirt left on his spade. "What's your name, young sir?"

"Seth Braxton. Benjamin Braxton's grandson from America."

The man's woolly eyebrows shot up and he threw open his arms. "Well, here you are, young Braxton. I hoped to meet you."

"Had you, sir? Why is that?"

"I knew your grandfather. Studied horticulture at his place once. He wasn't reserved in talking of you. He spoke with affection for your father as well. I knew him when he was a wee boy. You have his looks. Now I meet you at last. I can say you are as Benjamin described you."

"I'm surprised my grandfather would share his opinion of me with anyone."

"Are you pleased with Ten Width?"

"I haven't had time to decide. I've come at a desperate time."

"Aye, I know. How's your sister?"

"She's at home."

"I think I know why you've come."

Seth lowered his head. "Yes, to inquire after my nephew, young Nathaniel Kenley."

"Ah, the little boy. Such a lamentable thing. I was cut to the quick when the child's nursemaid came here with a sturdy fellow carrying him in his arms. What could I do? Your sister was in no condition to decide anything."

"Do you remember what the woman told you, anything she did or said that made you question what happened?"

"I cannot help you there. It was a dreadful day, and I was busy writing in my book. She came to me with him wrapped in a blanket, and I sent for the sexton to tend to what had to follow."

"And that was all there was to it?"

"Aye. All was written in the church record."

"There were no prayers? Did you see the child?"

"Look at him? I dare not, sir. I've seen much in my day, but as an old man, it pains me to see a person taken in their childhood. I said some prayers from the prayer book. Everything was done proper."

"Can I speak to the sexton?"

"Ah, well, I'm afraid he's gone north to live with his old mum."

"Was anyone else with this woman?"

"No, but she brought a note that explained what Miss Caroline's wishes were and they were carried out."

"I see." Seth's core twisted. He sensed all was not right. "How long have you been my sister's spiritual adviser?"

"I, her spiritual adviser?" The man stuttered. "Not I, young sir. Since she arrived here as a child, I've known her. I've been in this parish for twenty-odd years."

"You are the vicar, are you not?"

The old man stared a moment at Seth, then let out a cackle. "I beg the young squire's pardon. I'm but the caretaker."

Seth frowned at the man. "Why didn't you say so?"

"You didn't ask."

"I thought I had."

"You asked if I were caretaker of this place and I told you I was."

"Yes, but by the things you said, I thought . . ."

"I was a man of the cloth." The man let out a quick laugh.

"What's your name?"

"Loll Makepeace," he replied, straightening up.

"Well, Loll Makepeace, where is the vicar?"

"Gone, sir."

"An exodus at this parish, I see. When will he be back?"

"He's not coming back. Went to another parish. Things were too meager here to make any good living out of it. He found a wife and settled in Cornwall where a rich lord has given him a church."

"Is there a new vicar?"

"As soon as the bishop decides."

Pausing, Seth looked down at the mud on his boots. He drew out his knife and began to scrape it off. "So, when the child was brought to the church there was no vicar here?"

"That's right," Makepeace said.

"You should've sent for a clergyman in Clovelly and Dr. Yates."

Makepeace looked aghast. "No time, young sir. But that little grave is as hallowed as any other, I assure you."

He went a few paces and showed Seth the stone. It was all but a foot high, set beside Benjamin's, above a mound of tilled earth. Seth gazed down at both places. His heart lurched. The bitter pang of grief hurt more than a musket ball through the flesh.

His eyes read the names and dates. He choked back the surge of cruel emotion. Grave and silent, he set his mouth hard, squashed on his hat and hurried toward his horse.

Makepeace called after him. "I'll be of service to you if you need me, sir,"

Seth touched the brim of his hat to thank him. He turned the horse out onto the road and galloped off. Will followed.

Instead of entering the gates of Ten Width with Will, Seth rode on alone across the grassy fields of the country, his thoughts disturbed. Darkness deepened and a brilliant moon rose above the treetops. Wind rushed through the trees, caused them to sway, and forced a flock of rooks to burst forth. Seth raised his eyes. As if one, the birds took flight and landed in the hollows.

His horse sidestepped and reared. Seth looped the reins around his wrist, laid his hand against the hilt of his pistol, and steadied the restless horse with his other hand. He listened, staring into the darkness. A ragged howl broke the silence and stilled his pulse. His memory jarred. Wolves of the wilderness, hungry, stalking, waiting for a rebel to die. Waiting for the chance to draw close and steal away what they could. Wild flaming eyes. Gray fur matted with the sepia blood of a kill.

Wolf-like, a dog dashed into the road and stood with legs wide. It growled. Dusty black fur bristled, and yellowed teeth bared. Seth drew his pistol, aimed. The animal sensed danger and crouched. With a yelp, it shot off like a bullet. Before Seth could dig his heels into his mount, a figure stepped out onto the road. He cocked the hammer of his pistol.

With a shout, a man bounded forward. Calloused hands reached up to pull Seth off his horse. Jupiter reared and turned against the hands that grabbed his rider. Voracious, the wolfish beast raced forward. Snarling, the dog nipped at the horse's hindquarters.

Seth kicked Jupiter's sides. He urged him to race forward. Hands gripped the bridle and yanked at the frightened beast. Fingernails dug into Seth's clothing. They hooked into him, pulled him low on the saddle, and dragged him off. He twisted against the arms and hands that assailed him. Suddenly, he hit the ground with a thud, which knocked the breath from his body. His pistol fell from his hands. He groped for it, but the darkness hindered him.

Struck in the face with a fist of iron, Seth's vision blurred. With a stronger will, he fought his way back and shook off the sinking feeling in his brain. Like quicksilver, a knife flashed before his eyes.

The assailant pinned him down with one knee and pushed hard against Seth's chest. The dog barked in furious frenzy and bounded around them. Seth reached up and grabbed the man's wrist. With all his might, he squeezed. The knife came within an inch of his throat. The cold blade nicked his skin and drew blood.

Seth slammed his free fist into the grim, inflamed face above him, and the ruffian fell backward. Seth rolled and scrambled away.

The man shook his head, while his comrades urged him to carry on the fight and finish Seth off.

Back on his feet, the moonlight glinted across the barrel of Seth's pistol. He dove for it. Retrieved it. Cocking the hammer, he raised it at arm's length. He locked onto angry eyes, white clenched teeth.

"Stay where you are or I'll shoot," Seth shouted.

The man growled back. Heedless of the damage that could be done to him, he thrashed forward. Seth pulled the trigger.

The crack of his pistol, the yellow flash, pierced the darkness. The man jerked, tumbled and pitched forward. Blood gushed from his shoulder.

The smell of sulfur powder, the whipping of wind, assaulted Seth's senses. He watched as his attackers lifted their comrade and dragged him off into the dark asylum of the woods.

Seth reached for his frightened horse and hauled himself into the saddle. Blood seeped from his left side onto his shirt. As swift as Jupiter could carry him, he hurried back to Ten Width.

Grimacing in pain, he slid from the saddle and staggered up the stairs through the door. From an entry that led from the kitchen, Claire walked into the foyer with Will and gasped. Will stepped forward. "Sir, what happened?"

Seth did not want a flurry of activity over him. "I'm fine, but if you'd take care of Jupiter, I'll be grateful. Give him extra oats. He earned it."

Will hurried out the front door to do as his master bid and drew the horse away.

A left rib dug into Seth's body. It was either bruised or cracked. Claire hurried up behind him and helped take off his coat. As blood oozed against his palm, Seth pressed his hand against his side. He glanced back at her from over his shoulder. Shock and worry played over her face.

"You are hurt, sir," Claire hurried to the door. "I'll tell Will to get Dr. Yates!"

He forbade her with a lift of his hand. "There is no need for that, Claire. Bring me a fresh pitcher of hot water upstairs, so I may wash this blood off my hands. Do not disturb my sister." And he proceeded to go up.

"Yes, sir. But should I at least tell Miss Juleah?"

Juleah. If he needed help, he knew she'd give it. "She may need to know, yes."

He managed the pain until he got through the bedchamber door. A melancholy settled over him. He longed for home, for his fields, the mountains and forests, and the Potomac. So far away they were, and he now in England, among highwaymen and footpads, disappearing nursemaids, resigning vicars and sextons, and a doctor more given to spending time at the tavern than with his practice.

He lifted his hand away from the wound and stared at the blood on his fingers. Who were the ruffians that had attacked him?

He crossed to the window, unlatched the lock, and shoved the pane open. The frigid air smelled of rain, mud, and damp fields.

"It is not good that a man live alone," he murmured, thinking of Juleah.

He knocked his fist twice upon the windowsill and realized that coming to England presented more than he had expected: he was falling in love.

Humbled by this revelation, he let out a shallow breath and turned. His traveling clothes were laid out, brushed and cleaned, and a new bedcover replaced the old dingy one. The clothes cupboard door stood open, cleared of Benjamin's old clothes, replaced with the few Seth owned.

He laid his pistol on the table beside the mantelpiece. His waistcoat and linen shirt were blotched with crimson, the right sleeve torn at the seam. He unbuttoned the waistcoat, wanting to take care of this privately. It was but a scratch after all. A tap fell upon his door and it drifted open.

Juleah froze in the frame of the doorway. Seth could not help but gaze at her. She glanced at the bloodstains on his neckcloth and his shirt with quiet concern. Her eyes traveled to his right hand and to his fingers smeared with blood.

"I fell off my horse." A quick quiver of his mouth, he smiled over at her. He did not want to alarm her with the truth. But by the expression in her eyes, she knew he was lying.

"Claire." Juleah looked back over her shoulder at the wide-eyed girl. "Bring lint and bandages, sticking plaster, and ointment." Claire set the pitcher of fresh water on the table and promptly left.

Juleah stepped forward. "What happened? Who did this to you?"

"There's no reason for you to be concerned."

He wished she would not question him or stare at him in the way she did.

"There is reason." Defiant, she set her hands on her hips. "Caroline will be angry with me if I do not help."

"It would not be your fault. If she needs to be, she can be angry with me."

"She doesn't need you falling sick as well. She's had enough misery, don't you think?"

"She has, and I'll not add to it."

"Good. Then let me attend to you."

"I thank you for your concern, but I'll manage on my own."

Juleah's face flushed with frustration "You cannot dress a wound on your own, Mr. Braxton."

Seth lifted a brow. "I cannot debate you there, Miss Fallowes."

"No, you cannot." She gave him a satisfied look from under her lashes. Through the candlelit room, her eyes were dark as moon-drenched jasper. She ran her finger over the edge of the table. "I hope you left the men who attacked you with more pains than what their plans for you were worth." She walked over to the bowl and pitcher on a nightstand and poured the water into the bowl. "I doubt they were highwaymen. Highwaymen usually work alone and are not so violent. They demand money or jewels. These men wanted to hurt you."

A smile tugged at the corner of his mouth. "One has a bullet in his shoulder."

"I'm glad to hear it," Juleah said. "He deserved it."

Claire entered the room and set down the tray of supplies. She wrung out a cloth and handed it to Juleah.

"Thank you, Claire. You may sit with Caroline. She's asleep but if she wakes say nothing of this to her," Juleah said.

"How is my sister?" he asked, once Claire had gone.

"Asleep." Juleah's touch was gentle as she dabbed the cloth across the scratch. "She is trying to accept her grief, but the pain will be with her a very long time. How can it be otherwise for a woman in her situation? "

He winced in pain, both from Juleah's words and from the wound at his side. With gentle hands, she loosened the neckcloth around his throat. He studied her face, as his eyes followed the soft line of her jaw. He considered the lids of her eyes, how they were formed, how her dark lashes enhanced the shape, how the brows were evenly arched. She was even more attractive tonight with the way she wore her hair long and over her shoulders in a braid. She was close and her skin smelled of lavender and rosewater.

Her touch caused Seth to feel uncomfortable. She stood in front of him, he with his knees apart, feeling the whisper of her frock caress the fabric of his breeches. The urge to pull her against him grew strong.

Juleah picked up a jar of salve, opened it, and gathered up some of the ointment. With deft fingers, she applied it to the wound on his throat. Feeling the oval outline of her finger caress his skin, her hand near his face, Seth's pulse raced.

"It is not deep. But you may have a scar." She glanced into his eyes. "Let me dress the wound on your side."

"A flesh wound," he said. "Lucky for me, it was no more than that."

She stood back, glared at him with a plea. "Please, let me look."

Convinced by the expression she gave him that she would not relent, he lifted his shirt and she bent her head to see the wound.

"You're right. The blade grazed you." She pressed her fingertips over his skin and he winced again. "It struck a rib. You're fortunate. You could have been killed." She placed a piece of lint against the gash and lowered his shirt over it. "The bleeding has stopped."

She placed the lid back on the jar and set it down. She moved away. Seth cupped his hand at her waist and drew her close. He brought forward a loose strand of her hair, ran it between his fingers, and brought his mouth within a whisper of hers. He touched her lips tenderly with his. She trembled, and the thunder in his heart pulsated against the palm of her hand.

Wind stirred the trees outside, whispered down the flue of the chimney, and drifted through the open window. Juleah pulled away. "The room grows cold with that wind." Her cheeks were flushed, and her lips parted to take in a breath. She crossed the room, drew the window closed, and dragged the drapes over it. "I'll send Claire to build up the fire. I suppose we shall have more rain tonight and . . ."

Seth stared at the floor, instantly contrite. "Miss Fallowes." He interrupted her nervous chatter with deliberate firmness.

Juleah paused at the door.

"Please forgive me. I went too far."

She shifted her gaze away from his. In spite of the high emotions that passed between them, Juleah forced the tears back, and a trembling smile spread gently over her lips. "Let us say goodnight and not speak of this again."

He watched her step from the room. The urge to stop her overwhelmed him to the point that he headed down the hall after her.

"I am quite starved," he said. "Have you had supper?"

8

The following morning, dawn streamed through the window. Warmth alighted upon Seth's face and brought him back to the real world. The candle on the table, the tray of bandages, and the empty mug were reminders of the night before.

He struggled into clean clothes and pulled on his boots. A confusing mix of elation and pain troubled him. He splashed cold water from the basin on his face and dried it with a rough towel. For some time, he sat in a chair in front of the fireplace, stared at the embers that glowed in the grate, and prayed for guidance.

Part of him filled with chivalrous emotion, the other with overwhelming loneliness. The feel of her would not leave—the smooth texture of her lips, the warmth of her companionship. The thoughts they had shared opened her up to him. She had told him more about her family, the kindness of her mother, the dutiful father who had grown eccentric, energetic Thomas, Jane, and Peter, her brother who had died in America. She shared with him her love for herb gardens, how she wished she could study as men did and become proficient in horticulture.

He discovered she held deep spiritual beliefs, the greatest being hope of life beyond the material world.

Seth left his room and found Juleah out in the garden wrapped in her dove-gray cloak. As he approached, she yanked from the soil the dry remnants of a marigold plant.

"The garden has been neglected." Her tone was somber. He helped her up and she regarded him with forlorn eyes. "I know what you wish to say."

"You can read my mind?" He smiled lightly.

"The eyes of a man are the windows to his soul, Mr. Braxton. Do not say that you love me."

He drew her to him and cupped her face within his hands. "You want me to withhold my feelings?"

"It is too soon." She slipped out of his reach.

"On my life, I do not understand."

He marveled at her reaction, the change in her mood. "I am glad we talked last night. I remember the clock striking two before we said goodnight."

Juleah let out a heavy sigh and pushed back her hair from her face. "I received a letter from my mother. It has been more than a month I have been away, and she misses me. So, I must go home to Henry Chase."

Before Seth could reply, she turned and walked back into the house.

❧

Juleah shut the door behind her. She went to the window and stared across the span of green and beyond. Mist lay in glossy white ribbons in the lowlands. The scarlet light of morning touched upon the dew-drenched bracken.

She shoved aside angry tears.

Her feelings for Seth frightened her. How could she fall in love with a rebel? No doubt he longed for Virginia, would sell

Ten Width, and leave. If she allowed something more to grow between them, he'd break her heart.

Perhaps he cared nothing for her, and this was just a *moment*. Oh, but it had felt warm and wonderful the way he kissed her.

She flung herself down upon her knees at the bedside. Covering her face in her arms, she prayed for answers. Seth Braxton stirred up such strong feelings within her that she wanted to shout. What had drawn her to him? Was it his solid self-confidence, his sense of duty, his spiritual conviction? Or was it his ability to make her feel as if she'd known him all her life and that she deserved to be loved? What did she discover beneath his handsome surface that pulled her in?

She raised her head and stared at the letter that lay open on the bed from her mother. She took the rest of her clothes from the cupboard and folded them into her traveling bag.

A moment later, she heard a knock at her door. Caroline peered inside.

"I need to go home, Caroline," Juleah said, without stopping her packing. "My mother has written to me. You know how she frets when I am away."

"Yes, I know. I have been so comforted by you, Juleah, that I shall forever be in your debt."

Juleah put her arms around Caroline and squeezed. "You must promise to treat yourself well."

"It will take time, but I'll try to do as you say." Caroline gave her a broody frown. "Why are you behaving strangely?"

"I miss home." She gathered up an armload of snowy linens and tossed them on the bedcover.

Caroline, looking worried, touched Juleah's shoulder. "I believe my brother is fond of you. Is that why you are going? Is it because of Seth?"

Juleah sighed and tried to give Caroline a reassuring look. "My mother needs me, that's all. I've been here too long."

"Does Seth know?" Caroline sat on the edge of the rumpled bed.

"Yes." Juleah put the last chemise in her bag. She turned to Caroline. "He fell off his horse last night, so he says."

Alarmed, Caroline stood. "Is he hurt? He's no broken bones, has he?"

"None." Juleah bit her lip. He was hurt—inwardly.

"I must go to him."

Juleah clutched Caroline's hand. "You have no reason to worry."

"I wager he rode Grandfather's horse. Jupiter is high-spirited."

Juleah picked up her gilded horsehair brush and tossed it into her carpetbag. "I do not know which horse he rode."

"Oh, Juleah. Why did you not wake me?"

Juleah stumbled at the question. "I'm sorry, but he did not want me to disturb you. It was late." She closed the clasp on the bag and dragged it off the bed.

Caroline glanced down at the bag, then back at Juleah. "Has something happened between you and Seth? Do you not like him?"

Juleah laid her head to one side. "I need to go home, that's all." Was the pretense in her excuse obvious to Caroline? Caroline was not prying. Juleah was relieved she raised no objections and asked no further questions.

She hugged her dear friend good-bye, gathered her bag, and went down the stairs. She turned to see Caroline standing at the rail of the staircase. "I understand," Caroline said. "You must seek your heart, Juleah."

Juleah replied with a nod and left the house. The crisp morning air touched her face, and she breathed it in. Along the horizon, clouds streaked across a pale sky. Trees brilliant with autumn gold and scarlet swayed in the breeze. Jeweled leaves floated down to blanket the earth, and in the distance cows lowed.

When she entered the stable, the horses sighed in their stalls.

"I didn't expect to see you going, Miss Juleah," Will said. "It troubles me you are traveling alone. I ought to come along."

Juleah pulled her horse forward. "You needn't worry. Henry Chase is only two miles down the road. Help me onto my horse, and I'll be on my way."

Will lifted her up, and she secured her right knee around the pommel of the saddle. She gathered the reins within her gloved hands and nudged the mare on. At a trot, it went down the drive toward the massive gates of Ten Width. The urge to look back overwhelmed Juleah. She raised her face to the sky and kept her eyes forward.

ℋ❤

Seth stood at his window with his heart in his throat. He believed she was leaving Ten Width because of him. He watched her move the horse out onto the road, her cloak spread out behind her. He hoped she'd turn and look back. She never did, and he twisted his lower lip in disappointment.

The clock in his room ticked away. Minutes passed that seemed to gather into hours. Suddenly, he hurried from the room, rushed downstairs, and ran out the front door. With no time to spare, he threw a saddle on Jupiter's back and mounted, ignoring the pain in his side. He kicked the horse's sides with a fury, until Jupiter reared forward and shot off down the lane.

He turned to the right at the gates, looked for her, and snapped the reins for Jupiter to gallop on. He pushed his heels against the sides of his horse, until at a high point in the road he called out. She turned her head, but did not rein in her mount. Seth let out a breath of frustration. Shaking the reins, he urged Jupiter on, down the slope at a gallop.

Ahead, Juleah's horse whinnied. It reared and threw her from the saddle. She fell with a thud onto the hard ground, moved, and pushed herself up on her elbows. What had frightened her horse crept in front of her. A hound, maddened by the presence of the frightened mare, bared its teeth at her and growled. Crazed eyes marked Juleah. Gray, wolfish hair bristled on its back, while saliva dripped from its jowls.

Before Juleah's cry escaped her mouth, Seth vaulted off his horse, stood in the road, raised his pistol, and cocked the hammer. The beast turned toward him. It was the same mangy creature he had encountered the night before. It snarled, crouched on its haunches, and lunged. Seth fired. The hound yelped, twisted, and fell dead in front of Juleah.

When Seth reached her, she was gray with fear, but her eyes were brave. He fell upon his knees beside her. "Are you hurt?"

Her body shivered. "I'm all right, I think." She moved, and a sudden pain gripped her. "I have injured my arm," she said alarmed.

"Let me see." He pressed his fingers with care along wrist and forearm. He moved her hand back and forth. "You'll have a nasty bruise."

She reached her arms out to him. He lifted her and stepped away from the dead animal.

"Are you fit to carry me?" she inquired.

He ignored her question. "Henry Chase is not far. I'll escort you home."

"I have caused you enough trouble."

"Yes, you have."

"Why did you follow after me if I vexed you so?"

He paused in the road, to gaze down at her. "It was a good thing I did. Would you not say?"

She looked up at him. Her eyes were moist and sparkled with the morning light. Seth's heart moved within him, and his love for her deepened with each breath he drew. Why was she afraid to love him back? Had another man hurt her and caused her to fear love and mistrust men? Or was love new to her? Perhaps it was none of these. Perhaps she ran from him for being a rebel, a foreigner to her country, one who inherited what he had not been born to.

"We should go," she said, marking his hesitation.

He carried her over to her horse and set her up in the saddle. Then he put his foot in his stirrup and pulled up beside her to take her mare's reins.

When they reached Henry Chase, Lady Anna rushed out of the house. Chickens and dogs ran around her legs, clucked, barked, and yapped wildly. Children and husband followed her. Seth dismounted and helped Juleah down. Anna Fallowes cried out when she saw that her daughter was injured, though slightly. Questions flowed out of her like a breaking dam. She put her arm around Juleah and drew her away, but not before thanking the new squire.

"A wild dog, you say, threw her from her mare? Oh, Mr. Braxton, thank you for saving my Juleah from such a beast."

Seth bowed his head. "My honor, madam."

She leaned toward him as he walked alongside. "It's been terrorizing the neighborhood for some time now. You've done everybody a favor. No one has been able to kill the mean brute. It carried off one of my chickens two nights ago and frightened Sir Henry's dogs. I am grateful you killed it and have seen my Juleah safely home."

Sir Henry placed a firm hand on Seth's shoulder. "We are indebted to you, sir, in the most profound way."

"Come inside, Mr. Braxton. What shall we give you to satisfy your gallant deed?" said Lady Anna. "We've a warm pie on the table."

"I appreciate the offer, Lady Anna, but I believe your daughter needs more rest and less excitement."

Juleah glanced over her shoulder at him. Her mother gently drew her inside. She smiled lightly at him and was gone.

Seth inclined his head to Sir Henry, who gave him a swift salute. After a few congenial words, he remounted Jupiter and turned him around into the road. At a hard gallop he went, with longing raging in his heart.

9

Seth swung the sickle and violently sliced through tall grass and tough weeds. Just when he thought he was safe from the wiles of a woman, Juleah invaded his dreams, raced through his mind every waking moment, and disrupted his appetite.

His muscles ached. He tossed down the sickle and drew in a breath. Sweat soaked his shirt and it clung to his chest. The cool breezes of autumn mingled with it and caused him to shiver.

Placing his hand above his eyes, he looked out across the fields to the manor. Proud of what he had accomplished, he smiled. A man could do much when a woman captured his heart. In order to work off his frustration he had torn down ivy, repaired cracks in the bricks and the stone walls, and cleared out thickets of dead wood.

Will flopped down on a heap of grass and wiped the sweat off his brow with a dirty rag.

"Time to quit," Seth told him. "I'll ask Claire to make us a huge supper. We both deserve it."

Will squinted up at him. "I'll welcome a hearty meal, sir. Hard work's no stranger to this lad and whips up an appetite. But it's odd for me to work alongside you."

Laughing, Seth picked up the sickle and walked on. "Hard work is good for every man, no matter his station."

Will heaved himself up. "That may be, sir, but it ain't expected of squires or lords."

After supper and a thorough washing, Seth decided to swallow his pride and ride down to Henry Chase. He took care to wear his best suit of clothes, a dark blue coat with matching breeches. He had forgone shaving for days after Juleah left. Now his face was smooth.

His horse trotted beneath a sky that sparkled like a prism of color. Shreds of white clouds spread over a pale blue sky, and patches of brown leaves swished over the road. He spied a traveling coach rolling toward him and lifted his hand. The driver pulled rein. Juleah put her head out the window. A sad smile moved across her lips.

Seth approached her with all his powers gathered, calm and determined. "You are well?" He fixed his eyes upon hers, watched her breast rise and fall.

"Yes. Are you?" She struggled to button her left glove. Her wide-brimmed hat, tipped to one side, shadowed her left cheek, while daylight touched the right.

"I've not been myself since you left." He hoped she could see the pain in his eyes.

She did look concerned. "Your wound, is that it?"

"It is not my wound. *That* has healed." He nudged the horse with his knees and moved closer to the window. "I was on my way to see you. We should talk."

"I'm afraid I cannot delay."

He swallowed hard at her answer. Or it may have been how her eyes caught the light and sparkled. "Don't you think it is important we come to an understanding?"

A moment's pause and she looked at him with loving eyes. "I cannot wait," she said softly, and lowered her gaze. "I am on my way north to visit my aunt. She is not well and is expecting me."

"Then I'll ride alongside."

"Please, do not." Juleah fastened her hand over the window frame. "Besides, it is too far. Aunt Issy lives in Congleton, in Cheshire, more than two hundred miles away."

Running! He frowned.

"How long shall you be gone?"

"A month, perhaps longer."

"You're leaving without saying anything to me? Did you think it would make any difference?"

Her gaze, full of sadness, turned away. "I cannot explain." She leaned outside the window. "Driver, move on."

"No, driver. Stay as you are," Seth ordered. He looked back at Juleah. "Avoid me if you must, but do not be a stranger to my sister."

"I will write to her every day. Now, I must be on my way." She drew back inside the security of the coach, her face hidden.

Seth backed his horse away.

The driver snapped the reins and the horses plodded on. He wanted to hurry after her, fling open the coach door, and pull her out and into his arms. But it would look foolish. Instead, he turned his horse and watched the coach disappear down the shady road. He'd wait—and hope she would come back to him.

Juleah reached her destination three days later. She peered out of the coach window and saw Little Moreton Hall. On a plain of green grass, its black and white walls look subdued under a gray sky. Its crooked chimney puffed a bellow of smoke into the air, and Juleah thought of the hearth fires that she'd welcome at her aunt's home. Four more miles down the road, she leaned out to observe the bleak country house before her. It was a grand residence of two stories, made of gray wintry stone. Five years had drifted by since she had last seen her aunt. Still the house was silent and lonely, just as she remembered

The housemaid escorted her through the door to a sitting room cluttered with glossy dark furniture. In a high-backed chair sat Juleah's elderly kinswoman. Upon her lap was an orange cat. The dimness of the room could not conceal the wrinkles on her face, which were more plentiful than Juleah recalled. It came as no surprise that her aunt wore the same style of clothing she wore ten years ago, black taffeta gown, lace cap and shawl, black lace gloves. She was asleep, and the house-maid, a wisp of a woman no more than five feet tall, touched Issy on the shoulder.

Startled, the old woman's eyes shot open. "What do you mean? You wish to frighten me to death?" Aunt Issy, her name shortened from Isadora, shuddered in her chair. The maid apologized and pointed to Juleah.

"Hello, Aunt Issy. It is I, Juleah."

"My niece?" Issy shifted in her chair. Taffeta crunched against chintz. Her gray eyes stared at Juleah in disbelief. "You appear nothing like her. Come closer and let me have a look."

Juleah did as she was bid. Issy picked up her eyeglasses and looked her up and then down. Soon her scowl turned into a delicate smile. "On my soul, it is you. Take off your hat and gloves. Lay them aside, then come kiss my cheek."

With a gentle smile, Juleah untied the ribbon under her chin, took off her hat and gloves and handed them to the maid. She walked over to her aunt, leaned down, and kissed the wrinkled cheek, the skin soft, thin as oiled paper, scented with rosewater and rice powder.

"You look well, Aunt."

"You mean to flatter me. If you speak of my disposition, I agree. I have not changed that in the least. But in body? Thin and gaunt is what I am. Old."

"Only by a few years."

" 'Tis long enough, though it seems like yesterday I last saw you. Your mother agreed to allow you to stay the winter?"

"Yes, but no longer, I am afraid. She was remiss to have me away through Christmas, but did not want you to be so lonely. You know it is only a week away."

"Indeed, I know of it. We shall attend church and not make a fuss . . . have a goose for supper. Perhaps invite a few neighbors."

Juleah lifted her brows. "It would do the house good to have some holly about."

Issy pressed her lips together in a crooked smile. "Do as you wish, girl. How are your parents?"

"Well. They send you their love."

"And your brother and sister?"

"They are also well. I've brought a letter from Mother."

"Give it to me later." Issy waved the note away from Juleah's hand. "I am glad you've come. Your mother said you needed time away. I imagine it is over a man."

Juleah smiled lightly. "Is that what she told you?"

"Not in those exact words."

"She worries over me."

"And why shouldn't she?" Issy's eyes enlarged. "Young women these days read too many novels. I hope you have not read that outrageous novel by Burney."

"You mean *Evelina?*"

"Yes! That is the one." Issy shook her head and clicked her tongue. "So called *The History of a Young Lady's Entrance Into the World.* Bah."

"I admit I am guilty of it, and without shame."

Issy lifted a hooked finger and shook it. "Books like that give a young woman wrong ideas, not what the real world is about. They lead to disappointment. You'll find no such books in this house. You don't draw silhouettes do you?"

"No, but I would like to learn."

"They are a waste of time."

"May I read to you in the evenings?" Juleah inquired. "From a book of your choosing?"

"I suppose that would be acceptable. I prefer Shakespeare and the Bible."

It took some time, but Issy stood from her chair. Her cat jumped down and curled up near the fire. Issy was the same height as Juleah but thin. Her clothes hung loose and shapeless.

That evening, while they dined, Juleah could not help but notice how little her aunt ate. Perhaps, she would eat more if the food were better. Boiled fish and bland stewed apples were not the most enticing of foods.

"I do not believe in hearty conversation at evening meals, Juleah." Issy picked up her fork and pushed the food around on her plate. "It is bad for the digestion—puts off sleep."

With their meal concluded, Issy retired and left Juleah alone with her thoughts. For a time, she sat at the table that faced the window, glad the curtains were left open. Moonlight played over the lawn. The clock ticked away in the hall, seconds passed, never to be retrieved. The dishes had been removed, but the scent of the fish lingered, along with the cedar fire that burned low in the hearth.

She stood and loneliness gripped her. She wished to deny it, wanted to suppress the feelings, her longing for Seth. Pressing her hands against the table, her throat tightened and a sob escaped her lips. She could bear it no longer and retreated upstairs to her room.

When she opened the door, cold smacked her in the face. The fire in the hearth burned low, and her hands trembled from the cold. She stirred the coals, and soon the room glowed in an amber light.

The bed was old with a worn quilt. In the corner sat a dressing table and an ironstone bowl and pitcher. That was all there was to it.

When she woke in the morning, her feet and hands were frozen. The fire had gone out during the night. Wrapped in the quilt that she drew over her shoulders, Juleah swung her legs over the side of the bed. The floorboards were as cold as blocks of ice when her feet touched them. She hurried over to the clothes cupboard, slipped on a pair of wool stockings, and finished dressing.

At breakfast, her aunt eyed her from the other end of the table. "You mustn't flee from your troubles," she told Juleah, while she dipped her spoon into her plate. "Running away will add to them."

"I have not said I am running away, Aunt."

"No, you have not. But I know just the same." And she went on to eat her boiled egg in silence.

Weeks drifted by slowly. Sir Chester Bottomly rode over to the house from his estate four times in one week. He was older than Juleah, talkative, and the stoutest man she had ever seen. He had great whiskers along his jaw that he fluffed with his fingers. Then came two other gentlemen Aunt Issy had extended invitations to—a wealthy banker who smelled of tobacco and an untidy merchant with a lord's title, who was too thin and too pale to catch any woman's eye. All were bores to Juleah, their attentions insincere. They sought a wife, and she hated how they all wanted her.

Her aunt grew frustrated by Juleah's indifference. She summoned her to her chamber one night in the fourth week of her stay, before drifting off to sleep. Earlier in the day, snow had fallen, covered the ground, spread over trees, and deepened the chill of the house. Drifts lay against the foundation and the Roman walls in the fields. The landscape lay white, dotted with the bare blackness of trees. The fire in the hearth crackled and hissed. Warmth reached out in waves that quivered against the floor of the bedchamber.

Issy sat up in bed with a heap of bedclothes over her. She glanced up from her Bible when Juleah entered the room. "Why are you not more attentive to the gentlemen that visit this house, Juleah?"

"I am not rude to them." Juleah tucked in the sides of the covers beneath her aunt's mattress. "They ask questions and I answer."

"Yes, my dear, but that is all you do. Can you not smile or pay a compliment?"

"I do not know what to say. I find no reason to smile at them. That might give them ideas I do not wish them to have."

Issy marked her Bible and set it beside her. She sighed. "You are ungrateful. Here I have taken you under my wing and invited the finest gentlemen of my acquaintance to meet you. Though reluctant, I had hopes of helping you find a husband."

Juleah flopped down on the edge of the bed. "These gentlemen are amiable, but they are not for me. Besides, I did not come here for that reason."

Issy pressed the thin line of her lips together. "Well, why did you come?"

"To see you."

"I don't believe it. A girl of twenty-one has no time for elderly aunts. You are running away from something." The wrinkles beside Issy's mouth folded up like an ivory fan. "I've become a haven, haven't I?"

Juleah smiled in return. "Perhaps."

Issy dropped her hands upon her lap. "Is there a man among those whom have called that you like? Is not there one you would consider for a husband?"

"You would not want me to marry where I do not love."

"But you do love someone, don't you? A man has declared his feelings for you, and that is why you are running away."

Juleah lowered her head. "I suppose so."

"Do you love this man?"

"I believe I do."

"Then you must allow him to pursue you. Do you understand? Now I must write to your mother and apologize for my hard words. I was angry at first that she had sent you. I told her it was her responsibility to see you married, not mine. But I've seen the light."

Juleah leaned over and kissed her aunt's cheek. She turned to go, but when she reached the door, she paused.

Issy opened her book of Shakespeare's plays and lifted the lace marker from off the page. "Is there something more?"

Juleah nodded. "I have not told you everything."

"I thought so. You may if you wish, otherwise go to bed."

"The man is an American."

Issy's book fell from her grasp. The pages turned, and her place was lost. "An American, you say?" Her voice hissed in a somewhat humorous manner.

"Yes, from Virginia. He has inherited Ten Width."

"Has he? So this American is Benjamin Braxton's grandson and Caroline's brother. How interesting. I have never met one, and I cannot say I have heard good things about Americans, except that the men are more amorous than English gentlemen."

"He is a good man, Aunt," Juleah assured her.

"God-fearing?"

"Yes, Aunt."

"Do your parents know him? Are they aware of this attachment?"

"Father likes him a great deal. My mother doesn't care whom I marry as long as he's wealthy and has a good name."

"Any letters from him?"

Juleah felt her cheeks flush. "Two."

"Two is good. I hope he spoke of more than the weather."

"He did." She glanced down at her hands and felt a strange sensation flutter within her. "Caroline and I have been writing . . ."

"If it were not for the fact this Braxton is of English descent, I'd insist you see him no more," Issy interrupted "But, he does have the blood of nobles in his veins. Oh, it is a confusing matter." Isadore threw up her hands. "I shall leave it up to you."

Juleah was indeed surprised. "You do not disapprove?"

"I am not remiss in remembering my first amour, who was a Frenchman. Time will tell whether this is right for you or not."

10

At an hour when the light of day painted the sky magenta, a man on horseback rode through the gates of Ten Width. His hat shaded his face, and the tall black horse beneath him gave him the appearance of being taller than he was.

Although he was eager to see Caroline, he slowed the horse, reined in at the front of the house, and glanced up to the window above. With a brilliant smile, he drew off his hat and waved it to the lady behind the glass. He watched her with a quickly beating heart. She returned his smile and lifted her hand in greeting.

"Caroline!" he called. "Come down and welcome me." With a kiss, he hoped.

When she hurried away, he dismounted and paced. Will came out of the door to take his horse. "Welcome to Ten Width, sir. Been a long time."

"Too long." Michael Bray glanced over the front of the house. "What have you done to the old place? It looks changed."

Will squared his shoulders. "The new squire and I been fixing things up."

"I did not know you were such a craftsman."

"Nor did I, but it got me out of the stables." Will moved off with Bray's horse.

Through the door rushed Caroline. Her skirts floated above her ankles. Her eyes glowed as she thrust out both arms in greeting.

"Caroline." Bray hurried forward and kissed her hands. "You haven't changed at all. Still pretty."

She stood a moment gazing at him. "Michael, I have thanked God the war did not take you from us. When we heard no word, we thought you were lost to us. Have we not been as close as family?"

"You know we have."

"And yet not a single letter from you all this time?"

"After I left America, I went to Paris on business for my uncle. I confess my negligence. Say you will forgive me."

"I will, but I'll not let you forget how you have kept me worried and wondering."

"I should have written. But I thought your husband would object."

Her smile settled at the mention of Jeremy. "My husband died almost two years ago. My little son has died also. My heart is so broken over losing him, I dare not count the weeks since."

Bray stepped forward. "I'm sorry, Caroline, deeply. I did not know."

She looked at him, her eyes forlorn. "I shall tell you about it later." She gripped her hands around his forearms and looked up into his face. "I know what you did for my brother. He would be dead if it were not for you. How can I thank you?"

He smiled down at her. "A hot mug of cider and conversation will be enough."

Rounding the corner, Seth looked at the man who talked with his sister. His hands held hers. He was attired in a buff coat instead of a scarlet uniform. Seth remembered him as a lean man. Now he looked well-fed.

Seth waited, marked his sister's expression, a loving look that surpassed friendship. Bray glanced over at him and strode quickly across the lawn. Holding out his hand, Seth grasped Bray's and shook it.

"Seth, it is Michael Bray. Can you believe it?" she said.

Bray laughed and gave Seth a brotherly touch on the shoulder. "I had every intention of visiting Ten Width. But I must say I'm surprised to see you here in England, far from Virginia."

"Grandfather died, Michael," Caroline explained. "Seth inherited."

Bray's brows pinched into one line. "I'm sorry. I liked the old man."

"He lived a full life and died peacefully." She linked her arm in his and led him inside.

Bray spoke of France and the troubles that brewed across the English Channel. "I felt uneasy there, being English and well-off." He set down his riding gloves. "The poverty in France is reaching a crisis, and the king is too stubborn to do much about it. I'm afraid another revolution will grip the world, poor against rich, the lower classes apt to shed the blood of the upper."

"I hope you're wrong." Seth led the way to a sitting room. The sunlight spread through the windows, fanned across the floor.

"Well, aside from that, I've brought other news," Bray said.

"Good news? Since I arrived the wind has blown with nothing but bad," Seth told him.

"I heard in town that Benjamin's widow, hearing of his death, disappeared from her house near the coast, and when found she attempted to throw herself off a cliff into the sea. She has gone mad, they say."

Could grief have driven Benjamin's widow to such lengths? Seth had not yet met her and doubted he ever would. He had seen what the sting of losing someone had done to his sister, and thanked God that Juleah had been there to help her through.

Caroline's eyes narrowed with pity. "Though she was never warm toward me, I am glad someone prevented her."

"I believe a local man held her back in the nick of time." Bray breathed in through his nose and looked pleased. "Do I smell English beef?"

"Claire is setting out dinner, and you will stay," Caroline insisted.

Bray smiled. "I've been away so long that I forgot how good English beef tastes. I've had enough goose and hen to last a lifetime."

"Is that all you ate in France?" said Caroline.

"Most of the time. It is a far cry from the stale bread we had during the war. Am I right, Seth?"

"It wasn't bad though, for us who knew the woods," replied Seth. "There was plenty of game."

Bray nodded. "But as the war went on, even game became scarce."

Caroline lowered her eyes. "Seth told me what he thought I could manage." She looked up at him with her eyes moist and shining. "It pains me to think of the hardships you both endured."

Bray looped her arm through his. "Then we shall not speak of it."

Leaning her head to one side, Caroline gazed at him, her hair a nimbus of curls. "We can walk in the garden after dinner." She then looked over at Seth for approval. She needed none, but he nodded just the same.

Later, candles glowed under glass domes in the dining room. Claire carried in a roast and bowls of steamed vegetables. They ate, drank, and laughed together. But Seth's heart grew lonely, for there was one person missing. She was far away in windy Cheshire. When would she return? If too much time passed, he would go to her.

Before Bray left, he took up his hat and walked with Seth to the door while Will fetched his horse. "Perhaps it is too soon, but I would like to see your sister again." A strained look surfaced on Bray's face. "Aren't you going to ask what my situation is?"

"I suppose I should," Seth replied with a wry grin.

"Two thousand pounds yearly, from my inheritance on my mother's side."

"Good and well. But loving her is more important than money."

"Indeed, I would say as much. I met Caroline before she married Jeremy Kenley. I stepped aside when she made her choice. My feelings have not changed in all this time."

Seth nodded, while he lifted the right corner of his mouth into a smile. "That is the right answer."

"I hope to acquire land someday, good for farming. I want to build a house, attend church on Sundays with a brood of children, and grow wheat the rest of the days."

"Your goals are similar to mine, except I long to be in Virginia and raise horses."

Bray stared up at Caroline's bedroom window. "I've not declared my intentions, not since I left England years ago."

Seth gave the moonstruck Bray a smack on the shoulder. "If I were you, I would not wait too long."

Bray returned a broad smile. "You're right, Seth. I don't want her to slip out of my arms again. Caroline told me you are fond of Juleah Fallowes. I've met her on more than one occasion and found her amiable and pretty."

"She is all that and more, but prefers to avoid me."

"I would have thought the contrary."

"I am, after all, a foreigner here and to some undeserving of my inheritance."

"Juleah is not prejudiced."

"No, just cautious."

"It is nothing that a love letter wouldn't cure." Bray slipped on his gloves and picked up the reins of his horse. "I wouldn't doubt for a moment what Juleah wants is for you to pursue her. Women are indeed a mystery we men shall never solve."

As Bray rode off, Seth stood outside in the fading light. A mist rose from the ground, curled around tree and bush, and sank into the lowlands. Trees stood stark still, and he looked at their shadows slant across the fields.

He gazed up at the sky and whispered a heartfelt request. He missed Juleah.

Shifting his gaze to the darkened hills beyond, he saw a man on horseback, cloaked in black, his face concealed by a slouch hat. Seth squinted his eyes and felt as though he were being spied upon. The rider turned the horse with a jerk and galloped off over the hill into the lowlands.

11

After a late harvest, fresh hay lay in the stalls at Ten Width. The musty scent filled the air. The roof leaked and the walls were in need of repair where the stone crumbed. He'd fix them himself, beginning later in the afternoon, Seth decided.

When the stable door opened, Caroline, hooded and cloaked, walked in. Her gray mare swayed inside the stall closest to her and whinnied. Her gloved hand reached out, stroked the velvet nose, and rubbed the long face.

"Seth, I know you're working, but will you take me to the churchyard?"

He set the bucket of oats he carried on the hook outside Jupiter's stall and wiped his hands along his coarse work breeches. "I'll take you now if you are ready."

Caroline leaned her head into the mare's. "I'm brave enough. I was his mother."

Clouds stretched across the heavens, white as cream. Ribbons of mist touched the earth in silver pathways, as brother and sister rode alongside each other.

"I hope Michael comes to visit us this evening," said Caroline.

Seth shifted in the saddle, relaxed the reins. "You're fond of him, aren't you?"

"He gives me reasons to like him."

"Twice this week he visited you. A gentleman would not pay a lady much attention if he did not have intentions."

"We have known each other a long time. I would have married him if it had not been for Jeremy." She looked toward the hills. Wind rustled the woolly coats of the sheep that dotted the fields. Lambs huddled close to their mothers. "What about you, Seth?"

He shrugged. "What about me?"

"You must miss Juleah, and Cheshire is so far."

"It was her choice."

"Maybe so, but you should not delay to write to her. I received a letter from her this morning. She will not be back at Henry Chase for a long while."

Seth made no reply to his sister's suggestion. Instead, he kept his eyes fixed ahead, but thought about seeing Juleah again.

"It is the next step to take, if you love Juleah and want her. Otherwise another man will steal her from you and you will regret losing her."

Seth glanced over at his sister with an understanding smile. "I've heard that warning before. Don't think all this hasn't been on my mind."

Caroline sighed. "You have already decided what to do. You think I cannot see how you miss her? Ever since she left you have been moody. You're not yourself at all. You love her and cannot deny it—not to me anyway."

He reined in. "I won't deny I have feelings for her."

"Good. So, do something about it. Life is too short, Seth."

He nodded at her. "Pride will not get in my way, I promise."

Caroline lifted her face with a triumphant smile. "I'll hold you to your word."

"I have no doubt you will." He nudged his horse on with a gentle squeeze of his thighs. "There's the church."

They looked out across the green meadow that led to the churchyard. Caroline's eyes filled with tears, and she dashed them back with her gloved hands. "It is the wind, Seth, not tears," she said when he looked concerned.

He helped her down from her mare. Side-by-side they walked across a path of colored pebbles, long ago swept smooth by the endless caress of the sea. The hem of her skirts drifted over the walkway and onto the grassy plain. Seth went on ahead, stopped, and turned. He held his hand out to his grieving sister. Caroline took it and came beside him.

"Name and date—etched in stone forever," she said.

She knelt beside the brown sod speckled with grass. Reaching out, Caroline ran trembling fingers along the carved letters of her son's grave. Uneven breaths turned to sobs. Her frame shuddered beneath grief's cruel embrace. Seth's sorrow deepened, as he watched her. To quell his anguish, he pressed his mouth into a hard line. It did no good, for his soul flooded with despair. The reality that his nephew reposed beside his grandfather hit him hard. Ah, but it was only the body that remained, he tried to tell himself. They were in paradise, were they not? They were released from earthly bonds.

He touched his sister's shoulder in a wish to comfort her. Caroline wiped her eyes and stood. Seth put his arm around her to lead her away. He glanced over at the line of trees that bordered the churchyard and spied movement within them.

A figure crept between the trunks. Hooded in an old cloak, a woman moved back into the shadows.

Caroline gasped. "Hetty! Hetty Shanks!"

The woman's startled face jerked at the call of her name. She halted in her steps.

"Hetty!" Caroline lifted her skirts and hurried forward. "Stop! Stop, I say!" But Hetty Shanks hurried on, stepping clumsily over roots, branches, and twigs, in a pair of old cloth shoes.

Caroline gripped Seth's arm and looked at him with a plea. "Stop her, Seth."

He rushed forward. The woman turned on him with her hands up ready to strike. "Leave me be, sir. I know you not, nor this lady!"

"You're lying," said Caroline, upon reaching Hetty.

Hetty hissed back. "I don't lie."

"You know me well. You were nursemaid to my son."

"I'm no nursemaid to anyone's son."

Caroline grabbed the edge of Hetty's tattered cloak and shook it. "He was given into your care, as God is my judge."

With a look of desperation, Hetty whirled around and confronted Seth. "Sir, let me go on my way."

Seth stared down at her, his height setting a shadow over her face. "Not until she has finished with you. Is your name Hetty Shanks?"

"Aye, but that don't mean I know her."

"Why were you spying on us?"

"I wasn't."

"You were. Why else would you be standing in the woods hiding within the trees?" Seth stared at the woman and waited for her to speak. And when she did not answer he said, "Come then. Perhaps a constable will help loosen your tongue."

Hetty gasped and shook free. "I came to pray." Her lips pressed hard together and she turned to go. From her pocket, a leather pouch tumbled. The silver inside it tinkled when it landed in front of Seth. He bent, picked it up, and held it in his palm. Caroline caught her breath and stared at it.

Seth glared at the distressed woman. "Now will you admit you know this lady?"

Hetty gripped her hands together at her throat. "I know her in passing. Give me my money."

"You are not a wealthy woman. Where did you get this silver?"

Hetty stood back and rubbed her hands together.

"Tell us, Hetty," Caroline urged. "No one will hurt you."

Hetty's eyes roved to and fro. "Wagging tongues can be cut out."

Surprised at her remark, Seth stepped closer. Hetty staggered. "No one will do that, woman. Now, answer the lady."

Her face grim and strained, Hetty pressed her hands against her sallow cheeks.

"I don't want to die. They'll cut my throat if I tell."

Caroline gripped Hetty by the shoulders. "Tell me who you are afraid of, Hetty, or a worse fate might befall you."

"I saw you crying, Miss Caroline, over that grave. I can't stand it no longer." Hetty put her fist into her mouth, bit down on her knuckles with a sob.

"You know something more about my son? In the name of God, you must tell me."

Hetty braced her hands against the tree behind her. "Your lad isn't in that grave. They laid the child of a beggar woman there that had died from the fever, not yours, Miss Caroline. Your boy is alive."

Caroline's knees buckled. She sank to the ground. Seth lifted her up, his arm around her for support. The flood of joy and bewilderment that washed over him could not compare with the storm of emotions that overtook his sister. He set her back against a tree and turned to Hetty, who was about to flee.

"I swear if you're lying . . ." Snatching her by the arm, he moved her back.

Hetty cowered in his grasp. "No lie, sir. 'Tis true."

"Then who paid you?"

"I never saw the person's face. It was dark. They were inside a coach." She squirmed to free herself, but Seth held tight.

"What coach?"

"I don't know. There was a woman veiled in black, a man whose face was hidden in the dark. I only made out his eyes."

"What did they require of you?"

"That I give the boy over. I couldn't do it."

"What did they do when you refused?"

"The man tore him right out of me arms."

The muscles in Seth's face twitched. "How do you know it is a beggar woman's child in that grave?"

Hetty hung her head. "It was awful, I know. But they forced me to go with one of their servants, a mean man he looked to be, and I was quite afraid of him. He carried the child wrapped in a bundle, said I was to give a letter to the caretaker, say it was Nathaniel Kenley, or he'd wring my neck. I suppose they had some heart not to do the boy a harm. They gave me more money than I'd ever seen. You can't blame me, sir. I'm a poor woman."

Caroline's teary eyes were wide and incredulous. "So, you gave my son to a stranger for money? You let me think he was lost to me forever? You cared not that it broke my heart? You kept silent that he was kidnapped? How could you do something so wicked? You're an evil woman, Hetty Shanks!"

A long, shuddering cry escaped Caroline's lips, and she fell against Seth in tears. Hetty saw her chance and ran off. Fleet as a shadow she disappeared into the darkness of the woods.

Pained to see his sister in shock, Seth tapped her cheek with his hand. Shaken, Caroline stood in front of him. Tears streamed down her face. Sobs escaped her lips between quick breaths.

"My Nathaniel is alive?"

"Yes," he said. "And we will find him. I swear to you, we will."

12

Two days after Juleah's arrival home, on the fourth day of April, she sat in the window seat of her parents' sitting room and admired the scene outside the window. The meadows were beginning to green and the sun warmed the earth. Farmers had seeded the rich English soil with wheat, and the ewes had brought forth lambs. The woods, on the edge of Henry Chase, showed signs of budding. Pale green knobs decked each branch and twig. Wild fern peeked through the leaf-covered floor of the forest.

Juleah gazed at the sun-drenched hills. She would walk them later, stretch her limbs, and soak in the peace. Idle time had been afforded her at Aunt Issy's, but here at home the hurly-burly kept her mind from clear thinking. If it were not Sir Henry's boisterous voice booming above the clamor of his dogs, then it was Jane's pianoforte practice, and Tom running about like a wild pony, insisting she come explore his latest interest by tugging her hands until she gave in. Her mother did not give Juleah a moment's peace to herself.

Jane sat with her that afternoon, in a chair drawn up to the window, and read her French lesson out loud. Absently, Juleah listened as several letters were delivered into her hand from the housemaid.

"You are doing very well, Jane. That is enough for today." She left for her room, shut the door, and sat on the edge of the bed. After she stared at the address for a moment, she tore open the first letter in the pile and ran her eyes over it. She frowned at the signature, got up, and went to her writing desk. She took out a sheet of paper to pen a reply to Sir Chester and to make it clear to him she had no interest in being *his darling* as he had so eloquently put it. The second letter addressed to her had come from Benjamin's stepson, Edward Darden, at Crown Cove. Without reading it, she tossed it into the hearth.

Not being in love seemed a poor reason for breaking with years of tradition to some of her acquaintances. Marriage among the upper class was the bedrock of their existence, the carrying forward of a name and title that in years to come would mean nothing to the average person. Juleah was determined to marry for all the right reasons.

"Never mind that what is in a man's heart is most important," Juleah said to Jane when she peeked her head inside the door. Juleah dipped the quill into the inkwell and began to write. Jane stared with interest in her sister's love affairs and sat beside her.

"All they see is bloodline, Jane, and money. Hardly is love the sole reason to wed among the upper class." Again, she dipped the quill into the ink, lifted it, and wrote rapidly. "I feel sorry for all the women that have had to endure loveless marriages. I shan't be one of them."

The ink dangled from her white feather quill, and before it could stain the page, she shoved it back into the inkwell. After a quick glance over her missive, she wrote her name along the bottom.

"I wish mother would understand." She blotted the ink, folded the page, and dripped sealing wax on the edge to seal it. "Women are to have no ambitions in life according to her. I find that dull, don't you, Jane?"

Jane nodded. "Yes, Juleah. I have ambitions. I'd like to be a writer."

"My dear Jane." Juleah reached over and took Jane's hands within hers. "Who shall have you when you come of age, but a man good and true."

Juleah's sister gazed back at her and parted her lips.

"My prayer for you, Jane, is that someday a good man shall come along and love you for you and that you will write all the stories in your heart," Juleah said. "I pray that God will give you a man who will stand up to the face of ignorance."

She looked down at the next letter in the stack. "It is from Mr. Braxton. Caroline must have told him I have come home."

Jane scooted closer. "Open it, Juleah. What does he say?"

"I have a feeling it shall be of a private nature, Jane." She went on to read Seth's missive and pondered over his words. His confession of love captured her, caused her heart to lift, windswept in a storm of emotion.

She glanced over at Jane. "Tonight, I will write to him when the house is quiet and everyone asleep."

She knelt on the cushions of the window seat and gazed out at a sky that mimicked the sea. Her sister drew up beside her and pointed to the lawn and stable on the side. Juleah turned her sister by the shoulders gently. "Did you know, Jane, why Father calls our home Henry Chase?"

Jane shook her head. "It's his name, part of it."

"When asked why this name he tells people, 'I am Henry and I chase my hounds over hill and dale. They're wild as the foxes that roam my land and rarely are they caught. But they're great fun.'"

Jane laughed, kissed Juleah's cheek, and left the room with a skip.

The light fled. Juleah's reflection appeared in the window glass. Unlike a mirror, it was a translucent image, her eyes and face pale, her hair ghostly soft about her face. She saw one person, one woman, instead of a couple. How incomplete she seemed without Seth beside her. Her eyes filled and blurred the reflection before her. The horse chestnut trees her father had planted on the hilltop beyond the garden came into view. Lances of sunlight poured between them, made the grass luminescent, and matched the color of the lichen in the pond.

"I wish I could paint that scene, God," she whispered, and leaned her head across her arm. "But I shall never excel at watercolors."

❧

Juleah had fallen asleep with Seth's letter on her lap and woke when she heard people speaking in the hallway downstairs. One she knew. Her father's voice boomed deep as a well, mellow as aged wine. The quick replies to Sir Henry's questions arrested her. She knew his voice.

Her heart trembled, and when she rose, the letter fell from her hand onto the floor. She hurried to pick it up and went to the head of the staircase to listen. She paused and, hearing nothing more, went on down into the foyer to the sitting room. It was empty and she wondered if she had dreamt the whole thing.

The door swung wide and she turned. Sir Henry strode inside with his unruly mob of dogs. They sniffed everything and knocked the furniture with their tails. It was musical.

"There you are, Juleah. By thunder, if it's not raining like mad outside." Mud was upon Sir Henry's boots, yet his huntsman's coat showed not a dapple of rain. Boot prints etched the carpet, and brown paw marks littered the hardwood floor.

Juleah smiled mildly and went to kiss his cheek. "Thankfully it was a light rain and passed quickly." She helped him pull off his coat. Today, as yesterday, he wore his old brown waistcoat, breeches, and gray worsted stockings.

"The sun doth shine now, my girl?"

"Brightly, Papa."

Sir Henry bent toward her ear. "Our new neighbor stands by the door."

Juleah followed the direction of her father's eyes and met the gaze of the man who stood in the gloom of the doorway. His black riding coat and white linen shirt contrasted his dark hair. In his hand, he held a tricorn hat made of black felt decorated with a black rosette cockade and pewter button on the left side. He had taken a step up, and she liked it.

Quick to realize she was staring, Juleah looked away. She felt heat rise in her face. Never had she seen such eyes in her life, dark as earth, rimmed in gold, the whites brilliant. The last time she had gazed into them, he had met her coach on the road astride Jupiter. Now he stood in the haze of morning and looked straight into her eyes.

Sir Henry made a gesture with his hand in Juleah's direction. "Braxton, my daughter, Juleah, has come home. Is she not pretty?"

"Prettier than any woman I've seen." Seth kept his eyes fixed upon her.

"Braxton, as you know, Juleah, is the gentleman who resides at Ten Width," Sir Henry announced, with a military inflection in his voice.

"Yes, Papa. Mr. Braxton and I are acquainted."

A quizzical look spread over Sir Henry's face. "Well, he's here to tell us we must leave our home. A battle is soon to ensue. I shall stand my ground and serve my king, sir." Sir Henry squared his shoulders, puffed out his chest proudly. "Hi ho to Colonel Braddock. He'll get us out of danger soon enough."

Juleah touched her father's hand. "All battles are beyond our doorstep, Papa. We are at peace here, with no war for you to worry over."

"But Mr. Braxton met me on the road to warn us against the Indians and the French. I was in the way of his horse. It's true, is it not, Mr. Braxton? Juleah, where is my brace of pistols? Get them for me, my girl."

Juleah glanced over at Seth, and caught his troubled expression, aware that her own was one of sadness and despair for her Papa.

Seth stepped forward. "It is true my horse was in your way, Sir Henry, and I beg your pardon for it. However, your daughter speaks the truth. We are not at war. You needn't think you must leave your home."

Sir Henry's smile faded. "There you see, Juleah, Braxton set me right. Now where is your mother?"

"In the garden with Tom." Juleah hastened toward the door that led outside.

"Juleah. Stay here and entertain the gentleman until I come back. You are safe in his charge. No one will know whether we break the rules of polite society or not." Sir Henry whistled to his dogs and out the door they trotted with him in the lead.

"Please excuse my father," she said. "He is not always himself."

"I like him," Seth replied. "He has a keen sense of humor."

"You are right. But his humor leaves him when he retreats back to his youth—when he served under General Braddock."

"I don't doubt his courage. It was a brutal war most men preferred to forget. You're worried about him, aren't you?"

"Yes. There are days when he seems content and knows he is at home with his wife and children. He has little memory of my brother, but knows he is gone. To where he does not know."

Seth shifted on his feet. "Though a man's mind may fail, he is still a man. I have respect for your father, no matter what he says or how odd he may behave."

She smiled at his words and glanced at the floor. The palms of her hands grew moist and nerves prickled over her skin. She hadn't seen him in months, and it was indeed trying. For most of her life, Juleah had not been in the habit of concealing her feelings. Self-expression was encouraged in her family, not suppressed. But now, with Seth standing before her, she was at a loss for words.

❧

Seth remained in the doorway, his hat in his hand, and his gaze upon her. He controlled himself well, but fought against the pain of seeing her again, hoping she could see in his eyes what burned in his heart.

"It's been a long time since we last saw each other. Not a day has gone by that I've not thought of you."

She lowered her eyes. "How is Caroline?"

"She sends her regards and hopes to see you soon."

He paused a moment, feeling the sting of rejection. He wondered why she evaded him. To steady his emotions he took in a breath. "She had a visitor—Michael Bray. Do you know him?"

Juleah's eyes brightened. "Captain Bray is a most amiable man."

A tense pause followed, while a meadowlark sang in the wisteria vine that hung near the window. Seth wanted to tell her everything, but Caroline had asked him to be silent about her son, believing his young life was in grave danger.

Seth turned and walked back toward the door. "I was on an errand when I met Sir Henry on the road. I've already stayed too long."

She stood to see him out. Soon she reached him. When she lifted her gaze, love brimmed within them. He moved his arm around her waist and drew her close. She did not resist.

"I've missed you." He could not help but long to touch her lips to his and leaned closer. "I'll be back tomorrow and stop here on my way. When I return—"

From the open French doors, Thomas ran inside the room. His shaggy dog leapt alongside him. Startled, Seth and Juleah parted.

"Squire Braxton. Papa said you were here. Do you remember me?"

"Of course, Master Thomas. You were, after all, one of the first people to welcome me to England."

Anna Fallowes floated into the room as light and elegant as a vapor. The hem of her dress rustled along the floor, and she held her hands out to Seth. "My husband says you and he had an exciting meeting. He is not as steady upon a horse as he once was, but for a man of his age he is at least upon one."

Seth took her hand and bent over to kiss it. "Oh," she whispered, dropping it to her side. "We've not seen you since you shot that monster that tried to harm Juleah. How is your sister? I have meant to call but felt it best to leave Caroline to herself for a while."

Seth read in Lady Anna's expression honest concern. "Better, I'm happy to say." He watched her set her head to one side. She meant to study his reaction to her inquiry.

"I am pleased to hear it," she said. "Stay for dinner."

"Your ladyship's offer is kind, and I would like to stay. But I must decline."

Lady Anna sighed. "That is a pity. I am not accustomed to people turning us down for supper. We set a fine table in this house."

Food was the last thing on Seth's mind, and though she looked disappointed, he'd not be persuaded by a woman's somber look. "Perhaps another time," he suggested.

"But what is so important to take you away from us?"

"It is a private matter, my lady. I cannot delay, so I give you my leave."

Juleah followed Seth out into the hallway. There in the foyer, dark and cool, Seth opened the door to leave.

"Tell Caroline I'll visit soon now that I am home," she said.

He nodded a reply and waited, constrained. All the way from Ten Width, he had thought of her. When he met Sir Henry and was obliged to come with him to the house, he hoped she would be at home, that he would see her again.

The others were behind closed doors now and she, standing before him in the dimness, looked more beautiful than he had remembered. Their separation over the last few months had done nothing to dampen the fire that played between them.

"Did you receive my letter?"

"Yes, Seth."

"I meant every word."

She glanced up at him, and he watched a nervous smile spread over her lips. "Why do you look at me that way?" she whispered.

"I want to kiss you."

"You must go." She looked back at the sitting room door.

Wrapping his arms around her, he lifted her. The heat of her breath escaped across his cheek. He brushed his lips over hers, soft and tender; she trembled. Willingly, she allowed him to glide his mouth over hers, and she kissed him back. His blood surged like river rapids through his veins.

It was too much, for he wanted her, all of her. It was natural to feel this way, but he had to rein in his desire and curb his hunger.

"You will come back, won't you?" She ran her hand along the curve of his cheek. He turned to kiss her palm.

"How could I stay away with the way you kiss?"

They heard the others and drew apart. Reluctant to leave her, Seth stepped outside into the dazzling light.

Juleah stood inside the doorframe with her palm over her bodice.

"Yet you won't admit you love me." He gave her a tender smile and a nod of his head. He dug his boots deep into the stirrups, turned his horse, and galloped off through a soft mist that rose and wove through the land.

Juleah stood on the threshold until Seth rode out of view. She turned back inside the house, regretful that they hadn't had more time together. And this errand that he needed to attend to—it had an air of mystery. Juleah ran a dozen questions through her mind as to its nature and looked back at the crest of land he had galloped over. Then she closed the door.

In the sitting room at Henry Chase, Sir Henry sat in a chair near the window, smoking a long clay pipe. Lady Anna paced across the room.

"We must speak, Juleah. You have had four proposals of marriage within the last year, and turned every one of them down. Why?"

"Because I do not love those who sent them."

"Issy wrote in her letter that several gentlemen showed interest and you turned them away. She has me most confused, for she says I must give you more freedom to follow your own heart. What does she mean?"

"I believe she is suggesting you allow me to decide for myself. Other than that, I do not know."

Lady Anna threw out her hands. "You must know something."

"I suppose you will want me to make eyes at Mr. Braxton in order to charm him into proposing next." Juleah smiled, hoping he would.

Her mother's mouth fell open. "Oh, did you hear her, Henry? Did you hear what she thinks of me?"

"I cannot help but hear it, my dear." Sir Henry knocked the ashes from his pipe into a dish. "Juleah is right. You would like it if Mr. Braxton asked for her hand now that he is rich. But it will take more than pretty eyes to squeeze a proposal out of him. He's too occupied upon other matters."

"You are not helping, Henry dear."

"I am glad for it." He stood. "I have business with the king's men. They have waited outside too long, and if I do not speak with them, they shall die of boredom right out on our drive. His Majesty will have my head for it." Sir Henry threw back his shoulders and strutted out.

Anna pulled her handkerchief from her sleeve and dabbed her teary eyes. It grieved Juleah's mother to hear her husband speak so. At times he lapsed into the past, and when he did return to the present he was as young and spirited for adventure as Thomas. Age crept upon him, and he'd sit in his chair for hours to stare out the window, mumbling to himself, looking as though he was in a faraway place.

"Papa is all right, Mother. Do not cry," said Juleah.

"It grieves me," Anna said.

Juleah went to her mother and put her arms around her.

"Why does your father say such things?"

"We must be patient with him."

"There are no soldiers out on the drive, yet he believes them to be there." Lady Anna twisted her handkerchief between her hands. "One minute he is here, the next, somewhere else. He speaks of war and next he's walking in the fields hunting rabbits with Thomas."

"At least he is happy," Juleah assured her.

Lady Anna hung her head. "I hope that is true."

"You only have to watch him to know it is."

"Mrs. Pepperdine stopped me one day in the village and urged me to put him away, said he was no good to me, a burden. I shan't do it, Juleah. I'd rather die than send him away."

"We shall bear it together, Mother. Papa will abide with us and die in his own bed with his family around him. No one will send him away to strangers."

Anna snapped up her daughter's hand in hers. "You are a comfort to me, Juleah." She wiped her eyes dry. "As far as Mr. Braxton goes, I like him."

Juleah stood and leaned toward the window. Outside, Sir Henry walked along his drive, paused and looked down at a dandelion. "Papa likes him a great deal, too."

Lady Anna sighed. "He fought against England. And there is your brother we must think about. You have no idea how broken my heart is. My son enlisting to fight in that war, miles and miles away from home in some godforsaken wilderness. And for what, I ask? The king? What did the king care for my son? What did he care for a grieving mother?"

Juleah turned away from the window. "A pain no mother should bear."

"I shall see him again, for I do not doubt I am not long for this world."

Juleah rushed to her mother and sat close to her. "You mustn't say such things. It is distressing to hear." Her voice was etched with pain.

Lady Anna rested her handkerchief against her breast. "At times, I have shortness of breath, and my heart pounds. My skin grows chilled, my limbs weak. Doctor Yates says it is high emotions and the strain of life that plagues me. Grief, I say, plays havoc on a woman."

Juleah sighed. "Peter would not wish you to grieve long, Mother."

"I wonder what Mr. Braxton sacrificed?" Anna gripped the edges of her handkerchief as if to pull it apart.

Juleah's lips parted, and she found herself answering with sympathy. "He lost his father in the war. Was that not enough?"

Lady Anna settled back against the cushions. "I had forgotten about that."

"Families on both sides suffered, Mother. I will never understand why men solve their differences by waging war and killing one another."

Her mother nodded. "If the world would follow the Lord's command to love one another, life would be better everywhere.

Do you imagine Mr. Braxton feels homesick for his country and will return some day?"

This was an idea not to be considered. The thought of Seth leaving caused her much pain. "He has not told me."

"You like him, don't you?"

"I think he has qualities any woman would like," said Juleah.

Her mother took her hands. "I would not want him to take you far away."

Juleah recognized the look in Anna's face—one of worry and doubt. "There is no understanding between us, Mother. He has not asked me."

"Has he implied it?"

"That he take me away? Be assured—he has not." Juleah pulled at a loose thread on the cushion, twisted it between her thumb and finger.

"This conversation is most confusing," Lady Anna pressed her fingertips against her temples.

"Then we should not discuss this topic," Juleah told her.

"You are exhausting me, Juleah." Anna lowered her hands and slapped them on her lap. "Is there any relief?"

"Would you like to go for a walk? The day is fine."

Anna raised her brows. "No. What we shall speak of is the letter that arrived. I saw it on your writing desk. I refused to look at it, but I have a good idea what it says."

"Edward Darden sent it." She did not tell Anna she had not read it, but instead tossed it into the fireplace without a second thought.

"I thought so. Before he left England, he visited you often. Why has he stopped?"

"I asked him to stay away."

Lady Anna angled her head. "Why?"

"Something cruel is in his nature. He's changed."

"I've always thought Darden must be low on the aristocratic family tree, with the way he dresses."

Juleah smiled lightly at her mother's flippant comment about clothes. "Darden is selfish and arrogant, Mother. It has little to do with the coat he wears."

Lady Anna wiggled in her seat. "Hmm. Well, Mr. Braxton reflects his grandfather's pride. One cannot help but see in his eyes a disdain for us."

"That is not true, Mother. Mr. Braxton thinks the best of us. He respects Papa and likes you. He has affection for Thomas and Jane."

"That is kind of you to say, Juleah. It relieves my doubt. But I fear to think what will happen when he and Mr. Darden cross paths. They are of two opposing forces."

Juleah stared out the window. She hoped with all her heart, Seth and Darden would never meet. It would be disastrous indeed.

13

Seedlings shook free from majestic sugar maples and whirled down to earth. Seth rode his horse from the groves nine miles into green moorland. He reined in and saw Wrenhurst nestled in the lush valley below, the poplars casting shadows over a plain of lawn.

Eager, Seth searched for a child at play, but no person was in sight, at least not until a horse galloped across his path. The rider jerked the reins and his horse skidded to a halt. It reared and beat its hooves forward.

"Gad, young man! I almost collided with you! Steady that horse. Who are you and what are you doing on my land?"

"Paying Sir Charles a visit, if it is of any business of yours, sir. My apologies, that I startled your horse."

"You are a bold rider. You should be more careful. You are not a highwayman I hope."

"I'm Seth Braxton of Ten Width."

The man's face deepened into a frown. "Ten Width, you say? I suppose you've come to Wrenhurst for reasons other than a social call."

"I've come to speak with Sir Charles. Is he at home, do you know?"

The man shot Seth a proud look. "I am Sir Charles."

Seth steadied Jupiter and tightened the reins around his fist. "I'll not impose on you long, Sir Charles. But it is urgent we speak."

"Speak to me here and be quick."

"Do you have a rule of not allowing strangers by the name of Braxton to enter your house?"

"The name Braxton does have a certain aversion when I hear it. Besides, by your speech, I'd say you were no Braxton. What is a colonial doing here in England?"

Seth drew himself up. "My grandfather was Benjamin Braxton."

Sir Charles raised his brows. "Ah, I see. Well, I am not so ill-mannered not to extend my condolences on the deaths of your grandfather and sister. Caroline was my son's wife, as you may know."

Seth's brows pinched together. "My sister is alive and well. What made you think she had died?"

Shocked, Sir Charles's eyes widened. "I was told as much in a letter I received. You mean the fever did not take her?"

"You were deceived. Did you not receive word concerning your grandson?"

"I received no word of him."

"I'm surprised, sir, that you did not make inquiry into the welfare of your grandchild. What did you think happened to him with his mother supposedly dead?"

Sir Charles squinted his eyes. "I think, Mr. Braxton, we should go to the house and discuss this."

He turned his horse and Seth followed. Before him rose the grand house at the end of the drive. Not a spot of decay, not a brick out of place, the house had an atmosphere of perfection. A groom met Sir Charles to take his horse, while Seth dismounted and looked up at the bulwarks and the wide mullioned windows.

The door swung open and a servant stepped out and stood outside it. "We are not to be disturbed," Sir Charles said to her. With her eyes lowered, she gave Sir Charles a quick curtsey.

Heading into his study, Sir Charles waved Seth inside and shut the door. His gray hair had once been dark and the wrinkles beside his eyes showed his maturity. His tailored dress and scrubbed appearance were of no surprise, for he was a rich man.

"I'll get straight to the point," Seth began. "My sister was sick as you were told, with an infectious fever. Upon the advice of her physician, your grandson was removed from the house and given into the care of a nursemaid."

The muscles in Sir Charles's face twitched. "And where were you when this occurred?"

"Making my way to Ten Width. An earlier arrival might have prevented what followed. Do you know a woman by the name of Shanks?"

"I do not recall ever hearing that name. Why?"

"Caroline was told her son perished in Hetty Shanks's care. I arrived and found her wasting away with grief."

Sir Charles's eyes shifted from Seth's to the floor. "That would be distressful indeed. I am no stranger to grief."

"Then you'll understand the circumstances I'm about to unfold."

Lifting his eyes, Sir Charles's expression became one of anxious inquiry. "I am listening."

"I caught Hetty Shanks sneaking through the woods beside the church near Ten Width. She confessed she was paid for her silence, for the lie she told. She declared young Nathaniel is alive, and before I could get out of her where he might have been taken, she slipped from my grasp when my sister collapsed in my arms."

Sir Charles clasped his hands together and turned to stare out the window. "I cannot hide what is true. It would be cruel. The boy is indeed alive."

Elated, and relieved his search had ended here, Seth stepped forward. "Then he is with you?"

Sir Charles looked at Seth, aggrieved. "Yes. I assure you he has been well cared for."

Seth nodded. Indeed Hetty had lied about the boy being snatched out of her hands. It was she who brought him to Wrenhurst. But why?

Seth frowned. "You'd best tell me now, sir, what role you played in this."

"I had no knowledge of this conspiracy. Dare you question my role in anything?"

"Was it your idea to take the boy from his mother?"

"Of course not."

"Had you thought this was the way to injure my sister?"

His face flushed, and Sir Charles stepped away stiffly from the window. "What stupendous impertinence. I tell you, I had nothing to do with it."

"You were satisfied that the events told to you were true?"

"I was."

"Did you contact the authorities to make inquiry?"

"I had no reason to doubt the woman. She appeared honest enough. She gave me a letter penned in a feminine hand, signed by your sister. No doubt, it was a forgery. The letter entrusted Nathaniel to me and rightly, seeing I am his grandfather. I never would have thought anyone would bring him here under false pretenses."

Sir Charles lowered himself into a winged chair and ran his hands over his face. "I remember that woman standing in my hallway, her cloak dripping with rain, a look of false sincerity on her face. She had come in a covered farmer's wagon. I remember scrutinizing its driver, a robust, mean-looking fellow . . . perhaps her man, but I cannot say for sure."

"Yes, she mentioned him, said he was a servant, that he carried a dead child to the church for her. They lied and told the caretaker it was Nathaniel they had brought to be buried."

Sir Charles's face turned ashen. "This woman, you called her Shanks . . . she spoke to me in a sugary tone, extended her sympathies, and told me I must do my duty. She had the gall to put out her hand, that greedy palm covered in an old glove. I paid her for her troubles. God will pay her for her sins."

"At least she had enough heart to deliver the boy to you, Sir Charles. Others meant to harm the child . . . possibly end his young life."

Sir Charles shook his head and balled his fists. "You mean someone would have gone to such lengths as to murder an innocent child, my little lad that never harmed a thing?"

Seth looked into his elder's strained face. "It is hard to conceive."

With an oath, Sir Charles stood from the chair. "They do not deserve to draw breath!"

"Indeed not. God willing, they will be brought to justice."

"We've been played the fools. My wife was present when this took place. You may ask her if it will settle your mind and make you think better of me."

"I shall not trouble her. I believe you."

"Well that you did, for we must sort this thing out together. Agreed?"

"Agreed." Seth extended his hand and Sir Charles grasped it. "May I see him?"

"Certainly, but I will not give him over. Not until you bring Caroline to Wrenhurst. I must hear her story from her lips and see her face-to-face."

"We both are cautious men, Sir Charles. I assure you, I am whom I claim to be."

"If you were in my place, would you give over your grandson to a stranger?"

Seth took no offense. "No, I would not, sir."

With a troubled gait, Sir Charles paced. "Caroline and I have a breach between us. Yet, what we have in common seals that breach. She gave me a grandchild, an heir. It appears I have made a muddle of things by not inquiring about her. I am sorry."

Sir Charles gazed down into the garden at the side of his house. His stern face softened, and the lines near his eyes deepened. "Nathaniel is in the garden playing with his nurse."

Seth leaned forward and looked out. On the lawn tumbled a curly-headed child. A spaniel puppy romped alongside him. Though his stockings were torn across one knee and smeared with mud, he had the appearance in his blue velvet jacket and breeches, of a young heir. The nursemaid tried her best to keep him from racing about, but her efforts were futile. She kept her hands stretched out, as if wanting to catch the boy. He listened, stood, and threw a ball to the pup.

When Seth's eyes met his nephew's, the boy moved toward the safety of the woman. An inquisitive look swept across his face, and he raised a plump hand. The gesture shot an arrow straight into the heart of Seth Braxton.

"He looks every inch his father," Sir Charles said. "Except his hair is the color of Caroline's, and his eyes are as wide and green as hers. He has been a comfort to me having lost my son. She will let me see him from time to time, will she not?"

"Caroline knows what a grandfather can mean."

Sir Charles nodded, his eyes filled, and Seth watched him swallow his emotions.

"I cannot tell you how happy I am to hear she is alive," said Sir Charles. "Surely, for her to hear her son lives was tremendous—a miracle, in a word."

Seth shifted on his feet. "Words cannot describe it, Sir Charles."

Sir Charles paused to think. "We must discover who the other conspirators are. Hetty Shanks is not the mastermind behind this."

"I agree."

"I'd say you should go to the constable about this, have the woman arrested. But Latterbuck is useless. He'll say it is a misunderstanding."

Seth walked from the window to the doorway and donned his hat. "I have heard of this man. It would do no good for the moment to involve him, not until I have solid evidence. I'll return with Caroline in the morning."

Under a sky filled with bands of gray, Seth left Wrenhurst touched to the heart. He lifted his eyes to heaven, thankful he had found Nathaniel, healthy and whole.

✍

Sir Charles watched from his study window. His reflection showed a man struck a blow of a most devastating nature; his features sunk into an expression of complete despair. He could not be so self-controlled at that moment and not be touched with sadness; of releasing his grandson to a daughter-in-law he had not accepted. Yet, a sudden pity for this girl filled him, along with a strong sense of respect for her brother. Seth would bring Caroline to Wrenhurst, and Sir Charles would hear with his own ears the truth and see with his own eyes she lived. He'd know, without any room for doubt, this cruel plot had deceived him.

"Criminals all! I pray to God I see the perpetrators swing from the end of a rope." He slammed his fist hard against the window frame. Hetty Shanks and her expression of pity for the child sickened him. But at least she had brought Nathaniel to him, like Seth had said, in order to spare the boy a cruel end. Perhaps she thought the seclusion of Wrenhurst would buy her time to get away before the truth was told.

Still he cursed her and the persons who had planned such treachery.

14

*J*uleah slipped outside and paused to gaze up at the twilight sky. She drew in the scent of lilacs, watched purple blossoms drift onto the cobblestone walk. The orchard, through which she hurried, cast shadows along the ground. The horse chestnut trees quivered with the slightest breeze. She ran her hand over a trunk and ducked her head beneath the boughs.

Once she reached the bank of the pond, she slipped off her shoes and sat upon the cool grass. For a long while she watched swallows dip and circle above. She picked up a stone, threw it into the water, and watched the bands of ripples it made. The cattails quivered, and she brushed away a tear that slipped down her cheek.

She had to admit she was in love with Seth.

With her head thrown back, she gazed into the fathomless heavens. The warm night, the water, the purple sky above her beckoned. She pulled off her frock and stockings. In her chemise, she stepped into the water. She dipped her fingers along the surface, waded a ways out, turned, and bent her head until her hair was soaked. The soothing sensation caused her to shut her eyes. She moved her arms to and fro to feel the ripples against her and the soft mud that squished between her toes.

She spoke her heart to the One who had given her all this beauty and prayed that Seth would ask her the question that other men had longed for her to answer.

✥

On a hillside that overlooked the pond, Seth reined in Jupiter. Below, Juleah moved in the water with her back to him. The water reached her hips. Her hair caught the light and fell against her skin. The sight of her caused his heart to rear up. He enjoyed seeing her soaking wet, how her chemise clung to the curves of her body. Curling the reins tight around his fist, he wondered if it were wrong to admire a beautiful woman in this manner.

She stepped up, lifted the hem of her chemise above her calves and reached the shore. She picked up her frock, slipped it over her head, and smoothed it down. Her slim delicate fingers gathered up her hair. She squeezed the water from it, and pushed it back.

He rode toward her.

Jupiter shook his mane, and the bridle gear jingled. Startled, Juleah turned.

"Are you lost, Mr. Braxton?"

Seth drew off his hat. "I thought this way might be quicker. You're soaking wet."

She gave him a tilt of her head. "I . . . slipped in."

He dismounted, drew off his coat to place it over her shoulders. "You must be more careful."

"When I said I slipped in, I meant I had gone into the water." She leaned over, searched for her shoes. A lock of her hair brushed against her mouth when the breeze blew. Juleah lifted her hand and pulled it away, which sent something electric through Seth.

"I've come to tell you good news. Caroline's son did not succumb to a fever as you were told. He is alive."

Juleah dropped her shoes; her hand covered her mouth to stifle a cry. "Alive?"

Seth smiled and laughed. "Yes, alive."

"How can that be? How do you know this?" Her eyes revealed wild astonishment. "I do not understand. I was told . . ."

"Listen and I'll explain," Seth said. "I've been to Wrenhurst, and when I told Sir Charles the details of all that has happened he showed me the boy."

Numb with shock, Juleah shook he head. Seth could see she struggled to take this in.

"How did Sir Charles come by Nathaniel? Is this his doing?"

"No. Hetty Shanks took him to Wrenhurst and told Sir Charles that Nathaniel was now orphaned. She gave him a letter he believed was from Caroline bequeathing Nathaniel into his care. Naturally, he took the child. His one mistake—he failed to investigate whether what Hetty Shanks had told him was true."

For a moment, Juleah stared at Seth. Filled with excitement, a rush of eager questions poured out of her. He answered each one in turn, told her all he could, about his suspicion from the start, how he had suppressed it thinking he was in the wrong for doubting, believing that no one would ever lie about such a matter. What he omitted to say was who he thought was behind this cruelty.

"Sir Charles should have ridden to Ten Width and seen for himself," Juleah said. "But I suppose if he believed the letter was genuine, he would not have done more. He did not doubt you?"

"He was astounded, but willing to listen," Seth told her. "I'm taking Caroline to Wrenhurst tomorrow."

Juleah laid her head against his forearm. "Tomorrow cannot come quickly enough."

"I would be pleased if you'd come along."

She leaned up on her tiptoes, held Seth by the shoulders, looked at him with eyes bright. "Indeed I will. It is a miracle."

"Perhaps your father would allow me to escort you to Ten Width tonight." He gazed down into those beaming eyes and hoped some of her joy concerned him.

"Perhaps." She paused, removed her hands, and stepped back.

"Caroline will be pleased, and that way we can leave early without delay."

"Would you be pleased?"

"Yes, you know I would."

Shadows deepened. The breeze rushed through the cattails and lifted the ends of Juleah's hair. "I must get back." She stepped up the path. "I have to tell everyone what has happened."

Restraint broke as he looked again into her joyful eyes. He moved closer and took her by the shoulders. "Do you not love me as I love you?"

A breath slipped from her lips. "Do you not know, Seth? Do you not see?"

Seth drew her into his arms and brushed his lips over hers. She melted against him. "You'll not run away again?" he asked softly.

Her eyes softened. "No. Not again."

"I wish to speak to your father." Running his hand through her hair, he brought it forward over her shoulder. "It's important."

An even softer expression washed over Juleah's face. "Every evening he walks up on the ridge."

Seth picked up her hand, kissed it, and glanced toward the wooded swell of land beyond. "I'll find him."

He swung into the saddle and turned Jupiter out into the field. He looked back at Juleah. She stared after him. He smiled and waved his hand to her. With a gentle kick of his heels, he pushed Jupiter to a gallop in search of Sir Henry.

He reached the crest of green and reined in. He paused to look back at Juleah as she ran home barefooted, with her hair unbound.

As he rode down the dusky lane, Seth spied Sir Henry off in the distance. The old gentleman walked along with a smile, carrying a walking stick. Thomas bounced ahead of his father, chased something fluttering in the air, and stood still when Seth's horse snorted.

He cantered up to them. Jupiter shook mane and tail.

"It's Jupiter, Papa, the old squire's horse. The one named after that pagan god." Thomas took a quick step back.

"Aye, lad, and now he belongs to this gentleman." Sir Henry's dogs circled around him, wagging their tails like flags. "Down, you hounds."

Seth pulled off his hat and set it across his thigh. "Good evening, Sir Henry. Master Thomas."

Sir Henry looked up at Seth with a broad smile. "And to you, sir."

"I admit, Master Thomas, Jupiter may be an unfit name for a Christian gentleman's horse," Seth said. "But he's used to it."

"He's mean-spirited." Thomas scowled. "I hear he kicks and bites."

"If ill-treated, Tom. Here climb up." Seth bent over, held out a hand. "You can guide him to the house, while your father walks alongside us."

Tom shifted uneasily on his feet. He moved beside the right stirrup and lifted his hand to Seth, who pulled him up and set him in front of him. Jupiter sidestepped under the meager weight of the extra rider.

"Now, take the reins and lead him on." Thomas brought the reins together and gripped them hard. "Relax, Tom. He'll go easy if you nudge him with your knees."

"Well done, lad." Sir Henry clapped his hands. "You show that beast you're not afraid of him. Come in to the house, won't you Mr. Braxton?"

"Yes, come inside," urged Thomas. "I want to ask you about Indians."

"Well, the boy has asked you," said Sir Henry. "What say you, sir?"

"I'll stay. I wish to have a private word with you, Sir Henry."

Sir Henry raised his brows. "You have my undivided attention, sir."

The horse moved on beneath Thomas's gentle touch, toward the house before darkness conquered. The moon stood above the trees; grasses in the fields whispered and were covered with dew. Seth showed Thomas how to bring the horse forward, how to bring him to a halt, and move him on again. Thomas grew bold, nudged Jupiter harder, and forced the horse to pick up each step.

Outside the door, Seth dismounted and helped Thomas down. He walked proudly away, and Jupiter followed him. One quick shove sent Thomas forward and he stumbled.

"He wants whatever is in your pocket," Seth told him.

Thomas frowned at the horse. "It's my apple, sir."

"Well, don't spoil him with it unless you want to."

"If I give it over, will he like me?"

"Kindness wins a horse. Here, let me help you." Seth looped the reins tighter around his hand, and brought the horse to a standstill. "There, you see. I have him firmly."

Tom drew out the half-eaten apple. He stepped closer and held the treat out in the palm of his hand until Jupiter took it between velvety lips.

Thomas rubbed his hand against his breeches. "His nose felt soft, and he didn't bite me."

Seth smiled and handed him the reins. "Now that you have won him over, you take him. Loop the reins over the post." Seth looked up and saw Juleah leaning on her arms at the window, her head cocked to one side as she smiled at him, pleased by his attentiveness to Thomas. He headed for the door and knocked his fist against the wood frame. The serving woman pulled it open.

Lady Anna rushed forward with her hands stretched out to greet him. "Juleah told us the news. I'm overjoyed for Caroline. But, oh, what mischief has been afoot these many months to do such an evil deed. You must employ the constable at once, Mr. Braxton. Have the persons responsible arrested."

"I shall not let the matter rest." He gave her an assuring nod.

"I have no doubt. My daughter tells me you wish her to join your sister at Ten Width. I'd object to her traveling alone with you at this time of day, but under the circumstances, it is agreeable. You will take care of her for us?"

Seth bowed. "You have my word."

"Do not let her fall from your horse."

I'll hold her firmly. He regarded Juleah when she came down the stairs freshly dressed. "Shall you not ride your own?"

Sir Henry stepped forward. The dogs weaved in and out between his legs. "The old nag has gone lame. Be off before it grows too dark to travel." Sir Henry leaned toward Seth. "Keep to your pistols. There are highwaymen about."

Before Anna Fallowes could raise any objection at the mention of highwaymen, Juleah hurried off. Seth followed her out. Lady Anna pleaded with Juleah to take care not to soil her clothes, while Sir Henry said something about the king's men, and Thomas and Jane said their good-byes.

Before he climbed into the saddle, Seth turned to Sir Henry. "Sir, I wish to speak to you."

"What is it? Nothing serious I hope. No call to arms?"

Seth drew Sir Henry aside. "I love your daughter, sir."

A smile swept over Sir Henry's face. "You wish to court her?"

"I wish to wed her."

Sir Henry shrugged indifferently. "You have my blessing. I shall ask the king to give his as well. Perhaps he shall call you both to court. You will have to get a new suit of clothes if he does."

There he went, slipping away once more. Seth exercised great patience and compassion, and shook Sir Henry's hand to thank him. He mounted his horse and reached down. Juleah put her foot over the top of his boot in the stirrup. He drew her up to him. His arms went around her and she held tight.

Moonlight bathed the road and made the ride easy for the pair that traveled toward Ten Width. Juleah leaned back against Seth. They traveled on through the forest, beneath brooding, dark elms. An owl hooted and Juleah's hand tightened over his arm. He could have reined in his horse and turned her to him. Instead, he reined in his desire and relished the closeness of the woman he loved.

15

The following morning, a brisk wind drove in from the sea. Leaden clouds crossed the sky and threw long shadows over the land. A hired coach arrived by nine o'clock and made the journey bearable for the people within it. Soft, cushioned seats instead of saddles and shelter from wind and drizzle gave comfort. They passed whitewashed cottages, the square church belfry, and the crumbling Roman walls. Wheels churned along a road at the edge of the bluffs, above the sea, through the moors toward Wrenhurst.

Seth fixed his eyes upon Juleah. He sensed she could feel his gaze; and when she glanced back at him, he commented about the scene outside, the passing farms and fields, the beauty of the countryside. What he wanted to tell her was how beautiful she looked. The dark blue habit she wore fitted close to the curve of her waist. Its color heightened the ivory tint of her skin and the dark auburn tresses of her hair. He wanted to tell her that every time he gazed upon her a fire burned within. But he smiled instead and made light conversation. He told himself there would come a time when they'd be alone, and he'd tell her all that was in his heart.

"You say it is beautiful here. Is it like Virginia?" Juleah asked.

He shifted his gaze back to her. "In some ways."

"You miss it? Home and your river?"

"I've enough here to keep my mind off it." He smiled at the rush of scarlet that bloomed in her cheeks.

"You do not have horses like Jupiter, though." And she returned a coy smile.

"No, but I will someday. Every man has dreams. Mine is to raise horses and, hopefully, many children."

"You must first find a wife, my brother." Caroline laughed lightly. "It shouldn't be too hard."

"A wife, that is true. But will she have me?" He looked at Juleah warmly.

"I have no doubt of it," Caroline replied with a broad smile. "Speaking of marriage, Michael Bray has asked me to marry him."

Juleah turned to her with an embrace. "How wonderful!"

Caroline looked over at her brother. "Do you approve, Seth? Do we have your blessing?"

"I gave it long ago," he said. "He's a good man, and you deserve to be happy."

A tear slipped from his sister's eye. "It is good of you to say so, Seth. It means the world to me that you would call Michael your brother. We wish to be married quickly and quietly in the little church near Ten Width."

The carriage climbed a hill and made a sharp turn to the right. Irregular stone walls bordered each side of the road. The horses slowed and were brought to a halt in order to make way for a boisterous flock of geese. A girl with flaxen hair guided the snowy fowl along with a reed. She swung it to and fro, and once she managed to steer them to the other side the carriage moved on.

By the time the sundial reached ten of the clock, the coach slowed and drove into Wrenhurst. Seth got out first. When he reached the door a servant opened it. They waited in a large room, furnished with comfortable chairs and a settee, the windows set wide open to allow the morning breeze inside. A clock on the mantel ticked away the minutes, adding tension to excited nerves. Footsteps echoed out in the hallway. The door swung open and he entered the room dressed in black linen and gold trim, with gray silk stockings and buckled shoes. Beside him stood his stately wife, Lady Barbara Kenley. The moment their eyes rested on Caroline, they paused.

Caroline, Juleah, Claire in the background, and Seth between the women, bowed and curtsied.

"Dear Lord," cried Lady Barbara. "It is Caroline, Charles. She is as lovely as the day our son brought her to meet us." This was not a moment for formality, for introductions. Her ladyship opened her arms and embraced her daughter-in-law. "Dear girl, you have suffered so. I am sorry that we did not help matters."

With his brow furrowed and his eyes fixed upon his son's first and only love, Sir Charles stepped forward. "Can you forgive this old man? Can you pardon my stubbornness, my prejudice?"

A sob escaped Caroline, and she hastened to him. He kissed her cheek. She lowered her head, held his hand against her cheek. "How can I thank you both for looking after Nathaniel? What must I do to repay you?"

Sir Charles looked down at her. "Repay me? Dear girl, I should have done something, written to someone at Ten Width. Here you had to grieve all these months due to my stupidity." He turned to a door at the far end of the room as it opened. "Ah, here is the lad now. Nathaniel, come greet your mother."

Hand-in-hand with his nurse, the child's flaxen curls tumbled over his head. His large green eyes gazed up at the four adults, then rested upon his mother's face. He held out his chubby hand. Caroline knelt down and stretched her arms out to him. Tears streamed down her cheeks and she gathered her son to her bosom, held him close, and kissed his cheeks.

Seth stood behind her, and Caroline turned. "Oh, look at him, Brother. Is he not the finest boy you have ever seen?"

"Indeed he is, Caroline." Seth crouched down and tousled Nathaniel's head. Next to him, Juleah wiped her eyes.

"Give Juleah an embrace, Nathaniel," said Caroline, and he tumbled straight into her arms.

Sir Charles cleared his throat and ordered his serving girl to prepare rooms for his guests. "The best rooms, my girl. Fresh linens, you hear? And open the windows to let fresh air inside."

Caroline glanced up at him from the floor with her eyes glistening with tears. "Oh, Sir Charles, we cannot intrude upon you a moment longer."

"Nonsense," he said. "Your journey was a long one. I insist you all stay. It will break my heart if you refuse."

"May my maid stay?"

"Of course, she may." His eyes drifted over to Claire as she waited in silence in the shadow of the doorway. "What's your name, girl?"

She lifted her lowered eyes and curtsied. "Claire, sir."

Sir Charles held his hand out to Caroline and lifted her up. "We must have time together—get to know one another better. The nursemaid will show you and your girl to Nathaniel's room. You may stay with him if you prefer."

She nodded. "I would be very pleased. Thank you, Sir Charles."

She gathered her son's hand, and with Claire a step behind her followed Lady Barbara out of the room.

Sir Charles turned to Juleah. "I assume this is your wife, sir?"

A smile tugged at Seth's mouth. "No, Sir Charles."

"She ought to be. She is pretty enough."

Juleah blushed.

Seth drew beside her. "May I introduce Miss Juleah Fallowes of Henry Chase?"

"I recognize your name, Miss Fallowes. It is a pleasure." Sir Charles bent over and kissed her hand.

"My friend has suffered," Juleah said. "Because of you and Mr. Braxton, she is happy again. What a glorious ending to a very difficult time of mourning."

"Not all things are concluded, Miss Fallowes," said Sir Charles. "May I ask, did you pack a gown suitable for an evening promenade?"

The corners of Juleah's mouth gently lifted. "I did, Sir Charles."

"And Caroline, and you, Mr. Braxton, did you pack suitable clothes?"

Seth nodded. The navy blue suit he recently had tailored would do nicely.

"Excellent." Sir Charles slapped his hands together. "The vermin who caused this trouble will be flushed out. For I have a plan. Lady Barbara and I are to play host come this Friday evening. It shall be a large gathering. Invitations have been issued to all my acquaintances and to those who are in some way connected with the Braxtons. After we dine, I shall have you read over the guest list, in case I left anyone out. There is something about a country affair that brings secrets to light. I believe we shall learn more by way of it."

He escorted them upstairs and requested they come down after they refreshed for an early dinner. He left them in the hallway outside the room for Juleah.

"Sir Charles is determined," she said. "I hope his plan works. I am not sure what he is expecting, though. Would not those who planned all this stay away?"

Seth moved closer, lifted her hand in his, and played with her fingers. "Maybe, but I think they'll show. Curiosity, if anything, will draw them out."

Her eyes, wet and glistening, enticed. "Be careful, Seth."

"Do not worry about me."

He drew her into his arms and kissed her.

⁂

The next afternoon, the household gathered out on the lawn for lunch. The day grew quite warm, with a blue sky speckled with wispy clouds. Bird songs echoed in the woodlands, and it seemed as if since morning the buds on the trees had burst out into lime green, newly born leaves. Seth drew Juleah aside. "Care to take a walk around the grounds?"

She looped her arm through his and they strolled within sight of their hosts. A lily pond reflected the blue sky and the lush grass surrounding the water. Small white butterflies danced in midair before them, and a blackbird darted into the cattails and sang.

"There is a mockingbird that sings on moonlit nights back home, down by the river." Seth broke off and listened to a blackbird in silence. Its wings spread wide and it flew off as they drew closer.

"I have been meaning to ask you something." Juleah's hand pressed into his arm. "Were you able to have that talk with my father? You know, the day he was walking up on the ridge?"

Seth's eyes smiled at her. "Yes. But I cannot tell you what we discussed, not until later, when I know it is the right time."

She did not question why. "Tell me then, will you stay here in England?"

He stopped, and looked down at her. "It all depends."

"On what?"

"Many things."

A cloud passed over the face of the sun, and the light faded from her eyes, as did her smile. "I do not think I could ever leave England."

Seth frowned slightly and looked away toward the hills beyond Wrenhurst. Confused by her admission and whether she truly meant what she said, he grew silent and grave. Yet, within him, his love for her rallied. No matter what things she said that pricked him or caused him to doubt, he had sworn within himself to make her his wife one day.

Therefore . . . a man shall leave his father and his mother . . . and cleave unto his wife. This truth spoke a quiet promise into Seth's heart, that there'd come a time when he would hold her fast. He only had to be patient.

Coming up behind them, one of Lady Barbara's house-maids called to Juleah. "Post has arrived for you, miss." And she handed over a sealed letter.

The girl dipped and went her way, while Juleah looked down at the uneven handwriting that sprawled across the paper. She unfolded it and skimmed over the words. Seth stepped back to give her a moment, but when he saw the rose in her cheeks fade away, he grew concerned.

She glanced over at him. Her mouth parted, and her eyes blinked. She heaved in a breath, and then gave him a quivering smile. "It is of no importance."

"It has troubled you. Is something wrong?"

She shook her head and a lock of her hair fell forward. "For some reason, Edward Darden thought he needed to inform me that he has accepted Sir Charles's invitation. I don't understand why he thought I should care."

It suddenly occurred to Seth, that he might have a rival. He watched her step to the bank of the pond, fold the letter back up, and toss it into the water. A moment and it sank away. He'd never know exactly what Darden had written to her.

16

At sunset, after a sun-drenched Friday when Wrenhurst's servants had decorated the house with juniper garlands, and the cook had completed all the dishes, Sir Charles stood in front of his marble fireplace looking over the people that crowded his ballroom. Above the mantle hung a portrait of King George, and beside Sir Charles stood Seth.

Music mingled with the chatter of guests. Some argued politics, excited voices raised above the others. High-pitched laughter and exclamations from the less-refined ladies overtook them. Powdered hair, black patches against white faces, the stark contrast of rouge—they stood grouped together as life-like porcelain dolls.

Wrenhurst's elegance surpassed the quaint beauty of Ten Width and the charming family atmosphere of Henry Chase. High-backed chairs covered in scarlet velvet lined pale ochre walls. Banquet tables overflowed with country fare. Silver chargers held fruit of every kind, their luscious colors illuminated by candle-light. Platters of beef and fowl sat among bowls of vegetables.

The majority of gentlemen present were of a higher class than Seth. He rejected the whole idea of rank, believing what was in a man's heart mattered more. All men were created equal. High or low, rich or poor, in the end all would face the same judge.

Some argued over issues of Parliament and the king, clicked their sterling snuffboxes open and shut, sniffed their snuff, and sneezed into linen handkerchiefs. Titled people, old soldiers, young veterans dismissed of the regimental scarlet, grand dames, and wealthy ladies, those with titles not so wealthy, bankers, ship merchants, and landed gentlemen. Seth wondered where he fit in.

Agitated, he flexed his right hand. He was not accustomed to such gatherings. It was clear what the ladies thought of him when he caught numerous sultry gazes. He was set apart from unfamiliar faces and rich clothes. His navy wool coat, his shirt and neckcloth made of plain white linen, his dark breeches and waistcoat, were all a simple man's attire. Silks and satins were not to his taste, nor the square-toed shoes with bright buckles. Tonight he wore his best black leather boots. His ponytail hung at the nape of his neck, tied snug with an ebony crepe ribbon.

In a corner stood Mr. Banes with his wife, a bone-thin woman with rouged cheeks. She waited in her husband's shadow and spoke not a word, while Banes debated with two other lawyers.

At the banquet table, Doctor Yates filled a plate. Upon his arm hung a painted woman, her dress cut low, revealing an ample bosom. The wig piled high on her head flowed along her shoulders in heavy white curls. Seth imagined that beneath the powder and rouge there might be a pretty face—or perhaps an older one.

"Caroline has been happy these past few days at Wrenhurst," Sir Charles said. "I'm pleased she agreed to stay with us. I've grown exceedingly fond of her and have atoned for the way I treated her. I know this is how my son would have wanted it to be between us."

Seth inclined his head. "Your kindness toward my sister is appreciated, Sir Charles."

"Well, I have discovered how easy it is to be kind to one so good. Come, let me introduce you to my guests. The ladies are anxious to meet you."

"I'm not good at introductions."

"All you must do is nod to the gentlemen and kiss the ladies' hands. But I daresay you have eyes for one lady and here she comes."

Seth's heart leapt in his chest.

Catching the candlelight, her hair glowed with a burnished color against her throat. She lifted her eyes and her gaze met Seth's. A shy smile spread over her lips and he returned one of his own as a surge of desire pumped through his core.

His blood rushed, as his pulse quickened. The curve of her mouth proved fatal to his senses. The emerald gown graced her figure. He was pleased she was not the kind to rub rouge over her cheeks or wear wigs. Tonight her hair hung down her back in majestic curls and twists, and her face had a light dusting of powder.

He moved through the crowd toward her, through a sea of silks. Through the doorway, a man moved beside Juleah, bent his head, and spoke into her ear. She cast her eyes down, turned her head aside. Lifting her hand, the man looped it through the crook of his arm. Handsome and tall, dressed finely, the ladies unabashedly cast glances at the man. He returned nods in a manner given to a libertine.

In cloaked shock, Seth stood motionless. Instantly, he recognized the man's face. His limbs turned heavy as stone. He could not go forward, as Edward Darden dared to lift one of Juleah's ringlets and run it between his fingers. Seth's hands flexed tight at his side and then relaxed.

Sir Charles came up beside him. "Are you acquainted with that gentleman?"

Through the flare of candles, Seth encountered Darden's eyes. "I am not, though his face I know."

"Darden is a rogue, I do not mind saying."

A cold chill ran through Seth when he heard the name of that British, red-coated bully that had wanted him dead. "Introduce us, if you please, Sir Charles."

But more than an introduction raged in Seth's mind; a confrontation, a battle, a drawing of the line in the sand was more of what he had in mind. Never had he sensed so great an aversion toward anyone, not even to the enemy he faced on the battlefield.

For Juleah's sake Seth resigned to be in control of his tongue. He'd conceal his feelings for the moment and allow time to weigh everything out in its balance. But how was he to tolerate Darden's connection to his family, now that he knew who he was and the attention he showed Juleah? He wanted to laugh at the irony of it all.

Seth watched Darden follow the direction of Juleah's eyes. Had a flash of memory reeled within Darden's prideful stare? The rebel taken prisoner several years ago now faced him amid a gathering of upper-class English. With a scowl moving over his lips, Darden looked Seth up and down with his cruel eyes.

"Well, Darden," said Sir Charles. "You made it to our affair and with a beautiful lady on your arm."

Darden inclined his head. "Sir Charles, you are an observant man."

"More than you may think—Miss Juleah, Sir Henry and his lady have not arrived?"

She gave him a graceful curtsey. "They send their regrets, Sir Charles. My mother fell ill with a dreadful headache and could not make the journey."

Sir Charles took a step back and moved Seth forward. "Darden, have you met our American cousin, who is now the squire of Ten Width?"

Darden flashed Seth a haughty glance. "Rarely do I make acquaintance with Yankee rebels, Sir Charles. But seeing he happens to be your guest, I will at least be civil. Have you found Ten Width to your liking, Mr. Braxton?"

Seth fastened his eyes on Darden. "In some ways, yes."

"I have not been to Ten Width since my stepfather died. Your sister left me no reason to visit."

Juleah's eyes lifted to Seth's, and he marked the painful gleam that filled them. A step forward; he took her hand. Darden frowned.

"Ah, my wife stands by the punch bowl, speaking with Lady Moreland." Sir Charles held his arm for Juleah to take. "She is most anxious to introduce you."

Juleah looped her arm inside her host's and moved through the crowd in the direction of her hostess. "You, Darden, must stay." Sir Charles held him back with a firm hand. "Feminine conversation is best left for the ladies to enjoy without us hovering."

Darden paused in resignation. "I know better than to question my host's knowledge of women."

Seth inwardly applauded Sir Charles's conspiratorial actions and declined a glass of burgundy from the servant's tray. "I suppose it was time we met, Captain Darden. How does your mother fair?"

Darden's face stiffened at the question. "My mother is in a condition to be expected. Illness has plagued her since the passing of her husband. He left her little of his heart, let alone his money."

"I'm sorry for that." Seth turned in Juleah's direction. He watched her speak to Lady Barbara, run her fingers through a twist of her hair, and smile.

Darden straightened the cuff of his right coat sleeve and grinned. "Do you still hunt with a musket?"

"Not since the day I lost it to an Indian," Seth replied.

"Ah, yes. I remember now. A spoil of war."

"I hope he put it to better use. It was the best musket I ever owned. I felled my first deer with it."

"It felled several Englishmen as well."

"I care not to think of lost lives, sir. We were at war."

"Yes, I imagine it weighs heavy upon your conscience."

"I did it for my country, as you did your duty by yours."

Darden slipped his finger inside his neckcloth to loosen it. "All Americans who fought against England were traitors. Every one of them should've hung or been thrown in prison, their lands confiscated, their houses burned, before war broke out."

"No doubt those things would have occurred if you had won."

Darden twisted his lower lip. "We compensated in other ways. There were rebel houses burned that summer before it all ended."

"It is in bad taste to brag about it."

"I disagree. It speaks of our strength."

"Strength? It shows a lack of compassion for the women and children who suffered. I believe the king would not have approved if he had seen it with his own eyes."

"You are ignorant on what the king would approve and not approve."

Seth meet Darden stare for stare. "My father's house was spared but ransacked. Two slaves were carried off by redcoats and most likely pressed into their service. I suppose you believe that was justified."

"Indeed. Lord Dunmore filled his Ethiopian Regiment quickly after declaring freedom for any slave wishing to fight alongside His Majesty's troops. I recall that the American ships in the Chesapeake hoisted British flags in order to deceive the wretches and sent them back into slavery. What difference did it make to the slaves whom they served, as long as their bellies were full?"

"I do not defend what my fellow countrymen did, Captain Darden. Men desire freedom, regardless of the color of their skin."

Darden laughed. "Your father had slaves, and you speak of freedom?" He finished his glass of port and set the glass upon the table. "I must say, I never knew my stepfather had a grandson until he was dying. He never spoke of either you or your father in my presence. Apparently he had nothing of any importance to say."

Seth could not help but let anger flicker over his face. "Why should he have spoken of me to you? Clearly, I was of great importance to my grandfather, seeing he made me his heir. Now, if you'll excuse me, there is something I wish to discuss with a lady."

He strode away, hoping he left Darden burning.

He came up alongside Juleah. "Lady Barbara, will you excuse us?" Her ladyship nodded graciously.

Taking Juleah's hand in his, he drew her outside onto the terrace. The air blew fragrant with the scent of boxwood. The sky was studded with stars.

Juleah lifted her gown as they hurried down the terrace steps. "Where are you taking me? I mustn't leave."

He glanced back at her. "Why not?"

"It is rude. People will talk."

"Let them."

He took her across the stone walkway, over the dewy lawn toward a walled garden. The hedge within brooded over the paths, cast shadows that deepened the darkness. Spears of moonlight floated through the trees in veils of blue and purple. It brushed over lawns, stone figures, and latticed walls.

Seth hurried with her to a place hidden from view. He stopped, held her waist and moved her in front of him.

"You must be angry with me." She touched his face.

"I didn't expect to see you with Darden."

"I did not seek him out. He found me."

"What was I to think when I saw you with him?"

She touched the lapel of his coat and ran her fingers over it. "You are jealous."

"You have the right to be with whomever you wish. But I wonder, have I been wrong in assuming you felt anything for me?"

Juleah's mouth fell open. "Must you trample on my feelings, Seth? My heart is yours."

Cut to the quick, he gazed down into her eyes. "Forgive me."

"You have no cause to feel threatened by Darden."

"I'm glad to hear it. I love you."

Her eyes softened, warmed at his tender admission. "Perhaps it is foolish to love me."

"Love may make a man do foolish things. But I'm no fool for loving you."

She moved from him, walked a ways down the path with him beside her. "I have had something weighing on me that I must tell you about."

He stopped, his curiosity pricked. "I'm listening."

"The year before Darden left to fight in America, he pursued me. He asked if I would wait for him, told me he was promised Ten Width, that he could give me a good life. I did not love him, but . . . we've been secretly engaged since that day."

Seth could not help himself. He stared at her, speechless and hurt. She raised her eyes to his. Her gaze reflected the wish that he would understand and somehow rescue her.

"Engaged? To Edward Darden?" he asked.

She shook her head. "I was too young to know what I was doing."

"You should have told me."

"I was afraid I would lose you."

"Is there anything else I should know?"

"No, Seth. Please understand, Darden has never been, nor ever will be, my love. You mustn't doubt me."

"Mustn't I?" A rapid pulse beat inside his temple. A flash of heat coursed through his body. "That blackguard took for granted my grandfather's good graces. And here you were engaged to him, while I courted your affections, kissed you, and held you in my arms."

He jerked away, and she reached for him. She pulled him close and put her hand on his cheek. He breathed hard and looked into her face. Pain was there, and she fought back the tears.

"You will break it off," he said, stung with fury.

"Before he has not listened. Tonight I will make it clear to him. I swear."

Her look of sincerity, and the beauty of her face, melted his fury. He lifted a ribbon from her bodice and pulled her close. She settled against his chest.

"I need to do some explaining as well," he said. "Darden and I have met."

Juleah's eyes widened. "Where?"

"Remember the story I told you about my capture? Darden was one of the officers."

She let out a moan. "Oh, if only I had known." She hung her head.

He lifted her chin with the tip of his finger. "It doesn't matter."

He put his hands around her face and looked at her. Her tears were true. He wiped them from her cheeks and kissed her three times full and passionately.

She whispered in his ear. "Find me in the dark." Lifting her skirts, she hurried away, along the path hemmed in by boxwoods. He followed her.

She came around a bend. Her hair floated off her shoulders in the breeze. Her smile brightened under the moonlight, her breathing hurried, and her laughter light. When she made the turn, she bumped straight into Darden.

"What are you doing out here in the dark? Come back inside." His face appeared stern, lined, and hard against the moonlight. He stopped short when he saw Seth. The moment Juleah went to pass him, Darden stepped in front of her. "What are you doing alone with that *rebel?*"

She jerked away. "I can be with whomever I please. Do not touch me again."

Darden glanced between the two, his face livid in the moon's haze. He thrust out his hand for her to take. Juleah looked down at it, turned and hurried up the stairs.

Struck with insult, Darden's mouth twitched. He took a quick, angry step toward Seth. "Look, you Yankee blackguard. I order you to stay away from her."

"Order me?" Seth laughed, stepped forward, and looked Darden straight in the face.

"I warn you, I am an excellent shot."

Seth folded his arms. "Are you threatening me?"

"Absolutely." Darden turned on his heels and stamped up the stairs.

"Then let it be so," Seth whispered, even though it was not the time, nor the place. Heading up the terrace stairs, he turned back inside the room. The crowd, being gathered together, stood shoulder to shoulder. They craned their necks, while curiosity swept over the sea of faces.

"Ladies and gentlemen," began Sir Charles. "I know you're wondering why I asked you here tonight. I beg your pardon, dear ladies, for I have interrupted the dancing. And you gentlemen, my apologies for waylaying your feasting."

The men nodded, and a round of laughter rippled through the room. The ladies giggled behind their silk fans.

"Some of you may have heard that my daughter-in-law and her young son were both taken from this world by the fever. I invited you here to introduce you to my son's widow, Caroline, who in actuality survived her bout of illness." Restless, the crowd murmured. Then Caroline, her hand set on Michael Bray's arm, walked through an opening in the crowd and stood beside Sir Charles. He took her hand and kissed her cheek in a fatherly manner.

Seth glanced around the room to observe the expressions on peoples' faces. They drew in their breaths, stared in utter surprise.

"And now my friends, I wish to introduce my grandson and heir, Nathaniel Charles Kenley."

Sir Charles swept his hand out toward the doorway. Holding his nurse's hand, the lad came into view, his eyes brilliant and absorbing. He hurried to his mother. She lifted him up and people applauded.

Seth shifted his eyes from the bright, happy face of his sister and glanced over at Darden. He saw him jerk as if someone had slapped his face. He stared in disbelief, the creases in the corners of his dark eyes deepening. Malicious scorn spread over his taut mouth. Seth watched on as Darden bowed to his sister. She lost her smile, lifted her face, and turned away without speaking to him. Darden's face flushed with insult, with that dark look in a man's eyes when he has done wrong and realizes his plans have been foiled. His mouth turned into a sneer and twitched.

Easily, Seth read in Darden's bearing, this turn of events was too much for the man to stand. It was obvious the sight of Caroline and her son rattled him to the marrow as did the man who had inherited what he coveted.

Darden turned on his heels and stalked out. Seth caught Juleah's eyes. She nodded knowingly to him. She had seen what he had. Turning her gaze away, she followed Darden outside. Seth had to trust whatever she had in her mind to do.

He realized he should not gloat, but he was glad Darden had seen him alone with Juleah, glad he had seen Caroline and her son alive. He observed each gesture, each twinge of expression. The trap had been set. Darden was moving toward it more than anyone else in the room.

Now, Seth thought, they must wait for it to spring.

17

*C*ool evening dew brushed Juleah's face. Evergreens stood pale as granite carvings in the garden. It was what her eyes first beheld, that and the veils of soft moonlight that filtered through the airy pine needles.

She saw Edward Darden stride across the green and call for the stableboy. Darden's fists were tightly closed, his body stiff.

"Bring my horse now." Darden's firm demand caused the boy to cower. Off he ran in the direction of the stable. Darden turned toward her. His countenance changed in an instant, from anger to forlorn hope.

When he reached the place where she stood, he bent to kiss her. She turned her head, and her lips refused to meet his.

A corner of Darden's mouth turned downward. "When a woman is accustomed to the ways of a man, she welcomes his kisses. Obviously you have not reached that point."

"I do not wish to be kissed," she said.

He sneered. "Not by me, anyway. Why should you, when Braxton is here to make eyes at you? You seem fond of him, and not a'tall apprehensive to be alone with him. It is unseemly of you."

"It is no different from what I am doing now. We're alone, are we not?"

"Yes, but for a different reason. Tell me what it is."

Juleah moved away from under his dark shadow. "I need to dispel any idea you have had about having me."

"We had an understanding."

She plucked a leaf from the vine on the wall and tore it. "Yes, but I was barely fifteen then, and the years have changed us both."

He took a step toward her. His eyes blazed with infuriated emotion. "My affections for you have deepened."

Her body jerked, then she forced it still. "Your behavior speaks otherwise."

Darden took her by the arms. "You have left me disappointed."

"You expected me to keep a promise I made when I was too young to know any better?"

"I will never stop wanting you."

Juleah winced and shrank from his grip. She had not forgotten his cruel temper, how he'd strike back like a coiled snake if pushed. "I do not want you. I do not love you."

Darden dropped his hands, smarting under a bewildered sense of failure that showed on his face. "There was a time when you gave me hope."

She answered with sharp-tongued clarity. "I tried to protect Caroline. I thought you would throw her out with her son if you inherited Ten Width. Do you think I'd injure her by accepting you? You ignored her when she grieved for Jeremy. You sent her no word when Benjamin died. You have shown no compassion."

His eyes narrowed and he set his teeth. "I have done nothing wrong. You will regret your accusations."

"There is no regret when there is honesty."

"But not enough to admit to my face you love another man. You treat him as if he were born and bred in England. You should have nothing to do with him. None of us should."

"The war is over. Why can you not put it behind you?"

"Because it was in my rights to have Ten Width more than his."

She narrowed her eyes and stared back at him. The more he spoke, the more Juleah grew disgusted. "If Seth had refused, Nathaniel would have inherited, not you."

"It was mine before the will was changed."

"It was never yours. It belongs to Seth and is Nathaniel's legacy."

"That child has enough being Sir Charles's heir. Why should he have more?"

Juleah paused to compose her rage. "I saw your reaction when Caroline came into the room with Nathaniel. Your face paled, as if you had seen a pair of ghosts."

Darden pressed his lips together hard. "I was shocked, like the rest."

"Shocked, yes, but you did not rejoice like the rest of us."

"What are you accusing me of?"

"I think you know something. Who was it that planned this evil to have the child murdered?"

Darden guffawed. "You believe I had something to do with it? It is a mystery to me as much as it is to anyone."

She believed he was lying. "The truth will bring darkness to light."

"What kind of man do you take me for?" He grabbed her shoulders and shook her. When she raised her palm to strike his face, he cuffed her wrist with his hand. Juleah yanked free, but he secured both her wrists in an instant.

"You will be sorry one day. I can promise you that. And that Yankee of yours, he'll regret it in the deepest degree."

He released her, flung her back, turned, and walked down the stairs. The lad had brought the horse and stopped short. Darden mounted. He slipped the reins through his gloved hands and swung his horse around. She watched him dig his heels into the horse's ribs and gallop off.

Juleah went back inside the manor and heard laughter in the other rooms. She found Seth leaning against a wall.

"I had not the pleasure of a single dance with you," he said.

"I am sorry." She forced a smile.

"It's just as well. I lack the grace of the English when it comes to dancing. But I'm good at Virginia reels."

"Darden has left, and our understanding is over." She wove her fingers through his. "I fear he might try to harm you. He made threats."

A furrow formed between Seth's brows. He put his hands on her arms and moved them down to her wrists. He ran his palms up along her skin, beneath the lace that fell over it, to her elbows.

"He can do nothing to me."

18

Two days later at Ten Width, Seth opened his eyes to the gloom, sat up, and rubbed his face with his hands. He tried to shake the languor of the night from his body as he walked over to the washbowl and splashed cold water over his face and neck. The subtle patter of rain streamed on his window and he moaned. *The roads will be muddy.*

He pulled on his clothes and boots and left for downstairs. After he grabbed a hunk of bread slathered with butter and a mug of black coffee, he set off. When he climbed into the saddle the rain had lessened to a misty drizzle.

At the gates of Ten Width, a rider hailed him. It was Michael Bray.

"You're a godsend. I need a witness," Seth told him once they met out on the road. "I'm on my way to see Mave Proctor."

Bray squashed his hat down tighter against the drizzle that assaulted him. "A witness I shall be, yet a quiet one. I'm not good at getting answers out of old women."

Six miles later Seth stepped up to the door of a thatched house and knocked. The door creaked open and Mave peeked out. Her face appeared like an old man's, the beauty of womanhood robbed by age. Deep lines and brown spots covered her sunken cheeks and broad forehead. Her nose was crooked and scarred, and her eyes were gray with a lackluster stare.

"Are you Mave Proctor?" He stepped closer, with his boot near the door in case she wished to clap it shut on him.

Mave blinked up at Seth. "Aye, sir, I'm Mave. What's your business?"

"I've a few things to ask, if you'd be so kind as to open the door and let me and my friend inside."

She looked him up and down. "Business is it? You've a lady in need of a nursemaid?"

"Neither. But it is business just the same."

"I only speak to people if it pays well."

"How much?"

"Whatever you can spare from your pocket will do."

"I'll give you ten pence. Nothing more."

Mave wrinkled her nose and cocked her head to one side. She opened the door to let him in. "By your suit of clothes, I would say you are a wealthier man and can afford more. But I'm not one to take more than I should."

Seth removed his hat and glanced around. The place was neat, but poor nonetheless.

Mave led Seth and Michael to a parlor. Two chairs, a table beneath the window, and a rag rug furnished most of the room. An old brass candlestick with a tallow candle stood upon the table. A knitting basket sat on the floor. A desk hugged the wall near the window, its finish scratched as if a litter of kittens had handled it.

Mave sat down. A gray cat leapt onto her lap. She pulled it close and stroked its ears.

"This gentleman is Captain Bray," Seth told her.

Michael Bray nodded while he held his hat. Seth put his down and sat across from the old woman. "I'm Seth Braxton. Do you recognize the name?"

"Braxton is an old name in these parts. I knew your grandfather and his wife, Elizabeth. He worshiped her."

"Others have told me the same," Seth replied.

"I took the banns forty years ago. Thirty years my husband's been gone, and not once has the ring he gave me left my finger."

Seth caught the glint of gold on her left hand. She held it up, the ring on a gnarled finger crooked like the others, the skin thin and translucent, the blue veins raised and twisted.

Seth leaned slightly forward. "I was informed you had come to Ten Width to deliver distressful news to my sister. What would you say if I told you young Nathaniel Kenley is alive and that my sister is soon to marry this gentleman?"

Mave's eyes lit up and widened. "Why would you come here and tell me such a falsehood?"

"I assure you, madam, what I've told you is the truth. Now, tell me about the night you came to Ten Width."

Mave shifted in her chair, and with a raspy voice said, "It was Hetty Shanks that came here, to my house, and said I had to be the one to tell Miss Caroline."

"Why would she insist on that?"

"Since I was the one that found Hetty to care for the child. You see I find nursemaids and governesses for the upper class."

"How did Hetty appear? Was there anything out of the ordinary with her?"

Mave tapped her knobby chin. "Well, let me see. She twisted her hands in and out and looked frightened. It's a hard thing when a child dies while in a nurse's care. So, naturally I assumed she was upset."

"The child was taken to Sir Charles Kenley at Wrenhurst."

Mave's brows shot up. "Wrenhurst, Mr. Braxton?"

"Sir Charles was told my sister had died and he was to care for the boy, since he is his grandfather. Hetty lied about my sister, but I believe she meant to save my nephew's life. We must find her. Can you tell us where she is?"

Mave squinted her eyes. "What do you mean to do?"

"I intend to find out who paid her to carry out the unthinkable."

A gasp slipped through Mave's lips and she shook her head. "She'd never harm a child, sir, and Hetty might be too frightened to talk."

"I realize that. Nevertheless, you must tell me where she lives."

Mave twisted her mouth, stroked her cat harder. "She lives in a cottage outside Clovelly. It's the one with the brown thatched roof and red door."

"With her man?"

Mave paused. "I know nothing about any man of hers."

Seth thanked her and stood. Mave touched him by the coat sleeve. "I'm not a bad woman, sir. I didn't know Hetty lied. Please assure me that I'll not be held accountable for Hetty's actions."

He could not give her the assurance she asked for. He believed there would come a time when the sheriff would want to question her. "I'll do what I can."

When he reached the door, he turned back. "I understand Miss Fallowes paid you with something precious to her. I'll buy it back."

She nodded approval and once she fetched the trinket, she held it out to him. "Sixpence, sir? That's fair, don't you think, for all I've been through?"

Seth dropped the silver coin in her palm, took the choker, and shoved it into his waistcoat pocket. He and Michael put their hats on and left Mave Proctor's humble dwelling for the house with the red door.

✒

The drizzle lifted. The sky turned milky white and the breeze sighed through wet leaf and bracken. Seth walked his horse down the lane beside Michael Bray's. Drawing near a dwelling, a flock of rooks rose overhead from a crop of elms. Their unearthly screech filled the air. Hetty Shanks's cottage sat off a tree-lined road that led toward the sea and the cliffs above it.

They dismounted and looped their horses' reins over a rickety picket fence. Seth scanned the place. It was ordinary, like other cottages he had seen along the country roads. The thatched roof and red door was as Mave had described. An herb garden grew beneath a window and to the right sat a rain barrel, a crude wooden bench, and a butter churn.

The door sat open. Seth called, but no one answered. He moved the door in with the tip of his boot. It opened up to a single room, dark and homey, sparsely furnished yet clean. From an open window, the breeze blew back a pair of muslin curtains, the air laden with the heady scent of sea and rain.

Seth stood with his hand against the doorjamb. A cast-iron pot hung inside the fireplace on a hook. The coals beneath it were gray and powdery. He moved his hand over them and felt warmth emanate from the ashes. Careful to touch the side of the pot, he discovered it was still warm.

"She has not been long from home," he told Bray.

"Perhaps she's gone into the village." Bray picked up a tattered shawl and tossed it back on a chair.

"We would have passed her on the road if she had." He walked outside and looked up at the gray and forlorn sky, how the clouds whirled, how they oppressed earth, cliffs, and sea.

"What woman would leave a pot of stew over the fire unattended? Why would she leave when it looks as if the sky is about to burst?"

Bray came up beside him. "A sure sign she left in a hurry. These tracks show she had a visitor."

Seth looked down at the ground. Boot prints were beginning to dry in the wind. The outlines of horseshoes were pressed into the soggy earth. He lifted his eyes to study the road ahead. It was quiet except for the birds fluttering in the trees.

"Perhaps she is close by."

"She did not answer when you called her name," said Bray.

"I may have frightened her off." Seth glanced back at the red door. "No woman would leave her door unlatched."

"She may have been called away. Whoever was here before us gave her a lift into the village."

"Or harmed her."

Bray frowned. "I pray that not be so. We need her to answer some important questions, don't we?"

"I have a feeling she has either fled or fallen victim to this rider." Seth crouched down and ran his finger along the outline of a print.

Seth stalked away. Bray made a quick turn and followed. Mounting their horses, they moved them down the road. Seth leaned to the side of his saddle to observe the tracks left in the mud. In front of them were more footprints, scattered and confused, as if the person who made them had stumbled along drunk.

"These are the footprints of a woman." He straightened up and looked over at Bray.

"They lead off," said Bray. "Without a trace they are gone."

When they reached the bend, Seth reined in his horse and looked hard into the woods and then ahead. "You're right. There is no telling where they went." He paused, breathed deeply to calm the anxiety within.

"Do not be discouraged," Bray told him. "We'll find her, if not today then soon."

Seth believed him, yet replied in a grave tone. "What a mess of confusion this is. I fear it is the beginning of something more dangerous than either of us realizes."

19

The following Thursday, Caroline and Michael Bray were wed in the stone church outside of Ten Width. They had long awaited the arrival of a minister, and it was none too soon for the couple. They held a quiet ceremony, with only those closest to them in attendance, with no reception, and no delay to keep them from settling in London.

The Fallowes troop was noisy the moment they stepped out of the church door into the glorious sun-drenched day. Just as Juleah walked outside, she spied the carriage spiriting off the happy couple. Sir Charles and his lady's coach took the opposite direction homeward. She looked for Seth. He was nowhere to be seen. *If he wants me, he shall find me.*

Her mother gathered her younger children to the carriage door.

"I shall walk home," Juleah told her. "It is a fine day."

Anna Fallowes huffed. "Dear me, Juleah. It is another mile to home. And you have no companion."

Juleah brought her wide-brimmed hat down closer to shade her eyes from the brilliant sunlight and strolled down the tree-lined lane. When she turned at the bend leading home, she paused and glanced up at the streams of sunlight that poured through the trees.

Continuing on, the breeze caressed her face. It was good to be alive, to feel the sun on her skin, smell the scent of wild-flowers growing in the fields, hear the songs of birds. But with no warning, a horse galloped round the bend behind her. The rider reined in several yards from her and steadied his mount. He relaxed and put one hand on his thigh, while he held the reins with the other.

"Juleah." Seth spoke out of breath. "Do you always walk in the middle of the road?" Dark blue, his brave eyes met hers, and her heart leapt.

"Usually. I must take care from riders who ride so fiercely." She smiled and it caused his eyes to warm.

He dismounted and came to her. "I do ride recklessly. I'd never forgive myself if I hurt you. I would deserve to be hung from the highest tree and left for the birds to pick clean."

Juleah grimaced. "Ah, that is an awful thing to say."

"Yes, you're right. Tell me where you're going. I thought you had left with your family."

"I decided to walk home." She moved on. He followed her, pulling his horse along.

"You should have someone with you this time of day."

"I'm safe enough close to home."

"Do not be so confident. It was on this road I was ambushed."

"I have not forgotten. But it is not yet dark—and you are here."

He touched her arm, which caused her to stop. "I was headed to Henry Chase when I saw you had left. You may ride Jupiter and I'll lead. Or we could both ride."

A thrill stole up through her at the prospect of being close to him on horseback again. But it would invite sweet temptation and cause her nerves to grow tremulous. "I think for now we should walk."

"There's something I need to ask."

Juleah stared at the flame within his eyes and suspected what he needed to say was of a serious, intimate nature. She found herself at a loss for words.

Seth made a slight turn. "To look at you is like looking at a rose after it has rained."

She laughed lightly. "I would not compare myself to a rose, sir. I'm plain and more lowly born than you know." She bent over and pulled a dandelion head off its stem. "I do not deserve your compliments."

Seth frowned and looked amazed at her reply. "Why not?"

"Because I should have told you everything from the start." Lifting her hand, she released the soft white bracts into the breeze, and they floated off like the down of a bird.

"Here, perhaps this will help." He drew the choker from his pocket and put it around her neck. As she had anticipated, he encircled his arms around her, drew her under the bower of a weeping willow, bent his head, and brushed his mouth over hers four separate times. The wind rustled the delicate diamond-shaped leaves of the tree that shadowed them.

"Marry me," he whispered, holding her close.

She looked at him wide-eyed. "What did you say?"

"Marry me, Juleah."

It could not be helped. She gazed at him with eyes filled with loving him. "You want me, Seth?"

"Yes, I want you as my wife. Say *yes*." The expression in Seth's face grew desperate. "If you refuse, I'll go back to Virginia. I won't be able to bear not having you . . . you being near."

"Hush." She pressed her finger against his lips. "You know my answer. It has always been yes."

He grabbed her hand and kissed her palm. Sunlight pierced the trees and showered silver dust down upon the two lovers. They clung to each other, until the rumble of a carriage that drew near forced them apart. The carriage passed by, and the driver lifted his hat to them.

Seth breathed out heavily and smiled. "I suppose I should take you home. We are, after all, out here in broad daylight for all the world to see."

She laughed and he took her hand. "It is safer that way," she said.

They walked on past fields dotted with fleecy sheep. Beyond them, settled on a peaceful plain of green grass, stood her father's house made of white sandstone bricks and tall mullioned windows.

Seth drew her inside, and Juleah called her father.

⬧

On the twenty-seventh day of May 1785, a magnificent sunrise painted the sky magenta. Liquid gold edged the clouds. Barn swallows dipped and whirled. In a nearby field, sheep wandered close to the stream that cut through it. Trees budded, apple blossoms fell as if flakes of pink-white snow.

The new minister that now resided at the vicarage arrived by ten in the morning, dressed in rusty black. His Bible and *Book of Common Prayer* were cradled in his arm. An elderly gentleman, Reverend Simon's features were gaunt, with deep-set hazel eyes that reflected kindness and gentleness of soul.

He handed Claire his hat once he proceeded through the door. "I was sent for. Is there sickness here? Is someone in need of last rites?"

Seth smiled and stepped forward to greet him. "There are two of us here, sir, who are heartsick. You were sent for to wed us."

Reverend Simon wiggled his head and returned the smile. "Ah, I am relieved."

The ceremony took place in the largest room at Ten Width, commonly used for a chapel. It had been a tradition that all Braxton males wed at Ten Width beneath the roof of their forefathers. Juleah came to Seth, her hand upon her father's arm, her figure draped in pale rose silk. Blue ribbons dangled at her elbows where the sleeves fell in folds of cream-colored lace. Her hair fell long and soft over one shoulder. Her glossy lips parted when she lifted her eyes to meet Seth's. They glowed brighter than the stars in the heavens.

Rock doves cooed in the eaves of the house, as their hands joined before the minister and they spoke their vows. Seth slipped the golden band set with jewels that had belonged to his grandmother over Juleah's finger.

"With this ring, I thee wed, a band of gold for our past, our present, and our future. A ruby for love and diamonds for eternity."

Eager to seal the marriage, Seth glanced at the minister. Reverend Simon nodded, and Seth lifted his bride up in his arms and kissed her.

The guests stayed for a quiet supper, then departed by nine. Anna Fallowes wiped the tears from her face, kissed Juleah's cheek, and boarded the coach with her husband and children. Even Will and Claire hurried off, to leave Juleah and Seth alone.

In his bedchamber, which they now shared, Juleah slipped on her silk nightdress. Thin white ribbons laced the front. She sat at the dressing table brushing her hair. Tinted with the golden splendor of the candles, she smoothed it over her shoulder and ran her fingers down its length. Excitement filled her, tripped over her skin along with desire. She glanced around the room. How masculine it appeared. A fresh coat of paint would improve its appearance, and white curtains over the windows would bring it warmth and light.

She set the candlestick on the table next to their bed. The brass clock on the mantelpiece chimed out the hour. She paused to listen to the musical sound it made, while she pulled down the coverlet. The door drifted open. Seth came inside, shut it, and proceeded to pull off his waistcoat.

"Ah, have you seen the moon?" She opened the drapes wide to let the moonlight pour in. It bathed the room soft blue. "Is it not lovely, Seth?"

He joined her at the window. Wrapping his arms around his wife's waist, he stood close behind her. His breath brushed against her neck and she sighed.

He whispered in her ear. "Doubt thou, the stars are fire. Doubt, that the sun doth move. Doubt, truth to be a liar. But never doubt, I love."

It pleased her that he, a Virginian rebel, had memorized the beauty of Shakespeare's verses. Melting with longing, she turned to him. He took her into his arms. She reached up and pushed back a lock of hair that fell over his brow. "I will never doubt your love, not for anything in the world."

He brought his lips to hers and she strained against him. Love rose within each heart. He lifted her, and her feet dangled above the floor. Holding her, he kissed her, turned with Juleah toward their bed, and took his bride away from the window.

20

*W*ill and Claire strolled side-by-side on their way home from the farmers market, a half hour's walk down the main road. The forest seemed dark and brooding beneath a leaden sky that promised rain. Will paused, pressed his hand against his mouth, and yawned. Claire smacked his shoulder.

"You haven't heard a thing I said, have you?"

"Sorry, Claire. Can't we talk of something else other than woman things? Let me have a go. I'll tell ya 'bout that new filly I saw in the market that I mean to talk the master into buying."

"He already has a horse."

"But the mistress doesn't."

"That's true, Will. Then you must tell him."

"Aye, I will. You know, the squire's an excellent judge of horses. He told me he wants to raise thoroughbreds in Virginia someday. If he goes, we should think of going too. I hear Virginia is a grand place to raise a family."

Claire quit her stroll and stared at Will. "What's this about a family, Will? You got a maiden I don't know about?"

Will stared back at Claire, with a blink of his eyes. "No, you silly lass. I've been meaning to drop a hint." He leaned up and down on his boot heels.

She giggled and waved her hand. "Ah, go on."

"I'm fond of you, Claire."

"Fond? Is that all?"

"Would it help if I told you, you make my knees weak?"

"Hmm, it might. But a lass wants to hear more than that."

"What if I said I love you? Would that do it?"

She touched his shoulder. "You love me?"

"Since the first day I laid eyes upon that sweet face of yours."

"You think, Will, I might marry you?"

"If you'll have me."

"You haven't asked me proper yet."

Dragging off his hat, Will went down on one knee. "I'm asking, Claire. Will you be my Mrs.?"

"Oh, Will, you're the only lad I've ever had eyes for." She pulled him up, threw her arms around his neck, and kissed his cheek. "Yes!"

Yelping, Will swung Claire around. When he set her feet back down to earth, he looked deep into her bonny eyes. "I'll be giving you my betrothal kiss now, with no objections from you."

Claire lifted her face, eyes closed. He kissed her well, but with gentleness.

She let out a long sigh when he drew away. "Ah, you do kiss nice, Will."

"I'll tell the squire we're to wed, then I'll tell him about that filly." Will smiled broader than Claire had ever seen.

"Ah, so many weddings and people making merry these days, Will. I may only be eighteen and you over twenty, but we know what love is."

"I agree with that, my girl."

"What a nice present a mare would make for the new mistress of Ten Width." Claire held Will's hand and strolled on.

"I can see them riding over the hills together and into town to visit folks. I'm glad he married her."

Will stopped in his tracks. "Hush!"

"Ah, what now?"

He put up his hand to quiet her. "I heard something."

Leaves and twigs lying thick on the forest floor crackled like icicles that broke underfoot. The pair turned their eyes in the direction of the noise. From the woods shot a pair of ravens. They cawed, their feast interrupted. They spread their wings wide and flew off into the hemlocks.

A chill went through Claire. She reached over and dug her fingers into Will's arm. Will removed her hand and motioned for her to stay where she was. He took four paces forward, craned his neck, and sank back with a gasp.

Claire moved closer and peered over his shoulder. "What's wrong?"

"Don't look, Claire. It's someone on the ground."

Claire stepped forward and her eyes followed the direction of Will's stare. "It's a woman."

"Right ye are, lass."

"What's she doing?"

"By the look of them birds, I'd say nothing. I think she's dead."

Claire gasped. "Oh, God rest that poor soul."

Will approached the body. He stopped short, and gazed at what was concealed under drifts of leaf and fern. The arms stretched out as if on a cross, and a tattered dress fanned out above the ankles. The woman's white cap, a blatant contrast against the dark leaves, sat awry upon her head. Fragile light drifted through the tree limbs overhead, dusty, silent as the grave, and played over the gray face and unseeing eyes. Above, a crow squawked and flapped its wings.

"Be gone!" Will shouted with a wave of his arm, shooing off the irritating bird.

"She's dead for sure," whispered Claire. "Oh, Will, Hetty Shanks is dead."

Will put his hands upon his knees and bent down to have a closer look. "For days, I'd say. Ah, it would've been a shame if the birds had gotten her face."

Shivering, Claire looped her arm through Will's. "Perhaps she got sick and collapsed."

Will shook his head. "I suspect foul play." Will drew aside Hetty's mobcap and turned her head. The mobcap was stiff and black with gore. Her throat had bruises the size of silver sovereigns. The temple and ear were dark with blood. It matted her hair and made the strands stiff and tangled.

"No, you mustn't touch it," Claire cried.

"Hush, my girl. I know what I'm doing." His fingers shook, as he drew shut the gaping mouth and eyes. The horrible stare was hard to look on.

"Ah, Claire. I know for certain she didn't succumb to anything natural. This is murder."

"Murder you say? Why'd anyone want to murder Hetty? What could she have done to deserve that, Will?"

"I don't know for sure, lass. But I heard she had something to do with Miss Caroline's little lad. Have you ever looked upon a death such as you see now?"

"No never—and never murder." She gagged and stepped away. Sobs gurgled in her throat.

Will hurried after her. "I wish you had listened and not looked, Claire."

"What should we do now?"

"I'll stay here. You take the path back to Ten Width and tell the master what's happened. Tell him to come right away."

Claire glanced back at Hetty's cold, twisted face one more time. She hurried to leave, out of the woods and along the sun-dappled path. And then she ran.

The path widened the closer Claire got to Ten Width. She stopped, looked down the hill, and caught her breath. There stood the house, the brick washed with dew and morning light as if an ornament chiseled from an artist's hand. With her sleeve, she wiped the sweat off her face and moved on.

She rushed down the hilly path. The neigh of a horse caused her to glance up a few yards ahead where a rider pulled rein. His tall, black horse shook its wiry mane and looked at her with wild yellow eyes.

"Captain Darden," Claire said with a start. She wished to get past him without saying more. But his horse sidestepped in the road.

"Where are you going in such a hurry, Claire? Why aren't you at Ten Width attending your duties?"

Claire clutched her hands together. She did not think it prudent to tell him what she and Will had discovered. "I've been out strolling, sir. The morning is fine, though it looks like rain, and walking is good for the limbs."

"Is your master at home?"

"Indeed, sir, he is."

Darden scowled. "I heard your mistress married Michael Bray."

"She has, sir."

His jaw tightened and he ran the reins through his hands. "You best hurry. No doubt your master will wonder where you've gone."

"Oh, I doubt the squire ever noticed I've been away. He's with his bride and has no time to worry about me."

The crease between Darden's brows deepened and his face darkened. "Bride?"

"Yes, sir. He and Miss Juleah are married. You should've seen Miss Juleah. She looked pretty on her wedding day, and Mr. Braxton looking handsome."

Darden's horse made a restless circle in the road. He coiled the reins around his gloves. Anger colored his face. Claire stepped away from the restless horse as it snorted and pawed the ground. Darden swore and dug his heels into the horse's sides. The horse shot off, kicking up clods of dirt.

Claire stood motionless. Darden was hot-tempered the days he had spent at Ten Width. To her, his behavior was not anything out of the ordinary. When he was gone, she rushed down the hill toward the house with her heart pounding.

She pushed open the door and hurried inside. "Sir, come quick!"

ℒ❧

Seth emerged from the study with his shirt loose at the throat, and his waistcoat unbuttoned. He'd been going over the books that morning, and in his hand was a ledger.

"You must come at once." Claire struggled to catch her breath.

Seth looked past her. "What's happened? Where's Will?"

She gestured with her hand. "He's back there, not far down the road. Hetty Shanks lies dead in the wood. Will needs you to come right away. Oh, sir, it's awful."

"You're sure it is Hetty?"

"Yes, sir. Will thinks she's been lying there for some time. Oh, sir. She's been murdered!"

Seth tossed the ledger down. "I'll come at once. Tell Miss Juleah. She's upstairs. Stay with her until I return."

Now it was clear why he and Michael Bray had not found Hetty at her cottage, why the door was unlocked and sitting open, and why a pot of stew was left on the hearth. The one person who could have revealed the truth was dead in the woods.

After he saddled his horse, Seth swung into the saddle, dug his heels into Jupiter's girth, and shot off down the lane toward the gates and the road beyond. He rounded a sharp bend in the road. Will stepped out with a frantic wave of his arm. Seth pulled rein, and the horse skidded to a stop.

Seth slid off the saddle. "Where is she?"

"Over here, sir." Will led him through the brush toward the body. "A shame, 'tis this. We haven't had a murder in these parts in years. It'll be the talk for miles around, and every woman will keep her door locked from now on."

Seth leaned down and looked at Hetty's face. It ran through his mind that whoever hired her to carry out their plans had now paid her for disobedience and the wagging of her tongue.

He pushed down the repulsion, as he studied the corpse. "This was done in cold blood. Swift by such wounds, I'd say, but brutal."

"Aye. I'll go for the constable, sir."

"No, I'll do it. You stay here."

"It isn't proper the squire should go, if you don't mind me saying, sir. 'Tis a servant's job."

"All right, I'll wait at Ten Width. But first we'll mark the spot."

Without hesitation, he untied his neckcloth from around his throat and looped it over a branch. A spider's web, outlined with glassy beads of dew, fluttered beside Hetty's head. He looked at the delicate pattern of spiral mesh. Eight threads provided moorings, their strength unbreakable against wind and storm in their silken grasp. He reached down and touched one. It broke. One thread released from its anchor caused the rest of the web to flutter and weaken.

It was the same with the series of events that had come into Seth's life. He swore to himself he'd find the weakest link, break it, and thus cause the plot against his family to disintegrate.

Within an hour, Constable Latterbuck appeared at Seth's door.

21

Constable Latterbuck stood on the Persian rug in the foyer and waited for the master of Ten Width to acknowledge his arrival. Impatiently, he drummed his sausage-like fingers on the table beside him. He glanced over the paintings, the tapestry, and the way sunlight came through the windows. He tried to make an honest assessment of the place and wondered what the rest of the house looked like. Already he was bored, and a wide toothy yawn overtook him; he pressed a meaty palm over his gaping mouth. He had been in the middle of an enjoyable nap when Will roused him and entreated him to come at once, claiming a body lay in the woods, that a murder had been committed.

"A murder?" he had said to Will. "No murder happens in my district. More than likely an accident."

He recalled that the master of Ten Width had recently sent him a strange letter, where he claimed odd happenings were afoot at the old place, but Latterbuck didn't believe it. Being contrary to every person who claimed any knowledge a'tall of a crime being committed, he ignored the urgings of the squire to meet with him and his sister to discuss the matter.

What was done was done. Why bother with situations that have been resolved or come to a happy ending? More important matters needed attention in the immediate, namely keeping an unblemished record intact. If there were no crimes committed, people would believe he was responsible for the peace. He'd be a formidable force to those who would have mischief in mind.

Latterbuck stood in the hall and yawned a second time. He grew increasingly impatient and called out. "I say, is anyone coming or not!"

✍❧

Juleah came into the hallway. She paused when Latterbuck extended a clumsy bow. Upon his feet were large black shoes decorated with dull brass buckles. The light silhouetted his large frame. For duty, he wore a heavy buff coat with large whalebone buttons and gray stockings over bulging calves and thick ankles.

Latterbuck's stomach growled and gurgled. His stained waistcoat stretched over his enlarged belly, separating between the buttonholes, and revealed the dingy shirt beneath.

"Excuse me, ma'am," he said, stifling a belch. He pulled his watch from his pocket and looked at the time. "The day is getting away from me. Is your husband coming or not?"

"He is, Constable, and shall be but a moment. He is changing his clothes."

"Why? We are not going to a ball, ma'am."

"I suggested it. What he wore earlier is too fine for such matters at hand."

Latterbuck lifted a plump finger in the air. "Ah, not wishing to have them soiled is he? Well, he'll not touch anything he should not, ma'am. I'll see to that. But do not let the maid clean those clothes, for they may be evidence."

Juleah laughed. "Evidence, sir? I think not."

"You'd be surprised what a coat or a pair of boots can tell. But it's nothing for you to worry your pretty head over. This is man's work." Again, his stomach rumbled.

Juleah narrowed her eyes. "I would prefer you not reference me in that manner."

Latterbuck appeared confused. "I don't understand."

"You said I should not worry my *pretty head*, sir."

"Oh, I do apologize." Latterbuck gave her an awkward bow. "It was improper, but true, ma'am."

Juleah glanced back toward the door that led to the kitchen. "Would you like something to eat before you go?" She drew him away with a gesture of her hand.

"If it is no trouble." He stepped alongside her. "I must tell you it is hard to do this job on an empty stomach. I have no wife you know."

"Have you no cook?" she asked.

"Indeed, madam, I do. And a good one at that."

Juleah showed him through to the kitchen. Claire was gathering apples from the barrel into her apron.

"Claire, please set a plate for the constable," Juleah said.

Claire emptied the apples into a bowl and shortly plopped a plate of seared beef, bread, and potatoes in front of him. He stared at the plate of food, leaned over it, and sniffed to take in its aroma.

"No ale, my girl?"

Claire gave him a scowl and pulled a tin mug from off the shelf, yanked the tap on the keg, and made sure his portion was filled mostly with foam. She set it in front of him and waited.

Latterbuck licked his lips and wiggled his fingers. "This ale is better than what I'm accustomed to, even with the foam." Saliva formed in the corners of his broad lips.

Juleah watched him and wondered if he had the kind of mind given to detection. He smelled of rum and tobacco. He ate with his mouth open. Food fell on the front of his waistcoat and, to her surprise, he'd pick it off and pop whatever it was into his mouth. Repulsed by his table manners, by the gravy that dripped down his chin, she handed him a napkin. But he lifted his beefy arm and wiped his mouth across his sleeve. He slopped bread through the gravy and shoved it into his mouth. He picked up the last crumb on the plate, sucked each finger in turn, and then swiped his hands with the cloth.

"Have you more?"

Claire stood back with her hands over her hips. "No. Unless you wish a dish of stewed apples."

"I never eat fruit. It's bad for my digestion." He tossed the napkin down and rose from the table. "Don't you find fruit bad for the digestion, Mrs. Braxton?"

Juleah shifted in her chair and stood. "I cannot say I do."

"Well, I can, dear lady. I can." Latterbuck put his hand over his mouth, puffed out his cheeks, and burped.

✐

Through the door walked Seth. "Ah, Constable Latterbuck." He finished the top button to his waistcoat. "It's about time we met. You ignored my previous request. As fate would have it, Hetty's death drew you to reply. I'm sorry to have kept you waiting."

"Never mind, sir. Your good wife provided me with distraction and your girl a plate of food. The time has flown by delightfully."

Seth glanced at his wife. "Distraction?"

"A hardy meal and a pretty lady does a man's constitution good. A compliment to your good wife, sir." Latterbuck bowed.

She picked up Latterbuck's plate. "It is not to my credit, Constable, but to Claire's. You should thank her, for she's a better cook than I could ever be."

Latterbuck pushed out his upper lip and bowed in Claire's direction. "Well, a woman who is pretty as well as a good cook, I imagine has no lack of beaus. Right, Claire?" He rubbed her chin between his greasy forefinger and thumb. She frowned and jerked back.

"We should be off," he said, squashing on his hat. "Come, Squire. Show me the poor wretch that lies in your woods dead."

⁂

Will had run all the way to town to find Latterbuck and had hitched a ride behind Latterbuck's deputy back to Ten Width. Since he had no horse of his own, he jogged alongside Seth's.

Worried he would exhaust himself, Seth looked down from atop Jupiter at the energetic lad. "You can ride behind me, Will. Or perhaps behind the deputy again."

Will kept up his pace. "No, sir. A good run does me just fine. It wouldn't be proper for me to be seated behind you, sir. I don't mind telling you that oaf probably hasn't had a proper washing in a year. I can't stand the smell of him."

Seth laughed.

When they reached their destination, he dismounted and looped the reins over a branch. Latterbuck slipped from his mount and followed Seth and Will into the woods. His deputy waited beside the horses.

Latterbuck heaved a breath. "What is tied to the tree?"

"My neckcloth," replied Seth. "I thought it best to mark the spot."

"Ah, good thinking." When Latterbuck spied the body, he put on his steel spectacles and placed a dingy handkerchief over his nose. He paused for several minutes, looking but not touching.

"Obviously an accident." He grunted and turned away.

Stunned by his rapid conclusion, Seth stepped up to him. "How can you say that? It is obvious the woman was murdered. Do not tell me you cannot see it."

"An accident, sir." Latterbuck stepped over a thick root that protruded from the ground.

"I'll have you know there hasn't been a murder in my district since 1776, the year the Colonies revolted against good King George, God save him. It's always an accident. They leave the tavern intoxicated, or they travel in the dark and fall over a cliff, or wander into the sea. Or like here, they take a shortcut home through the woods, fall, hit their head on a rock, and are found a few days later dead as a doornail. Nay, sir. No murder is done in my district."

Agitated by Latterbuck's avoidance of the truth, Seth moved in front of him. "I do not agree. Look at her again."

Latterbuck huffed. "Who appointed you in charge?"

Seth set his mouth and stared hard at Latterbuck. "It doesn't take much to see what happened to this woman. Look at her face and throat. She's been hit and hit hard. Look at the bruises on her wrists and arms. Would you not say they are indicative of a struggle? She was fighting back."

Latterbuck shrugged. "Women easily bruise. Those are but marks from heavy work."

Seth let out a breath of extreme irritation. "What kind of heavy work would do that? Besides she was a nursemaid, not a farmhand."

Latterbuck groaned and moved past Seth. "This poor wretch's mortal remains shall be taken to the sexton at the church for burial."

"That is all you will do?" Seth cried.

Latterbuck turned on him. "Give the poor woman some respect, young sir. She died before reaching elder years and should be given proper treatment. There's nothing more to do."

Latterbuck turned on his heels and headed for his horse. Once he reached the road, Seth glanced back at Hetty and swore under his breath. "A false witness shall not go unpunished."

Hearing this, Latterbuck stopped and whirled around. "What was that?"

"Hetty Shanks was a false witness. I can prove it."

"Go on, not that it matters now."

In detail, Seth proceeded to retell Latterbuck the sequence of events that led up to his conversation with Mave. "Captain Bray was with me when we stopped at Hetty's cottage. The door was left unlocked and she was gone."

"Many folks leave their doors unlocked. It's nothing unusual."

"We followed footprints in the mud until they trailed off, one being that of a man, the other of a woman, and there were hoof marks as well."

"Ah, Hetty had a sweetheart." Latterbuck smiled cynically.

"Yes, so it seems."

"A name?"

"I do not know, only that he was a large fellow."

"Look here, young lad, let me deal with this. I'll go to her cottage and have a look around. But you must rein in your urge to do my job."

"It would give me ease if you saw this for what it is, Constable."

Latterbuck shook his head. "I've been doing this job for twenty-five years. I know the difference between a murder and an accident. As for the former events you've unfolded, I see no reason to go into it any further. Sleeping dogs must lie, good sir."

Seth frowned at Latterbuck. "Sleeping dogs that have committed a crime?"

Latterbuck threw up his hands. "I see no proof of any crime. You must understand, we do things differently compared to wherever it is you are from."

Seth set his mouth. "I'm from Virginia, sir."

"Of course you are. And here in Devonshire life goes by at a slow, quiet pace. That is how people like it. Sometimes folks make mistakes of identity, children are misplaced, and facts are misunderstood. I'm sure that's all that happened with Hetty and your nephew. It was a mistake and not a conspiracy."

"You are as blind as you are gluttonous," Seth told him.

Latterbuck turned red in the face and let out a puff of air. "I advise you to watch what you say. Speak no more what might incriminate you."

Seth flexed his hands. "I've said nothing to implicate myself in this foul business."

"You've admitted to seeking this wretch out for a misdeed done to your family."

"I did, sir. You may recall I sent a letter to you weeks ago. You preferred to ignore it. I've nothing to hide."

"Bide your time, sir. In the meanwhile, hold your tongue."

Seth folded his arms across his chest in defiance. "I hold myself ready to answer any questions you have, Constable. Is that clear to you?"

Latterbuck twisted his mouth. "Indeed it is. Have no doubt I shall have them ready for you."

Seth viewed this advice as a means to tighten the ropes that already bound the truth. Outraged at Latterbuck's blindness, he stood aside. Could Latterbuck ignore what his eyes told him in order to protect his unblemished reputation? How could he not desire justice for Hetty? If she had been a lady of quality, Seth wondered if Latterbuck's deduction would be different.

"George, lift it," Latterbuck ordered. His deputy moved to obey.

"Will, put her in our cart," Seth said.

Latterbuck countered the order. "Bind the body to the saddle, George. Go gently. Steady."

Seth notched the earth with the heel of his boot. Will, equally incredulous, kept his eyes on Latterbuck, then glanced at Seth. They watched as the droopy-eyed deputy lifted Hetty from the ground and swung her stiff and swollen body over his shoulder. His knees buckled under the weight. He carried her over to his horse and tied her body to the saddle. The constable's horse blew out a snort when Latterbuck put his foot in the stirrup and, with an effort, hoisted himself back into the saddle.

He bid Seth a good day and touched the rim of his hat. Beads of sweat stood out upon his domed forehead. Seth watched him turn his horse out onto the road and ride off with a slackened rein, with his servant on foot to lead the burdened horse.

22

*D*isconcerted by the flippancy over such important matters as a death and by the constable's offhanded remarks, Seth, with Will beside him, watched Latterbuck and his mate disappear down the road. He balled his fists and strode hard over to his horse. He sent Will home and rode over the fields at a brisk pace.

An hour later, when he turned on the road back to Ten Width, another rider galloped toward him. The man reined in, drew off his hat, and set it across his thigh.

"Sir, is this the road to Ten Width? I'm uncertain if I should have taken the turn north a half-mile back."

"You're on the right," Seth answered. "What brings you to Ten Width?"

"A letter for the gentleman who lives there."

"I am he." His restless horse sidestepped and he looped the reins around his gloved hand to control it.

The messenger looked at him warily. "Are you?"

"Yes, my name is Seth Braxton."

At ease now, the messenger settled in his saddle, drew the letter out of his saddlebag and handed it over. Then he turned his horse and galloped off. Curious, Seth broke the seal and read the message. His expression softened. He folded the page and tucked it away inside his coat.

He galloped closer to the gates that greeted him, gazed at the house. Loneliness for his father's land seized him. He missed the quiet murmur of the Potomac, the ancient trees of the forests, the meadows of wildflowers and bluegrass. He recalled when the wind blew through the mountains, it whispered of ages past and smelled of laurel and leaf. He glanced up at the sky and wished he could leave this place and go home with his beloved.

Someday.

Juleah met him at the door. A soiled apron covered her dress; a smudge of dirt marred her cheek. Smiling, she pushed back her hair from her face with the back of her hand. In the shade of the ivy she gazed at him, and his heart raced. She was the reason he had stayed, the reason he lived.

She reached up, smoothed back a lock of hair from his forehead, as was her habit to do. "What is it, my love? It did not go well?"

Seth hung his head, lifted up her hands, and pressed his lips upon them. He could not describe his outrage. "Latterbuck believes it was an accident," he said. "I know different. But there's nothing I can do."

Juleah sighed. "Time will reveal the truth. God is not slack in such things."

"There is something else." He removed the letter from his breast pocket. "I've received a letter from Michael asking us to come to London immediately. He says it is urgent. We should go. Can you be ready in an hour?"

Juleah looked worried. "Less than that. It may not be anything to fret over, do you think? Otherwise, he would have said so. Perhaps he has some business he wishes to discuss with you."

Seth held her about the waist. "No matter what it is, I've wanted to take you away. I'm sure there'll be more exciting things to do in London than in the country."

"London has its diversions, that is true. But I prefer the quiet life we have here."

"You mean you are not bored?"

"I keep busy. Come and see what I have been doing." She pulled him by the arm to the back of the house, past a row of boxwood and yews, until they reached a plot of tilled soil.

He was indeed pleased at her industrious nature. "What have you planted?"

"Herbs. They were growing in the hothouse, and I thought it such a waste they had been neglected. Thyme, sage, and parsley are here. Spring onion and rosemary there. The lavender I have kept separate by those stones."

Seth did not know why, but an overwhelming sorrow rushed through him, and he felt some dreaded thing would come between them. She bent to touch the tender plants. The man within him broke and he lifted her, held her against his chest in a strong embrace. His hands encircled her face, and he kissed her cheeks until he found her lips.

He walked with Juleah into the house, where sunlight flowed through the windows in dusty shafts. She removed her straw hat, and her hair tumbled around her shoulders and down her back. It caught the light and Seth caught his breath.

She touched his cheek with her fingertips and lifted her skirts to hurry up the stairs. Seth set the letter on the table beside him. Claire came out into the hallway with an armload of laundry.

"We're headed for London, Claire. Be a good girl and help your mistress pack."

Off she went upstairs. Seth went to his study. His grandfather's will lay on his desk. He took it and set it in a drawer. Before he turned the key to lock it, he looked down at the deed to Ten Width and the ledgers that lay open. Even now, he could not shake off the feeling he had been shackled, indentured to a piece of land he did not desire. Duty bound to take it into his hands, he had managed to clear all debts. Now the fields were planted, the sheep bore their lambs, and the promise of money would come. Yet, emptiness clung to him while he longed for Virginia and hoped his life would not be spent in a place he had less heart for.

A knock at the front door roused Seth from his thoughts. He found a man on the doorstep, dressed in clothes too big for his frame. With a flourish, the man drew off his plumed hat and bowed. Tufts of greasy, steel-gray hair fell forward over his shoulders.

"Good day, sir," he said.

The man's eyes were bleary gray, etched in the corners with heavy lines, each cheek careworn with pockmarks. In one earlobe hung a golden ring. Around his waist and diagonally over one shoulder, he wore a leather baldric. Tucked below the buckle was a flintlock pistol. Bucket boots reached up to the man's knees.

"Who are you?" Seth inquired.

"James Bonnecker. Sailor by trade, known aboard ship as Billy Bonecutter, but me friends call me Jim."

Amused, Seth smiled. "Well, which name do you go by?"

"Bonnecker, sir. It wouldn't be fitting to call me by my Christian name." Bonnecker leaned forward and winked his right eye. "Some call me a pirate cause I served Cotton-eyed

Jack. Aye, what adventures the sea gives a man, sir. Perhaps sometime I can join ye in a mug of ale and tell tales of the sea, pirates, and buried treasure."

Seth was skeptical of Bonnecker, and no degree of friendly conversation would persuade him. "Why have you left your life of seafaring?"

Bonnecker rubbed his bristly chin. "Well, sir. Privateering has gone downhill. It's not like it was in earlier days. The glory's gone."

"Well, Mr. Bonnecker, if you're hungry, then go around to the backdoor. I'll be sure you get a plate of food. No one can say the poor go hungry at Ten Width. I am on my way out and have no more time to talk to you."

"I thank ye, sir. But a beggar, I'm not. I've come to deliver a message to . . ." And he pulled a letter out of his pocket and read the name inscribed upon it. "Mistress Juleah Braxton of Ten Width. Is the lady home?"

"She is. Who's the letter from?"

"I don't know, sir. A man saw me passing down the road and offered to pay me money if I were to bring a message to Ten Width."

Seth held out his palm. "Give me the letter. I am her husband."

Bonnecker passed it over and set his hat back on his head. With a swing of his arms, he whirled on his heels to go. "Wait," Seth called. Bonnecker turned, and Seth reached inside his pocket. He tossed the privateer a sixpence for his troubles. Bonnecker caught it in his fist and nodded his thanks. He then went on with a whistle down the road.

When Seth gave the sealed letter to Juleah, she opened it. "I cannot go to London." Her eyes flooded with worry.

Seth touched her cheek with the back of his hand. "What's wrong?"

"My mother has fallen ill and I must go to her. I will take Claire with me."

She looked up at Seth with eyes that pleaded. He took the letter from her hand and read it. She threw her arms around his neck and kissed his cheek. "Oh, Seth."

"I'll send word to Michael that we are delayed."

"There is no worry to keep you away. You go on ahead alone."

"Juleah, you are certain?"

She nodded. "My mother has bouts with her health often, you know. I shall see her, stay a few days, and then Claire and I shall travel to London. We shall come by my father's carriage."

"If Lady Anna is too ill, then please stay with her."

Again, she drew her cheek up against his and sighed. "I shall worry about you the whole time."

"Me? I've a brace of pistols."

A slight smile spread over her lips. "I forgot that you lived in the wilderness and traveled over ocean and land to Ten Width. I should not worry."

"If your mother is not better in a week, send me word. Kiss her for me," he said. "And tell your father when I return I'll take him and Thomas fishing, like I promised."

23

*T*en Width had yet to own a carriage. Juleah ached already from all the bumps in the road as they traveled by cart down the two-mile stretch of road. Fresh wind caressed her face, and she listened to it blow through the trees. A gray curtain fell, the sun was extinguished, and she hoped it would not rain. A moment later, it parted as quickly as it had come, and the sunshine softened over the land once more.

The horses slowed and Will drove the cart down a hill to level ground, where on the heights ahead Juleah saw her father's house. She stared long at it, worried over her mother's condition. She remembered how her mother loved tending the herb garden and hoped this illness was not something serious that would end her life.

The cart turned into the drive. Will jumped down and when Juleah took his hand and stepped out, she glanced up at her mother's bedroom. Window glass sparkled between lead mullions. Ivy clung to the brick that framed it.

Claire followed behind her into the foyer. The window within faced east, and warm sunlight and soft shadows fell through it as they crossed the polished floor. Jane hurried out to greet Juleah. Thomas followed at a quick pace, then Sir Henry, who bowed.

"Papa." Juleah kissed her father's cheek. "Where's mother?"

"In her room." Sir Henry patted her shoulders and gazed into her eyes.

Thomas tugged on Juleah's dress. "I've got a bullfrog in a jar. You won't be afraid to look at it, will you? Jane is."

Juleah caressed her brother's curly head. "No, I shall not be afraid. I would like to see your frog, but after I visit with Mother." Juleah looked over at Claire, and with her eyes told her to take the children outside. Claire rounded the pair up and went out the back to the garden.

"How ill is Mother?" Juleah asked her father.

"Well, you ask her, child," he answered. "Woman things, I suppose."

She stopped him on the stairs. "Yates sent me a message, Papa. He made it sound serious."

"Did he?"

"Yes, Papa. That is why I have come."

"Anna hasn't said a word to me about it. I have noticed she cries for no reason a'tall. That is why he wrote, I'm sure."

Disturbed her father had nothing more to tell her, Juleah slipped by him and headed up the stairs. One of Sir Henry's dogs lay on the carpet and rolled over at her approach.

When she reached Anna's room, her maid squeezed through the door with a bowl of water and an arm draped with towels. Sarah's mousy brown hair peeked out of her cap along the nap of her neck in wispy brown threads.

"Is she awake?" Juleah asked.

"Oh, yes, and bossy as ever, if you don't mind me saying so. I've done all I can for her in the way of comfort, and she still complains. After listening to her, I think she's got every ailment known to man."

Ready to ignore Sarah's pertness, Juleah let her pass. Water slopped out of the bowl onto the Persian runner. "I'll clean it up, miss," Sarah called back. "Not to worry."

Juleah pushed open the door and went inside.

"Juleah, what a pleasant surprise! I wasn't expecting you." Anna lifted her back away from the chintz chair. Her features froze in an expression of somber delight, and she gestured for Juleah to enter. The room had a warm, womanly scent to it, of lavender and spring rain.

If this were the sickroom of an ill woman, it fooled Juleah.

Anna's hair hung about her neck in soft ringlets streaked gray. A shawl lay across her shoulders. "There's nothing wrong, is there?" Anna's eyebrows pinched.

"I received a letter saying you were sick." Juleah folded a blanket and set it at the foot of the bed.

Anna straightened in the chair. "I am well enough I suppose, considering my age. Who sent you such a letter?"

"Yates."

"He has not stepped foot inside this house in weeks." Anna rang the silver bell on her table. Sarah entered. "Sarah, did Yates visit Henry Chase recently?"

"He was here a week ago, ma'am."

Anna sighed. "So strange. I have no idea why Yates would have troubled you. I am worried now."

"Well, don't be. It must be a mistake."

"How can it be? He must know something I do not."

Juleah went toward her, and her mother's arms went around her in a light hug. "Oh, do not make assumptions, Mother."

"What else can I do?" Lady Anna pulled back and beheld her daughter's face.

"Papa said you have been quiet and have complaints."

Anna smiled gently. "There are things a wife does not tell her husband, woman things. Have you come with your handsome husband?"

Juleah sat beside her. "He has gone to London."

Anna raised her brows. "Without you?"

"I was told you were ill."

Anna clasped her hands together. "Dear Juleah. You chose to come here instead, to look in on your poor mama because of a mysterious message?"

"How could I ignore it?" Juleah studied her mother's face. She looked tired.

"I am furious with Yates. I shall stew over this until I see him again, and then give him a good talking to. The nerve of the man, upsetting you like that." She tossed her shawl from off her shoulders and stood.

"He will have an explanation." Juleah did not want to upset her mother, knowing Anna's mind would race every which way. Yet, uneasiness settled within her, and she began to think something was terribly wrong. Or someone had played a cruel joke on her.

"Let us change the subject," her mother insisted. Back into her chair she flopped. "Has Seth made you happy?"

Juleah smiled. "Yes. He is good to me and . . ."

"Romantic? Protective?"

"Indeed he is all that and more."

Lady Anna picked up her needlework and pulled at some threads. "I am glad you married for love, Juleah. Few women do. They want a husband of quality and means, and for good reason. You were lucky and found both. I have changed my mind about Americans."

"I am pleased to know it."

Lady Anna shivered. Juleah reached for the bell. "I shall call Sarah and have her set a fire."

"That would be good. One moment I'm chilled, the next flushed with heat. Some days the room goes round and I'm tired. My bones ache, and I wake in the middle of the night in a sweat."

"Then you are ill," Juleah exclaimed. "I shall have Will ride into town and bring Yates."

Anna put out a comforting hand to Juleah. "Do not despair. These are woman's ways. It comes to all women. Tell me what news you have."

Anna threaded a needle with scarlet floss and thrust it into the cloth. Juleah paused, watching her pull the needle through the linen.

"Hetty Shanks was found dead," said Juleah.

Lady Anna dropped the cloth onto her lap. "What terrible news."

"Seth believes she was murdered, but Latterbuck argued with him, insisting it was an accident, that if Seth did not stop speaking of it, he would cite him with interfering with the law."

"It would be best if he were to have no further dealings with Latterbuck."

"Indeed, but Seth wants justice for Hetty, no matter what she has done."

"Your husband is a good man, and his principles run deep. It shall be water under the bridge soon enough. Perhaps it really was an accident and you have nothing to fear. I will try to think of that, instead of the possibility of an assassin being about."

Juleah bit her lower lip and twisted her hair between her fingers. It suddenly frightened her, the idea that a murderer could be near Ten Width.

*

As darkness fell, Seth's horse wearied. He found a carriage inn near the village of Gastonbury, paid his shilling, and ate a huge supper. After he pulled off his boots, he fell to sleep without undressing, upon a mattress stuffed with straw. He barely noticed its discomfort or how low the night wind blew through the brick hearth. His dreams took him back to Juleah and Virginia.

Dawn broke clear and he climbed into the saddle and headed east. He rode past Gaston Abby and took the high road that led toward County Wiltshire. Trees were heavy with leaf. Spring wheat sprouted in the fields. Grassy meadows were emerald in the sunshine, and he wondered how green the pastures of Virginia must be.

His heart grew heavy, and he longed for his land, his oak, and his river. *England will never be home.*

Neither rider nor carriage met him on his journey thus far. At a bend in the road, he traveled southeast, made his way through Hampshire and Surry, through leafy forests that led him toward the bustling city of London.

The capital was unlike any city he had seen. Larger than Williamsburg and Annapolis, it was a hurly-burly of activity, a city filled with diversions. Thames Street bustled with merchants and travelers as Seth made his way toward Fleet Street and The Strand. Vendors hawked their wares. Carriages and coaches lumbered over cobblestone streets and parked outside elegant townhouses. Tea and coffeehouses, inns and shops, were filled with patrons.

Soon Seth found himself passing through the lowly east end. It was dark and sooty, the people poverty stricken, in tattered castoff clothing. Troops of orphans huddled in doorways, begged on the streets. It saddened him, and he handed what coins he could spare to as many as he could.

Closer to the better part of London, the startling contrast between rich and poor was evident. Along the streets, they mingled. Gentlemen purchased bouquets for their ladies from poor flower girls and had their boots polished by barefoot lads. Messenger boys waited on the corners for an assignment. Ladies in fine dresses and hats moved far from the reaches of scummy hands.

Woven between both classes were missionaries that ministered to the poor, the drunkard, the homeless, the prostitute, the orphan, and the infirm. When he turned one corner, two Methodists helped a one-legged man into a cart.

"Worry not," one said. "There'll be a bed for you tonight and a hearty meal."

The missionaries' compassion convicted Seth. There were people in the country who were needy, and he wondered what he could do to ease their plight. He decided, as he rode farther into the heart of London, they could use another physician in the country. Perhaps he could persuade a young man to leave London.

Presently the somber gates of Newgate heralded a darker side of the city. Seth glanced at them briefly. He moved his horse on and headed into the heart of the west side. After he acquired directions from a street vendor, he was glad to find his sister and her new husband living in a fine house sandwiched between blond-bricked homes.

He left his horse moored to the iron ring out front and stepped up to the door.

A servant pulled it open. Her face was round as an apple, freckled, and she was no beauty. Her brows were thick, joined as one above a pair of almond-shaped eyes that sat back in her head. Her mouth extended in a thin line and her teeth did not show when she spoke. But her gentle manner, faint smile, and pleasant lilt of her voice made up for what she lacked in looks.

"This way, sir," she said. "Mistress Caroline is away, but the master of the house is at home."

Seth stood in the brightly lit study that belonged to Michael Bray. He waited, and a sparrow flew to the windowsill. For a moment, it stared back at him, spread its wings, and flew off.

"Seth!" Bray bounded into the room. "It is good to see you."

Seth turned. "And you. Are Caroline and my nephew well?"

Bray glanced back out into the hallway. "Very well. You have come without Juleah?"

Seth pulled off his riding gloves, noting Bray's surprise. "She's with her mother."

Bray's smile vanished. "She hasn't left you, has she?"

Seth's grin glided over his lips. "No, we are happy. Lady Anna is ill, and she thought it best she stay at Henry Chase until she recovers."

"Then we are two men alone. Caroline and Nathaniel are visiting my aunt in Bristol." Bray poured Seth a glass of ale and handed it to him. "She is old and alone, and Caroline, after learning of her, asked to visit her."

Seth took the glass in hand. "Something of importance kept you from going with her?"

"My business prevented me. We've decided to settle some-day in Virginia. It is Caroline's true home, after all. Riches we shall never have, but we shall be happy."

Feeling envious, Seth smiled, and grabbed Bray's hand to shake it. "Grand news indeed. I hope to see home again as well with Juleah. There's enough Braxton land there to divide between us."

Bray shook his head. "Oh, no. I never meant to imply—"

"You implied nothing, Michael. It is my father's legacy and he would want Caroline to have part of it. Think of it as a wedding present."

Bray blinked his eyes. "I'm speechless, Seth."

"Five hundred acres will do for you, but you'll have to build a house."

"With all my sweat and blood, I shall."

"Believe me, it shall take every ounce." Seth proceeded to a chair. "Now what was so urgent that you called me to London."

Bray's countenance shifted to bewilderment. "I sent you no letter."

Something dreadful jerked inside Seth. "It is signed by you."

"Do you have it? Let me see."

Seth handed it over. He watched his brother-in-law's expression grow troubled. The note had not come from him. Something was wrong.

"This is not in my hand," Bray said. "What person would send you this and forge my name?"

Seth's heart lurched with fear, and he set his mouth hard. A sudden sensation, as if his body had been plunged into icy water, shot through him. He stood. "It is clear I've fallen into some scoundrel's trap."

He hurried out into the hall, strode to the front door. "I must leave at once. Juleah could be in danger. She also received a message and no doubt it too is a lie."

His hand trembled as he reached for the brass door handle. He would have gone out into the street to his horse, but Bray thrust his body between the door and the jamb.

"I'm going with you." His voice was determined, his face taut. "If there is danger, two are better than one to face it. Ella!" She appeared from the back of the house. "You must pack me a change of clothes. I'll saddle my horse and bring it around front."

Her eyes enlarging, Ella nodded. "When will you return, sir?"

"I do not know. Tell Cook, I shall not be needing dinner tonight." Bray pulled on his leather riding gloves and hurried out the back.

Seth sprang into the saddle and pulled Jupiter away. Impatience overwhelmed him. His heart pounded in his chest hard and rapid. The palms of his hands were slick with sweat beneath his gloves.

A moment later, their horses' hooves pounded the earth as darkness swallowed the last glimmer of twilight. Out of the city, the wind shoved against their bodies, as if unseen forces prevented them. Keeping to the high road toward the west, they rode with swiftness, beneath a night sky darkening with ponderous clouds.

✐❧

On the evening Juleah left Henry Chase, the sun sank below a ragged horizon flushed violet and gave way to the descending night. The cart rattled over the road misty with twilight.

Juleah pinched her brows and stared out at the fields. "Why would Yates send me a message claiming Mother was ill and it not be so?"

Claire shook her head. "Lady Anna would never conceal an illness from you, Miss Juleah."

"I must write Yates a letter as soon as I arrive home. He owes me an explanation."

"I never trusted that man." Claire crossed her arms over her bosom. "He has shifty eyes."

Darkness fell along the rim of the sky. Two bright stars rose in the east, and a brilliant moon tripped above the horizon. For all the stress of the recent days, the beauty of creation caused it to ease. But along the horizon, a dome of clouds darkened the sky. Cold wind blew against Juleah's face.

When they passed through the gates of Ten Width, the house looked empty to Juleah, for Seth was not there. She stepped over the threshold and entered the dark foyer. She drew her cloak from her shoulders and handed it to Claire. A rush of loneliness filled her with longing for her husband.

Candle in hand, Claire went ahead of her mistress up the staircase. The flame caused shadows to quiver over the walls and along the floor. Inside Juleah's room, she lit the fire in the hearth, for the night had grown chilly. The fire crackled, seethed, sparked, and glowed as if a thousand stars had been born within it. It warmed Juleah's skin.

She slipped off her shoes and tossed them aside. "You must be tired, Claire. It has been a long day. Go to bed. I can manage on my own."

Claire picked up Juleah's brush. "But I haven't brushed out your hair."

"I am accustomed to brushing out my own hair. Wake me in the morning for breakfast. Good night."

After Claire left, Juleah stretched her arms upward and sat on the bed. She lifted her skirts to roll down her stockings. The silk felt smooth against her hands as she pushed the first one down. It made her think of her wedding night, how warm Seth's hands were, how gentle his touch as he rolled each stocking down her thighs, over her calves, and slipped them off her feet.

"Oh, Seth," she whispered. "How I wish you were home."

Wind blew down the flue of the fireplace, stirred the ashes, and rushed along her legs. She was seized with the sense of eyes watching her. A chill ran up her spine. She shivered, and then froze.

Her gaze drifted toward the window. The green satin-lined border of the curtains quivered and a figure, shrouded in shadow, stepped out from behind them.

24

Seth could not reach home and Juleah quickly enough. He decided to make for Ten Width first. It was closest, and if he did not find her there, he'd go on to Henry Chase.

Anxiety mounted in his heart, as he and Michael rode on, until they reached the lands that bordered Ten Width. Shadows swayed over the road, swept across the stretch of dirt and sand. He twisted the leather reins through his hands. His body ached from the journey, as his eyes grew accustomed to the darkness.

The moon rose full that night, large and brilliant, an opal specter set against a cold, ebony sky. A moon dog surrounded it—a huge ghostly swath in the sky that washed the heavens. It prophesied rain, though a silver light trembled over the fields and illumined the path.

He urged his mount forward where the road broke through woodland bathed in grim moonlight. The air filled and reeked with what he believed were hearth fires, for it was a chilly night. Yet, the closer they drew to Ten Width, the heavier the air became. He frowned. It was unlike the homey scent of a warm sitting room fire, of mellow cedar and heady oak. Rather it became the distressed smell of danger, smoke, and burning wood.

Uneasy, Seth glanced up at the top of the hill before him. A band of gold rimmed the dark edge of the mound. It appeared as if the sun was beginning to rise. He glanced above to see the clouds illuminated with an eerie ocherous glow. Beneath them stretched a milky sheet of what appeared to be fog. Baleful light quivered, and his heart slammed against his ribs. Fear gripped him hard and fast.

He suddenly realized what his eyes beheld, and he snapped the reins. He pushed his horse to a gallop up the shimmering hill. He reached the summit and looked down. His heart tightened in his chest and pounded against his ribs. A chill rushed through his body as if a cold winter blast struck him naked.

Seth raced his horse down the hill and across the dewy grass. He yanked at the reins and the horse skidded to a halt. The smell of danger wafted in the air, and Jupiter reared and beat his hooves down into the spongy ground. Before the horse could steady, Seth leapt from the saddle and ran toward the house. He heard, over the roar of the blaze, a woman's soft, mournful cry.

Intense heat seared his skin. He raised his arms across his face. In the east wing, windows glowed from within. Glass cracked and shattered. Tongues of flame spouted from the casements like the tongues of demons and licked against brick and mortar. Wind blew from the north against the blaze and pushed back the pyre. Soot blew against his eyes. A dry, hot taste coated his tongue. Relentless, the heat exhaled against his face.

"Juleah! Juleah!"

Bray pulled him back. Seth struggled free and stumbled ahead. Will fell on his knees beside him, his face smudged with charcoal, his shirt scorched.

Breathing rapidly, Seth fixed his eyes on him. "Where's my wife?" The words choked in his throat. Will stuttered, trying to reply. Seth reached down, grabbed Will by the front of his shirt, and yanked him to his feet. "Where is Juleah?"

Will shook his head. "I don't know, sir. I tried to reach her, but the fire was fierce." He put his hands over his face and trembled. "I called and called. I tried, sir. I tried hard."

Seth hurried forward. Bray and Will held him back. As if it were meant to deepen the crush in his soul, clouds shut out the moon. Then rain began to fall in a torrent. Thunder boomed and shook the earth. The fire seethed and hissed. Steam rose. Smoke vanished as it stretched higher. Charred wood crackled. Flames fought against the deluge, but the storm conquered.

Numb with shock, Seth stared at the ruin before him. "It's dying out. She's inside . . . somewhere safe."

Seth broke free from the arms that held him. He hurried into the smoldering ruins. He called her name and coughed from the smoke and weightiness of the air.

A tongue of flame leapt from a piece of charred wood. From beneath it, a blackened hand stretched out to him. A body lay a short distance away at the bottom of the staircase. As if run through with the sharpest of rapiers, Seth's heart tore and bled out grief.

The stench of burnt wood and seared flesh filled his nostrils. He staggered toward the body. It could not be distinguished, yet a blackened gown still covered her form. Juleah lay face down with one hand flung over the back of her head, as if to protect it. Her glorious hair had been burned off. He dared not look at her face.

Violently, Seth's body trembled. If he did not look away, he'd go mad staring at her body lying in a heap of debris and ash, molested by fire, emptied of her spirit. His crazed mind agonized over how she suffered. To lose her in this way! His anguished cry echoed through the empty house.

Blinded by his misery, Seth saw Michael move toward the grizzly body. Bray shoved the seething wood away with the toe of his boot. A ring glinted against tarnished flesh. The ruby and pair of diamonds sparkled through ashy dust. Bray pulled it loose from the scorched finger it encircled, careful not to break and tear away the charred flesh.

At first, Seth fought the hands that urged him back, but weakened as they dragged him out.

Latterbuck stood out on the lawn. Rain dripped off the edge of his hat. "What is that you have in your hand?" he said to Bray.

"A body lies within, a woman's body. I believe it is Juleah Braxton. This is her ring." Bray went to leave, but Latterbuck put his hand on his chest to stop him. "If you fear God, Constable, let me pass."

"I sense this fire was no accident. Give it to me."

Bray refused, and jerked away. "I shall not. It belongs to her husband and he shall have it."

Bray hurried to Seth and handed him the ring. "I am sorry, Seth."

Heartbroken, a cry clawed its way up his throat. "Juleah! Juleah!" If ever a man like Seth Braxton were to cry, it was at that moment, when his world collapsed around him in one hailstorm of misery, as if the hands of hell reached up from a molten abyss to rend his heart from his body.

Bray put his arm around Seth's slumped shoulders. "Do not look any longer, Seth. Come away."

He gasped in agony and sobbed. He staggered into the darkness, as a cold moon, crueler than the dark, broke through the cloudy sky. Its beams touched the earth, and mist coiled around his boots.

Seth gripped Juleah's ring in his palm. The image of her body could not escape his mind and the wound deepened. Anger rose with the want to destroy, to beat something.

"Juleah," he whispered through his tears, his teeth clenched. "Juleah, my love."

He stared down at the ring, put it to his lips, and with a trembling hand, he slipped it inside his breast pocket beside his heart.

"I should not have left you."

He balled his fist and struck a tree. Rough bark tore his skin and left his knuckles raw. Again and again, he struck it, until his hands bled, until all strength emptied from him.

He reeled away, drunk with sorrow, possessed by grief. The roar of the sea surrounded him, and the taste of salty air mixed with the salt of tears.

Rain battered against the cliffs high above the cove. Stricken beyond measure, Seth stared down from the edge. Through the haze, he watched raindrops fall downward and splash onto the rocks. He wished he were one of them, to fall, smash, and spread into oblivion.

Rain drenched his hair and matted the dark strands that touched his shoulders. It covered his face, blurred his vision, and deafened his ears. Wind blew with the pulse of the sea and moaned through the crags.

At the cliff's edge, Seth fell to his knees and stared out at the dark water. A maddening mix of emotions gouged out his heart and left him weak and broken.

He stared out to sea. The lantern lights of a ship, set against the backdrop of the horizon, faded and the vessel disappeared.

So was her life.

As she had died, so had he. His hell was to stay behind and face the agony of living on without her.

Burying his face within his hands, he moaned and rocked as he wept. The pain was unbearable. A double-edged sword turned within. Razor sharp it ripped into the chambers of his heart, plunged deep into the hollows of his soul to destroy him.

Michael Bray called to Seth, and when he reached him, he touched him on the shoulder. Seth turned to see his friend and stood.

"I don't care about the house." He breathed hard, his face tense with feeling. "It can burn to ash. I wish I'd never come here. If I had stayed away, she'd be alive. I should have known not to go to London without her."

"You cannot blame yourself." Bray took a step forward.

"Tell Will and Claire they cannot stay."

"It is not their fault, Seth. They were fortunate to get out in time. Be kind to them."

"I cannot stay here. With her gone, there is nothing left."

Soberly Bray nodded.

Seth raked his hands through his hair. "How shall her family be told? How am I to do it, Michael? How can I face them? I pledged to protect her, and I failed. How will I live without her?" His body shook. "I loved her. I loved her!"

Bray's face twisted with emotion. "I know, Seth." He put his arm over Seth's shoulder and helped him down the rocky expanse.

They did not follow the path back to Ten Width, but instead followed the road leading away from it.

25

*W*ill and Claire stood by the roadside. With stunned faces and bewildered stares, they waited in grim silence. They had the horses with them and helped the grieving patriot climb into the saddle and put his boots into the stirrups.

They took him down to The Sea Maiden, after passing under the shadow of the ruins of a Roman tower. A great flurry of activity arose when they came through the door. Men put their mugs of ale down and stood.

"What's happened?" asked the tavern-keeper.

"Ten Width caught fire," said Will. "The squire needs help."

Through the strands of hair that covered his eyes, Seth glanced at Will's desperate face. Claire let out a stifled cry and the tavern-keeper's wife gathered her into her arms. Then she ordered the men to carry Seth upstairs.

"Take the poor lad to the room at the far end. 'Tis my best." She then turned to Michael Bray. "Open the windows, sir. The air will bring him 'round."

As Seth stumbled up the stairs, Will spoke in a low, strained voice. "The squire's wife is dead. She didn't get out."

Seth moaned deep in his throat and hung his head.

Upstairs, in a room darkened by heavy timber beams, where no fire glowed, and where the latticed window seemed too small to let the moonlight in, Seth lay across the bed and covered his face with his hands. For an hour, he forced back the tears that stung his eyes and the sobs that raked his throat. Lying with his face covered in his arms for the space of an hour, feeling he'd go mad, finally he wept quietly. When he lifted his hands away, he glanced over at Michael Bray. He sat in a chair beside the empty hearth, his face ashen with pain.

"I will send for Yates," Bray said, breaking the silence.

Seth frowned hard. "I don't want him. I must go." He threw his legs over the edge of the bed and strode to the door.

Bray grabbed his arm. "You are not fit to go anywhere, Seth. Let me."

The corner of Seth's mouth twisted, and he drew himself up. He stepped out of the door and clattered down the dim staircase to the smoky room below.

Out into the damp night, he stumbled. Finding Jupiter, he pulled himself onto the steed's back, flicked the reins, and moved him out into the darkness onto the winding road from the tavern.

The moon, an ivory disk set against black mourning cloth, lit long stretches of grim clouds. Wind braced Seth's body, smacked his face, and whipped the horse's mane against him.

The roads were muddy, but not enough to delay him. His breath hurried along with the cadence of Jupiter's hoofbeats, and he cried out to God for strength.

By the time he reached Henry Chase, the lower lights of the house were absent. Although he regretted the duty he must now perform, he headed toward the house, his trembling hands slick with sweat.

A candle passed a window. He supposed the thud of hooves had awakened the occupants. The door swung open and Sir Henry appeared in his slippers, nightshirt, and cap, holding a lantern high over his head.

"Who is it?" he called out through the dark.

"It is I, Sir Henry." Seth climbed down from Jupiter's back.

"Why, Seth. 'Tis late, lad." Sir Henry took a few steps out onto the grass, his face pinched with alarm.

"Forgive me, sir, but I . . ."

"You smell of smoke. Has there been a battle? Should I fetch my pistols?"

At those words, Seth pressed his hand against his eyes to forbid what he did not want his father-in-law to see. Troubled, he stared back at Sir Henry, saddened to see what was in the old man's eyes. How was he to tell him his daughter was lost to him, that she had died a painful death, and that he felt responsible?

He searched and prayed for the strength to do it.

"I must come inside and speak to you and your lady," he said, and turned Sir Henry back toward the front door.

26

*W*hen the moon dipped below the zenith of the sky, Edward Darden's hackney rolled over the high road toward The Sea Maiden. Trees swayed and shadows quivered along the eerie, windswept road. Above, cold stars peeked out from the clouds. Fog lay low in gullies and curled over hedgerows.

His body stiffened with impatience when the horses slowed to a halt, and he climbed out. He had heard of the place, but had never stepped foot inside, not until the day Benjamin Braxton left this world, when drink became his friend and numbed him from the inner demons that raged within.

Tonight he needed a pint of ale before going on. It would steady him, he believed, make him a braver man. But drink mocked him and made him a fool. The lantern outside the tavern flickered. He walked past it and sensed the fan of yellow light spread over his shoulders. The tavern was thick with tobacco smoke, and a roaring fire burned in the hearth.

Darden took a seat in a booth hidden from the rest of the patrons and waved over the serving girl.

"Evening, sir. What is your fancy?" she asked, her flaxen hair falling forward over bare shoulders.

"You." He took a quick inventory of her with his eyes. "What is your name?"

She threw back her head and laughed. "Pen, short for Penelope, and I am not for hire. I'm promised. My young lad wouldn't like you making overtures at me."

Darden leaned his broad shoulders against the back of the bench. He wiped his hands along his breeches and then reached for her. "You'd give in if we were alone." He drew her close.

The girl's mouth fell open, a sweet, pouty mouth that Darden liked. She gasped and shoved away. "Perhaps I would, but you'll never know."

She whirled round and left him. Upon her return, she plopped a mug of ale in front of him. Every instinct urged Darden to down his pint and take her outside. Being with a girl might drive out the tension that raged within and allow him to escape reality for a brief time.

Pen leaned forward, and he hoped she would permit him to touch her and have his way. He imagined what pleasure it would bring. But *Juleah*—her firm body, soft lips, her alluring voice. He trembled and cursed her.

With his hands tight around the mug, his muscles constricted. What had happened to the strength he once possessed? Juleah caused this. Juleah, and her rejection of him. Juleah, and her love for Seth Braxton.

Darden swallowed some ale and stared at Pen. "What is it?"

"You've gone quiet. Is something wrong, sir? Is it a lady that makes you sad?"

Darden clenched his fists as a slow pain burned through him. "If it were, would you pity me?"

"Maybe. It'd depend on what you did to make your lady treat you badly. Some men can be cruel."

"What if it were my lover who had been cruel?"

"Then you're better off to forget her and find someone else."

He reached out, caught Pen's arm in a tight grip, and pulled her down on his knee. "You could help me forget. I know you're promised, but he'd never know." He lifted her arm to his lips and kissed it. He looked at her eyes. How they glazed over with desire.

The tavern-keeper, keen to see what was going on, called to Pen. She shot up and smoothed her apron. "I have to go." With a sweep of her hand over her hair, she went back to work.

Darden's heart had never encompassed tender love. He had never known such feelings, only that he wanted to possess Juleah and own Ten Width. Since Benjamin's death, he had lived at his dead father's home, a crumbling country house, with a mother who had gone out of her wits and demanded much of him. How could he bring a wife to such a place? Juleah would have never accepted it, but she may have accepted him if he had inherited Ten Width.

In an effort to find a good wife, he resumed courting Juleah after he returned from the American revolt. Certainly, a uniform, his loyalty to the king, and the battle scar over his left cheek would have caused her to think him brave and to want him. But he was wrong. Juleah wanted more. Darden rarely sought to know her mind. He believed a woman's thoughts were unimportant and could not match the intellect of a man. A gentleman needed a wife of good reputation and breeding only to satisfy his desires and provide an heir.

What he knew of her he'd learned through his eyes—the pretty face, the sensuous lines of her body, the faint fragrance of her hair, the silky appearance of her skin. He'd looked no deeper than the surface, and jealousy and pride consumed him.

Seth Braxton had stolen everything from him. Juleah preferred Braxton, and Darden hated her for it. She answered the letter he had sent with a refusal and made him look like a fool at Wrenhurst. His mug empty, he slammed it on the table and called for another.

Pen carried her pitcher over and poured the ale to the rim. "It's a shame what happened at Ten Width." She spoke in a hushed voice. "Everyone's talking about it. Did you know the lady?"

Darden shot her a startled glance. His face stiffened. "I knew her."

"She and the new squire had been married such a short time. He's gone to Henry Chase to tell Sir Henry and his lady. So sad for them. Captain Bray is left upstairs to wait. I suppose I should go see if he needs anything."

Darden gripped his mug of ale. "Perhaps you should."

"Folks say Seth Braxton should've never come to England, being a rebel and all. I think they're wrong. I thought him a perfect gentleman. I can't imagine losing my love newly wedded. I'd die from a broken heart. Folks say he's crazed with grief."

"Do you think I care what people say or for his pain?"

Her mouth fell open at his cold comment. "No, I guess you don't care what people say, but you should feel sorry for the gentleman. What if it had been your wife?"

Darden looked up at her with a start. "Don't say that. I'd not care to think of it."

She set the pitcher on her hip and glanced over at Will. Darden followed her eyes, and leaning from his seat, he saw Will with his head nestled in his arms. His mug sat beside him on the table. Claire with her back to Darden had her arm over Will's shoulder. They sat on the other side of the room, and

Darden moved back, deep in the shadow of the corner, so as not to be seen.

Pen leaned down and whispered, "First the old squire dies. Then those goings-on about Mistress Caroline and her child. Then Hetty Shanks is found dead. Lord knows where the man ran off to. And what do we have now, but Ten Width burning and the new mistress killed in the fire. Why do such things happen all at once, you suppose?"

Darden's mouth twisted. He hung his head. "I do not know. Now, leave me alone."

Pen's sweet smile faded, and she turned away. Darden cared not that he had hurt her by his abruptness. Tormented, he raked his fingers through his hair. His lips curled, and he downed his ale.

A quarter hour into his time there, three men came through the door. They swaggered to his table, and he bid them to sit with a gesture of his hand. Briefly, they spoke and he paid them money. Darden stood, pulled on his hat, and left the tavern.

When the door closed behind him, the night air rushed against his face, the moistness feeling like a woman's tears. His driver opened the hackney door. Darden climbed inside to sit beside a sleeping woman. Moonlight touched the lids of her eyes, and her face looked pure and young. She shivered and he drew the blanket on her lap up to her shoulders. He leaned out and ordered the driver to move on. The gloom of the night grew oppressive as the hackney rambled down the road. The crunch of the coach wheels and the pounding hooves mingled with the rapid beat of his heart.

His coach drew near the coast and he listened to the waves sweep the stony shore. A ship's bell anchored in the harbor struck out the hour, and he turned to the woman beside him.

27

*A*nna's face paled when she heard the news delivered to her and Sir Henry in the gentlest manner. She collapsed into her husband's arms and wailed. She did more than cry. She screamed in agony.

Seth picked her up in his arms to carry her upstairs to her room. Sir Henry, equally crushed, appeared to steel himself from the slaughtering grief and said he would wait in his study.

Seth left Lady Anna with her maid Sarah and went back downstairs. His father-in-law stood at the window, staring forward into the darkness. A tear slipped down his cheek and dropped onto his neckcloth.

"Sir Henry . . ." Seth paused, not knowing what more to say.

Henry Fallowes turned his head. "I would prefer you call me Father, Seth." His voice quaked under the strain. "Call me that from this day hence. It would please me."

"I fail to deserve to be called your son. Before you and God, I swore I would protect her."

"You cannot be blamed. How were you to know what was to come?"

"I should not have left her."

Sir Henry lifted his eyes. The candlelight from a single wick etched his drawn face. "Yet if in this life only we have hope, we are the most wretched of men." He lowered himself into a chair, bowed his head within his hands, and wept.

Seth could not bear to stay at Henry Chase and listen to Lady Anna's wails and the weeping that went on behind closed doors. He rode back to The Sea Maiden along a road drenched in eerie moonglow. In cadence with the pain that pulsed through him, the wind moaned.

A gust bore the stench of burnt wood to his senses. He groaned and struck his horse with his boot heels. The musty scent followed him, and his heart tore within him as he pushed Jupiter to a hard gallop.

The tavern was quiet when he walked through the door and up to his room. All night he tossed and turned, unable to sleep. Several times, he got up and paced the floor. More than once he fell on his knees with his hands clasped tight.

The sorrows of death compassed me, and the pains of hell gat hold upon me. I found trouble and sorrow. . . . Then I called upon the name of the Lord; O, Lord, I beseech thee, deliver my soul. . . mine eyes from tears, and my feet from falling.

Sweat beaded over his brow. He trembled and prayed until, exhausted, he could pray no more. By four in the morning, he drifted off into a restless sleep.

Dawn crept through the window. Shades of magenta and yellow struck the walls and caused him to lift his eyes. He needed to face the day, but regretted he ever woke. Why could he not have stayed asleep? He wished he had slipped away and escaped the world. He wished he could be with Juleah in eternity.

That morning, Latterbuck made his way over a foggy country road toward Ten Width. His deputy followed alongside him, yawned, and shook his head. Latterbuck, on the other hand, appeared alert in his saddle. He had drunk a quart of strong black coffee, eaten a scrap of bacon, and a huge bowl of mush before he left his house.

"Wake up, George. We've work to do." Latterbuck smacked George on the shoulder and squinted his eyes against the wind.

He turned his horse through the gates of Ten Width, pulled rein, and drew off his hat. "Will you look at that, George? What a woeful sight for the eyes. I don't like it."

He squashed his hat back on his head and poked his horse with his heels. Then he moved down the lane. "A sad business this. That house stood for hundreds of years. Now look at it."

When they reached the threshold, Latterbuck slid off his saddle. "This deviltry must be rooted out."

George looked perplexed.

"You don't understand, do you, George? Well, I'll say this. What happened here was meant to harm. Now a woman is dead. I never thought I'd say it, but this was no accident."

28

Seth and Michael Bray waited outside the church door with Reverend Simon until the caretaker, Mr. Makepeace, showed up with the key. Comfortless, Seth watched him shove it into the iron lock. The door creaked on its hinges. Wind blew leaves from the churchyard over the flagstones.

Sunlight poured through the church window above the altar and caught Seth's eyes when he walked inside. Streamers floated through the colored glass, across the granite floor. Dust motes flashed in their beams against shadow. Before the altar stood a funeral table. Upon it sat a simple wooden box with bright brass hinges, and within lay a body wrapped in a linen shroud.

"I'm so sorry, sir." Makepeace stood apart from the pair and turned his hat in his hands. "Your lady had a beautiful soul and shall be missed."

Seth thanked him for his sentiments. "It is good of you to speak of her kindly." He stood in front of the box, with a black crepe band tied to his arm. No more would he see her beauti-ful face, her hair, her elegant mouth, or her glowing eyes. He clenched his teeth as agony filled him. He bit down on his tongue to stifle a cry.

No, this is not the end, for we will be together one day. But until then, I will have to live out long and lonely years without you unless the Almighty would be merciful.

If he could bring her back, he would do so; he willed it with every fiber of his being. But it was not in his ability to do. He stepped closer and glanced over the words on the brass plate fixed to the top.

Herein lies the body of Juleah Fallowes Braxton
August 10, 1764–June 30, 1785
Beloved wife of Seth Braxton
of Ten Width, Devonshire, England

Seth's chest tightened, as if gnarled hands squeezed the life breath from him. He swallowed the pain and reached out to touch the brass plate. His hand trembled as he ran his fingertips over the words; he pressed his palm against the wood to leave his mark. When the church door opened, he lifted his eyes to the light and turned along with Bray. The village pallbearers entered the church and carried Juleah's coffin out of the church to the cemetery.

Outside, he watched the group that came toward him— Lady Anna in black satin, Sir Henry holding her to his side. Thomas and Jane were behind them, Claire and Will in the rear. Caroline lifted tearful eyes to her brother. Upon their faces were such looks of unspeakable grief that a heart of stone would melt beneath such stares, especially Lady Anna. Shadowy circles lay beneath her eyes.

To see Juleah's family in this way intensified Seth's sorrow. *If only it had been possible to spare them. If only I had taken her place.*

Wind rustled the heavy folds of Lady Anna's mourning clothes and whirled around Sir Henry's shoes. Thomas and

Jane were too young to throw themselves into the meaning and finality. Yet, for their youth and energy, they looked older and walked with the gaits of sick children.

Reverend Simon, a man of the cloth accustomed to marrying and burying his flock, read the words from the prayer book. Yet, even he was affected and wiped away a tear from the corner of his eye with his finger. He paused while reading Psalm 23, swallowed hard, and went on.

Gut-wrenching agony seized Seth as he watched the men lower his beloved into the ground. Tears stung his eyes as he watched the pallbearers cover her with earth. Cold grief seized every inch of his being.

"Underneath this stone doth lie, as much beauty as could die," he mournfully quoted an epitaph by Ben Jonson, "which in life did harbour give, to more virtue than doth live."

Lady Anna buried her face against her husband's shoulder and sobbed. Sir Henry moved her away to the coach that awaited them. Jane and Thomas followed and boarded once Lady Anna was settled inside. Caroline, accompanying them, leaned out of the window and called softly to her husband.

Seth turned to Bray. "Please attend to the family at Henry Chase."

"Where are you going, Seth?"

"Ten Width."

Determined to conquer his pain, he waited until everyone had gone. He stood alone, staring at the mound of tilled earth, and crouched down to lay a fistful of wildflowers upon it. Beaten down with grief, he pressed his hand over his eyes. It felt as if he had been run though the heart with the sharpest of spears. His tears slipped through his fingers and dropped onto the grave.

"Juleah. Juleah," he cried.

With a heavy heart, he finally stood, wiped his face, and strode to his horse to mount it. He rode across the fields away from the road. Lush grass waved in the wind, and the air smelled wild. He slackened the reins and spurred the horse onto the road that led to Ten Width.

Coming around a bend, he reined in and the horse reared up. Latterbuck raised his hat. "My condolences on this sad day, Mr. Braxton." He drew his horse alongside Seth's. "Have I missed the service?"

"Yes." He had to catch his breath. "You must excuse me, Constable."

"Where are you headed? If it's the tavern, I'll join you in a mug of ale."

"I am on my way to Ten Width."

"I've just come from there. Steel yourself for what you are about to see in the light of day, sir." Latterbuck lifted his bleary eyes away from Seth and craned his neck to look down the road. "Where is your sister? I expected to see her coming from the church."

"She is with Lady Anna."

"Your wife was her closest friend, was she not?"

"Yes. They were like sisters."

"Then this is a great loss to Miss Caroline as well." Latterbuck scratched his chin. "What do you intend to do?"

"Repair the house, of course." Seth steadied his restless horse and wished to move on. "Or pull it down," he murmured under his breath.

Latterbuck frowned. "I hope you have not considered returning to Virginia."

"It is a greater possibility than before."

Latterbuck's slim eyes narrowed. "A man's duty can be far-reaching, unconfined to borders. If there has been a wrong done, duty will find a way to settle it. Restitution must be made. Justice served."

In an instant, Seth tightened and coiled the reins within his hands. The subtle accusation was more than evident.

"I have just buried my wife. This is neither the time nor the place to discuss anything. You'll find me at Henry Chase if you have questions."

"Then I shall meet you there at two this afternoon after dinner," Latterbuck said. "I cannot do my job on an empty stomach."

"I imagine not." Seth urged Jupiter forward.

He went on at a gallop and felt Latterbuck's eyes boring into his back. Digging his heels into the horse, he turned at a place where the trees stretched overhead in a canopy of green. Cold despair and loneliness worsened when he saw the chimneys of Ten Width looming above the treetops.

He had been warned what he would see, a grim ruin of naked stone, surrounded by green. The damaged wing stood windowless and depressed. The untouched portion of the house brooded over the landscape. Ravens flew between the charred beams and perched at the highest points. They cackled and their throats gurgled a mysterious chant. Their feathers glistened like wax in the warm sunlight.

Seth sat in the saddle and stared hard before him. Sorrow rippled over his skin and he moved his eyes over the edges of the walls, the door, the charred bricks, broken glass, and stone facade. Then he dismounted to go inside.

At first, the door would not budge. The heat from the fire had warped the jamb. Leaning his shoulder against it, he shoved hard. It skidded open, and he stepped through into the hallway, grimy with soot.

From the west wing, Seth took the servants' stairs, which was now the only way to the second story of the house. The door to the room he had shared with his wife sat open. He stepped in, looked with a weary sigh around the chamber. Without thinking, he pushed the latticed windows of the balcony open. He stepped out and looked at the hills. The memory of Juleah wrapped in his arms, with her back to his chest, suddenly flooded his mind. Here is where they would watch the sun set and the stars brighten, sometimes to see the northern lights dance across the night sky.

He turned back inside. The bedcovers were pulled down. His heart sank to think Juleah had been preparing to go to sleep before the inferno took her life. The scent of lavender and rose still lingered.

He took out a clean shirt and breeches and shoved them into a saddlebag. He expected he would stay at Henry Chase several days, perhaps weeks. The idea crossed his mind that he might never return. His Bible sat on the night table. He picked it up, held it in his hand, and placed it with the rest of his things.

When he finished, he went over to Juleah's wardrobe closet and opened it. Her clothes were gone—every gown, every frock. Her teak jewel box was empty. Looters had moved quickly, and it caused Seth's heart to sink lower.

He rummaged through drawers and searched for what he did not know. Her undergarments were there, her stockings and garters, the pair of pink silk slippers he had bought her. But what was this on the floor behind the chair? He reached over and picked up the gown she had worn the day they were married. The right shoulder was torn and the front of the bodice shredded. He clutched it within his hands, and his heart slammed in his chest as a startling revelation filled him. He pressed the folds of the gown against his face and wept.

A lock of Juleah's hair, held together by a silk crimson ribbon, lay on her dressing table. Seth picked it up and gazed at it as it lay in his palm, the chestnut color, the silkiness and beauty. He closed his hand over it and put it in his pocket beside his heart in the same place he kept her ring.

Out in the hall, he walked along the Persian runner back to the servants' stairs leading to the kitchen. From there, he went back to the hall and toward the east side of the house. He brushed his hand along the wall, where the paper had peeled back from the heat. At the far end, near a window that had reached the ceiling, a brass candlestick lay upon the blackened floor. Leading from it, an even blacker thread spread like distorted fingers up the wall.

Seth bent down to study the pattern. Questions raced through his mind. Why had the fire started here? Someone had a candle in hand, passed down the hall in the night, and dropped it. He supposed it could have been Juleah. She might have grown restless and gotten up to go downstairs. But then, perhaps someone or something had woken her. Perhaps she was going down to answer the door.

Seth stood and turned toward the place where the staircase had been. He dare not go any farther, for the house was unstable at this point. The Delft vase lay broken on the floor, the table it had sat on overturned. Had Juleah struggled to get out, or had she fought to get away from someone?

He tried to visualize the candle falling, flame catching the curtains afire. He shook his head and thought that Juleah would have had time to get out by way of the west wing. Then, a reality both frightening and freeing, gripped him.

Who have I buried—my wife or an intruder?

He pressed his palm against the wall and slipped down to his knees.

Show me the truth, Lord. Show me the way. Have I gone mad with what I'm thinking? Has grief blinded my reason?

Struggling to his feet, he hurried out the front door, grabbed the edge of his saddle, and hauled himself up. Off he raced toward Henry Chase to find an answer, a confirmation, a hope.

29

*J*upiter was lathered from the hard ride and blew out his nostrils as Seth dismounted. Before he reached the front door, Sarah drew it open and stepped aside for him to enter. He was told Lady Anna had taken to her bed, stricken by grief, and was unable to bear company. The children were out hiking with their father over the hills with his hounds, the Brays and little Nathaniel for company.

Sarah motioned to Seth to follow her to the kitchen. "And the constable is here, sir," she whispered. "He'll eat us out of house and home if he don't leave soon."

Latterbuck sat at the table feasting on cold chicken. When he looked up at Seth standing in the doorway, he tossed down the picked-over bone and leaned back against the chair, which creaked against his weight.

"You look flushed, Mr. Braxton. Had you a hard ride coming over from Ten Width?"

Seth moved to the table. "We need to talk."

"Indeed we do." Latterbuck wiped his grimy hands across the front of his waistcoat, and glanced over at Sarah. "You, girl. Bring the gentleman ale, and refill my flagon."

Sarah curled her lip and did as he bid her. Seth was even more annoyed by Latterbuck's rude behavior. "This is not a tavern, sir. Be mindful of where you are."

"I beg your pardon?" Latterbuck bent forward and shoved the plate aside.

"You heard me. The girl is not required to wait on us hand and foot. Lady Anna is upstairs with a broken heart and needs this girl more than you or I." He turned to the wide-eyed young woman. "Go on, Sarah. Attend your mistress."

With a bob, she left.

Latterbuck settled back in his chair. "Hmm. I had forgotten you colonials are more tolerant. Obviously, our way of treating servants is different from yours."

"I'll not have you ordering that girl about as if she belonged to you." Seth slapped his palm on the table.

Latterbuck guffawed. "You own slaves and indentures where you're from. At least we promised to free them if they fought on our side. Your constitution would not."

Barely did Seth hear Latterbuck—his heart, mind, and soul twisted with pain. "I'm not here to debate with you."

Latterbuck wiggled his head. "Not about politics, anyway. I've spoken with Sir Henry and Captain Bray. Both think highly of you. Bray vouched for your whereabouts the night of the fire. You are fortunate to have a witness in that regard."

Seth frowned and crossed his arms over his chest. "If I had not, would you have clapped me in irons by now?"

"Is that what you think?"

"You have given me that impression."

"Have you something to hide, Mr. Braxton?"

"No, Constable." Seth paced the room.

Latterbuck scraped his fork over the plate, put it in his mouth, and licked it. "Bray said you received a message requesting you come to London, and you found it to be false. Is that so?"

"It was a forgery."

"Who sent it?"

"I do not know. A forger does not reveal his true self."

"Indeed that is so. And Miss Juleah, she was called away as well?"

"Yes. The letter said her mother was ill."

"I spoke to Yates, too. He claims Lady Anna was indeed having difficulties, of which details he would not divulge. He did not recall sending your lady word of it. So, we can assume it may have been Sir Henry that sent the message. He denies it, but he is forgetful of what he may or may not have done. Whoever it was must have been concerned for her ladyship."

"Juleah would have recognized her father's handwriting. He would have signed it." Seth kept his eyes fixed on Latterbuck, annoyed at the shoddy deductions of a man who claimed to be a professional.

Latterbuck appeared unmoved. "I'm curious about one thing. Why did you not go with your wife, with the hope of finding all was well enough for you both to travel on to London together?"

"The message was urgent. We agreed I'd go to London and she would join me later."

Latterbuck paused to rub his chin. "I see. I spoke with Mr. Banes. He claims you asked to view your grandfather's will a week or so ago. Have you had some concerns about your inheritance?"

"Indeed not."

"A formality, I suppose. Banes gave it to you then?"

"It is locked away at Ten Width."

"May I have the key?"

"What for?" Seth stared at him incredulously.

"It would be best if you allowed me to remove it from the house for examination."

"You question its authenticity?"

"It is standard procedure in this case."

Against his better instincts, Seth handed him the brass key he kept in his pocket. "You'll find it in the right-hand drawer of the desk in the study."

Latterbuck gave him a smug smile and took the key from Seth's hand. "I'll return it once I'm through with my investigation."

Seth gave him a wry smile. "It is not the only copy, I'm sure."

"Nevertheless I wish to view the one in your possession. You've been to Ten Width. Why did you go there so soon after burying your wife?"

"To see the damage . . . and to grieve." Seth filled a mug of ale and ignored Latterbuck when he pushed his empty flagon across the table.

"On my way here, I passed some workmen," Latterbuck said. "They informed me they were hired to clear the debris and start rebuilding the damaged wing."

"Why waste time?" Seth told him. "I'll not be staying at Henry Chase, but going back home. Looters stole my wife's jewelry and clothes."

"I'm sorry to hear it."

"I believe there was a struggle between my wife and an intruder. Look at this." He pulled the gown out of the carpet-bag and showed it to Latterbuck. "It is torn, here and here."

"So, looters fought over the gown and damaged it. What of it?"

"I believe that fire was no accident. Juleah would have had time to get out. I'm not sure things are as they appear."

Frustration built within him, tightened his muscles, and prickled over his skin. One corner of his mouth twitched. Sweat beaded over his forehead. What he was about to say was risky, but he had to speak his mind, even if the constable would think he was crazy.

He put his hands on the table, leaned forward, and looked Latterbuck straight in the eye. "I believe Juleah is alive."

Latterbuck pinched his brows together. "Did you not identify the body?"

Seth stared at the garment. "I could not look at it. You should understand the reasons why."

"But upon the finger of the corpse was her wedding ring."

"An intruder stole it, placed it upon her own finger, and perished in the fire."

Latterbuck stared back at Seth with a skeptical gleam in his eyes. "Then who is the person you buried, Mr. Braxton? Where is your wife now?"

By Latterbuck's expression, he did not believe a word of what Seth said. That slight curve of his lips and the way his eyes narrowed said everything. "You think I'm mad?" Seth said.

"Grief makes a man do and say what makes no sense."

"It makes perfect sense."

"Your wife is gone, sir. You must accept it."

Seth slammed his fist onto the table. How could Latterbuck be such an idiot? "I am right about this, and as the squire of Ten Width, I demand you investigate my claims. Otherwise, Constable, I'll go over your head, report your incompetence, and take it upon myself to find my wife."

"You'll do nothing of the kind, sir!" Latterbuck shouted back. "Leave it to a professional to sort things out. I've ways of discovering the truth you have not even thought of."

Seth could have taken Latterbuck by the neckcloth and shook him. But he held back, for it would do no good to use force. He took in a long breath to calm his anger.

"Then do your job," Seth demanded. "I'll take care of what I, as a husband, know I must do."

✿

James Bonnecker lumbered up the steep limestone slopes that led from the beach. He paused to catch his breath and glanced back at the waves that brushed over the shore. For once in his life, or perhaps twice, Bonnecker decided to do something meritorious. What he had seen with his own eyes, heard with his own ears, had set his teeth on edge. Leading the pirate's life, he had seen much in his day. But this beat all. He tried, but he could not sit idle and do nothing. Was there not a code of chivalry left in England? Shouldn't a man, no matter how high or low he may be, defend the helpless? And wasn't it wicked to take blood money?

When he reached the top of the precipice, he glanced back to the inlets along the coast. The sea mirrored a dark blue sky. A balmy wind blew heavy with the scent of salt.

In order to keep the stiff breeze from blowing it off his head, Bonnecker squashed down his ragged tricorn hat and crossed the road. He went up a grassy hill pocked with young trees. A footpath through the woods led to the other side and was a shortcut to Henry Chase.

It'll be safer going this way, instead of walking in the wide open.

Yet with all his gathered bravery, Bonnecker could not keep his eyes from widening at the slightest sound. A covey of quail flew up before him. His heart skipped a beat and he leaned his back against the trunk of a tree to gather his tremulous nerves.

Steady there, mate. You've faced foes at sea, and you let a dumb batch of birds scare the living daylights out of ye? Gather your courage, man. Don't be squeamish.

He took a deep breath and moved on. His eyes darted here and there, hoping no one had followed him. He passed the place where they had found Hetty Shanks. A cold chill ran straight up his spine. Aye, it was the place, for someone had painted a cross on the tree to ward off evil and make Hetty rest quiet. Bonnecker made the sign of the cross over his chest and strode on.

A few miles more and he turned at a bend in the path where Henry Chase would be on the other side of the hill through the trees. The land opened up before him, misty, and forlorn. He left the brooding woods and hurried into an open plain of grazing land.

Plowing his way through a herd of sheep, he crossed the field and headed toward the house. Ewes and tups crisscrossed in front of him, bleating and leaping as he shooed them away. Once he reached the door, Bonnecker pounded on it and waited for someone to open up.

☙

The family sat together in the sitting room. A fire simmered in the hearth and set the room aglow. Lady Anna, on the settee with Jane wrapped in her arms, stared at it in silence. Sir Henry smoked his clay pipe. Thomas sat Indian-style upon the floor and read aloud from a book of poems his sister had given him on his birthday. They spoke of pirates and treasure, adventure and heroism. The words reinforced in Seth his desire to search for Juleah. He would have left hours ago if it had not been for Lady Anna's plea that he linger with them.

Michael Bray, in an armchair near his wife, propped his boots up on the fireplace grill. Caroline sat in the chair to the right of him with Nathaniel asleep in her arms.

Growing impatient, Seth took a turn about the room, and paused to look out the window at the misty land outside. In his hand, he held a list—events in sequence, names, places, conclusions, and his plans to find Juleah.

Then, as his heart tore in his chest, he crumbled the paper in his hand. Was he mad for concluding she lived? If she were alive, Juleah would have come to him. She would not have left him to grieve and to bury a nameless person in her place. She would not hurt him in that way or hurt her family. He had to accept she was gone. But how?

He ran his hand over his face. A part of him fought against doubt once more, and he opened the paper and stared down at it. Footsteps out in the hall echoed. Sarah entered and approached Seth.

"There's a man says he wants to talk to you, sir."

He entered the kitchen. James Bonnecker sat at the table. It was a surprise indeed. Bonnecker shot up from his chair. His face was pale and his eyes wide.

"Are you hungry, Bonnecker?" Seth had no doubt food would loosen a famished tongue. "If you are, help yourself to what is left in that pot on the table and the bread as well."

"Aye, thank ye, sir. I'd welcome a home-cooked meal any day." Bonnecker grabbed a plate and spoon and scooped up what remained of the stew. His hand shook. "I guess you're wondering why I've come."

"I am."

"I heard about the fire at Ten Width. A shame that." Bonnecker loaded his mouth with food. "Then I heard someone at the tavern say you'd come here to Henry Chase."

Eager to know the purpose of Bonnecker's visit Seth drew up a chair. "I imagine people will be talking. But what of it?"

"Aye, people are dunces." Bonnecker tapped his foot on the floor.

"You're nervous," said Seth. "Is something the matter?"

"Food will ease it. Now, I need to go slow with what I got to tell ye. It'd be of a shock for me to blurt it out all at once."

Bonnecker swallowed and waved his spoon close to his face. "I may hang from the longest yardarm for what I'm about to tell ye, but I hope you'll find it in your heart to be kind to an old seadog like me. I've not many years left, and I'd like it if I could live 'em out to my appointed day. So, if they come after me, I expect ye to give me aid. But, I'll take whatever the will of God is."

Seth dropped his hand from his chin. "Get on with it, Bonnecker. I'm listening."

"I took money for the letter I brought to your lady. People pay other people lower than their class to deliver letters to folks, and I've no problem with that, as I'm sure you don't either, sir. But what haunts my brain is that the letter parted you and your lady."

"Why should you feel bad? It wasn't your fault."

" 'Cause I just does." Bonnecker wiped his mouth with the sleeve of his coat. "The man who gave me the letter said it was from a doctor, but I never did ask him who. I kind of assumed he were the doctor's servant, you see. He was dressed in that form of clothing, sir. Late last night some of my lads and I went to the tavern. We sat near the door, when who'd enter but some fellow named Captain Darden."

"How do you know it was him?" Seth was curious as to where this was leading. He had a gut feeling he was about to find out if his suspicions about Darden were correct.

"I heard the serving girl call him by name. 'Evening, Captain Darden,' said she. 'What ye be havin'?'"

It was a crude imitation of a female's voice Bonnecker made, but effective.

"When she came back with his ale, I heard her say how sorry she was that Ten Width caught fire and that the mistress died. His face turned fierce. Aye, he drank and drank with his head bowed. At times, he'd run his hand over his face and tremble like he'd been frightened by something. I thought maybe he were sick or grieving for Miss Juleah, since he loved her once, and I know that 'cause folks talk. Next three men came—rough-looking fellows. They sat with Captain Darden and he paid each of them money."

"Do you know who the men were?"

"Aye, they're seamen, I can tell you. I was making my way to the tavern, when I saw a coach pass by on the high road. That same coach was at the side of the tavern when I reached it. A woman was inside and there were those lads. Ah, now here's where it gets tricky."

Bonnecker paused to taste the ale, smacked his lips, and ran his sleeve over his mouth a second time. A chill ran through Seth when he mentioned the woman.

"I heard one man say, 'Mind yer own business, lads. Not a one of ye will go near the lady. Yer not to touch her, nor speak to her. If ye do, ye'll get the lash, every last scurvy dog of ye.' When I realized what kind of men they were, I got away as quick as jack and come to find ye."

Like a flood, understanding swept over Seth. It welled up inside and he knocked over the chair when he stood. "It was Juleah, my wife, wasn't it?"

"I can't say who the lady was for sure, sir," Bonnecker told him. "But it's some poor lass. I should've tried to rescue her, but they'd have beat me to a bloody pulp—maybe even killed me."

As if lightning had struck him, Seth reached over and pulled Bonnecker up by the shoulder. "Show me where they have gone."

"I can't, lad. The men took off, and the coach rolled away down the road and vanished in the gloom."

"Where to?"

"I ain't sure, but they were headed up the coast. If that lass has been taken against her will in the night, someone doesn't want folks seein' her traveling over land in the light o' day. And those lads, they were shady-looking fellows if I ever saw. And if it be your lady in that coach, then who was burned up in your house?"

Every muscle in Seth's body stiffened. A chill charged through him, and he let go of Bonnecker. For a moment, he allowed what the old pirate had told him to sink in. Struggling between the possibilities, he stared at the floor. Then he hurried from the house.

Outside he swung into the saddle of his horse and gathered up the reins. There was no time to tell anyone where he was headed to or why. With a fury, he dug his heels hard into the horse's sides. Jupiter reared up and shot off. Over the fields, Seth raced his steed, crossed a bridle track, and plunged the horse into the path through the forest, toward the limestone precipices above the sea.

30

*O*n the road that skirted the cliffs, Seth turned his horse full circle, uncertain of which way to go. He looked out at the sea. The wind blew through his hair and ruffled his clothes. The jingle of a harness preceded a horse that stampeded up the road toward him. He tried to move Jupiter on, but the horse refused, reared up, and beat the air with his hooves. The rider, upon reaching Seth, pulled hard on the reins. His mount stomped its hooves to a halt.

Bray slid off the saddle. "Bonnecker told me everything. You should not have left without me, without saying anything. I want to help you, Seth."

Seth dismounted and went toward Bray. "My wife is alive, Michael."

"Seth—"

"You saw her gown, how it was torn. You heard me out about the fire. Bonnecker's story makes sense of it now."

"The woman he claims to have seen could be anyone. It was cruel of Bonnecker to have told you such a tale. Do not listen to him. Come back."

Seth raked his fingers through his hair, his hand trembling under the strain. "Who it was I buried, I know not."

Bray put his hand on Seth's shoulder. "It was Juleah, my friend. I know. I took the ring from her finger."

"Did you see her face?"

Bray paused and frowned. "No."

"Neither of us did. The ring was stolen and the intruder put it on her own finger."

Bray looked back at Seth, grieved. "Please, come back with me."

"Not until I speak to Darden and shake the truth out of him." Seth took hold of Bray. "Where does he live? Tell me!"

Shocked, Bray stared at Seth. "Somewhere north of here, an old place called Crown Cove."

"I have to go there." Without hesitating, Seth turned to leave but found his way barred by Latterbuck, his deputy, and three of his officers armed with muskets.

"Seth Braxton," said the constable, "I arrest you in the name of the law for the unfortunate death of Juleah Fallowes, your wife. You are also charged this day for having Ten Width manor set alight."

Bray charged forward. "This is absurd!"

Latterbuck drew back his coat to reveal the flintlock pistol in his belt. His men took aim. "I suggest you not interfere, young sir. Step away and let me do my duty."

The words were too unbelievable to comprehend. Had he heard wrong? Had the roaring of the sea tumbled Latterbuck's words? With his will fixed upon one thing, Seth went forward for his horse. George put forth his arm and stopped him.

"No, Mr. Braxton," said Latterbuck with a grim frown. "You must return with me to the gaol in the village. From there you will stand before the king's magistrate."

"I am innocent and you know it," Seth recoiled.

"Hmm. Well, you'll have to convince him of your innocence."

Bray stepped between them, his face taut with emotion and his eyes ablaze. "Constable, you know I was with Seth when Ten Width burned. He and I were returning from London and saw the fire together as we came over the hill. He loved his wife and never would have done her harm. I demand you let him pass."

"I must deny your request," Latterbuck said. "I suspect Mr. Braxton hired a pair of ruffians to set Ten Width afire out of revenge. We caught one lingering in the woods near the estate."

"Where is he?" Seth demanded. "Bring him forth and let him accuse me to my face."

Latterbuck shrugged. "I cannot. He tried to escape and was shot dead."

Seth set his teeth. "Then you have no proof of anything."

Latterbuck's face reddened. Saliva foamed in the corners of his plump lips. "The will was not where you told me it would be. That's all the proof I needed to know you are behind this, robbing the rightful heir of a fortune."

"Impossible. Banes gave it to me and must have a copy."

"Well, he does not."

"He sent letters to America saying I had inherited."

"Do you have these letters?"

"I've witnesses. My sister knows what changes my grandfather made."

"What is in writing is more binding than the word of a woman."

Seth's face flushed with outrage. How he would convince the pig-headed constable to see otherwise, he had no idea. In

Latterbuck's eyes was self-exaltation, a glint of pride that he would bring a rebel to his knees.

He drew near until the foul odor that came from Latterbuck, of sweat, rum, and weeks without bathing, moved him back. "Can you be the kind of man so blinded by ambition and loathing for another that you would accuse me of murdering my wife, the woman I loved with every breath of my body?"

"I've no sympathy for you."

"I am not asking for your sympathy, just reason."

"You've brought this on yourself. Did you think I'd not look upon you with some disregard? You are a rebel, an insur-rectionist, a blasphemer against God and king, who came here claiming to have inherited his loyalist grandfather's estate. You wed an Englishwoman and tainted her with your American ideals. You learned of the true inheritor and worked out a way of destroying that inheritance. This story of your sister's child, I've no doubt that too was part of your plan. Perhaps you had something to do with Hetty Shanks, too?"

Outraged, Seth trembled. "How far will you go?"

"It is my duty as an officer of the king to take you into cus-tody. If you are innocent, as you claim to be, produce the truth. There are those among us who believe otherwise."

Latterbuck made a slight gesture with his hand and his offi-cers stepped forward. At first, Seth faced them without a word more. He glanced at Bray, whose face was desperate with what to do.

"You must listen to Seth," Bray said, giving rein to fury.

"He'll have his day to speak, young sir. Give way, or I'll have you arrested for obstructing my duty," Latterbuck warned.

"My wife is alive," Seth said, while he stared hard at Latterbuck. "Ask James Bonnecker. He'll tell you Edward Darden is behind this."

Latterbuck looked at Seth with mock pity. "It seems regret has caused you to go mad. Your wife is gone, buried in the churchyard. Grieve for yourself, Mr. Braxton, for no doubt you shall die a traitor's death after all."

If wisdom could have ruled Seth, he would have resigned to the constable and his officers with willingness and confidence. Yet a stronger, a more aggressive will surged within when the reality of what he was about to face, and how it would delay his chances, overtook him. Inside his belt was his pistol. His horse was out of reach, the bridle being held by one of Latterbuck's men. Behind him roared the sea. Its dark depths swelled with the wind. The precipice hung thirty feet above Bideford Bay and was covered in grass. There was nothing there to hinder, no trees or rocks in the way.

With a quick jerk of his head, Seth glanced behind him and measured the steps he needed to take. He stood back and held his arms out in resignation.

The deputies rushed forward. They caught him about the arms.

He twisted and turned. He clenched his teeth and rallied his strength. Breathing hard, he looked up through the strands of hair that fell over his eyes. He caught sight of Michael Bray. One deputy had his musket pointed at his chest to hold him back from aiding Seth.

Swinging his body to the left, he broke free, turned, and rushed to the edge of the cliff. He jumped out away from the perilous crag, fell, and plunged into the cold sea.

31

Many waters cannot quench love; neither can the floods drown it.

—Song of Solomon 8:7

*M*oonlight poured through leaded glass, alighting on Juleah's face. Her eyes moved beneath translucent lids, and she opened them. Startled to see she lay in a stranger's room, in a bed she did not know, her breath caught. Surrounding her were dingy white, plastered walls, crisscrossed with hair-thin cracks like the threads of a spider's web. Above her, a canopy of olive-green damask stretched across the bedposts. Cream-colored curtains fell along the sides of each stilt.

Warm beneath the down quilt, her bare legs gathered the softness of the sheets. She drew them up against her as a sudden surge of fear swept through her mind. Why had she not awakened in her room at Ten Width? Where was she?

"Seth?" she whispered. "Where are you?"

She put out her hand and wanted him to take it. She glanced around the room and searched for him. Then she remembered. He had gone to London. Perhaps that explained things. Had he sent for her? Did she now lie in a carriage inn along the Thames Road? Or was this a room in Caroline's house?

Her head hurt and she turned to raise herself up. Pain shot through her temples. A flood of dizziness washed over her.

She tried again, slipped her legs over the side of the bed, and touched the planks of the floor with her bare feet. The wood felt cold against her toes and heels.

She made her way to the window. Her hair hung about her face and neck, and she pushed it away from her eyes. The window stood open. She drew in a deep breath, leaned against the sill, and felt the warm breeze caress her face and throat. She gazed out at rolling fields turned sapphire in the moonlight. Lines of trees grouped from hill to hill, and a pond glimmered in the evening haze as still as a looking glass.

Juleah turned when she heard the door swing open. In stepped a woman she did not know. She wore a gray homespun frock, cut high above the bosom. From the sleeves poked a row of plain ruffles, framing delicate ivory hands with closely cut nails. The woman's hair was orange as a fox's fur, as were her lashes and brows.

"Who are you, and where am I?" Juleah said. "Where is my maid?"

The woman set on the bedside table a spoon and an amber bottle with a brown cork stopper. "There is nothing to worry about. You're safe and here to rest. Now, come lie back down."

"Where is my husband?"

"Away."

Juleah put her hand over her eyes and a flash of memory came forward. She rubbed her temples and hoped it would relieve the throbbing. "I remember now." Her eyes widened. "A fire!"

The woman set her hand upon Juleah's shoulder. "I know nothing about that. You might have dreamt it. Your gentleman brought you here and I'm to look after you." She guided Juleah back to bed. "Now, try to please him by doing everything the doctor prescribed. Understand?"

The woman yanked the cork from the bottle and poured amber liquid into the silver spoon. She set it at Juleah's lips, and Juleah swallowed. It tasted bittersweet, thick like honey, and soothing as it slid down her throat.

"Where is Claire?"

"I do not know her. Whoever she is, she isn't here."

"Claire is my maid. You must send for her."

"I will tell your gentleman. For now, you have me to look after you."

"By what name shall I call you?" Juleah began to feel sleepy again.

"Judith Dirk." She tucked in the bedclothes. "Born and raised in Kincardine O'Neal in merry Scotland."

Juleah glanced about the room. "This is not my room. In whose house am I?"

"Why you're in your gentleman's house. Don't you remember?"

A flood of uncertainty overwhelmed Juleah. Her head ached so bad that the depth of Judith Dirk's reply did not sink in. "I am at Ten Width." Then she closed her eyes and fell asleep.

Later, when she woke, a bell counted out the hour from a clock on the mantel. She looked over to see Judith Dirk laying out clothes. On a table sat a glowing candle in a brass stick.

Judith Dirk turned her head and smiled over at Juleah. "Are ye hungry? You should eat something before we leave, for there's no telling what kind of food we'll be offered on *The Raven*."

"*The Raven*?" Juleah's voice barely reached above a whisper.

Judith Dirk slipped a hanger out from the shoulders of a gown. "A fine ship from what I'm told. Your gentleman made plans for us to sail in her."

Juleah put her hand up to her forehead. "I do not understand. I need to see him."

"He's not at home."

"When will he be back?"

"I'm not sure."

Juleah struggled to rise. "I want to see him. Oh, why does my head go round?"

"If you don't lie still, you'll sicken." Judith Dirk spoke with arresting firmness and pressed her hands on Juleah's shoulders to make her lay back down.

Juleah shoved away. She stood and rushed to the door. "Seth! Seth!" She jerked and rattled the handle. A moment and she heard footsteps and relaxed. Seth was coming. The door opened, and there stood the tall figure of a man in the darkness of the hall. She gazed up at him, unable to make out his face. Her knees buckled. She felt his arms go around her, lift her, and carry her across the room to the bed.

Having no will to fight it, Juleah sank lower, deeper into unwanted sleep, where neither dreams nor nightmares invaded.

32

$\mathscr{S}$eth shot down into the chilly depths. The strength of the tide pulled at him. He'd stay under for as long as he could, hoping Latterbuck and his men could not see him below. His lungs were about to explode, and he slowly released his breath. He swam toward the surface and battled the hold of the sea.

Close to the shore, blank fog surrounded him. He groped with his hands until they touched stony edges and he pulled close to them. He glanced up from his rocky shelter to see the dark and silent sky frowning above him. Within the breaks, a myriad of stars stood out. High in the heavens the moon broke free from the embrace of clouds.

Farther down the beach, he spotted the restless sparkle of lanterns. Latterbuck's men were searching for him. Their voices were faint, but Seth could tell they were weary of their quest.

"Nothing's here," he heard one shout. "We'll find a body in a day or two."

They believed he was dead, drowned in the sea, crushed against harsh rocks, a man so grief-stricken that he took his own life. He was glad for it, at least for now, at least until he found Juleah. What would Latterbuck say to him then?

He hoped nothing hard had befallen Michael Bray. It grieved Seth to think Bray might believe he had died and that he would tell his sister.

A moment passed and the searchers turned back. They gathered together like a troop of fireflies and mounted the stone steps that led to the land above the cliffs. He watched them move off until atop the hill their lanterns grew small and disappeared into the darkness.

Those who searched for him were gone, save one man, who without the aid of a lantern climbed down the rocky slope. Moonlight grew strong and Seth watched him walk along the beach. The man paused and looked around. A moment later, he moved into the shadow of the cliff face where Seth could no longer see him. A twig snapped, and a bird started from its nighttime perch. It mounted the wind and merged into the deep indigo heavens. Seth's heart pounded against his chest and his breath came in short, silent gasps.

He slipped from the huddle of rocks and all but stumbled into the man outside it. He grabbed him, threw him back, and raised his fists to strike.

"Thank a merciful God." The man grabbed Seth by the shoulders.

When he saw Bray's face in the moonlight, he lowered his fist. "Michael."

"Latterbuck thinks you're dead, and I feared it were so. Are you hurt?"

"Cold. You must think I am out of my mind for what I did."

"Aye, I do, and I could strike you down for it. You could have been killed."

"I couldn't let them take me, not when I know my wife is in danger. I thank God the sea here was deep, though it was not without a struggle for my life."

Bray slipped off his coat, threw it over Seth's shoulders. "They've been searching for your body. Be relieved they are gone now."

Seth glanced up at the cliffs above. "You are certain?"

Bray nodded. "Yes, follow me. I know these cliffs as well as my own face, having climbed them as a boy."

Exhausted, cold, and silent, Seth followed Bray up the slopes toward the heights above. With care, they set their feet upon slippery stones carved into a steep staircase centuries ago by fishermen. It was indeed an age-old path, covered in green lichen, its wanderings capricious with loose and crumbling stone, banked by the walled fortresses of the cliffs.

Closer to the top they came to a place where trees and shrubs crowned the precipice. Seth looked back to realize the height to which they climbed.

Bray put his hand over Seth's shoulder. "We must hurry back to Henry Chase. Sir Henry and Lady Anna will help."

Seth took Bray by the sleeve. "I do not want to cause Sir Henry and his lady any more problems."

"Then where will you go? I can take you to London, hide you."

"No, I must go to Crown Cove. I'll find Juleah there."

"Someone at the tavern might know the way. I have had time to think, and because you are adamant that Juleah is alive, I now believe it may be possible. I'm coming with you."

They set off into the darkness and took the road less traveled. Seth hung back a ways from Bray's horse if by chance he were stopped by Latterbuck's men. But no one was in sight.

The tavern sat at the bottom of the hill. Lights glimmered in the windows. A lantern swung on an iron staff outside the door. They moved their horses to the back, hidden from view. Bray went to go inside to make inquiries, but was stopped when Pen stepped out through the back door. She emptied her bucket of wash water into the grass and glanced up.

"Pen," whispered Bray. "It is I, Michael Bray, and a companion. We need to talk to you."

With startled eyes, she stared at him through the gloom. Cautioning her to raise no alarm, Bray hurried to her, while Seth remained atop his horse.

"Captain Bray," she said in a hushed voice. "Why you about scared the life out of me, sir. Who's the gentleman with you?"

"A friend, Pen. Now, you must listen. It is important. We need your help."

"I'll try. I'm muddled tonight, Captain Bray. Have you heard the news? Folks are sayin' the squire's dead."

Bray glanced at Seth, then back at Pen. "No doubt the news spread fast, since you know already."

"They say he jumped into the sea. His heart must've been so heavy it drove him to it. We should pray for his soul, sir."

When the flame from her lantern flared, she recognized Seth and she rushed forward with a sighing breath. "Mr. Braxton!"

Seth leaned down to her. "You mustn't tell anyone, Pen. Understand?"

Though she looked bewildered, she nodded and gazed at him with doe-like eyes. "I think so."

"You mustn't let anyone know you saw me, especially the constable."

"Yes, sir." She put her lantern down and drew closer.

"You will not betray us, will you, Pen?"

"I'll not breathe a word. What must I do?"

"I'm bound for Crown Cove. Do you know the way?"

"Aye, sir. Crown Cove is eight miles north of here. You must follow the main highway for several miles until it comes to a crossroad. A cage hangs from a gibbet. It's a startling sight you can't miss. From there, head west across the moors. Crown Cove is a large old house with four chimneys. You'll see it down in a vale. You'll know the hill above it by a great heap of stones set atop."

"You have my thanks," Seth said.

Pen bit her lower lip. "Edward Darden was here, if that matters. He was out of sorts, nervous."

"Thank you, Pen."

"I'll be your eyes and ears, sirs. But how will I get word to you if I learn anything?"

"You'll see me here, Pen." Michael Bray walked back to his horse and mounted. From his pocket, he handed her a gold piece. "Your information and silence is well worth the cost."

She moved back in refusal. "Nay, sir. I'll not take your money. Now hurry in case the constable and his men come here."

They moved off into the darkness, Seth took hold of the horse's bridle and stopped Bray.

"You mustn't come with me. I don't want you implicated in anything. Your first duty is to your wife, not me."

Bray looked over at Seth, grieved. "As much as I want to argue with you, I find I cannot. And though it makes me feel a coward, I'll do as you've said. Send me word when you find what you are searching for."

"I swear it. Take care of my sister."

"God go with you, my brother."

Inflamed with urgency, Seth turned his horse out onto the moonlit highway and galloped off into the fog-cloaked darkness.

33

*L*ater that night, when the ship's bells set the hour, Juleah woke with a shudder in a narrow cot, huddled under a blanket that smelled of sea air. Why could she not fully wake? Why could she not clearly think? Again her eyes closed, and she lay in quiet fear.

Overhead, footsteps and timbers creaked. The sounds frightened her, and she wanted Seth with a heart that ached. Tears slipped from her eyes onto her cheeks, and a prayer whispered from her lips. Why was she alone? She must be ill, perhaps with a fever, or something stronger, and it had made her confused by way of its force. She supposed it would pass in a day or two. Then she would be well again. There was no need to worry or fear. Seth would take care of her. Soon he'd walk into the room, sit with her, and explain everything.

Thirsty, she skimmed her tongue over dry lips. Her stomach twisted with hunger. She turned to see a table on the other side of the room. Upon it sat a bottle of wine, a pewter plate, a bowl of oranges, and an amber bottle. Orange peels lay on the plate, and she could smell their scent. She grew ravenous for food and drink.

The room moved and shifted to one side, then back again. She stood and groped her way to the door. It had a metal latch, and when she tugged at it, it would not budge.

Realizing the room she was in was no bedchamber at all, but a ship's cabin, a rise of dizziness swelled in her head. She reached for the bedpost, wrapped her arms around it, and held on.

Her eyes caught sight of that amber bottle again. Sunlight streamed through the cabin window and shone upon it like tiny stars. Whatever the content, it was her saboteur. She moved toward it, snatched it up in her hand, wiggled the cork loose from the lip, held it to her nose, and sniffed. She recalled the odor, for her mother had a bottle set aside in a cabinet at home.

A sleeping draught made from the Gaelic poppy lus a' chadail, the herb of slumber. Who would do this to me?

Her hand closed in a tight fist around the bottle. She crossed the room to the window and shoved it open. The sea wind hit her face and blew back her hair. She threw the bottle into the waves. She leaned from the window and watched it sink into the inky depths. From the leaded casement, she gazed out at the vast expanse of ocean. The landless horizon and the white foam churned from the drive of the ship. Despair gripped her, and a sob slipped from between her lips.

Shaking free of the stupor brought on by the opiate, she gripped the sides of the window and tried to think. Her hands tensed and shook as she tightened her hold. Slowly her memory returned.

Judith Dirk, that mysterious woman, no doubt administered the potion. Then she remembered she was told they were to go on a voyage—aboard a ship called *The Raven*. The man at the door—his face was not clear, but she wanted to believe it was Seth. His voice—no it was different and unmistakably English. He claimed to love her, said he had saved her from the ravages of the fire.

Darden. It had to be.

Her mind drifted back to the glare of a candle, to the house cat curled around the edge of the curtain. She had sighed and shaken her head with relief. The clock on her mantle chimed—a noise, a whisper. Footsteps.

She remembered she had picked up her candle, slipped out her door into the hall, and gone down the staircase. She had reached the third stair and out from the gloom two figures moved forward. Her hand froze around the silver stem. Her throat tightened—she could not call out.

Juleah, a voice had spoken to her through the shadows.

At the foot of the staircase stood Darden and his mother. A chill charged through her. The horrid words of the old squire's widow came ringing back. "Take the ring off her finger. It should've been mine. To think, that usurper thought he had a right to give her Benjamin's treasures."

He had said it mattered not, for he had found what he had come for. Benjamin's will was all he wanted. She watched him turn and toss it into the fire. Benjamin's widow snatched at Juleah's hand. In a struggle, the ring was taken from her, pulled with such force that her skin bruised. The candle had been knocked from her hand. The awful fire spread, and the world went black.

She had been carried off against her will. Panic rose anew and her breath snatched in her throat. She gazed out at the wanton sea and knew there was no telling how far from Seth she was, where they were taking her, or if she would ever see him again.

"Oh, my love!" she said, tears slipping from her eyes.

Waves tossed and beckoned. With her heart drumming, Juleah hauled herself up. Wind pushed against her, as if to say go back, that there was hope yet. Her hair blew about her and mizzle from the sea covered her face. She prayed, and as she whispered to heaven, something within her rose—strength of will—her love for Seth.

Tightening her grip, she climbed back down, shut the window, and fixed the latch. A chest lay near the bed. She hurried over to it, opened the lid, and stood back. These were not her clothes. She went on her knees, rummaged through frocks and linen petticoats. At the bottom, she found an iron ring of keys. Perhaps one would open the lock.

At first, she hesitated, unsure if opening it were wise. But what choice did she have? She laid her ear against the door and listened. A faint suggestion of movement, then a dull thud followed the creaking of the ship's timbers. She placed one key after another in the keyhole, until a faint click freed the latch and she opened the door. Before her, a companion ladder led up to the main deck. Spears of sunlight fell between the slats from above. She slipped out and pressed her back against the wall. Cautious, she approached the steps and glanced up at a clear azure sky through the riggings in the sails.

A slow breath slipped from her mouth as she set her hand on the stair rail. She climbed the steps and came out on deck, in the full glare of the sun. The breeze rushed through her unbound hair, and her gown of pale blue muslin wrapped about her frame.

All eyes nearby turned and men halted in their work. Silence fell, and they drew together to stare. The crew was a fearsome knot of seamen; some barrel-chested, others thin as bowsprits. Most dragged off their caps to her and nodded.

"I wish to speak to the captain," Juleah said to the man nearest her. Meeting the man's eyes, she raised her face. "Please take me to him."

He stepped forward. She stared at him, and he took off his tricorn hat, swept it in front of his chest, and bowed low. She was taken aback by his pirate-like appearance, the gold rings that sparkled through sagging earlobes. A pair of bucket-top boots covered his thick legs, and a red silk scarf surrounded his throat. His hair hung long about his shoulders. It was the blackest she had ever beheld, streaked gray and adorned with thin braids. His face held an expression of courtesy, though lined and bronzed from the sun and salt air.

"At your service." His dark eyes looked into her face and his right brow arched.

Juleah forced fear down. "I've been taken aboard your ship against my will. If you are a God-fearing man and a loyal subject to His Majesty and his laws, you will turn your vessel around and return me to England."

A round of laughter rippled through the crew, which caused Juleah to clutch the fabric of her dress.

"I can't do that," he said. "We're far out to sea. You can disembark with your servant when we reach land."

"Servant?" Juleah stepped forward. "She's a fraud. She drugged me." Still the effects of the potion were with her. She raised a trembling hand to her face. Then she stamped her foot. "I demand you return me home."

The captain held out his hand. "Let us discuss this in my cabin, not in front of my crew." Some of his men shifted on their feet and murmured. Their leader threw a fierce look over his shoulder at them. "To work you scurvy dogs. Give the lady leave. Away, I say! Or I'll have your ogling eyes plucked out and fed to the gulls."

Juleah disliked this man and his threatening manner, but she was glad to hear his bold threats, for it told her he would protect her. The sailors turned away, except for one. His eyes met Juleah's. He looked like he wanted to come to her aid. With a brief smile, he nodded to her and turned back to the ropes he coiled.

Inside his quarters, the captain bid Juleah be seated at the table. He poured her a glass of Madeira and offered it to her. She did not accept, but he took a swallow. Its heat colored his cheeks. After another taste, he set the glass on the table, over which a brass lamp swayed to the gentle heave of the ship.

"Be at ease," he said. "No one shall harm you aboard my ship."

"I thank you for that, Captain . . ."

"Roche."

"Well, Captain Roche. Are you willing to help me?"

He covered his heart with his hand. "As I'm a loyal subject of the king, and a God-fearin' man, I'll do my duty."

Juleah looked at him with a plea. "Then you must see me safely home."

"I would, if we were closer to it."

Her eyes flashed. "What difference should the distance make, sir?"

"It makes all the difference in the world, ma'am. For one, we wouldn't have enough provisions to last the voyage. Secondly, America's shores will be in our sights soon enough with this wind."

"I do not wish to go there."

"Let Mistress Dirk explain. Perhaps you'll change your mind."

"Are you a pirate, sir, that you'd carry me off like this?"

"*Pirate* is too harsh a word, ma'am."

"How else should I think of you?"

Roche's face stiffened. "You should think of me as the captain of this fair vessel. Stay on my good side, and all will go well. Call me a pirate again, and I may not be apt to help you at all."

Juleah set her mouth and heaved a breath. "I apologize, Captain Roche. I do not understand what has happened and why I am here."

"You must ask the fair Judith." Roche poured another glass of wine and drank it down.

A rap fell upon the door and it drifted open. Judith Dirk hesitated at the threshold, until the seaman who had accompanied her moved her inside.

Now Juleah viewed her with a clearer mind. Streaks of gold ran through Judith Dirk's red tresses, her skin pale and freckled, and her eyes large and of a golden-brown. She stared back at Juleah with an expression that swayed between anger and trepidation.

"Mistress," Judith cooed like a dove. "You're feeling better and are up and about. Aye, 'tis 'bout time, and ye have met our bonny Captain Roche."

Juleah stepped swiftly up to her. "Stop your pretense. Why am I aboard this ship? Why did I find a bottle of sleeping draught on the table? Why was I locked in?"

Judith Dirk pinched her brows. "The medicine was to help you sleep. I kept the door locked for your safety. Ye wouldn't want any wayward sailor getting any ideas, now would you? And it was your good gentleman who booked us passage. Once his business is concluded in England, he intends to join you. He thought it'd do you good."

Juleah slapped her palm down on the table. "You are lying."

Judith Dirk shrugged. "Now why would I do that? What could I gain?"

"Give someone enough money," Juleah said, "and they'll do anything."

Mistress Dirk threw Roche a quick glance and shook her head. "She's not in her right mind, Captain Roche."

Roche also shrugged.

"I am in my right mind, especially now that I got rid of the potion you were giving me," Juleah said.

Judith wiggled her mouth. "You mean medicine, miss."

Juleah shook her head. "Lies. I remember the fire at Ten Width, and that Edward Darden and his mother were there. She took my ring. She forced it from my hand. And in the struggle, I dropped a candle."

"I don't know anything about that." Judith set her mouth and looked away with her eyes closed. She muttered under her breath and glanced over at Captain Roche. "I heard this tale before."

Juleah took an abrupt step closer. "You must know something."

Judith stood back with a frown. "Why? I'm a servant."

"Then explain to me when I first woke, why I was in a strange house."

"The reason you were set up in different lodgings was never explained to me. I suppose it was due to the fire you speak of."

"I remember seeing Darden there. Why? He should've been the last person to see me after what happened."

Judith jerked her head upward. "I do not know this man. You may have dreamed you saw him. There was never a man by that name that came to see you."

Juleah stared back at Judith unconvinced and with a look that caused her to lose her beguiling expression.

"I do not believe you."

"Here's a letter from your gentleman. It was left to give to you when you were feeling better. I suppose this is the right time."

Juleah hurried around the table, snatched it from the woman's hand, and tore it open. Her heart thumped to see Seth's handwriting. Words of love and affection penned out on the page could only be his, for he said things only the two of them knew. It was a brief missive, but he told her he had dreams of building their lives together back in Virginia, of raising horses, and having children together. It was dated the day he left for London.

She dropped her hand and tears fell from her eyes. With a heavy sigh, she pushed them aside, and folded the letter.

Judith put her arm around Juleah. "There, now all shall be well."

"He would not send me on without him."

"He said it was urgent, he had business to attend to, that he needed to get you away from a dangerous man."

"Darden," Juleah whispered.

"Maybe so."

Juleah's heart lurched within. "What am I to do when we reach land, Judith Dirk?"

"We'll travel by coach to Virginia. Now won't that be fine for you to get his house in order before he arrives?"

Juleah stood still and silent. She shrugged out of Judith Dirk's arm and stepped away. She hurried out, back to the cabin. She shut the door and threw herself across the cot. Even if Seth had sent her on this journey, he had not explained it enough and to be without him was unbearable.

The Raven gave a sharp pitch, and she grabbed the side of the cot. The light in the cabin faded to gray, as the sky filled with heavy, windswept clouds. With a sinking heart she listened to the timbers moan. She closed her eyes and kept them shut.

You are not alone. You are not forsaken. When she heard the words spoken into her heart, she drifted toward sleep, comforted, as if angels soothed her brow.

34

$\mathcal{I}$t was exactly as Pen said. Seth reached the crossroad, where an iron gibbet stood. Suspended by a chain hung an iron cage. Shrouded in a moonlit darkness, it swung and squeaked in the wind. The full moon hovered above it, high, golden, and brilliant as a watchman's torch. Through its light, Seth stared at the decomposing body of a highwayman. Whomever he had been, an awful end was his reward for robbery.

They hanged him, coated his body in tar and placed it in the body-shaped cage made especially for him. Seth could tell the corpse had been there several months and knew it would remain in public view for at least a year, until there was nothing left to see. Then his bones would be scattered. It was a fearful thing for a man, to think he'd have no proper resting place, that his spirit would wander the moors in a purgatory of agony for ages to come.

So it was believed among the common folk of that land. But as for Seth, the man was no longer there. He'd gone on to stand before a merciful God, finally released from the troubles of an earthly life. But what had pushed the man to rob others? Was it a hungry brood of children, or an ailing wife? Whatever it was, compassion filled Seth and he uttered a prayer while staring at the lifeless, tattered remains of a face.

The hollow eye sockets stared back in horror, and the mouth gaped in a frozen scream of penance. The highwayman's clothes, shredded and torn, stained and rotten along with flesh, rippled in the breeze. Birds had feasted, and even now in the dark under grim moonlight, a crow landed on the post, pecked and plunged its beak through the iron slates until it pulled out a strand of bloodless, gray flesh.

What Seth's eyes beheld caused a wave of sickness to rush through his belly. Jupiter flared his nostrils and reared at the sight. Seth calmed him with a pat of his hand, and with a gentle nudge of his knees he moved on.

Seth passed under the gibbet and remembered he was now considered a lawbreaker. If he could not solve the mysteries that surrounded his life, he wondered if he would meet a similar fate if captured.

He lifted his eyes to the stars and murmured, "Have mercy upon me, O God."

Exhaustion overwhelmed him, and a mile later he dismounted and drew Jupiter to the side of the road. There he found a shallow stream. From it he splashed water over his face and neck, and then drank. He remounted and galloped along the high road surrounded by endless fields and woodlands.

Once he reached a hillside thick with knee-deep meadow grass, he reined in atop it and gazed into a valley blanketed with fog. From there, he could see the ancient house of Crown Cove bathed in moonlight, with one window that shimmered with the light of candles from within.

Seth drew closer. His heart pounded. Perhaps Juleah slept even now in that upper room, beyond that mullioned window facing east. Ivy clambered up the walls, spilled over deep window-sills, and concealed the stones beneath with glimmering green.

Again, he reined in his horse and paused to catch his breath and to think. A moment later, he slid off the saddle and walked to the front door. Vague ochre light from a lantern beside it fell over his hand as he pushed it in. A flood of light came from a room at the far end of the hallway. A young woman's laughter followed a man's, but it was not Juleah's.

"You have been a bachelor for too long, Edward," he heard her say. "You need a woman to guide your house. Where is your mother, by the way?"

"She has quit England for the south of Spain," Seth heard Darden reply.

"Whatever for?"

"The warmer weather is better for her health."

"I hear southern Spain has sun all year round. I imagine it would be ideal for one's health. I wish your dear mama well, Edward. Will she be returning soon?"

"No. This is a permanent arrangement."

Seth's upper lip twitched. How he despised the sound of Darden's voice—so calm, so self-assured.

With a heavy heart, he moved closer to the doorway, and when he stepped inside the room to make his presence known, Darden leapt from his chair with an oath. The woman seated beside him raised her hand to her throat, where a pearl dangled from a gold chain.

"You leave your door unbolted?" Seth asked.

Darden set his teeth. "Braxton."

"Is he a highwayman?" the woman asked. "He shan't have my jewels. You must protect me, Edward." Seth glanced at her. Excitement and lust glowed in her eyes. She was tall and lean, with a head of lush brown curls. Bright vermilion blotches covered her cheeks, and rice powder dusted her face. A tiny black patch inched near the left corner of her painted mouth. The rich burgundy gown she wore hung low about her bosom and shoulders. He had no doubt of what kind of woman Darden entertained.

"Are those the clothes of a highwayman, sir?" She laughed at him and scanned his person with her wanton eyes. "They are torn, muddied, and stained, giving you the look of a brigand. I had imagined highwaymen dress more finely and masked."

Seth bowed. "I am no highwayman, ma'am."

"I do not believe it," she said. "You will have to get past Captain Darden to take this pearl from my throat."

Darden shot her a stern glare. "Be quiet, Fanny!"

She threw her head back and laughed. "Shall you have this man ravish me, Edward?"

Seth fixed his eyes in reproof on her fine blue ones. "Be assured, I do not seek worldly riches or *you*."

Flushed with insult, Darden stepped forward. His eyes narrowed and his mouth twisted. "How dare you walk into my house unannounced. What is the meaning of this?"

"I've come for my wife," Seth told him. "Where is she?"

Darden stared back at Seth a moment and laughed. "Are you mad? She's not here, but buried in the churchyard."

The desire to take Darden by the throat and shake the truth out of him surged through Seth, but he held back his hand. "She's alive and was seen with you in your coach after Ten Width was set afire."

Darden turned to his guest. "It appears Mr. Braxton has played the fool. It is commonly known Yankees possess a gullible nature."

"Fools are blind to the truth," Seth exclaimed.

"It was not Juleah anyone saw. The woman in the coach was Miss Lovelace here. I do not have to answer to you, Braxton." Darden put his hands on the table and glared at Seth with an insolence that was intolerable.

Miss Lovelace's eyes pooled with sympathy. "It is true that I sit and wait, while he has his ale, Mr. Braxton. The tavern is hardly a place for a woman to take her leisure. I can assure you, your wife is not here, nor has she ever been inside Edward's coach. That is a privilege left to me."

For a moment, doubt flooded Seth and his heart sank to the soles of his feet. Determined, he shook it off and turned out the door.

Darden spread his hands outward. "Search every room and you'll not find her."

Seth glanced back over his shoulder. Unconcerned and bored, Darden sat back down and lifted his glass. "I could shoot you for coming into my house the way you did, and the law would say nothing. A man has that right. So, I suggest you leave before I take your life."

Miss Lovelace took a gentle but desperate hold of Darden's arm. "Let him go, Edward. Obviously, he has not accepted his wife's death. Let him look, and when he has not found her, he shall be forced to accept the truth that she is dead and gone."

Darden set his glass down. "She's right, Braxton. It may be the only way to be rid of you. Since I am a gentleman and we are no longer at war with one another, I'll concede to her request."

Seth stepped forward and faced his enemy. "Ah, but you are wrong. We are at war, you and I."

Darden huffed and called for his manservant. "Escort the squire of Ten Width through the house, Habbinger."

Habbinger looked confused. "May I ask why, sir?"

"He's in search of a ghost. Can you handle that?"

With a nod, Habbinger picked up a candle and led Seth upstairs. Seth called Juleah's name. He stood in the gloom and waited to hear her answer, but no reply came. From room to room, he searched for her. He found two bedchambers lit by candles in sconces. The beds were made, the rooms plain. A decorative tower graced the west wing, and when Seth climbed the winding stairs and pushed open an oaken door, he found a void space. Mice stirred and scurried off upon his sudden presence.

The cellar proved no different from the rest of the house. Dusty wine bottles sat in racks covered in cobwebs. A few ale casks sat on the dirt floor among a few old pieces of discarded furniture. The air within smelled of age, musty and damp, and cold as a tomb.

"There's no one here," said Habbinger.

Seth did not like the tone of the servant's voice, for it smacked of mockery. "You don't remember seeing any woman other than the one your master is presently entertaining?"

"No," he replied. "Besides, the master is rarely at home. He's been away in London for several weeks with Miss Lovelace. There's been no one here save for myself. If you don't mind me saying so, the house has been as quiet as a grave."

Frowning at his words, Seth turned away and stood in the dark. He felt alone and defeated and wondered what he had done. His belief that Juleah lived slipped away. He had searched Crown Cove from top to bottom and there was no sign of her. Bonnecker's information was mere words and speculation. The old seadog could not identify the woman in the coach.

Seth's love for Juleah, and the unwillingness to let her go, had caused him to run from the king's law and play the fool in front of his nemesis. For all his efforts, he found a courtesan at Crown Cove, who claimed to be the woman in Darden's coach while he paused at the tavern. Grief rose anew within his heart, pulsed through him like a raging current, and swept away all his hopes.

"You have my apology," he said, facing Darden alone in the hall.

Darden smiled from one corner of his mouth. "Perhaps you should return to that rebellious country of yours and lick your wounds."

With his teeth clenched, Seth strode out into the misty night. His heart ached and his soul reached for solace as he rode off at a slow pace. He uttered the words out loud to accept what he wanted to deny.

"She is gone."

35

*O*nce more, Seth reached the hilltop, then the gruesome gibbet. He rode past it with thunder in his heart, reached the precipice that loomed above the sea, reined in his horse, and stared out at the foamy tide that washed over the moonlit shore. Anguish weighed upon him and dragged him down in the saddle. The tranquil sea was peaceful no longer. Moonlight turned dull and grim, and the moors and cliffs appeared barren. Above him, the stars were no longer bright lights of heaven. They were swallowed by somber blackness dark as a tomb.

He turned the horse back to the road and paced him. His desire to leave Ten Width and return to Virginia was a certainty. But for the moment he needed a sanctuary, a hiding place, until he could steal away without Latterbuck nipping at his heels.

He entered his father-in-law's house, went up the stairs toward an unused room. He could not bear to return to Ten Width, to stay in the place he had shared with his wife, where he had held her in his arms and made love to her. Her scent would be on the pillow, the sense of her would permeate every inch of the room.

Quietly he shut the door behind him. Weary in body and mind, he slumped into the armchair drawn before a cold and blackened hearth and shut his eyes. Juleah was gone, and he was left behind to bear the years without her. *How long, Lord? How long?*

He covered his face with his hands. Then the passion of tears poured out of him until he slept. He would accept whatever plans the Almighty had for him and take whatever bend in the road he would be led to tread.

✐

The next morning, the din of galloping horses jolted him awake. He stood, strode to the window, and peered out. A coach and four rumbled down the drive.

The horses slowed and were brought to a standstill. A figure stepped down from the driver's perch, and then someone pounded with force upon the front door. Seth picked up his pistol and headed downstairs. The household stirred. Feet pattered over the floor above him.

A man dressed in a forest-green coat stood outside on the threshold. "Permit me, sir. Is Seth Braxton here? It is of the utmost importance."

Seth eyed the stranger with caution. "Who asks?"

"I'm Sir Charles Kenley's gentleman servant. Sir Charles and Lady Kenley sit within his coach and wish to speak to the squire."

Seth glanced at the coat of arms, of rearing steed and stag, mace and sword, upon the coach door. He hurried down the steps and approached the window. Sir Charles moved forward to reveal himself.

"We have come to warn you. Latterbuck is on his way here."

Seth ordered himself to be calm.

"He thinks I am dead, Sir Charles."

"Apparently not, lad. I was told Captain Darden came to see him this morning and informed Constable *Dunderhead* that you had barged into Crown Cove last night, raving mad, and insisted that you search his house for your late wife."

"Indeed it is true. I had to see for myself, Sir Charles. I found nothing for my pains. Why would Latterbuck intrude upon you?"

"My lady and I were on our way to visit, after your sister had sent us word that the family was abiding at Henry Chase until such time Ten Width was livable again. We wished to come and extend our condolences. We understood the funeral was private."

A muscle in Seth's cheek jerked, and he raised his hand out to her ladyship. "It was, sir. It was kind of you to travel so far, so won't you come inside?"

Sir Charles shook his head. "You must understand, Seth. Latterbuck stopped us on the road, not more than three miles from here."

"Near Ten Width."

"Indeed, yes. He said he was headed there first. He dared to demand my lady disembark with me and to search my coach. The imbecile."

Seth shifted on his feet and frowned. "I had guessed word would reach him soon enough that I had been to Crown Cove, but not this soon."

He stepped away, with his fists clenched at his side. "I'll face him. I am no coward. My mind is clearer. I'll not run this time."

At this, Sir Charles stepped firmly from his coach. "Indeed you will not face him, unless you like the feel of hemp about your throat. You must leave at once."

Seth's heart galloped so hard that for a moment he could not utter a word. He glanced back over his shoulder to see Michael and Caroline standing in the doorway. Concern shadowed their faces.

Seth turned back to Sir Charles. "I am not sure where to go, Sir Charles. But go I shall."

"I know of a ship headed for America." With his expression going from worry to relief, Sir Charles pushed open the coach door. "*The Reliance* is a stout vessel and her captain an honorable man. He'll see you safe to Virginia, for you can no longer stay in England."

Virginia. Home.

Seth shook his head. "I don't know what to say, Sir Charles, except to offer my thanks."

"Say nothing except your farewells to your family. Let us waste no more time."

With haste, Seth kissed his sister's cheek, wet with tears. He looked into her jade eyes, saw understanding, and then embraced her. After clasping Michael's hand, he hurried into the foyer brightened with morning light. He bid farewell to Sir Henry, and when he looked into his eyes, it occurred to him he might never see the old man again.

"We shall tell the children that you have been called away on an adventure, Seth. Write to us soon," said Sir Henry. Seth thanked him.

After he kissed the cheek of his mother-in-law, he pulled on his hat and stepped out.

"Seth!" Caroline hurried to him and fell into his arms, tearful. "Seth, how I shall miss you! Please . . . be careful."

He handed her back to her husband and climbed inside Sir Charles's chaise. The driver cracked his whip over the heads of the horses and set them at a canter. Louder grew the breath of wind across the moors, the beat of the horses mingling with the turn of coach wheels.

"Thank the Almighty for the lack of rain." Sir Charles peered out at the open sky. "Otherwise the roads would be difficult."

Seth, too, peered out. "Latterbuck's pursuit will be easier too."

Sir Charles laid an assuring hand over Seth's shoulder. "My driver knows this route well. He'll get you through. Steel your courage."

"Courage I lack not, Sir Charles. It is the idea of leaving her. Not even the chance to visit her grave . . . and losing the chance to clear my name."

"You mustn't think of that. She'd want you to flee for your life, Seth."

They had driven out as far as a mile when the coachman called back, "Riders in the rear, Sir Charles!"

"Let the horses loose," Sir Charles ordered.

The canter picked up to a full gallop over the high road that led toward the Devonshire coast. Seth reached inside his coat, drew out his pistol, and set the barrel on the window frame.

"When we reach the shore, you'll be let out," Sir Charles said. "A skiff will be waiting to take you out to the ship. Tell them Sir Charles has sent you. I'll delay Latterbuck if he should stop me. I wish you well."

The coach rolled to a stop and Seth jumped out. With no time to speak his thanks or say farewell, he leapt over the crumbling Roman wall and went on a way before crouching behind a hedgerow. With concern, he peeked over the edge and watched the horsemen surround the coach.

"Constable, fancy seeing you twice in one day," he heard Sir Charles say.

Latterbuck's voice rose above the wind. "Didn't you notice we were in pursuit?"

"My coachman is not attentive."

Latterbuck moved closer to the window. "Why did he pause?"

"Must I explain to you of all my business? It is my stomach, sir. The roll of the coach, you see. You stopped us once already. I insist this is the last time!"

Latterbuck set his fist against his lips and stifled a belch.

"I've been to Ten Width and found Seth Braxton is not there. No one at Henry Chase seems to have seen him. His family had nothing of significance to tell. I surmise he is in hiding."

"I have no advice to give you, Constable," Sir Charles said. "Good-bye."

Seth waited with his breath heaving. Once he heard the coach roll off and the horses gallop on, he slipped away from the hedgerow and hurried down a steep embankment of trees that met the shore.

Through the fog, he spied a pair of men waiting beside a small rowboat. Silently, they motioned to him to climb in, then pushed off into the sea. He stared back at the land, and loneliness swept over him. The salty breeze caressed his face. The wind rose and rushed through the darkness as the skiff mounted and fell over the swells.

He reached inside his pocket and drew out a silver locket containing Juleah's portrait and a lock of her hair. He closed his hand over it and held it fast, relieved he had not lost it.

36

Juleah stood at the rail of the ship and gazed out at the ocean. She wondered, with yearning for Seth, how much longer it would be until they reached land. In her hand, she held the letter, opened it, and read it once more. The edges were frayed now from so much handling.

She tucked it away in her sleeve for safekeeping and saw the seabirds whirling near the forecastle.

Four weeks into the voyage, she befriended a seabird. Of what kind she did not know, having never seen one like it before. The head and underbelly were pale pink among a mantle of chalky gray. A thin black ring encircled the bird's head. Its scarlet legs looked too thin to hold up its body, but it managed to stand upon the sill against a lusty breeze. She saved scraps of bread; in the mornings and before sunset, the bird would swoop from the masts and land in her window. From her hand it took the morsels, and she grew attached.

Back in her cabin, she stood at the window waiting for the seabird until the sun slipped behind a crimson line of thunderclouds. By late afternoon the sky turned leaden, and she knew then why she had not seen the bird. Above decks, she heard Captain Roche shout. She went topside, felt the wind strengthen, and saw the sea churning. No longer did it appear shimmering verdigris, but angry black granite.

The sails filled with the gusts and the ship heaved forward and cut into the waves. The timbers creaked and moaned. The sea crashed against the hull, lifted the ship, and brought it down again into the sea's dark embrace.

She looked up at the threatening sky with her heart racing. Clouds covered the vaulted heavens in great swirling masses of blue-gray and coal. Tepid air brushed over her skin. Pushing against her, the wind howled. She felt its power to do harm descend out of the sky. Seamen climbed the riggings to furl the billowing sails that strained against the ropes and whipped back and forth.

She caught the eye of one particular seaman. While he pulled hard at the ropes he fastened, he glanced about, then proceeded swiftly toward her.

"A great storm approaches."

Juleah shoved back her hair against the wind and with a steadfast soul gazed up into the stormy swirl that loomed above. Streaks of lightning scored the sky. Thunder pealed. She raised her face to the wild and brooding heavens, then looked at the old seadog standing before her.

"We are in great danger?"

His eyes, sober and grave, locked into hers. "Aye. Great danger."

"Are we near land?"

"Off the Carolinas. I've been at sea long enough to know we're in for a rough time."

She glanced at him with a start. Deep concern mounted in his eyes. "But it is only a storm, and Captain Roche knows what he is doing."

The seaman leaned forward. "Beneath these treacherous waters, hundreds of shipwrecks lay in a tangled web. It's the graveyard of the Atlantic. By the force of the wind and current, we've sailed straight into Diamond Shoals."

Juleah gripped her hands together as a chill tapped over her spine. "Then we are doomed."

"I'll watch over ye." The old seaman moved closer and leaned toward her ear. "I know your husband and I owe it to him."

She clutched his sleeve. "You know Seth? How?"

"It's a long story. My name's James Bonnecker, at your service." And he bowed to her quick and smart.

"Tell me, James Bonnecker. Did my husband send you?"

"I serve on this ship by my own doing, ma'am. Now ye must go below. The water's looking mighty rough, and it'll get rougher by the minute."

She hoisted her skirts and hurried back to her cabin. Inside she went to the window, pulled the pane shut, and pushed down the latch. Wind shoved against the glass, as if angry to no longer have entrance. Panes rattled. Timbers moaned and trembled as the yawning sea lifted the hull.

Huddled in the corner of her cot, Juleah drew in her breath. With each heave of the ship, each rise and fall, she waited for the full force of the storm's fury. Judith Dirk had not come and Juleah's dislike and distrust for her deepened.

The woman has abandoned me. But you are with me, O Lord.

She buried her face within her arms and prayed for her life and all those on board to be spared. She could not see the mammoth wave that towered over the ship, but she could hear it. Its roar peaked and then it slammed onto the decks. The force vibrated through each timber and beam. She listened to the hiss the wave made as it poured over the rails, swept over the deck, and ripped the rigging.

Her door was flung open. Within the threshold stood James Bonnecker, soaked and breathless, with eyes huge with fear. He rushed inside, grabbed her by the hand, and took her out of the cabin and up on deck. Glazed with foam, the water receded, pulled and tore at the ship, and made way for another swell. She lifted her eyes, and a dark image loomed before her. The terror of it bound her speech. It was the sea mounting up on all sides.

"The ship is sinking. Many will die. But not you, lass!" Bonnecker shouted over the roar of ravaging wind and gulping waves. He put his arms tighter around her and helped her forward.

"Take me back," she cried. "The sea will sweep us away!"

"Do you want to be entombed in the sea?"

She shook her head, with her frightened eyes wide upon him.

Bonnecker turned her to the rail. To the west, dark forms jutted up out of the sea as if broken castle walls. "We'll be hitting those rocks," Bonnecker said, "and when we do the ship will be torn in pieces."

Juleah clung with numb hands to the rail. She watched the helmsman struggle to turn the ship's wheel. The wind shoved against him. His hands slipped from the pegs. He fell, but held on. Captain Roche came to his aid and wrestled with the wheel to right it. The ship turned as the rudder moved. But due to the strength of the wrathful sea, it made little progress. Cold black granite loomed ahead. It grew closer, until the side of the ship struck. The rocks tore at the hull. From below men scurried like drowning rats up to the deck. Some jumped overboard into the sea and swam for the rocks. Others clung to whatever they could.

With her rain-drenched hair clinging to her face, Juleah glanced at Judith Dirk. The woman's eyes were huge with fear. Captain Roche hurried to her, and Juleah saw him lift her in his arms and carry her to a lifeboat. He drew out his knife to cut away the cords that secured it. At that moment, a most frightening sound crackled in the wind. The main mast snapped and crashed down upon the deck. Stunned with horror, Juleah saw it strike the boat, split it in two, and throw Judith Dirk and Captain Roche into the sea.

The ship listed to port, and as the water came up Bonnecker freed Juleah's hands from the rail and carried her over the side. She clung to him, and he leapt out from the ship with her in his arm. Together they shot down into the sea, and Bonnecker swam with her to the surface. Juleah gulped for air and spit the saltwater from her mouth. He held onto her, swam toward a plank of floating wreckage, and dragged her body up onto it. Men around them were drowning, as they cried out to God and their mothers.

"Hold tight," cried Bonnecker. "Shut your eyes and pray."

Rain pelted her face. Her limbs went numb, but she kept a firm grip on the raft of wood that held her above the water. As quickly as it had come, the rain lessened and finally ceased. Shivering, she listened to the crash of the water against the granite fortresses.

"James Bonnecker!" she called several times, but no reply followed.

With the meager strength she had left, Juleah hauled herself up, until her body was out of the water. She did not know which was worse, the cold of the sea or the wind. If the sun came out, it would warm her, dry her clothes. She raised her face and drifted farther away from the rocks. A new fear gripped her that she would be lost in the sea, to die atop a piece of wreckage.

Seth. Seth.

Laying her head between her arms, she prayed, *I beg you, God. Do not let me die here. Please, let me live. Let me find Seth again.*

The clouds drifted off. Twilight fell over the sea. Fog snaked around her. She raised her head and strained to listen. A sound echoed across the way, far at first, but now closer. A bell clanged and a voice called out. A light, small and feeble, pierced the curtain of mist.

Rallying herself, Juleah called back. "I am here!"

"Ho there," came the reply. "We're coming!"

A moment later, a boat slipped through the sea toward her, and a pair of strong hands reached out to lift her inside. Safe at last, she lay in the bow, her head pillowed upon a bundle of gear. Too weak for speech, she closed her eyes and wished not to see the ocean that surrounded her.

37

The boat that carried Juleah slid over the beach, and the men within it jumped out. A strong muscular fellow lifted her into his arms and took her away from the surf. He was a black man, and when she glanced up into his rugged face she feared him, for she had never seen an African before.

"Now you are safe here." His voice, deep and baritone, comforted her. "There's nothin' to fear from any of us folk. My name is Juba. We'll take care of you."

Juleah felt like a child in the man's arms. He had allayed her fears, and she rested her head against his powerful chest and heard the beat of his heart. Soaked through, her clothes clung to her body. Exhausted, she shivered and her lips trembled with cold.

A fishing village of ramshackle shanties stood back from the beach, at the border of wooded land. Nets, the color of sea-weed, were spread to dry among upturned fishing boats drawn up on the beach. Broad-winged gulls wheeled overhead. The air smelled clean, unlike the brackish breeze of the Devonshire coast. Barefoot children and turbaned women moved along the shore and gathered up wreckage. Barrels of ale and crates of oranges rolled in the surf and washed up onto the sand.

Juleah looked past Juba's massive shoulder. Men had begun the sad deed of pulling bodies from the surf. Juleah moaned and looked away. The coolness of the wind brushed against her cheek. Children gathered around, their voices calling.

She saw a woman of great age at the opening of a shanty. Her faded calico dress fluttered in the breeze. Tight wisps of steel-gray hair floated around her face and red kerchief. She stepped aside as Juleah was carried into the humble dwelling. The woman followed. Laid in a hammock, Juleah gathered the old woman's patchwork quilt around her.

"Poor chil'," the old woman cooed. "You been through an awful thing. Praise da Lor' you made it. It's a miracle, and you be in da sea."

"You nurse her, Lucy. Make her strong again. She got a husband or a mama and papa somewhere." Juba leaned down to get a closer look. "She looks like an angel, don't she?"

"Deed she do, Juba," Lucy said.

Juba turned and headed for the outside. "There be work to do. Burials. We need to hide those barrels and crates so Master, when he come, don't find them and take it all 'way."

Juba's large frame blocked the doorway, and when he went out Juleah watched the silver light of the outdoors return and felt it alight upon her face. Lucy patted her forehead with a tender hand.

"You go to sleep, chil'. You needs rest, 'cause you been through a terrible thing."

Juleah closed her eyes and drifted back into a world of dreams, where Seth waited for her.

The following day the sun bathed the surface of the ocean and caused grains of sand to sparkle like gems. Blue sky shimmered through the doorway and Juleah lifted herself up. Her body ached, but she was at least warm under the quilt. Lucy had hung her dress and chemise on a hook to dry. She got up and slipped them on. No longer did they smell of the sea. Instead, the scent of lye soap was upon them.

As she dressed, Juleah paused to study the hovel. It had a single entrance with no door. A woven mat covered it, thrown back and tied with a cord. The walls were made of rough-cut logs and old boards. A mix of sand and dirt made up the floor, packed down hard and even. A table, a chair, a tin plate, and bread bowl were the worldly goods Lucy owned.

While she laced the front of her dress, pulled the ribbons and tied them, tears pooled in Juleah's eyes. She combed her hair out with her fingers and turned to the opening where she laid her hand upon the side to peer out. The beach was white as the wings of gulls, the sky as clear and peaceful as the twilights at Henry Chase.

In Devonshire she was used to the stony beaches and grassy cliffs that brooded over the sea. Here the sand looked smooth and soft as cotton. She stepped out and her bare feet sank into it. The sand felt cool and she remembered how the grass at Henry Chase felt surrounding the pond.

Mama. How grieved she must be without her.

Dear Papa. How confused he must be by her absence.

Jane. Thomas.

Seth, my beloved.

Her heart ached for him, troubled as to how far away she was from him. She had been foolish to believe Judith Dirk. Seth would have never sent her away without him, and the letter made no mention of her journey. Would he discover what happened and search for her?

No. Darden will see to it no one knows.

Twelve slave women sat together on the beach sorting out the morning's catch. They talked of this and that, put their children on their knees. Each was dressed in calico with her hair hidden beneath a bright kerchief—some red, others a fanciful orange.

Lucy stood and waved to Juleah. "You hungry, chil'? You come here and I'll give you something." She pushed breakfast around in a skillet over the fire. "I thought the good Lor' were gonna take you, but you is better now, but not strong yet."

Juleah shoved aside her hair when the wind blew it across her eyes. "You took care of me?"

"I take care of all the sick folk round here."

"Thank you. I wish to thank the men who rescued me as well."

"Slave folk ain't used to being thanked."

Juleah took hold of Lucy's hands. They were rough against her soft ones. "I owe you and them my life."

Lucy's eyes glistened, and she snatched her hands away. "You's a good woman, I can tell. But you ain't from here, and you don't know the ways of white folks and slaves."

"Indeed not, but I know the ways of God," Juleah said. "And that is all I need."

Lucy set her head side to side. "Some folk have their reward in dis life. Ours comes later when we go to heaven. What's your name, chil'?"

"Juleah Braxton. I've come from England."

"Why'd you leave England for this place?"

"It is a long story."

"I got time." Lucy handed a wooden bowl piled with roasted fish to Juleah. "If you be wanting to tell me."

Juleah unfolded to Lucy the events that led her to the fishing camp. When she was finished speaking, Lucy pinched her brows and puckered her lips. "Folks treated you bad, Miss Juleah."

For a moment, Juleah looked at the old woman's wrinkled face and kind brown eyes. Touched by the slave woman's kindness, and her patience to listen to such a tale, Juleah laid her head in her arms and cried.

Lucy touched her shoulder. "Crying is good for da soul, Miss Juleah. And the Lor' knows you've had your share of sufferin'. That storm must've been terrible, and to be tossed into da cold sea with da waves crashin' and lashin' must've made you mighty scared. You cry as much as you want. We slave women know what it means to cry. We got bottles overflowin' with tears, and the Lor' he know."

Three boys raced up the beach toward the campfire. A man, dressed in a buff suit of clothes and an old tricorn hat, brought his horse to a halt and dismounted. Mud and sand were upon his boots, and she imagined he was the overseer of these poor souls.

A corner of his mouth curved and he drew off his hat and bowed. "You must pardon me, ma'am, for not arriving sooner. I'm the overseer, Corben. The slaves have treated you well?"

Juleah nodded. "They saved my life. I am indebted to them, sir."

He glanced over at Lucy and the other women. "You owe them nothing."

When Corben drew close, Juleah felt an aversion to him.

"What's your name, miss, and where are you from?" he asked, eyeing her.

"Juleah Braxton, from England, sir," she said.

"Well, you're a long way from home."

"Yes, and I wish to return. My uncle lives in Annapolis and is a prominent lawyer there. I would like to go to him. If you could arrange transport for me, I would be grateful."

"His name?"

"John Stowefield."

Corben looked away toward the grove of evergreens. "Mr. Martin owns this land and these slaves. His house is not far, on the other side of those trees. But he's away from home, in Charleston on business, and there are no servants in the house."

"Then I should stay here," she said. "At least until your employer returns."

He lifted his brows and laughed. "Among slaves? That's not done. Not for a white woman." Corben stood back with his riding crop poised in his hands. "Lucy will go to the house with you. You hear, Lucy? You are to go to the big house with this lady."

Juba dropped the net he was mending and hurried over when Corben called to him. "Help the lady into the saddle, Juba." With his great hands, Juba lifted her up and stood back.

Corben walked beside the horse, and when Juleah glanced down, she saw the hilt of his flintlock protruding out of his belt. They turned off the beach to follow a white pebble path that wound through tall grass into a crop of pines. The roar of the waves faded. No longer did she hear the sound of wind over the water. Instead, the land hummed with bees that worked over the wildflowers and with cicadas that twilled. Dusky willows bowed over the sunlit path in the heat.

Juleah looked ahead, hoping to see a clearing or the plantation house. Something moved in the trees. She turned her head, saw Corben pull his pistol from his belt and raise it beside his shoulder.

38

Corben's horse twisted under Juleah. She fought to keep the reins tight in her hands. The towhead of a boy peeked out from behind some bushes. Two more followed. They were handsome lads, each with ruddy cheeks and hair bleached blond and sandy by the sun and sea, yet poorly dressed, shoeless, and thin.

Corben shoved his pistol back inside his belt, stepped forward. "You lads want to be shot, is that it? What'd you mean coming up on us like that? Get back home, each one of you, before I tan your hides."

The young lads' eyes widened, and without a word, they sprinted off.

Juleah had no idea who the children were and thought to ask, but when Corben urged his horse on, she assumed he did not want to speak of it. She followed him in silence to a bend in the road, where they came upon a house made of rough-cut timber. Sunshine fell warm upon a front garden, changing the tassels of maize into golden plumes. A child played by the door and paused to look at the lady riding sidesaddle. The girl was holding a doll made of cornhusks, and next to her lay a heap of plucked wildflowers.

Within the doorway, a woman spun, and when the thread snapped in her hand, her humming ceased in her bronzy throat. For a moment, she gazed with troubled eyes at those outside her threshold and then sprang to her feet. The child set her doll upon the bed of blossoms and fled to her mother to cling to her skirts.

A light breeze wrapped the mother's homespun dress against her limbs and lifted her hair around her face. Her hand rested upon the head of her child until a baby's cry from inside the dwelling caused her to turn. Without speaking, she went to her infant. The child was left alone and plopped back down on the porch. Tiny hands gathered up the doll, and she cradled it against her chest. Juleah gazed at the girl sitting cross-legged on the porch and thought how pretty she was, even in a tattered dress too big for her tiny frame.

Corben turned to Juleah. "Those are my boys, and the child on the porch is my girl. The babe's our seventh. We lost two last winter."

She looked back at the doorway. "The lady is your wife?"

"Aye, that's my Abigail"

Abigail's eyes were upon her husband. Within her gaze sparkled adoration for the man she called husband, but a jealous glow when she looked over at Juleah. She stepped down and walked toward him. He leaned down, spoke into her ear, as her large brown eyes remained steadfast on Juleah. Her baby squirmed in her arms and whined.

Corben took hold of his horse's bridle and moved them on, with Lucy walking alongside. Beyond the poor hovel stood a grand plantation house. A gracious portico with white beveled columns graced the front. A colonnade of poplars swayed in the breeze along the drive.

Juleah craned her neck to view it. Corben helped her down, and she studied the lonely mansion. She hoped with all her heart she would not stay long.

❦

That night, Juleah stepped outside onto the lawn. An opal moon banked high over the shimmering pines, the stars too numerous to count against a black velvet heaven. The breeze rippled through her hair and she gazed heavenward. The constellations were above, and she watched Jupiter rise over the treetops. Her heart longed for Seth, and she prayed that Mr. Martin would return soon. Her mind fixed on the day she'd leave for Annapolis. A slow breath slipped between her coral lips as she thought of it. Her uncle would help her home. He would book passage for her on the first ship headed to England.

She imagined her homecoming. Seth would see her, sweep her up into his arms, kiss her face and throat. They would laugh together and never be parted again. Her family would gather and they'd have a great dinner together, laugh and sing and dance until dawn.

Despite her ordeal, she opened her eyes, smiled, and lightly laughed. What would Seth think of her hair, unbound, hanging below her waist in heavy strands? She had no ribbons to tie it with. Her dress was now the only one she owned, the seams at the waist apart, the laces on her bodice now a dingy yellow, whereas before they were white as cream. She had no shoes, for they were lost in the sea. Her stockings were torn and not worth keeping.

The sound of footfalls over the sandy lane drew her out of her thoughts. She turned and saw Corben walking toward her.

He screwed up his face. "Why are you out here so late, madam? You waiting for someone?"

"I could not sleep," she told him.

She turned to leave, but he reached out and took hold of her arm. "There's no reason to go back inside."

Juleah frowned and, frightened as she was, she looked down at the hand that held her arm. "Let go of me."

The tightness of his fingers lessened. He leaned closer, and his black eyes stared hard into hers. Rum fouled his breath. Repulsed, she turned away.

"If you do not let me go, Mr. Corben, I'll scream for Juba. He will hear me."

Corben laughed. "Do it and I'll shoot him."

By his tone, and the fact his inhibitions were lowered, he meant it, and she went quiet and still.

"That's better." He moved her away from the front porch stairs, further into the shadows.

Juleah let out a whimper, as his hand tightened. "I'll tell Mr. Martin how you have treated me."

"I'll deny it. He fought in the Revolution against your bloody country and he'll believe me over an English."

She jerked her arm free and headed toward the house. Corben seized her by the waist. She twisted, flung her arms and smacked his face. He let go and rubbed his bruised cheek. She ran. Corben sprinted after her. He caught her about the shoulders and they fell together. She kicked and clawed. He grabbed her arms and pushed them back. His weight upon her pushed the air from her lungs. She could not find the strength to cry out, nor did she wish to see death that night in the camp.

He ran a dirty finger along the curve of her throat. "How could you not think a man like me would be drawn to a woman like you?"

She squirmed from beneath him. "Let me go!"

Moonlight fell over his face, and the wanton look in his eyes ignited, as if a flame of lust possessed him. Her body shook with fear and strained from him. She lashed out with her fists, turned to get up and run, but he grabbed her ankles and pulled her back. She kicked her legs, and when he had drawn her closer, she swung her arm and struck. He let out a groan and reached for her again. She dug her fingers into the earth, gathered a fistful, and flung it into his eyes. He cried out and recoiled.

Seeing her chance, she scrambled forward and snatched his pistol out of his belt. She hurried backward and struggled to her feet. His teeth were clenched and his fists raised against his eyes.

Obscuring the brilliance of the moon, a figure lurched behind Corben. A hand reached out and grabbed him by the shoulder, lifted him, and left his feet to dangle in midair. Juba drew back his mighty fist and struck Corben, shook him, and tossed him to the ground.

Juleah saw Juba's face go blank with fear. "I had to help you, Miss Juleah. I saw what he was doin'."

"Go back, Juba before he comes to." Fearing it could mean death for Juba for striking an overseer, she shoved him away. He crept back into the darkness and hurried off.

Corben moaned, shook his head, and soon got up on all fours. He struggled to his feet, sand and dirt dusting his clothes. Juleah planted her feet firm and raised Corben's pistol. Her chest rose and fell with rapid breathing. Her hand trembled as she held the hilt of the pistol. The idea of shooting a man sent a chill through her. "Come closer, Mr. Corben, and I will shoot you."

Corben rubbed his jaw and leered at her. "It couldn't have been you that laid me out. I know one man strong enough to do it, and that's Juba."

"There's no one else here but you and me," she said. "I warn you well, that if you come one step closer. . . ."

He lifted his hand in compliance. "I believe you. But I want that pistol back. I paid good money for it and carried it with me through the Revolution."

Did he think her a fool? Juleah narrowed her eyes. "Empty your powder and shot."

He dismissed her demand with a short laugh, took a step forward. She cocked the hammer and kept her aim steady upon his heart. The slow movement of his eyes shifted with fear from her face to her finger curled around the trigger. Hesitating, he pulled the strap from over his shoulder, yanked the plug free from the horn and emptied the gunpowder into the wind.

"The shot will do me no good without powder, woman."

Juleah lifted her chin and stood her ground. "Even so, toss it away."

His mouth twisted and he untied the pouch. With his eyes fixed upon her, Corben obeyed.

He thrust his hand out to her. She waited. Staring back into his eyes, she cocked the hammer, turned the weapon toward the pines, and fired. The blast shook her frame, and the smell of sulfur wafted against her face. At arm's length, she handed the flintlock back to Corben.

She thought she heard him sob, as he shoved the pistol back into his belt, and then rake his fingers through his hair. "If it does any good, I regret that I . . . if you'd pardon my. . . ." He broke off, made a quick distressed gesture. "Please say nothing to Mr. Martin. I need my job—got mouths to feed. It was the drink. I need to repent and give it up." Slowly, he moved off into the darkness, and she knew, back to his poor cabin, to his wife and children.

Juba hurried forth from the shadows. "Are you all right, Miss Juleah?"

Juleah wiped her hands along her dress, as if something mucky clung to her palms. "I think so. I told you to go back, Juba. But you kept watch over me."

"Yes, miss. Corben might come back when you is sleepin'," Juba said. "I'll sleep in front of the door tonight, Miss Juleah."

"He won't be back." She walked up the steps, across the porch, and to the front door. "You are the kindest of knights, Juba. Stay if you wish beside the door. I shall fetch you something for your head."

"Where is Lucy, miss? Corben, he didn't hurt her, did he?"

"She is fast asleep. No harm was done."

She went inside to the gloom and heat of the mansion. Softly she whispered a prayer that the slave would be safe from the vengeance of his overseer.

39

The following day, Juleah opened a pair of French doors that led to an upper balcony. The room she had chosen faced east, toward the ocean, and she could see it clear and bright in the distance. Dunes of white sand and tall shore grass glistened in the sunshine. The surf, lined with milky foam, swept over the coast in time with the wind. The sun warmed her face, but her stomach growled with hunger.

When she heard Lucy clear her throat, Juleah turned to see the old woman carrying a tray of food. She hurried to it.

"I'm starved, Lucy. So good of you."

Lucy blinked her eyes. "I'm not used to being inside the house, Miss Juleah. I don't know what I can and cannot do."

Juleah patted the chair next to her. "Well, you can sit and talk to me."

Lucy broke into a laugh and proceeded to make up the bed with its tumbled bedclothes. She shuffled over to the window.

"A wagon loaded with goods from the shops in Charleston comin' down the lane," she cried. "And there's the master's coach behind it, Miss Juleah."

Juleah leapt to her feet and looked out to see a hackney rumble down the lane in a cloud of dust. The wagon circled up to the front, and beside the driver sat a slave woman. She appeared middle-aged, refined by the way she sat straight with shoulders back and with her hands clasped over her apron. Her dress looked new, crisp and clean, in calico pink flowers. Upon her head, she wore a white turban.

Mr. Martin dragged off his hat as he exited the coach. "Good day to you, Miss Juleah," he called up to her in the window. "I hope you are well on this fine day."

She nodded and smiled. "I am, sir, though anxious to leave for Maryland."

She hurried down to meet him. When she reached the bottom of the stairs, she found him in the foyer giving instructions to the wagon driver. He turned on his heels and bowed low to her. His clothes were fashionable, but simple. His hair was neatly tied in a ribbon, and his face clean-shaven. He appeared no older than her father, but leaner in body and brimming with youthful energy as he hurried over to her and lifted her hand to kiss it.

"Corben explained everything to me, how you were shipwrecked." He shook his head sympathetically. "A harrowing experience to be sure. I am so honored that you made my home your own."

Juleah gave him a polite curtsey. "I cannot express my thanks, sir."

Martin turned his body this way and that, as if he sought what to do next. He finally paused and said, "Your frightful event left you in rags, Miss Juleah. You may have any of my wife's dresses and whatever else you need. You're about her size I would say."

Although the offer was a kind one, Juleah could not take his lady's clothes unless Mrs. Martin were home and offered them to her. Even then, she'd feel obligated to repay in some way. But if she hinted of reciprocation, that would be an insult to their generous hospitality.

"It is indeed a kind offer, sir. Excuse my English manners, but I feel strange taking your lady's clothes."

"She'd insist. I'll be in trouble enough with her when she finds out you lived out here in a shanty among my slaves. You must allow me to offer you suitable attire for your journey as a way of making amends."

"Well, I would not want your lady to be angry with you, sir. I accept your offer."

Martin's face beamed. "That is fine, Miss Juleah. Now, in addition to proper clothing, my coach shall speed you north to your uncle. However, I hope you might consider staying longer."

Juleah's heart leapt in her breast. She was one step closer to Seth, and the silver lining to her plight would be to see her dear Uncle John again. She did not wish to seem ungrateful, but had to make her desire known.

She stood aside as the wagoner carried in a wooden box. "I am quite anxious to make my journey, sir."

"I understand." Martin moved to the door and motioned for the slave woman to come inside.

Juleah pressed her lips together in thought. She had to speak up. "Mr. Martin, your slave Juba pulled me from the sea. If it had not been for him, I would have perished. Is it wrong to be grateful to the man who saved my life?"

"Indeed, I would say not."

"And Lucy has cared for me very well," Juleah told him.

He looked about for Lucy. "Has she?"

Formality aside, Juleah put her hand out to him. "Promise me you will treat them well, Mr. Martin."

Mr. Martin looked at her bewildered, then grasped her hand. "I've no reason to do otherwise, I assure you."

She wondered, could she leave without telling Mr. Martin what Corben had tried to do to her? Did he not have the right to know what kind of man he had in his employment? It was a risk to tell. She thought of his wife, Abigail, and their children. No, she would stay silent for their sakes and pray that one day Corben would relent and give up drink.

With a graceful glide, Mr. Corben's slave came inside the house and paused in front of Juleah.

"Miss Juleah, this is Jenny. She's my wife's maid." Martin dropped his gloves in his hat and set it on a table. "Jenny, find this lady something appropriate to wear for traveling."

Jenny turned and led Juleah up a winding staircase to a grand bedroom done in white. A large canopy bed sat to one side done up in eyelet lace, cluttered with pillows that had golden tassels. A dressing table and mirror were beneath the window, stocked with brush and comb, powder and ribbon boxes. Jenny opened a clothes cupboard stuffed with gowns, day dresses, riding jackets, and more. She drew out several items and laid them on the bed.

"These are fine clothes." Jenny shook out the hem of a satin gown. "You can choose whatever you wish. I'll pack them for you."

"I can take one," replied Juleah. "These are Mrs. Martin's clothes."

Jenny spread the gown over the bed. "Well, she wouldn't mind. She don't need them."

Jenny's comment puzzled Juleah. "Why?"

"She's been gone six months."

"A long time to have been away. Mr. Martin said she would be returning soon."

Jenny shook her head and clicked her tongue. "Mrs. Martin died over the winter. Pneumonia. Mr. Martin, he been grievin' fierce. I think it did something to his mind. He tells folks she's away and coming home soon. I guess it gives him comfort."

Jenny shut the cupboard door and turned the latch until it clicked. "You need to change out of those awful clothes, miss. The driver will be here any minute."

"Already?" Juleah pulled loose the ties of her bodice.

"Yes, Miss Juleah." Jenny walked over to the window and threw open the sashes. The breeze rushed inside. "I heard what happen to you, about the ship sinking and you bein' in the sea. Good folks they are down on the beach. They'll take care of anybody needin' help. I imagine you can't wait to get back to your folks."

"Yes, I am lonely for them, especially my husband."

Jenny poured water from a china pitcher into a washing bowl. The lavender soap smelled heavenly. Juleah ran the silky foam over her skin, through her hair, and inhaled the heady fragrance. "I have taken such things for granted."

She chose what she believed was the least expensive of Mrs. Martin's clothes. It'd be wrong to take advantage of the situation. It fit her to a tee, a pale blue dress of lawn with modest lace and a linen chemise. Jenny took out of a box a pair of silk opaque stockings with matching shoes.

The moment Juleah had finished dressing she hurried from the room, downstairs to the front door. She wanted to thank Mr. Martin, but he was not in the house. In the distance, she saw him as he walked across his field toward the woods, his hand stretched out as if to clasp another.

The roomy coach and four awaited her.

"Miss Juleah," said Jenny. "Mr. Martin wanted me to give you this. It is for your journey." She held out a leather pouch filled with coins.

Tears filled Juleah's eyes. "It is too much."

Jenny pressed her lips together and stepped back.

"I cannot take it."

"Would you like to go hungry on the way, miss?"

Juleah hesitated. "Well, thank him for it. One day, I will pay him back." She boarded the coach, and her heart moved within her. The only payment she could offer she offered in prayer for Mr. Martin.

Lord, be kind to him and ease his grief.

She lifted her hand in farewell to Lucy and Juba, who stood by the side of the lane, Lucy in her faded dress and Juba with his straw hat in his hands.

Seated inside the coach, she closed her eyes. Relief to be leaving filled her. When the coachman's whip cracked above the heads of his steeds, the coach jerked forward and rolled on. It swayed and glided over the sunlit road through the Carolina dust. Locusts shrilled in the trees, and pine groves shaded the road.

Hours later, as the day strengthened, she went to draw down the window shade where the sun was strongest, but paused to see fields of corn wilting in the heat. Hedges of pokeberry and wild sumac mingled with snowy Queen Anne's lace along the road. She pulled off her hat and gloves and laid them on the seat beside her. Then, she raised her skirts up over her calves and kicked off her shoes. The breeze whisked inside, brushed against her skin, and she drifted off to sleep and dreamed of Seth.

Twenty miles from Virginia, they left fields of corn for sunny fields of tobacco. It took several days to go through Carolina and the Commonwealth. Twice they were delayed at tollhouses, but the toll-keepers were at least helpful. They informed the driver what lay ahead the next ten miles, the streams to cross, what bridges were out, and where they would find a modest inn to spend the night.

When the left rear wheel caught in the mud after an evening rainstorm, it took a half-hour for the coachman and his fellow to pull it out. It had been a deep hole and sucked the wheel down within it up to the hub. The horses strained, but soon the coach righted and they were on their way once again.

They crossed the James River by barge near Williamsburg, then the York and the Rappahannock, where the bridges were in good repair despite a heavy winter. Heading east, they traveled along the St. Mary's River, into the town that bore its name. The church steeple loomed above the treetops, and the road that led through the town lay dusty that morn and hard as stone.

Breaking at a roadside inn, Juleah sat alone near a window where daylight poured golden through glass. A plate of food was brought to her, and she glanced at the innkeeper and thanked him with the grateful expression of her eyes.

The window where she sat faced east. The fatigue in her body caused Juleah to set her chin in hand and stare out at the bay and a stormy horizon beyond it. Through the mist that gathered, she saw a tall ship with stark white canvas sail toward the wharf. Had it come from England or some other faraway place? For a brief moment, she observed the passengers that stood at the rail, women in broad hats, men in felt tricorns. Alone at the bow, stood a young man dressed in a dark suit of clothes. She could not make out his face at such a distance, but imagined he was handsome.

For a moment, she dreamed he was Seth.

40

The choppy water, the shoreline that hugged clay bluffs. Forests of spruce and elm, marshlands filled with seabirds and cranes, caused Seth's grave blue eyes to stare on with longing. Sadness seized his heart, for in the majesty of this place, one thing lacked—the company of his wife. Life was empty without her. With a struggle he leaned against the rail under the weight of grief.

Gulls glided in the rigging of the vessel. Snowy clouds mounted the sky. Breathing in the air, the coming rain merged with the scent of the water. The Chesapeake had a certain earthy fragrance, as if the life within it meant to flaunt its abundance to the one who passed over it. The water in the bay turned pallid green in the sunlight. Where it merged with the warmer waters of the river, a deeper blue fingered through the viridian hues like intertwining vines. Here Seth disembarked.

Turning up the collar of his coat, he stepped into the street. The thump of hooves and the churn of wheels made him step back. A coach rumbled down the road toward him. The horses' manes whipped in the wind, and their nostrils flared. He caught a brief glance of the woman inside as it rolled by.

Her profile, the soft curve of her cheek, the shade of her hair as it fell in twists over her shoulder, and the wide-brimmed hat that shadowed her eyes fled past him.

His heart gripped in his chest. Like a hammer, its rhythm pounded, while he strained his eyes to comprehend the face. He stood motionless, shaken, his muscles tense, with his hands flexed.

He whispered, "Juleah?"

He frowned and pressed his lips together against the pang of sorrow. He told himself what he had seen was a mere coincidence. What else could it be? Juleah was dead.

Gathering himself together, he crossed the street and looked up at the shingle outside the inn. He hesitated, not sure about going inside, for his conscience pricked him. Perhaps he should go to Annapolis first before returning home. It wasn't far, and he could be there in a few hours if he had a swift horse or could find a boat going up the bay.

He headed back down to the docks. Fishermen lingered on the wharf, smoking clay pipes. "Is there a man among you willing to sail to Annapolis? I'll pay you well."

One man stood forward and accepted the offer. When they passed the mouth of the Potomac, the wind increased, billowed the sail, and sent the boat off like a startled deer. Lightning flashed across the horizon, leapt higher, and thunder rolled. Rain fell in misty sheets along the opposite shore. The rain never reached him, but the cool wind brushed against his face.

Soon enough, the town rose along the shoreline. He imagined Mr. Stowefield was enjoying the afterglow of a sabbath's rest. Seth regretted he would bear him bad news, but knew his duty. Perhaps a letter from Henry Chase had arrived by now and would make his meeting with the old gentleman easier.

After he paid the charitable fisherman, he made his way to Stowefield's house. The windows stood open. Curtains flapped in the breeze, while bluebottle flies landed on the broad sills. Partridge stepped outside the front door, broom in hand. She swept the front stoop with vigor, but when Seth approached the bottom step and drew off his hat, she stopped with a start.

"Mr. Braxton!" Her eyes enlarged with disbelief and she gasped. "My word. What are you doing here?"

"I've come to visit your employer." Seth smiled.

Partridge put her hand on her ample hip. "Hmm. England didn't work out for you, sir? Well, you know what they say? The grass isn't always greener on the other side of the hill."

"You are keen at supposition, ma'am."

"I've been told that before, sir. Come inside if you will." She opened the door and passed through it before him. "I shouldn't be sweeping on a Sunday, but some child threw mud at the porch." She set her broom aside and hurried into Mr. Stowefield's sitting room. He drew off his spectacles when Partridge entered.

"A surprise, Mr. Stowefield. A gentleman of your acquaintance to see you, sir."

Stowefield closed the pages of his Bible and looked up. He stood as quick as his legs would allow. He'd grown thin, his head of hair white. His hands shook, and his eyes were a misty gray. In the doorway stood Seth.

Shocked, Stowefield threw open his arms. "Seth! What brings you back so soon? You have not been gone a year. Don't tell me the place was a shambles and heavy with debt."

"No, sir, but it was not what I counted on."

"Hmm, it never is. Your sister is well?"

"Yes. She has a son and is happily married."

"I'm pleased to hear it. And how is my favorite niece?" Stowefield glanced toward the doorway.

Seth could smile no longer. "I married her."

Stowefield's mouth fell open with a thrill. "Yes, I know. She wrote to me and said she was happy. Ah, the surprise of seeing you pass over my threshold has muddled my brain."

Seth did not know how to respond; he nodded and tried to smile. He looked upon the older man. How would he break the news to him without breaking his heart? But something else drew his eyes—Juleah's portrait. His heart swelled as he looked into her face. How could he ever forget the soft touch and honey taste of her lips?

Stowefield strode to the door. "You have brought her with you, no doubt. Where is she? Bring her in, Partridge. Juleah, where are you, child?"

Seth rested his hand on Stowefield's shoulder. "Juleah is not with me. There is more to tell and it is not good news. Please sit. I'll tell you everything."

At Seth's words, Stowefield's expression fell to worry. "Why? Has something happened?"

Moving him back inside the room to his chair, Seth drew up another in front of Stowefield. He went on to explain, spoke slowly at first, telling him about the fire, how he denied Juleah's death, how it could have cost him his sanity if not his life. He hated this. It caused him to remember the night he went to Henry Chase to tell her parents, the stunned looks on their faces, the scream of agony, the tears. Now he had to tell her uncle, whose face became more and more drawn and distraught as Seth unfolded the series of events.

Stowefield shrank back in his chair and moaned. "Tell me she lives, or that someone took her far away and you seek her. Tell me anything other than she is gone."

"I wish it were otherwise, sir." Seth watched the color drain from the old man's face. "If it were so, I would have brought her here to see you, and I would have taken her to Virginia, to my river and mountains. I do not know how I'll go on living without her. . . . I'll grieve a long time." Seth felt every muscle tighten, tremble, and surge with emotion.

Shaken, Stowefield rose and shuffled to the window. He stared out at an empty street. Seth looked at the floor, gripped his hands together, enraged at the thing that took her from him, that forced his mind to reel with despair and rip into him the reality of her loss, of living without her the rest of his life.

"Poor, child," Stowefield said, soft and painfully. He lifted his spectacles and wiped his eyes. "The last time I saw her was before the war. So pretty a child was she." He turned to Seth and let out a ragged breath. "You loved her?"

Seth looked up. "More than my own life." He ran his hand over his face and hung his head. "I had to leave England. I couldn't stay any longer."

"I'm sorry. God knows I am." He put his hand on Seth's shoulder. "I'll write to my sister. Oh, how I grieve with her and Henry, though their grief no doubt is far deeper than my own."

"Lady Anna took it hard."

Stowefield sighed. "I understand why she has not written, for it must be too painful to put it in a letter. What will you do now?"

"Go back home, build my father's estate, raise horses." He could not continue. Sadness swept over him in waves.

"Stay with me a few days before you move on," said Stowefield.

Seth looked over at him. "I would, sir, and I'm grateful for the offer. But I hope you understand the need I have to be alone. I would add to the melancholy of this house."

"Nonsense. You know you are welcome here. But I do understand. When my Mildred passed on, I, too, wished to be alone, to grieve for her in my own way and in my own time without others chattering on and on about her, filling my ear with their sympathies, no matter how sincere. Is there anything I can do for you before you leave?"

"I haven't eaten since yesterday," Seth answered. "Shipboard food is not the best, and I find my strength waning."

Stowefield rose from his chair and called Partridge. She moved into the light of the doorway from the shadows. She'd been listening, her eyes sad and weepy. She brushed away her tears and hurried Seth off to the dining table. She carved and poured for him, then cleared the dishes when he had finished.

They walked together to the front door in silence. Stowefield took a moment to set his hand upon Seth's arm and pull him forward. Seth's own father had never embraced him, and though it seemed awkward, he understood when the old man put his arm around him.

Before he rounded the corner on King George Street, Seth turned and raised his hand in a sober farewell.

✍

Back inside his house, Stowefield went into his parlor and stared at Juleah's portrait for several minutes. He'd give it to Seth. She was his wife after all, and it should go to him. He spent the rest of the evening writing a letter to his sister Anna.

When Partridge inquired about how he was feeling, Stowefield told her he could not shake off the sadness. She brought him a strong evening cup of chamomile and warm milk to help him sleep. After he had drunk it down, he stood to take to his bed. But before he climbed between the sheets, coach wheels passed over the cobblestones and stopped outside his front door.

He peered out the window. Under the glow of the street-lamp stood a boxed-shaped coach, drawn by dappled horses. Curious, he watched the coachman drag the reins through his hands to steady the horses. The footman jumped down from his perch, placed the step down and opened the door. From this height, Stowefield spied the top of a lady's hat exiting the coach.

Annoyed, he moaned. "Who could that be at this hour?"

41

Stowefield's house was dark and solitary when Juleah arrived. An amber spray of moonlight brushed over the window glass. The flame in the streetlamp near the door glowed against red lacquer, causing the brass handle to twinkle.

When the footman handed her down from the coach, the mist-laden air stroked her face and the scent of the bay enveloped her in its seductive ambiance. Her knees weakened, and she gazed up for the first time at the two-story house. In an upper room, the glow of a candle passed before the window. She had not seen her uncle in years. Would he recognize her? What would his reaction be to finding her on his doorstep?

Lifting her skirts, she turned and asked the driver to wait. She glided up the stairs, lifted the door knocker, and let it fall. A moment later, the click of the lock, and the door opened. Around its edge, Partridge peered out in her nightcap and robe, with candle in hand. The flame shimmered over her rosy cheeks.

"Yes, what is it?" Partridge looked Juleah up and down, attempting to make out her face in the dark.

"Forgive me for this late intrusion, but is Mr. Stowefield at home?" Juleah said.

"Yes, but he's abed," Partridge said.

"May I see him please?"

"He opens in the morning for matters of the law, if that's what you wish to see him for. Come back at nine."

Juleah stepped closer. "Oh, I did not come to see him for that reason. I am his niece, Juleah Braxton."

Candlelight spread over Juleah's face. All at once, Partridge's knees wobbled and she let out a gasp. "It's a miracle!" With her hands shaking, her expression a mix of confusion and amazement, she threw open the door and fumbled to set the candle on the table next to it.

"Mr. Stowefield!" she shouted in alarm. "Mr. Stowefield, come quick!" She hurried to the stairs, her arms and hands stretched out as if to take hold of him.

Juleah stepped inside and watched Partridge head up the stairs. In the shadows above, the shape of her uncle came down the corridor.

"Dear me, woman. What's the ruckus? Who's that lady at the door?"

When Juleah heard her uncle's voice, she too hurried forward and stared up. Partridge stopped at the top of the stairs. She slapped her hand over her chest, and her bosom rose and fell.

"Mr. Stowefield, your niece is downstairs."

"Oh, that is cruel, Partridge. It cannot be. Go see who it is and tell her I open for business in the morning."

He turned to go. Partridge grabbed his arm. "You must go and speak to her at once."

"Oh, very well." Stowefield headed down the stairs. Boards creaked under his weight, and Juleah gazed up at his face through the gloom. He had aged, but still had the same kind face, ever noble.

"See here, young woman. What kind of joke is this to play on an old man in the throes of grief? How dare you come to my house and claim—" He stopped short at the bottom of the stairs. He trembled and reached for the banister. "Can it be? Do my eyes deceive me? Am I seeing a ghost?"

Juleah smiled and put her hands out to her uncle. "I am no ghost, Uncle John. Do you not recognize me?"

Stowefield froze. His eyes widened. He struggled to speak. A sob escaped his lips and he reached out to pull her into his arms.

"I am glad you are happy to see me." She kissed his cheek and laughed.

"Happy? Words cannot describe." He released her and in a rush, took her hand. "Come into the parlor and sit. Partridge, bring my niece something to eat. Are you hungry, child?"

Juleah nodded. "Very. Have you any tea?"

"As much as you wish." Stowefield's voice quivered with excitement. "I cannot keep my eyes off you, child. You are worn out from your journey?"

"Indeed, but my journey was broader than the sea."

Stowefield rumbled his brow. "Was it?" He looked confused, elated, and looked as though he wanted to ask her questions. Yet, he held back. She untied her ribbons, then drew off her hat and laid it aside. It troubled her, his mood, the teary eyes and the shock.

"Uncle, you are disturbed by my arrival?"

He snatched up her hands. "I was told—"

She squeezed his hands. "What were you told? Have I upset you?"

"No, child. Tell me everything." His eyes were intent, although they filled with tears. He cocked his head. "What evil befell you?"

She released his hands. Where was she to begin to tell him all that had happened? "I was taken aboard a ship against my will, drugged, and kidnapped."

Stowefield let out a long breath. To calm him, she put her hands on his shoulders. She went on to tell him of the strange house, of Judith Dirk and her potion. "Then the ship met a storm off Carolina and sank. I clung to life until fishermen pulled me from the water."

"Rescued. God be praised you came through this unharmed, dear Juleah." He began to cry and drew her swiftly into an embrace.

"There is more to tell you, especially about Seth," she said.

Stowefield moved her back. "I learned the most awful thing tonight. I was told you died in a fire at Ten Width, but here you are alive." He pressed his fingers against the corners of his eyes.

Shock coursed through her and Juleah stared at her uncle. "They believe I am dead?"

"Yes, that is why I looked the way I did when I first saw you, why I spoke of grief. I could not believe my eyes. Wake me at once if I'm dreaming. Oh, God, be merciful to me if it is not true you live." And he lowered his head against her hands and wept.

Juleah drew her hands out from his and put them on his cheeks "Oh, you are not dreaming. Do not cry."

Stowefield looked at her with a joyful smile and a light laugh slipped though his trembling lips. "God's miracles do not cease. But what reason would anyone have to tell me my beloved niece perished in a fire?"

"Indeed there was a fire, and I was taken. That is the reason."

He nodded. "Indeed, that must be it."

"Did my mother not write you? I have been worried about her, and Seth and the others. I have no doubt Seth is searching for me in England and has no idea that I am in America. I must go to him without delay, Uncle John."

He looked at her with a start. "Seth was the one to tell me you had died. He is beset with grief."

"My darling Seth!" Juleah cried. "What did he say in his letter? Is he all right?"

Stowefield shook his head. "His letter? No, child, he told me here, today. He's come back to start again in Virginia."

"He is here?"

"Yes, he's in the city." Stowefield stood and paced the floor. "Where he is lodging, I do not know."

A wonderful feeling of elation filled her, overflowed from her. "I must find him."

"But it is past midnight."

"The time matters not. I must find him at once"

Stowefield placed his hands gently on her shoulders. "I won't have you going out into the night alone, Juleah."

He was right, but the idea of waiting drove her crazy. "Can you not send a messenger to the inns?"

His brows rose. "At this hour? Business is closed until morning. Taverns and inns are locked and the keepers abed."

She squeezed his arm. "But there must be someone, Uncle. Please, I cannot bear to think Seth is near and I must wait hours to see him. Please, there must be a way."

He paused and rubbed his chin. "You're right, child. What am I thinking? I shall go find him myself, or my name is not

John Stowefield." He hurried from the room out into the hallway. "Partridge!"

Partridge, with her cap askew, tottered forward. "Where are you going, sir?"

"To the inns, in search of Seth Braxton."

Stowefield squashed on his hat and ushered Juleah out the door. "Ho, there, good man," Stowefield called to the driver. "I'll pay you well if you take us through the town to the inns."

"Indeed you will, sir," said the coachman, swallowing down the ale and brown bread Partridge had provided. "For my mate and I are dog-tired."

"I'll pay your lodging. First, take us to the taverns on Market Street along the city docks. "

The coachman tipped his hat, and the footman opened the coach door to help Juleah and her uncle inside. The horses whinnied and pranced. Then the coach wheels rumbled over the cobblestones.

The streets were quiet and blanketed with fog. All windows and doors were shut for the night. Street lanterns glimmered. Stowefield tapped on the coach roof to alert the driver. He put his head outside the window when the horses slowed.

"Be a good man, footman, and knock on that door. Ask the innkeeper if Seth Braxton abides within."

The footman jumped down, ascended to the door and knocked. A moment and it opened. A man stood inside with a candle in hand. The footman turned back and shook his head. "No one by that name here, sir."

"Let us go on to the next," Stowefield said.

Juleah turned with desperate eyes to her uncle. "What if we do not find him."

He patted her hand. "Do not worry, my child. We shall find him soon enough."

They stopped at two more inns, The Gray Fox and The White Crane. Still they had not found Seth. Next, the coach drew up in front of a stately inn, The Flagship.

Determined to find Seth, Juleah and her uncle exited the coach and followed the footman through the gloom up to the door. It was unlocked.

"The innkeeper will not like getting roused from his bed at such an hour. But it is of no consequence. We are on a mission." Stowefield looped Juleah's arm through his, proceeded with her up to the door and stepped inside to the quiet great room. An oil lamp burned on the counter near the staircase.

"I know the innkeeper well," Stowefield went on. "No doubt he shall grumble beneath his breath as he slips out of bed, landing his bare feet upon the floor."

Stowefield patted the bell on the counter several times, until a creak in the floor above signaled the innkeeper had been awakened. Down the staircase, he tottered in his robe, slippers, and tasseled nightcap, holding a candle. He rubbed his eye with his fist and stared at the couple standing in the misty gloom. "It is well after midnight, sir."

"I am aware of the time, Mr. Randall, and I beg your pardon for this intrusion, but it is paramount I speak with you. You know me. I am John Stowefield."

"Dear me, sir. Don't tell me you and this lady are here for accommodations? I have no room for such goings-on."

Stowefield frowned. "This lady happens to be my niece. She has come from England after a harrowing journey and seeks her husband. Have you a lodger this night by the name of Seth Braxton."

"I believe I do, sir. Let me check my book."

Juleah's heart skipped and she reached over to grip her uncle's arm. Mr. Randall pulled the heavy ledger up on top of the counter and opened it. He then ran his finger down the pages.

"Yes, he is here. Should I alert the gentleman, or does Mrs. Braxton wish to go up?"

Juleah turned to Stowefield. "Uncle, let us go up together. You must tell him, first."

42

Agonizing time had passed since the night Michael Bray had told Seth the thing that had sunk his heart into a perpetual night. Even though he had put a great distance between himself and England and was set boot-firm upon the land he loved, he could not remove Juleah from his mind and heart. Upon a knoll thousands of miles away lay that fair shell from which a gentle soul had flown. Forever, he trusted, she would live within his.

He thought of his father's house; the oaken door would meet him, where he had hoped she would have stood, her hand held high as he walked from his fields. Her face would have been aglow with the Blue Ridge's golden twilight, the Virginian breeze whispering through her unbound hair.

An armchair sat beneath the window, and he drew himself to it before the blackness outside and the feeble light within offered by a single candle. If only she could have been with him now, the moonlight shining on her face, in her eyes.

He drifted off to sleep, but at length raised his drawn face, roused suddenly by footsteps and softly spoken voices out in the hallway. An owl hooted somewhere in a distant marsh, and Seth put his arms across his knees, and hid his face.

When they reached the room, Stowefield rapped on Seth's door and waited. The door drifted open, and in the faint candlelight that came from within, Juleah's husband stepped forward in his linen shirt with his hair loose about his neck.

She stood behind her uncle. In the shadows she trembled. The desire to run into his arms overwhelmed her, and she forced down the sobs coming up in her throat.

Moonlight made its way through a side window near Seth. It shone on his face, and though Juleah could not see how worn he was with grieving for her, he appeared more handsome than she remembered.

"Mr. Stowefield?" Seth hurried to tuck in his shirt. His brows pinched together, surprised to see the old gent. "What is it? Is something wrong?"

Stowefield smiled, stood aside, and swept his hand in Juleah's direction.

Seth eyes locked onto Juleah's. She smiled. Tears pooled in her eyes. Her heart thumped with such elation that a cry slipped from her lips.

Stowefield nudged Seth on the shoulder. "Wake, man! Your eyes are not dreaming. She's not dead. She'll wear your ring still, bear your name, and live with you many, many years. Speak to her. Your eyes do not lie."

"Juleah!" Seth rushed forward, reached for her, touched her, snatched her up into his arms. She threw hers around his neck, pressed her cheek against his. Joy took possession. He spun her around, and they laughed and cried together.

Stowefield stepped away toward the stairs. "Good night, my children," he called back. "God give you peace."

Juleah glanced at him, warm and tender. "Thank you, Uncle John."

Seth cupped his hands around Juleah's face. He kissed her cheeks, her eyelids, her lips, wove his fingers through her hair, breathed in the scent of her, and took in the feel of her body against his.

"I should have never stopped believing you were alive." He whispered through her locks and gathered them into his fists. He lifted her up and carried her inside the room. He held her close and kissed her until they were breathless.

"Hold me in your arms, Seth. Hold me and never let me go," Juleah said.

The silky feel of her rushed through him. The ribbons in her hair pulled loose from the hastening of his fingers, and her locks fell in a cascade of bronzy silk down her back.

The candle on the bedside sputtered, and the flame died. Pale moonlight floated through the window and dusted over them. She sat on the bedside. Seth fell to his knees in front of her, wrapped his arms around her waist and wept.

"Juleah. Juleah."

"I am here."

"I stood beside your coffin and watched them lower it into the ground and cover it with earth. I waited until everyone had gone. I wept over what I believed was your grave. My heart was torn out of me, and it felt worse than death."

Juleah lifted his face to hers. "Oh, Seth, my love!" And she drew him up and hung her head against his shoulder.

Long into the night, they spoke of each other's harrowing stories, often with tears, frequently with an embrace and a kiss. Then they grew silent and their loving spoke of deeper things.

A ship's bell clanged out in the harbor. The moon dipped low in the starry sky. The breeze whispered and swayed the curtains over the window. Night, moon, and wind surrendered to a misty dawn.

When Seth woke with Juleah in his arms, he gazed over at her and outlined the curve of her fingers with his. The pale morning light fell over her face. He gathered her up against him and fell back to sleep contented, thanking God for this miracle of love.

43

*T*wo days later, Seth hired a pair of horses and left Stowefield's house after partaking of a hardy breakfast. He had bought Juleah a wardrobe, and today she looked fair in blue and white calico with a straw hat that shaded her love-lit eyes. They traveled toward the Virginia glens. Seth's heart swelled, and he glanced over at her riding sidesaddle upon a gentle chestnut mare. Juleah's eyes were shining with wild, elusive grace, and her laugh charmed as the songs of birds echoed through the woodlands.

Upon drawing closer to his land, he reined in his horse. Juleah steadied her mare beside him. A stout oak stood at an enormous height. Beneath it grew a patch of ferns. Green lichen speckled its protruding roots.

"There." He pointed to the tree and its vast canopy. "This oak is like the one I sat under when I first met Michael Bray, when I learned his name and that he loved my sister. I escaped with my life that night, and that brought me to you."

He nudged his horse on with a touch of his knees, and together they rode under the tent of trees. Cicadas whirred and dragonflies danced over purple thistles.

Below the greening heights, the Potomac murmured over rock and boulder. A hawk cried and circled the sky. Juleah watched it dive toward the water, skim the surface, and come up with a fish in its talons. "Your country is wild indeed. I've never seen such a river as this."

"There is more," he said, and she followed alongside him, until they saw the house his father had built. Juleah measured the height and breadth of it with her eyes.

"It is a large house, and to think you lived here alone."

"I preferred it, but not any longer."

He helped her from her horse and took her hand to lead her up the stairs. Hand in hand, they walked into the foyer. From it, they entered a room of whitewashed walls and tall mullioned windows that faced west. Magenta light from the setting sun filtered through blown glass and shone against the oak floor. Within the room sat a large table with four chairs, each of which was scarred with time. A clock, a tall cupboard with brass-work handles, and a rough-hewn box for firewood made up the furnishings.

Juleah walked about the room, stopped to run her hand over the table and the back of a chair. She rested beside the window-sill where she could see the Potomac, reddened by the descending sun. Seth grabbed her hand and hurried her upstairs, took her through each room, ending with the largest.

"This was the room my father shared with my mother. It is ours now."

"May I make cream-colored curtains for the windows?"

"Indeed, you can do whatever you wish."

"I would like a blanket chest to hold the quilts I shall make and perhaps sometime in the near future a cradle."

Seth picked her up and whirled her around, kissing her lips and laughing. They spent the night in that room. The moon hung outside the window and the hoot owls called through the trees. He promised her they'd return to build a life there, have lots of children, raise chickens and horses, plant corn and wheat. He loved her that night, in the quiet wilderness. Their two souls breathed; their two hearts beat as one.

In the morning, he took her to the river. The stones she stepped over were smooth, and he held her hand as she crossed them. Slipping her into the water, he wrapped his arms around her and kissed her. He admired the way her eyes sparkled, the way her hair fell in wet tendrils, and the way her skin shimmered in the sunlight.

"It is paradise here," she breathed in, and pulled close to him.

"With you." His hand caressed the curve of her back.

"There is no one else around for miles." An afterthought struck her and she looked at him with worried eyes. "It is true, isn't it? Unless there are Indians nearby."

"You needn't worry." He did not wish to tell her about Logan's War, how the Indians had massacred settler families from the Virginias to the Hudson. The tribes had moved deeper into the wilderness, yet the threat still existed from lone bands of warriors.

Seth put his hands around her face. "I'm glad we're alone. No servants to interrupt us. No unexpected guests."

"You have me all to yourself, Mr. Braxton." She pressed her lips to his, eased down in the water.

"I am selfish when it comes to my wife. I refuse to share her with anyone."

Juleah laid her head against his shoulder. "I do not wish to leave, but I know we must."

"Only for a short while."

"I shall miss Braxton Hall while we're gone."

"Is that what you call it?"

"A place should have a name, Seth. Do you not like it? We can think of another."

"No, Braxton Hall does well."

She touched his cheek with her palm and smiled. "Let us leave soon. For the sooner we do, the sooner we can come home."

For a moment, Seth gazed into her eyes, studied her face, and his desire for her mounted higher than the bluffs shadowing them. His arms encircled her. Under a blue heaven, the water whirled about them. He brought his lips to hers, the kiss urgent, sweeping, and ecstatic.

"Seth." She sighed, and her eyes closed as he moved his mouth away.

He lifted her out of the water, carried her up to the heights, to the cool grass under the shade trees. Later, when the sun skimmed the ridge of the mountains in the west, and bathed the river in ruby light, she lay within his arms, the golden light playing over the curve of her shoulders. When the sun sank lower, she went barefoot with him up the hillside.

That night she slept curled up against him, her hand sedate over his heart, her head nuzzled on his chest. With no curtains on the windows, the moon poured inside the room. The shadows from the tree branches outside danced over the walls.

Seth lay awake, thought of the future, and wished they did not have to return to England. But it was the honorable thing to do, and he settled his mind upon it. Her family must see her again, for the sake of their broken hearts.

And he had to face Darden for what he had done.

44

*W*ith the coming of autumn, Crown Cove grew reclusive, more than in recent years. Having been a house of mystery to its neighbors, the windows went unlit in the evenings, and rarely did a passerby see smoke rise out of its chimneys. By day, when rain fell, eerie streaks of black rippled down the bricks. Withering vines clung to the mortar. Inside its walls, jealousy had fueled the fires of envy. Now regret and depression held it at siege.

By now, Darden had come to believe women were witches in lace and silky garb, eye-fluttering vampires sent to suck a man dry of his fortune and dignity. His mother had dragged him through the dregs with her headstrong ways and ambition, insisting he take, by hook or by crook, anything that would make him wealthy. He could never live up to her standards, and she was against his infatuation with Juleah from the start. Juleah was not rich, but how dare she throw him off for a Yankee usurper and take over the house that should have been her son's.

And finally, Miss Lovelace broke off their affair when she discovered how small a fortune he owned, telling him she had tried but failed to grow accustomed to his sullen moods and fits of anger. In truth, she made it clear she could not abide a man who lacked self-control and had no prospects, nor enough money to keep her in silks and satins. Her other patrons were more accommodating than he.

Now Edward Darden lived alone in his ancient house, save for his servant, with his money drying up and his debts increasing. He wondered, with a great deal of discomposure, why Judith Dirk hadn't written to him as he had ordered her to do. He had not heard a word from the woman since *The Raven* had sailed for America. Surely they had gotten there by now. His hunger to know how Juleah suffered in the heat of a Carolina plantation drove him to madness.

Sitting in the dark, his brows pinched, his stare stoic, he feared they had met with disaster at sea. Perhaps a storm had overtaken them. The nightmare came and he dreamed of raging waves that swallowed up the ship and Juleah crying out, her beautiful face disappearing into the murky depths. He woke in a sweat. His heart beat in his ears and his breath heaved. He admitted to God his intentions were dishonorable, evil, and he trembled at the price he would pay in the end.

He rose at noon, drank early, and shot sparrows outside his window with his pistol. Habbinger showed him some concern, but kept his eyes and head low, and spoke only when spoken to.

That chilly evening, the fog lay thick and brought a damp, morose feeling to the house. Habbinger piled a log onto the fire and shoved the coals back with a shovel. "I was in the village today and heard some interesting news, sir."

"Why should I care?" Darden grumbled.

"I think you would be most curious to hear it."

"Has Miss Lovelace found someone else? A rich lord perhaps?" He threw back a dram of Irish whiskey.

"I've heard nothing concerning Miss Lovelace, sir, but rather Juleah Braxton."

Darden looked up with a start. He stood and felt a rush of fear. Clenching his teeth, he threw the empty glass he had held into the fire. Flames shot up as it shattered.

"Do not speak her name. I cannot bear it." He put his hands to the sides of his head to block it out.

"But she's returning to England, and with that rebel husband of hers."

The angry flush in Darden's face all at once vanished into a white pall that he saw reflected in the dark windowpanes. "What's that you say?"

"She's returning. The village is a hornet's nest of gossip; everyone is amazed by the news, for she was thought to have died in that fire at Ten Width. Braxton was believed to have drowned. Now she'll show up pretty and hale with her upstart."

The corners of Darden's mouth twisted. "It cannot be true."

"Oh, but it is, sir."

"How?"

"Who knows? I went to vespers this evening, and Sir Henry stood in the church and announced it to those gathered. The minister had them all bow their heads and give thanks to Almighty God for the miracle."

"Miracle!" Darden spat. "It is a lie, and the old fool is insane."

"Ah, but it is true, sir."

"Stop saying that. They're speaking lies, I tell you!"

Calm as his manner ever was, Habbinger lifted the jug and poured his master another dram. "I doubt Lady Anna and Sir Henry would make up a story about such a thing."

Fearful he could be wrong, Darden crimped his brow hard and put his fist up against his lips. He had no idea how his plans could have gone wrong. He had paid well for their execution.

"Folks are wondering who's buried in the churchyard in her place," said Habbinger, "and why this is a case of mistaken identity."

"They'll never know."

"That is certain, sir."

"The body cannot be identified."

"True enough, sir."

"It would be a sacrilege to dig up the dead."

"Indeed, it would. I took the liberty to wish Sir Henry and his lady well, thinking it would shed good light upon you, sir."

"Good light?"

Habbinger nodded. "Yes, sir."

Darden sneered. "I doubt it. They hate me."

"What will you do, sir?"

"If she accuses me of anything, I'll deny it. I've your oath, as well, that you'll swear by every word I say?"

Habbinger inclined his head. "I've been faithful to you and the members of your household, sir. I'll not say a word of what goes on behind these walls. I believe you did what you thought was right."

It grew, as if a black tumor dug its roots into his mind. The idea he'd kill Seth Braxton was most appealing. How and when was another matter altogether. He cared not that Habbinger noticed his worried gestures, the wringing of his hands, the twisting of his mouth.

"Not to worry, sir." Habbinger stood with his head held high. "No matter what anyone says, they can prove nothing. Your mother is away for her health. I've been with you the entire time and have seen no one here but you, and Miss Lovelace from time to time."

Darden stared at his servant and dropped his hand. "How shall I repay you for a sealed tongue?"

"Faithfulness need not always be rewarded, sir."

"I disagree." From his pocket Darden drew out the gold watch that had belonged to his father. "Here, take this. You'll get some money by it."

Habbinger did not argue. He took it in hand, tucked it away in his waistcoat, and stepped from the room.

45

When the trees in England changed color, the sea turned from murky green to dark blue along the coast of Devonshire. Swells of clouds, swirls of gray and white, chilled the air in early morning. Evening fell. Frost hung in the air. Gusty northeast winds swept southward with the scent of the coming winter hoarfrost.

Great purple cloudbanks loomed over earth and sea, bidding a gentleman to draw his lady close in his arm while traveling. Their coach lumbered over the high road and turned into a narrow drive that led to a house that, for some time, had been a forlorn place, where miserable sorrow had gripped parents and stifled children. From the front door, Sarah emerged and called back inside. In a flurry of skirts and stomping boots, the others appeared, Lady Anna dressed no longer in dreary black, Sir Henry smart in his hunting attire. Thomas jumped up and down, waved his hands and kicked the stones with his boot. Jane, in her ankle-high boots, woolen dress and apron, lifted her face and waved.

"They've come out to meet us." Holding her hat down with her gloved hand, Juleah leaned out the window. Seth looked out as well while he held his wife's hand. The coachman turned the horses, drew in the reins, and the footman opened the door for the lady and gentleman within.

Juleah stretched her hands out to her parents and hurried to them. Tearful at their reunion, they trembled with the overwhelming reality that their daughter had been restored to them. Jane and Thomas, too, threw their arms around Juleah. Her mother mopped her eyes with her handkerchief, and Sir Henry kissed her cheeks. His hounds bounded and bayed around their legs.

"Down you beasts," he scolded. "Can you not see you may spoil my dear daughter's skirts? Away with you." Yet, they did not obey.

As Seth stepped out, dressed smartly in a new suit of buff and blue with matching tricorn hat, he watched as the family, save for Sir Henry, who lingered behind, went inside the house. Turning upon him with a grateful smile, Sir Henry put his hand out. "Thank you for bringing my daughter back to us. I am in your debt."

"No, there is no debt owed, Sir Henry."

"Well then, you shall rejoice to know that I received a note this very morning from your dear sister. She and Michael and young Nathaniel have stopped at Ten Width and await word of Juleah and your homecoming."

Without a moment's hesitation, Seth paid the coachman an extra pound to ride over to Ten Width to fetch the family residing there. The coach rolled off, and before the clock in the hall chimed out the noon hour, it returned with Caroline, her son, and Michael Bray.

Long into the night, while the candles burned low, did the family sit together, listening to Juleah's story. It was overall a sad tale, but adventurous beyond the wildest of imaginations. Thomas sat on the floor enraptured, admiring his brave sister in stunned silence. Jane laid her head on Juleah's shoulder. Juleah's mother and Caroline clasped their hands tight against their hearts in amazement, and Sir Henry looked on proudly.

A late tea was brought in, and while the family partook, Bray pulled Seth aside and inquired what they were to do about Edward Darden's involvement, whether Latterbuck should be informed.

"Will you seek revenge?" Bray asked.

"Vengeance is not mine, Michael," Seth answered. "I want justice."

Bray leaned toward Seth after catching his wife's eye. "I believe the best course of action is not to provoke a confrontation. Wait until he crosses your path or informs the constable. You have witnesses."

"I cannot be sure of ever meeting Darden by chance. As for Latterbuck, I doubt he'd listen, though he will be shocked to find us both living."

"I'd like to see the look on his face. At least he has nothing now to accuse you of. Your name is clear in the eyes of the law, I have no doubt."

"Well, perhaps Latterbuck will be pleased after all. As he says, there is no murder done in his district."

"Yet he forgets the body found in the fire and one Hetty Shanks. It is due to her station in life, I'm sure."

"I have not forgotten. I'll ride to Crown Cove tomorrow."

"We'll ride together this time and make him confess. Then we'll summon the constable."

Juleah lay awake with the pillow next to her untouched. She sighed, and thought Seth and Michael had stayed up a long time talking and having their ale by the fireside with her father. Juleah did not mind. It was good for a man to sit with his fellows and talk of things he perhaps could not share with a woman. She glanced at the clock on the bedstand. He told her he'd be up in an hour, and the time drew near.

She lay her head back, ran her fingertips over his pillow, and soaked in the coolness of the room. Tomorrow they'd bring the family back with them to Ten Width, and for the next four days spend the hours picnicking on the green, walking in the garden, and playing with the children. The fire damage had been repaired, and Caroline described to her how well Ten Width looked amid the autumn colors.

She got up and drew the curtains back. Leaning against the sill, she gazed at the moon and admired how it spread its haze over the boxwoods. Beyond the house, she saw the pond she so loved gleaming in its light.

An idea sprung into her mind. She could leave Seth a note on the pillow and ask him to meet her there. He would be coming up to their room any moment. It delighted her senses. She donned a dress over her chemise and drew out paper and quill. After setting the note in place, she slipped out onto the moon-lit balcony and down the staircase that went into the garden.

Through the grove, she weaved and walked down the grassy slope to the mossy bank.

She started at the whinny of a horse, glanced up, and saw on the road above a coach with a pair of bays harnessed to it.

"Juleah," a voice called, and she whirled around. She could not see his face. He called again and a chill ran up her body. The mystery of it filled her with fear.

She turned back toward the house and ran. Arms grabbed her, pulled her against a man's body. She could feel the roughness of the cloak he wore against her arms. She cried out and he covered her mouth with a gloved hand and squeezed. She shrank in his grasp, twisted and turned, as terror seized her.

He dragged her to the road and to the coach. Thrown inside on velvet cushions she scrambled into the corner and watched him climb inside, his hat pulled down, hiding his face in the dark. With a crack of the whip, the horses bolted forward. Juleah's heart went cold within her breast. The world reeled, and she struggled to scream, to call for Seth, but it caught in her throat.

The face she beheld belonged to Edward Darden.

46

"Let me out!"

Juleah balled her fists, struck Darden across his broad shoulders. He grabbed her wrists and held her back.

"I want to talk to you," he said, with a pleading tone that sickened her. "You have nothing to fear from me, you know that. I've much to tell you, to convince you of. This was the only way."

"We have nothing to say to each other. Have your driver turn around. Return me home."

Darden set his mouth and looked away. "I cannot do that."

"I will scream. He'll know I'm in trouble and stop."

"Habbinger obeys me. Don't you see?"

"Where are you taking me?"

"For a ride, so we can sort this out. I'll explain everything."

His expression softened, like a lover's, and he skimmed his eyes over her beauty. Juleah pressed back against the cushions and looked away.

"I'm happy you have come back to England."

"You shouldn't be."

"I worried about you while you were away."

"I was away by your doing."

"Mine?"

"I remember everything."

Darden shifted closer. "I feared what had become of you. You can ask Habbinger, I was packed to leave, until I heard you were home."

Tears slipped down Juleah's cheeks, yet she did not sob. Instead, she threw him an angry glance. "Judith Dirk drowned in the sea when the ship met with a storm."

Darden's brows pinched. "That is unfortunate." Then he turned away with his chin in his hand. "You need not tell me the details."

"Indeed not, for you'd have no stomach for it."

His jaw shifted. "You think me a weak man?"

"You may not care to hear it, but I too would have drowned if hadn't been for the bravery of a seaman and the goodness of a fisherman."

"I would have blamed myself if you had drowned." He turned to her, attempted to lift her hand in his, but she jerked away.

"Why did you let everyone go on believing I had died at Ten Width when you knew it wasn't true?" she said. "Why would let them go on hurting?"

"I'm sorry for causing your parents pain, but it could not be avoided."

"Oh, what a cruel thing to believe."

"I wanted to hurt Braxton more."

"You have hated him from the start."

"Yes."

"Because he inherited what you wanted?"

"He won you, Juleah, and if it hadn't been for Braxton, you would have been my wife. I saw my chance to get you away from him and took it. Do not hate me for it. I acted as any man deep in love would."

"And what did you, *a man deep in love*, intend to do with me by sending me off against my will?"

"Judith Dirk was to take you to Carolina and care for you until time passed and people forgot. I was going provide for you," he said.

Juleah shouted at him. "As your mistress, in a country you think low of?"

"No one would have known you were not my wife."

"I would have." She shook her head, kicked at the coach walls, and pounded him with her fists.

He grabbed her wrists and wrenched her down. "In time, you would not have cared about that."

She glared into his eyes. "And live an adulterous life? How little you know me."

"A comfortable life you would have accepted, eventually."

"Under lock and key?" She struggled beneath his hold.

He stared at her and pressed his lips together hard. "It may have stayed that way for some time, until you forgot *him*."

"I could never forget Seth."

"You would have if I had told you he had leapt into the harbor and drowned. That's what everyone believed happened."

She shrank back. "I once thought I knew you, but now I know what kind of man you are—cruel, selfish."

He released her and relaxed back against the seat. Juleah could not see how stern his eyes had become, but his breath hurried.

"I suppose by now you learned they buried someone in your place." His tone went cold. "If you knew who it was, you'd never call me cruel or selfish again. I am surprised you have not asked me about that night at Ten Width."

She gripped her arms together and spat at him. "You'd only tell me lies."

"Listen to me." He took her by the shoulders. "A candle tumbled over and caught the carpet afire. Do you remember how I carried you out, how my mother fell?"

Juleah's eyes widened and a heavy breath slipped between her parted lips. "It was she that died?"

"Yes, and I'm glad. She was a wicked woman, and I despised her."

Stunned at Darden's lack of remorse, Juleah pressed herself closer to the window. "She was your mother."

His eyes narrowed. "In name and body—never in her heart."

Juleah frowned at his confession. How could any man loathe the woman who had borne him into the world? If she had been the evil woman he claimed her to be, she had masked her intentions well those times Juleah had seen her. Yet, she remembered she never smiled, nor did she speak to anyone unless necessary. Juleah had mistaken her demeanor for shyness, when it was aloofness. She had thought her a reserved woman, when in truth she had always worn a proud expression and scrutinized people with her wintry eyes.

Juleah ventured deeper. "What about Hetty? What about the night Seth was attacked? Had you anything to do with that?"

Darden let Juleah go. "I know nothing about Braxton being attacked. But it was my mother who paid Hetty to take Nathaniel away. She wanted me to have Ten Width and was convinced he was a bastard child. When she discovered the woman had softened and taken him to Sir Charles instead, she—"

"Killed her?" Juleah murmured.

Darden laughed. "Yes. She hired some ruffian to do it. Hetty's man, so she said. I was against it."

This twist, that an English gentlewoman would stoop so low, was more than Juleah could comprehend. She shook her head in unbelief, incredulous of his mother's malevolence.

Her eyes pooled with tears, and she spoke with haste. "Take me back, Edward. You are in no danger of anyone knowing what has happened, for we are going back to Virginia. You'll not see either of us again."

His face turned pale in the darkness, his eyes glazed with sadness. "I cannot have it, Juleah. I cannot bear to be without you. I'm taking you to Crown Cove with me, and if you want to, we can go anywhere you wish—to America or France. I'd even tolerate Ireland if it meant being with you."

"You haven't any right. Let me go, or I'll throw myself out." Frantic she grabbed the latch and tried to open it.

Darden yanked her back, took her in his arms, and pulled her near. "Don't be foolish. What is done is done. Now you must listen. I promise to make you happy, to care for you, to give you anything and everything you want."

"It is my husband's place, not yours."

"If he hadn't come here, none of this would have happened. We'd be together. It is his fault!"

A fierce yearning and hopelessness possessed his voice and the contorted features of his face. Though her strength was no match to his brute force, Juleah would not release herself to him.

She clenched her fists at his vehemence. "I will not listen!"

His eyes ablaze, he yanked her wrists forward. She twisted away to keep him from seeing fear in her eyes and failed when he rallied his strength against hers and pulled her to him. Juleah cried out to the driver for help. The whip cracked and the horses galloped on over the high road. The coach swayed, her heart pounded, and her breath rose up in ragged pants.

"I will not let you go," Darden twisted his mouth. His eyes blazed that she rejected him yet again. "Do you hear? I'll not let you go!"

✐❧

Seth found the coverlet turned down. The sheets were tumbled and Juleah's nightgown hung over the chair. He picked up the note, smiled, and went into the garden down to the pond. He called to her, but she did not answer. Twice more he called and heard only the lapping of the water among the rushes.

Orbs of moonlight sparkled atop the pond. A gentle breeze rippled the cattails. He stopped short. His eyes searched for her, while his heart thumped in his chest, and he hoped that any moment his wife would appear. Wind whispered in low, forlorn tones through the willows and he called to her again.

He stepped away and had not gone five yards when he noticed two sets of footprints in the ground leading up to the road. Crouching down, he studied them in the brilliant glare of moonlight. One set belonged to a man, the other a woman.

Swiftly, he stood and traced them up the hillside. When he saw the grooves made by coach wheels and the imprint of hooves, he stood stunned looking down the road, his eyes following the trail.

"He's taken her," he whispered, distressed.

He swung around, raced down the hillside, through the grove to the stable. There he saddled a horse without saying a word to the family. It was best to leave them as they were. They'd been through enough. He'd bring her back, and none would be the wiser for it.

He jammed his foot into the stirrup, hauled the reins through his hands, and drove his heels into the horse's sides. It stomped its hooves, then shot off. Wind blew through Seth's hair, against his face, and struck him like an open palm. It grew colder, shoved a sea of gray clouds over him, blocked out the moon, and cast long shadows across the ground.

Long into the ride, his horse wearied. Foam lined its mouth and coat. Seth pulled rein and ahead of him was the crossroads and the gibbet with its gruesome contents that hung above it. The gibbet creaked in the wind, and the crows cawed nearby. He nudged the horse with his knees and hurried on.

Seth's heart raced like the clouds above him. He looked in vain for the house, and thought perhaps he had made a wrong turn. In his rising anxiety, he mounted a hill. From there, he stared down into a valley. Off in the distance sat Crown Cove, grim and gray in the mist, four chimneys rising against a stormy sky.

Juleah is there. He was convinced of it, and it sent a cold chill that ran up and down his spine.

A gust of wind frightened his horse, and it stomped its hooves and snorted. Seth snapped the reins and pushed it into a hard gallop. He forced it through a belt of tasseled willows, along the thread of a meadow stream. Crossing it, he plunged his mount forward and struck it with his heels. He turned onto a narrow, overgrown lane lined with gnarled trees.

When he reached Darden's doorstep, he dismounted. Violently, he shook the locked handle and pounded upon the door with a heavy fist.

A side window grated open. He stood back and looked up. Habbinger stuck his head out. On his gaunt face a frown deepened. Slapping his hand on the sill, he leaned out.

"You again? What do you want? Away, or I'll put the dog on you."

Seth pressed his lips together hard and strode toward Habbinger. His stride alone was enough to give the man reason to shiver.

"I know my wife was taken here in the night. Open the door or I'll break it in."

Habbinger grimaced. "How many times must you be told she's not here?"

Seth raised his arm and pointed his finger at him in warning. "I'll come for you as well." He rushed back to the door and pushed against it with his shoulder. The lock bent. He rammed the door and kicked it in.

He went through into a dark hall. A shadow passed against the papered walls and streamed forward. Juleah appeared, her hair loose about her, her eyes anxious to reach him. She rushed down the staircase, and he met her halfway. She fell into his arms and he held her close.

As one, they turned to leave, then stopped short. On the threshold stood Darden, silhouetted by the misty light, pistol in hand. In his eyes leapt a strange fire, one that locked onto Juleah. That he loved her with a great and evil passion, Seth had long known and now saw.

"Let us pass." He held Juleah close. With his other hand he drew out his flintlock. "If you refuse to move aside, I'll shoot you where you stand."

Darden's face twisted. "You broke my door in, and now you threaten to shoot me?"

"I do, and I will, if you do not do as I say."

A spark of light glinted off the barrel of Darden's pistol and caught Seth's eye. He gripped Juleah tighter and moved her behind him.

"I never meant to hurt her," Darden said. "I tried to protect her."

"By causing others to believe she was dead and then abducting her, twice?"

"No, by saving her from the fire. I sacrificed the life of my mother for her. What have you sacrificed? What did you do to protect her?"

With an oath, Seth sprang forward. Juleah caught him by the arm and begged him to move back. "No, Seth!"

He raised his pistol and cocked the hammer, with his eyes fixed on Darden's heart. "In the name of God, man, stand aside. I don't wish to kill you, but I will if I must."

Darden's face darkened. "Spill my blood on my own threshold?"

"I have no doubt."

Darden shifted his stare. "Juleah, do not leave me again." He held his hand out to her. "Stay with me. We once loved. We can again."

Juleah looked at him with pity and shook her head. "No, we cannot."

His face stiffened. "If that be so, then he shall not have you either." He raised the pistol and fired. The sharp snap echoed around the walls surrounding them.

The bullet cut through Juleah's sleeve, hit the banister, and splintered the wood. She let out a cry and fell against her husband. A cold chill filled Seth. Swiftly, he turned and gathered her up. A thread of blood oozed out onto her arm.

Seth jerked his head back to see Darden. Fury coursed through him, his body stiff with it. The pommel of his flintlock was hot in his hands, cocked and ready. His heartbeat raged against his ribs, and his temples pulsated with the desire to pull the trigger.

Darden, seeing what he had done, and that Seth meant to kill him, threw his weapon down as if it were a blistering firebrand. He covered his face with his hands. He raked trembling fingers over his face, begged, and turned his head side to side.

"Leave me!"

"I have no right to take your life, Darden." Seth leaned down to him, his mouth twisting. "Men will be here to arrest you. No doubt, you'll hang for kidnapping my wife, or spend the rest of your miserable days in a prison cell."

From the shadows, Habbinger crept forward, his face pale and drawn with fright. "I've had a change of heart, Captain Darden. After seeing you would have taken the lady's life, I want nothing more to do with all this. Your plan went too far for my stomach and conscience to handle."

With a heavy tread, Habbinger stumbled past Darden, as Seth carried Juleah in his arms out the front door. Upon the dewy grass he set her down and dragged his neckcloth from around his throat.

"Here, my love," he spoke softly to her, wrapping it around her arm. "This will stop the bleeding."

She trembled. "It is only a graze, Seth. . . . Hurry. . . . Take me home, away from here."

He lifted her and set her on his horse, then climbed into the saddle behind her. They rode off through the autumn moonlight that lingered through the trees and listened to the whisper of wind murmur among the branches.

When they reached the top of the hill, Seth paused and reined in his horse. He turned it around and they looked down upon Crown Cove bathed in the moon's glow. At first, it appeared smoke rose through a chimney. It grew black and twisted upward in a broad funnel. Below it, tongues of yellow flame grew. Then in its ravenous fury the fire spread.

Juleah let out a ragged moan, as they watched with startled expressions the old house transform into a pyre. Stones blackened as it ate away withered ivy and crumbled the mortar.

Crown Cove burned to the ground that autumn of 1785. Edward Darden was never found, and it was believed he had set the fire and perished within it. Or had he escaped?

Her nature being one of compassion, Juleah could not help but feel sorrow for a man she once believed was stronger. But there was naught she or Seth could have done to change the course of the Almighty's plans. For a man reaps whatever he may sow.

Epilogue

 $\mathcal{A}$ bove the stony shores of the Potomac lay tracts of green fields and lush forest. When the sun set over the mountains to the west, veils of magenta light spread over blooming meadows, over the mounting crests of the river. The north-born wind blew through the elms. Deer grazed in the fields, as they had for hundreds of years.

Overlooking the river stood Seth Braxton's house. Its rooms were vast yet gently furnished. The doleful chant of the Potomac droned, while the great horned owls answered, hooting in the pines one to another.

The years rolled on. Children came screaming into the world. Foals were birthed in the stable and suckled the mares. The land prospered, and so did Seth and Juleah, in their love, their faith, and fortune.

Content this twilight, Seth sat with the one he loved and watched her with love-lit eyes bounce their baby girl on her knee. They sat beside the clematis on the porch, listened to the hum of bees, and watched the moon rise above the treetops. His son raced about the green grass with his dog and caught fireflies in a glass jar.

He imagined, if his father-in-law had lived, he would have been content to lean upon a walking stick and lend gentle instruction to his grandson and his son Thomas on a day like today. Lady Anna, now a widow, and Jane, who seemed to have blossomed into a young woman overnight, sat nearby under the shade of Seth's tree.

In Seth's hand were letters from England. He opened them and read aloud to Juleah. Next month Caroline and Michael, with their two children, were due to arrive and settle on a tract of land near Braxton Hall. They'd bring Will and Claire and their daughter, one-year-old Ella, with them.

Ten Width had been let go. It was time to pass the old manor's woeful existence on to another and let the dregs of the past die. Henry Chase remained in Thomas's name, lent out to a retired admiral and his wife. It, too, would eventually pass into other hands.

And so, time descended through the misty twilight, while the sweet waters of the Potomac flowed year after year under the clustered stars, and those who loved it lived out the remainder of their lives in peace.

They now lie in dusty tombs long forgotten. Yet, their love is remembered in the Eternal.

Surrender the wind to one who holds its bands
Surrender the wind into His loving hands
Surrender the wind
Your burden lay down
Surrender the wind
Surrender the wind
—Rita Gerlach

Discussion Questions

1. How is the title of this novel symbolic? At what point in the story did the title *Surrender the Wind* have meaning to you? What does it mean to "surrender the wind"?

2. Discuss Ecclesiastes 2:18-19 and how this gives a prelude to the story.

3. To what extent does Seth's upbringing as an American patriot shape his character? What changes take place in Seth from the prologue to the conclusion of the story? What kind of man would you describe him to be? Dutiful? Kind? Heroic?

4. Why did Seth find it difficult to forgive his grandfather? Were his reasons valid? Have you ever been in a similar situation where you found it difficult to forgive someone?

5. What were the reasons Seth hesitated to accept his inheritance? What were the reasons that compelled him to go to England? How did this change his life? What made his inheritance a blessing? What made it a burden? Have you had times in life where you had plans, and then unexpectedly were faced with a major change? How did you deal with those changes?

6. What expectations did you have for Seth and Juleah when they first met? Did they fulfill them? What hopes did you have for their future together?

7. Seth was not expecting to fall in love with an Englishwoman. Have you experienced unexpected love?

8. In what way did faith help Seth and Juleah survive their trials? How did faith strengthen their relationship?

9. What are Juleah's strengths? In what scenes did she need Seth the most? Have you ever been in a situation where you realized you could not get through a trial alone and needed the person you loved the most to help you find your way back?

10. What was your first impression of Edward Darden when you met him in the prologue? What did his actions foreshadow? Did he ever gain your sympathy? What forced Juleah to change her mind about him?

11. For what reasons do you think the author left Darden's mother nameless?

12. Finally, how did you profit from reading *Surrender the Wind*?

Want to learn more about author
Rita Gerlach and check out other great
fiction from Abingdon Press?

Sign up for our fiction newsletter at
www.AbingdonPress.com
to read interviews with your favorite authors, find
tips for starting a reading group, and stay posted on what
new titles are on the horizon. It's the place to connect with
other fiction readers or to post a comment about this book.

Be sure to visit Rita online!

www.ritagerlach.com
www.inspire-writer.blogspot.com